Brenna
Lyons

Hunter's Moon

Night Warriors
Warriors, Book 4

FIREBORN
PUBLISHING

Fireborn Publishing Copyright

Statement

PUBLISHER

FIREBORN
PUBLISHING

**PO Box 5216
Haverhill, MA 01835**

Dedicated to...

The things that no one but the shadow knows. They are sometimes the best stories there are.

Never saying never. Your words will always come back to bite you in the end.

Second chances...everyone should have at least one in life.

Author's Note

In the twenty-four years between *"Swordbearer Reborn"* and *"Hunter Born"* in *Night Warriors*, a lot happened in the Hunter household. Some of it was hinted at in that book. Since this book delves into the hidden history of the Hunters, if you haven't read at least *Night Warriors*, stop right now and do so. You can follow this book without it, but I will be brutally honest with you. You aren't going to get half of the in-jokes, and you certainly won't pick up on the nuances shaded by the other books.

Some of the smaller pieces will look familiar to long-time Night Warriors readers. The first two sections of *"Playing Games"* and all but the last chapter of *"The Lord's Daughter"* have released before. Initially, I added them to this book to put them into the timeline and to connect them to the larger events happening in the Hunter range.

Then I made a discovery. In connecting it all together, I realized that there were more secrets and twists connected to them that would become important later. For instance, what happens when Corwyn has to offer protection to people after Polero's attacks? And...what happens when Stephanie goes to Armen range? These sorts of questions had larger implications than I'd originally given them credit for. In writing the full saga, that became all too clear.

That is one of the reasons the series has slowed down. My apologies, but I want to give you a complete understanding and a true representation, as much as possible.

Happy reading!
Brenna

Glossary of Warrior Terms

Beast- Beasts are what humans erroneously refer to as vampires. The stories humans tell are obviously not correct, but you can't expect a human to get everything right.

Blutjagd- The "blood hunt." Warriors crave battle with the beasts, as the beasts crave blood. Warriors are tied to beasts in that they sense many of the beasts' special powers. A Warrior can feel the use of coercion, feeding, and other controls of humans. They also feel other Warriors engaged in *Blutjagd*, the death of beasts and Warriors in their range, and the presence of nearby beasts that are not fully ghosted. Rigorous battle training will quell the *Blutjagd* for short periods of time.

Elder- One of the original beasts, the Stone stealers who were damned for their crimes against the Stone and the Warriors. The elders are gifted with powers turned beasts are not, including the ability to reproduce with a *Blutjagdfrau*, the ability to turn other beasts, and the inability to be killed by anyone but a Warrior.

Endspiel- The point in printing when a Warrior must either seal printing or go insane. A Warrior who feels printing may not progress should break printing long before this point. Note that they are rarely smart enough to do so.

Fluch- The Warrior's curse, passed from father to son or daughter. The *Fluch* may be removed from a daughter but never a son. If the *Fluch* is not removed in the *Zeremonie der Freiheit* by the time the menses begin or the *Zeremonie des Schutzes* is performed before freeing, the daughter is cursed to become *Blutjagdfrau*, a female Warrior. Because elders target *Blutjagdfrau* as mates, Warrior fathers will go to any lengths to free a daughter not marked by the Stone.

Ghosting- A talent that both beasts and Cursed Warriors learn to harness. Ghosting can hide the physical form of Cursed Warriors or beasts and all they hold or carry from each other and humans. In a lesser strength, it can "blur" the image of the user so that humans do not note the passage in particular but still see a person there, which avoids accidental collisions. Even a ghosted beast cannot hide uses of power that a Warrior can track. Warriors sometimes ghost in tandem to remain visible to each other but not other Warriors or beasts.

Krankheit- The "sealing sickness." In the final stage of the transformation between human and Cursed Warrior, at or about the sixteenth birthday in males and a year after the start of menses in females, the sickness strikes. The young Warrior will suffer nausea, vomiting, a high fever, disorientation, dizziness, and may become incoherent. It is usually the only time in a Warrior's life that he or she becomes ill, save morning sickness in a *Blutjagdfrau*.

Printing- Like imprinting, a Warrior becomes tied to his mate for life. He cannot choose another if she's lost, cannot be unfaithful while she lives, and cannot ever divorce or otherwise dissolve the union. A printed Warrior is the most stable of men, unless his mate or children are endangered or lost. Then he will suffer the printing madness and may have to be killed by his house. Likewise, a Warrior who breaks printing, even early printing, will suffer for it. A Warrior who breaks printing too close to *Endspiel* will face the madness.

Veriel- The Mad Elder. The Destroyer of Lives. The Mad Deceiver, who led the traitors and freed the elders from the Stone. The most hated and hunted of all the beasts. Fixated on one woman, he would destroy the world to own her. At least, that's what the stories say of him.

Warriors- Also called Cursed Warriors, *Krieger der Nacht, Soldat der Nacht*, or Sons of the Stone. The Warriors were an ancient race of protectors who spawned the beasts and now are driven to hunt their former brothers to extinction.

Zeremonie der Freiheit

Bei den Göttern, die uns alle geschaffen haben, erbitte ich, dass diese einer zur Sicherheit aller die menschliche Form erhält. Blut meines Blutes; sei frei von meinem Fluch für jetzt und für alle Zeit.

Ich befreie dich von der Schuld meines Fluchs und nehme die Pflicht, die die deinige gewesen wäre, auf mich zurück. Ich schwöre, dass ich an deiner statt und für deine Ehre kämpfen werde, bis der Tag kommt, an dem ich die Ruhe der Krieger finde.

Translated:

By the gods who forged us all, I ask that this one be transformed unto Human form for the protection of all. Blood of my blood; be free of my curse for now and all times.

I free you from the obligation of my curse and accept back into myself the duty that would have been yours. It is my oath that I shall fight in your stead and for your honor until the day that I join the Warrior's Rest.

Zeremonie des Schutzes

Bei den Göttern, die uns alle geschaffen habe, stelle ich dich unter den Schutz des Hauses [Name]. Ein jeder unserer Art und Sippe wird sein Leben geben um deines vor dem Bösen, das unter uns weilt, zu bewahren. Wandele nun gesegnet in unserer Mitte.

Translated:

By the gods who forged us all, I grant you the protection of the House [name]. Any and all of our kind and kin shall lay down life to preserve yours from the evil that walks among us. Walked blessed among us, now.

Section One

Stephen's Salvation

Chapter One

June 25th, 1982

"You smell wonderful," Antoñio Polero informed her in his heavily-accented English.

Gabby Farris giggled as Antoñio nuzzled her neck. The tall, blond European was incredibly playful. She sighed as his lips caressed the skin of her neck, beyond warm to scorching and insistent. He pulled back for a moment.

"Oh, God. Don't stop," she groaned. His mouth felt incredible.

Antoñio wasn't her usual type, and Gabby still wasn't convinced that this date would last past a goodbye kiss at her car. In fact, she was fairly certain that it would end there. Playful or not, Antoñio's eyes lacked some essential warmth that she preferred in men.

"As you wish."

Antoñio ran his tongue over her throat in a little circle and started to drop his face to her again. Her blood heated at the attention.

"Back off," a strange voice ordered.

Gabby retreated in shock, her eyes opening wide in the darkness. She tried to turn to the sound of the voice, but stopped in confusion as a warm splash plastered her shirt to her body. Antoñio backed away with his hand over what appeared to be a deep knife wound at his throat. Gabby jerked a step back with a squawk as a giant of a man brushed past her.

"Back off, Polero."

Antoñio's eyes widened in fear as a knife blade the length of a ruler flashed up in the moonlight. Gabby pulled her own knife from the sheath behind her back. It was a pitiful little piece of metal that her brother had given her years ago, the blade about the length of her palm, but Jeff believed a woman should never be unarmed.

Without thought of the size of his weapon, Gabby struck the stranger in the ribs, brushing past his heavy leather jacket. He recoiled, dragging her along in her surprise. Gabby gasped as he met her eyes. Fury burned there. For a moment, she was incapable of leaving that locked stare.

She forced her gaze to Antoñio, pleading for an explanation, anything that would help her find the ground beneath her feet. Her blood ran cold at the fangs clearly visible in Antoñio's grimace, the red eyes glowing in the near-black night. She might have thought she was hallucinating were it not for the fact that one of the fangs was broken. That was too much detail to explain away.

What have I done?

Gabby squawked again as Antoñio disappeared into thin air. He didn't run or hide. One second, he was there; the next, there was nothing as far as she could see. Gabby jumped back, feeling her knife slide free from the giant's body.

Her rescuer screamed that time. It was less in pain than in pure frustration.

Her knife clattered to the ground, and the smell of the blood on her shirt struck her, making her retch. Gabby backpedaled, shaking while the man cleaned his knife on the grass and sheathed it. She wasn't sure exactly what she just did, but it had been the wrong choice.

He turned to her, ran his hand over her throat slowly, and nodded. "I'm sorry for frightening you," he told her in a gentle voice.

Gabby stared at the growing stain of his blood on his jeans. "Oh...God." She dragged the denim scarf from her hair and tried to staunch the flow from the wound she'd caused. "What did I do?" She couldn't keep the tears from falling.

His hand covered hers, the other patting her back in comfort. "It's okay. You need to calm down and come with me."

"Yes. We have to get you to a hospital. Right now." She hadn't realized how severe the bleeding was.

"I have a doctor waiting for me." That sounded sincere.

"You do? But—"

He didn't let her finish. "Do you have a car nearby?"

She nodded. "In the lot."

"Okay." He reached down, retrieved her knife, wiped the blood on his jeans, and settled it into her sheath for her. Then he took her by the elbow and guided her back to the lot, while she tried to keep pressure on his wound. He walked quickly, as if he hardly noticed the fact that he was bleeding everywhere.

Gabby steered him toward her car with every intention of taking him to a hospital, but he shook his head.

"You have to go. Go home and wash your clothes immediately. Get a shower. If you don't wash it off right away, it will burn your skin like harsh chemicals."

"But—"

"No need to worry about me. I'll be fine."

"You're bleeding."

He ran his fingertips over her tear-stained cheek and smiled at her, a carnal smile that made her heart flutter. "It's okay," he assured her. "This is what I do, Gabrielle."

Gabby felt the air leave her lungs and fought to find the strength to answer. "How do you know my name?"

He shrugged with a sheepish grin and handed her wallet back. His dark eyes glittered in amusement and a black curl fell over his eyes in a boyish look. "How else was I supposed to find you later?" he asked.

She managed a weak smile. "Planning on getting even?" she joked.

He laughed softly. "With a strong, beautiful woman like you? Never. I just wanted to let you know that there was no permanent injury, at a later date."

Gabby blushed, her eyes scanning down his body to the slight bulge in his jeans. "If you show up with news like that, I may be tempted to make you prove it. After all, a big, strong man like you—"

What am I doing? I was just attacked by some creature. I'm nursing my personal knight in shining armor, who I just stabbed, and all I can think about is getting him into bed.

The man rose to her challenge in more ways than one. "Promise me that, and I will be on your doorstep in one week to collect on it." He checked his watch as if marking the time for that date.

Gabby licked her lips slowly. "Next week, I will be eagerly waiting for you. But, I warn you, I intend to make sure every inch of you is in full working order."

"I wouldn't stand for less."

His perusal of her made her knees week. "So, do you want me to call you 'he' forever, or is there something else I should call you?"

"Stephen."

"Until next week, Stephen." She slid into the seat, and he held the door for her. *A gentleman to the end.*

Stephen closed the door behind her and motioned her away. He stood and watched her leave, not moving from the spot he occupied until she was almost out of view.

Gabby groaned, not at the offer she'd made him but at the fact that she'd stabbed him in the first place.

* * * *

Stephen Hunter pressed his left hand to the stab wound in his ribs while he drove with his right. His black Firebird hummed under him, and he was glad that he went for an automatic. He'd bleed out if he had to shift. His mind was split: one part on ghosting so the beasts wouldn't converge on him in his weakened state, one part on reaching the manor house, and one part assessing his wound.

The knife had been tiny compared to a sacred weapon, maybe four inches of blade but wickedly sharp, a woman's blade. He laughed harshly that the damned beast Polero hadn't laid a claw on him, but a woman had nailed him well. It was an impressive bleeder. He would have left the blade in place to minimize bleeding, but Gabrielle had been so startled when that baby-stealing beast dematerialized that she pulled it out before he could stop her. She shouldn't have nailed him, but he'd been so intent on getting a deathblow on Polero, he had let his concentration on anything else falter. Worse, the time she'd cost him had allowed Polero to escape again.

Still, Stephen couldn't blame Gabrielle for her reaction. He had unghosted and landed his bleeder on Polero as he saw the beast go for her throat, but she hadn't seen his fangs. Gabrielle had believed the man was about to lay a playful kiss on her throat. It was a ploy the turned had learned from Veriel, courting a woman before using her.

Had she waited an instant longer to strike her blow, she might have realized that the blood covering her was the foul, black blood of a beast. She hadn't, but Stephen was sure that she wished she had.

He replayed the shattered look in her pale blue eyes, the swollen, tear-stained cheeks. She was lovely and strong, and that heartbroken expression had convinced him to show her she had done no real harm.

His body remained in a fierce arousal at her offer. He wasn't sure if he'd take the young woman up on it. Not that he'd complain about a night of sex with the spirited lass, but it smacked of deceit in getting her to bed. Was it honorable to accept an offer given under such duress? He'd have to consider that carefully.

Stephen pulled up to the gate at the manor house and reached his left hand out to the access panel. He had to reset the machine once when he hit a five instead of a two with his shaking, blood-slicked fingers. Bleary-eyed, he made it through the gate and into the underground garage.

He'd stumbled from the car and was halfway to the stairwell when Corwyn burst out. Stephen had only a moment to consider when he had let his ghosting slip before he lost his balance and landed in a heap on the concrete, cursing under his breath.

Corwyn flipped him to his back and pulled his jacket away to check his wound. His brother swore fluently, then ordered Colin to call Michael, one of their doctors. Stephen cried out as Corwyn applied pressure to the wound.

"It's all right," Corwyn assured him. "We've seen worse. Why didn't you let us track you?"

"Had to protect her."

Corwyn nodded in understanding, but his eyes burned in *Blutjagd.* "What beast did this to you?" he demanded.

Stephen barked in laughter, then grimaced as it jarred the wound. "No beast. A woman," he panted out. He smiled at the memory of the petite blonde with the flashing blue eyes and the spray of freckles over her nose and cheeks.

"A woman?" Corwyn asked in disbelief.

Stephen's smile spread. "What a woman," he quipped as he slipped into the darkness.

* * * *

June 26th, 1982

Corwyn smiled as Stephen opened his eyes. He could tell immediately that his brother was lucid again. "Good evening. It's nice to see you looking better."

Stephen winced as he shifted on the bed. He scowled at the IV line in his arm. "Get this damned thing out of me. You know I hate them."

"You didn't give us much choice." Corwyn started peeling the tape from the shunt, removing the apparatus and leaving Stephen with a gauze pad on his arm while he ditched the IV in the bathroom. He sliced the bag of fluid into the sink before dumping the empty shell into the trash can.

"How long have I been out?"

"About twenty hours. Next time, let us track you. We actually had to transfuse you."

"I couldn't," he decided miserably. "I needed to protect her. By the time I knew she was safe, I was in no shape to take on a beast. I had to keep ghosting until I got home."

"Gabrielle?"

Stephen looked at him in shock. "Yeah. Gabrielle."

"You talk in your sleep."

Stephen darkened.

"She made a real impression on you."

"Yes, I suppose she did." He ran his hand over the injured spot on his ribs. "All four steel inches of it."

"I wasn't referring to her blade. I was referring to the petite pixie you've been talking to for the last day." Corwyn raised an eyebrow suggestively. "I never realized you were so—inventive with women."

Stephen smiled weakly. "She has a body made for adventure," he admitted.

Corwyn nodded. "Would you prefer to eat here or in the kitchen?"

Stephen scowled as he rolled stiffly to his feet. "You know the answer to that."

"I'll see you in the kitchen." Corwyn didn't wait for Stephen's nod before heading down the hall. He took the stairs two at a time, considering Stephen's wild ramblings.

His youngest brother was only twenty-four, far younger than modern-day Warriors typically chose a mate. Still, Hunter needed heirs. With Anna lost to them, it was up to his brothers to provide those heirs as soon as possible.

Corwyn sighed. There would be no heirs from Colin. Had Colin not had his own disastrous brush with printing, he might someday submit. Short of Stephen dying without heirs, there was no chance of that happening. If he did submit, Colin would approach mating as a loathsome duty to be fulfilled. Corwyn shuddered at the thought.

No, the heirs would come from Stephen. If his mad ramblings were the beginnings of printing and Ms. Farris would have him, Corwyn would facilitate the match in any way he could. Gods forbid, if Stephen's printing turned as sour as Colin's had, Corwyn would let Stephen have his healing time. Eventually, one of his brothers had to print and produce children, else Hunter would die.

Chapter Two

July 2nd, 1982

Stephen walked down the hall toward the entryway, his nerves vibrating in anticipation.

He gave himself a mental slap. Gabrielle's promise had been given in a moment of stress. He shouldn't be set on it. Stephen prepared himself emotionally to assure her he was healed and check on her before leaving her in peace. In the intervening week, she had surely decided that offering her body to a complete stranger, even one she'd injured while he was saving her life, had been a mistake. He'd say a final goodbye and go find a willing woman for the night.

For some reason, the thought of satisfying himself with anyone but Gabrielle depressed him. Stephen smiled at the arousal that the thought of her promise had kept him in all week. Daydreams of her had filled every unguarded waking moment and engendered erotic dreams while he'd slept.

Stephen was passing the library when he heard Corwyn call for him. He sighed and made his way into the room.

"Yes, Corwyn?"

"I need you to do some tracking for me," Corwyn informed him. "Paper trail work."

His heart sank. *Not tonight. Any night but tonight.* "Umm. Can it wait one day or is it urgent?" Stephen tried to keep his voice neutral, but he could guess that he failed.

Corwyn's head shot up, and he scanned his gaze over Stephen critically. "You have something more important planned for tonight?" he asked with a raised eyebrow.

Stephen felt his face burn. "I... No, Corwyn. Of course not. My duty is more important." *Damn it!*

Corwyn sat back in his chair and furrowed his brow, swinging his pen as if he was considering something. "It's a woman, isn't it?"

Stephen averted his eyes. It had been less than five years for Corwyn. His brother still had nightmares of Anna's death, of Veriel taking her, and of his missing child being stalked by beasts. Stephen couldn't admit that he was begging off for a woman to Corwyn.

"Is it serious?" Corwyn interpreted his silence correctly. "The truth, Stephen," he warned.

"I don't know," he admitted. He chanced a look at Corwyn nervously. He *had* been arguing how insane his fascination was with himself on the way down the stairs.

"What's her name?"

"Gabrielle Farris."

Corwyn smiled. "The woman you saved last week. Your check said she was a clerk at the courthouse."

Stephen nodded, feeling on safer ground. "Yes. She is."

"How appropriate," Corwyn drawled, hooking his hands behind his neck.

"Is it?" His confusion had to be evident on Stephen's face.

"Oh, it is," Corwyn decided. "You don't remember what you said to Anna after she planted my blade in Veriel, do you?"

Stephen groaned at the memory. "Woman sticks a blade in me, I'd think twice," he parroted his words from that night.

"Which makes it poetic justice that you're burning for her."

"Corwyn, I—"

"Get going. You can't know if it's serious discussing it with me. If it is serious..."

"Yes?" Stephen asked.

"Don't come back for a week, if she'll have you, and bring her home as your mate as soon as she'll let you."

He nodded in relief. "Thank you, Corwyn."

"Don't thank me. If you're printing, don't let anything screw this up."

* * * *

Gabby glanced at the clock for the tenth time in an hour. Stephen wasn't coming, she decided miserably. What had she honestly expected? After all, she had stabbed the man while he was trying to save her from a vampire. Even if his wound was healing well, why would he want to come within miles of her?

Still, the bad boy smile he'd gifted her when she'd suggested he stop by had seemed sincere enough. His smile had been heart-stopping. She still wondered what was wrong with her that she had been standing there, covered in vampire blood and nursing Van Helsing embodied, and all she could think about was sex. It wasn't her typical response, but there was something undeniably sexy about the man, something that made her head swim.

She sucked in her breath as the doorbell rang and she forced herself to walk to answer it when she wanted to run. Gabby pulled the door open and smiled at the sight of him in one piece.

Stephen raised an eyebrow and tapped the spy hole. "You didn't check," he chided her.

Gabby laughed in spite of herself. "I wasn't aware that vampires rang doorbells."

"Beasts aren't the only dangerous creatures in the world. Plenty of them are human."

"Point well taken. Won't you come in?"

He glanced at her uncertainly. "Gabrielle—"

"Gabby," she corrected him.

"Gabby. I just want to say up front—if you don't want to go through with this—if you've changed your mind, I understand. You don't owe me anything. This is my life. This is what I do. My...payment comes in other forms, from other sources."

She looked at him, shocked by the speech. Gabby stepped to him on tiptoe and wound her hands around his head to draw his mouth down to hers. He was here, and he'd have to be really disinterested to avoid her advances.

Avoiding was the last thing he seemed intent on doing. From the instant her lips touched his, Stephen took over, lifting her with one arm while his other held her mouth to his. His hunger was like a living thing, his mouth seeking more than a simple kiss from her.

Gabby barely heard the door close as he carried her inside. The hand on her scalp disappeared momentarily, and she heard the lock snap shut. The wall was suddenly at her back, and his mouth left hers as he straightened and pressed the hard ridge of his cock to her.

Stephen groaned and looked at her with a longing that shook her. "I've dreamed of this all week," he admitted.

Heat pooled at the apex of her thighs. Stephen closed his eyes and pressed to her again, as if he felt that miniscule change in her.

"So have I, Stephen."

"Tell me what you want," he requested. "Anything you want."

"Next time." *God. Please, let there be a next time. This time is sure to be over far too soon.* "I promised you anything you wanted this time."

He managed a strangled laugh. "Gabby, you don't understand. I want you so badly that I'll take you here. Like this." Stephen sank his face to the deep vee of her silk shirt, pressing kisses to the cleavage she'd left clearly visible to him.

Gabby undid the buttons, baring herself to his seeking mouth. She gasped as he sucked at her nipple through the lace of her bra. "Undress me without putting me down, and you have your wish," she invited.

Stephen met her eyes. His smile spread, and he captured her mouth with a fever. Her shirt disappeared off the ends of her arms and her bra from between their bodies in a blur that made her head spin. His mouth left hers, and Gabby shivered in anticipation of what he would do to grant her unconventional wish.

She groaned as his hands slid up her thighs, pushing her skirt ahead of them until his fingers rested on the lace of her panties. His knee edged up as the skirt did, balancing her while he undid the button and zipper at the waistband and pulled it off over her head.

He removed her heels and thigh-highs, tossing them over his shoulders with a smoldering look. His fingers played at her panties while he surveyed her body and considered his next move.

Gabby moved against him purposefully, the sensation of his jean-clad thigh through the slick lace making her feel weak and empty. "Stephen, please. Rip them if you have to. I don't care. Really, I don't."

He chuckled. "Now why would I ruin such a lovely piece of clothing? If I can manage it without tearing them, what will you promise me?" His fingers teased inside the crotch of her panties, and he shuddered as she groaned, his thigh muscles clenching under her. "Tell me, Gabby." His voice went hoarse at that.

"Anything. Please."

"What will you give me?"

"All night long," she decided suddenly. "As many times as you can."

"You may regret that choice."

"I doubt it," she breathed, arching to him as Stephen slid his hand down the back of her panties and cupped her buttocks skin-to-skin.

"Does that mean you'll cooperate?" he teased, pulling her to the rigid length straining at the front of his jeans.

She nodded shakily. "Tell me what to do."

"Hold onto my shoulders."

Gabby wrapped her arms around his broad shoulders, nipping at his jaw and ear while he dropped his knee and stepped back from the wall. He supported her weight easily with his left hand while his right worked the panties off, pulling this way and that until they slid to her ankles.

Stephen pulled them away with one last tug, swung them on his fingertip, and flipped them toward the door. "All night," he mused. He shot her a hungry look. "And against the wall for a start."

Before she finished her internal commentary on how much strength what he just did took, Stephen unbuckled his belt and dropped his dagger to the floor behind his ankles.

"Afraid of a repeat?" she teased.

Stephen laughed as he opened the button fly of his jeans with a single pull. "Do I need to be?"

"I'm content to leave the weapons to you."

He slid his left hand down her thigh slowly, lifted her at the knees, and pulled her legs around his hips. Stephen pressed her back to the wall, and she felt his jeans retreating against her thighs. He paused, pressing against her for a moment before he surged up into her.

"Second thoughts?" she panted out, trying desperately to think clearly.

His laughter choked off into a groan. "Not on your life," he assured her as his movements speeded.

Gabby arched to him, offering her breasts to the mouth exploring her while he filled her, stretching her around him. Stephen moved in her urgently, anchoring her hips to him as he possessed her.

She felt herself spiraling away under the attention of his mouth and his thrusts deep inside her. Gabby knew it would be like this when she made the offer: hot, mindless, addictive. Was he mindless for her? He hadn't asked if she was safe, if she was taking the birth control pills that made her comfortable with something so crazy as inviting Stephen home with her and promising him a night like she planned to show him.

Stephen brushed his lips over her forehead, then straightened his body to push deeper into her. Gabby cried out, suddenly at the edge of an orgasm she hadn't seen lurking so close.

"Come for me," he whispered against her hair, moving one hand to tease at her clit.

She shattered, screaming at her loss of control to his gentle hands. Stephen followed her. His cry was ragged as he tensed inside her, filling her with an incredible wave of soothing heat.

His hand cupped her head, and he kissed her gently. "Gabby, tell me what you want," he pleaded again. "Anything you want."

Gabby laughed, amused by his comment. He couldn't possibly be ready again that quickly. "You don't need to recover?"

He surged into her, groaning as his still-erect cock hardened further. "With you? I don't think sated or recovered are words that will come readily to mind. Did you really mean all night?"

"I think I mean forever."

"Don't use that word yet. You don't mean it." He suddenly seemed serious.

Stephen kissed her again, his tongue caressing hers as he slid gently back and forth. He brought her up slowly, his body almost careful in his handling. He didn't release her mouth, nibbling and sucking at her between deep, drugging kisses. He exploded, filling her with a searing release that set off her internal contractions again.

He pulled back, his eyes fierce and his arms shaking around her. "Tell me what you want," he ordered in a low, gruff voice. "I will not take you against this wall a third time."

"My bedroom is upstairs," she whispered, lost in those eyes as she had been when she'd stabbed him.

Gabby held to him as Stephen walked. She shouldn't be sure about forever. She hadn't had more than thirty minutes in Stephen's company since the shout that made Antoñio Polero recoil from her. But, she was sure. Gabby hoped that the night wasn't all he wanted from her.

* * * *

Stephen's mouth quirked up in a faint smile as Gabby's fingers trailed up the underside of his balls, and he hardened in response. He thanked Ani that she seemed as insatiable as he was. Stephen opened his eyes a slit, watching the intense expression in her blue eyes as she played at his body. He ran his hand up the curve of her spine to smooth the riot of blonde curls that brushed her neck.

"What are you doing?" he asked.

"Considering tying you to my bed."

A wave of pure pleasure shot through him at that bold statement. "I'm not saying that the idea holds no appeal, because I would love to be at your mercy—"

"But?" she asked, enticing him with a kiss on the swollen head, promising him more of her delicious mouth.

"What brought this on?"

Gabby flashed him an impish grin, and her nose crinkled on the adorable spray of freckles he found himself nuzzling as he took her. Everything about her—from her pink painted toenails to her soft pixie cut that formed her wild, morning curls—fascinated him.

She dropped her head and kissed the pink scar left from the wound she'd given him a week earlier, then straddled him smoothly. "The sun's coming up," she informed him with a pout.

"And? I'm not a beast. I'll take you out on the balcony and make love to you as the sun rises if it would make you happy."

"I said all night, but I don't want you to leave. I thought, if I tied you to the bed..." She blushed. "I wonder how long it would be before someone came looking for you."

"A week," he answered simply, privately cheering that she didn't want him to leave.

Gabby furrowed her brow. "You're serious."

Stephen nodded, rubbing his thumb over her nipple while she considered his announcement.

"Why a week?"

"My oldest brother told me not to leave you for a week if I decided to marry you. He ordered me not to come home for that long if I decided I was serious."

She worked her mouth as if she didn't know what to ask first. "You told your brother you wanted to marry me?"

"No. He told me. He knows the look of a man who is far-gone well enough to know I have it bad for you.

So he ordered me to decide if I was serious and bring you home with me if I was."

"And?" she asked nervously.

"And what?" he teased, knowing full well what she was asking. He cupped her breast in his hand and watched the nipple harden for him.

"Are you serious? Do you intend to stay the week?"

"Do you want me to be serious?" That was the important question, after all. Stephen had known what he wanted when she'd toyed with the magic word *forever*. He had to know she was willing to consider forever as a reality very soon. Stephen was already further gone than he liked to admit.

Gabby nodded quietly. "Can I say forever yet?"

"No. Not yet." He drew her toward him and sucked in the nipple, fondling it with his tongue. Stephen released it with a playful lick. "When I ask you for forever, you have to mean it. I take forever very seriously."

"When. Not if," she noted breathlessly.

"My mind is made up. I need to be sure yours is, too." He moved to the other nipple, reining himself in as her core heated, slicked for him again.

"What's involved in forever?" she asked in a dreamy voice.

"You know what my life is. I hunt. Sometimes, I would have to go on trail. You've seen what I'm like when I'm protective. I would be very protective of you." He slid her further down his body, his cock screaming to sample the heat gathering in her while he talked. Just talking about making her his mate was driving him crazy.

"Go on," she whispered, her fingers massaging at his male nipples.

"You would move to the manor—or one of the smaller houses with me. In matters of your safety, you would defer to myself and the other Warriors."

He kissed her neck at the spot where Polero had intended to take her blood. The smell of their sex on her skin made him crazy for her.

Everything about her makes me crazy for her.

Stephen wanted to mark her, to leave an outward sign that she was his. He'd never wanted to do that. It smacked too much of what the beasts did for his tastes, but Gabby was different. She was his. He nipped at her, sucking her skin into his mouth gently.

Gabby moaned, her heat intensifying against his stomach. "Yes, Stephen. Please."

"I want to mark you," he admitted, his words muted against her skin.

"I know."

He groaned as he pulled at the sensitive skin of her neck, holding her still for his intimate assault on her. Stephen was surprised by how quickly he managed to leave his sign on her. He was more surprised by how excited it made Gabby to be marked as his.

"Do you want me to be serious?" he asked again, kissing at the love bite he'd left on her.

"My work?" she asked, continuing the questioning she had every right to engage in. Mating with him was a permanent move. She should be sure before she agreed to it.

"If you wish. You won't have to, and you can travel with me if you don't work. It's your choice."

"What is the manor?"

Stephen smiled. "It's huge and beautiful but lived in. If you hate it, we can use one of the smaller houses, but you would be safer at the manor."

She bit her lip lightly. "Do you like children?"

He hardened further at the thought of Gabby carrying his children. Stephen ran a teasing finger through the patch of curls at her pelvis. "Love them. Do you want children?"

Gabby nodded, blushing again. "Absolutely. Right away, if you're willing."

Stephen laughed lightly and moved the finger from her curls to rub circles around her clit slowly. "The day you promise me forever, you have my permission to throw away those nasty little pills you're taking and let your body prepare for a baby." *My baby.*

Her eyes widened. "How did you know?"

He slid his fingers lower, teasing the engorged slit and sliding inside her. Gabby's eyes closed, and she moved against his hand slowly. Stephen watched her taking her pleasure with a thrill.

"Your body tells me quite a bit," he assured her. "Now. Are you sure you want me to be serious? I can be very serious."

"Is this the moment that you ask me for forever?"

"No. This is the moment you find something to tie me to your bed. I intend on taking the week. I'm going to make love to you until I can't help but ask you for forever. How does that sound?"

Stephen groaned as she shattered around his fingers.

Chapter Three

July 6th, 1982

Two days later, Stephen thought he wouldn't survive if he didn't ask. Still, he held off until Gabby came home from work on that third day. He met her at the door, then swept her off of her feet and into the living room. He cradled her to the sofa beneath him.

"I have to ask," he breathed. "Give me forever."

Gabby's eyes glittered. "Take me to the manor."

"Why?"

"You're going to make love to me after you ask, right?"

"Yes. I am."

"Then I want you to make love to me in the bed we're going to share. Will you do that one thing for me?"

"I would do almost anything you asked. Pack an overnight bag. We're spending the night there."

"Convince me to call in sick, and I'll pack for the rest of the week."

His smile spread. "You have my word."

Stephen was practically carrying her when he swept her into the manor house. He nodded to Colin as they passed the library, ignoring his brother's questioning look. Gabby preceded him into his room, and Stephen dropped her bag on the floor, reaching for her.

She stayed him with hand on his chest and a laugh. "Not so fast, Warrior."

"What?" Stephen masked his frustration as best he could, but he was nearly crazed in his need to complete printing. His body was taut in preparation.

Gabby reached into the zippered pocket on her bag, pulling out a pack of birth control pills. She waved them under his nose, then turned to saunter through the open door into his three-quarter bath.

Stephen followed her in confusion. What did the pills have to do with anything? Gabby waited for him by the sink, the round container open in her hand.

"What are you doing?" he asked.

Gabby turned to the sink, leaning to outline her delectable bottom against her skirt. "You said I could throw these away when you asked," she purred.

Stephen snuggled his body behind her. "You want me to ask, then wait while you poke out those little pills and throw them away?"

"Who said anything about waiting?"

Stephen groaned. "I thought you wanted me to make love to you in my bed."

"Next time." She was breathless, and her scent increased in her excitement, testing Stephen's resolve to take her slowly. Gabby spread her legs and pushed back against his erection in invitation.

Stephen placed his hands on her hips, meeting her gaze in the mirror. He slid his hands down the front of her skirt, stopping as he reached her knees. Her silky skin teased his fingers. Gabby had removed her nylons while she'd packed her bag, a fact that had escaped him in his rush to get her here.

He eased his hands up her thighs, cupping his long fingers on the inside curve and spreading her further as her skirt retreated with his hands. Stephen knew before his fingers reached her core that he would find her bare beneath the skirt.

Gabby moaned as he teased inside her wet slit. Stephen slid two fingers inside her, and she grasped the edge of the sink. He eased his hand out slowly, and she whimpered at the loss.

Stephen kissed the back of her neck while his hands worked to free him from his jeans. Once they were pushed over his thighs, he unbuttoned her blouse to her navel, noting that she had removed her bra along with her other underclothes. He seated the head of his cock in the sweet cream between her thighs and surged into her, cradling her body to his. Gabby cried out, already nearing climax. Stephen stilled, his fingers massaging her nipples while she writhed against him.

"I want you, Gabrielle. Will you be my wife and mate forever?" he gasped.

"Yes. Oh, Stephen, don't stop."

"The pills," he crooned.

Gabby made as if to throw the whole container into the trash. Stephen stopped her, cradling her wrist in his hand.

"One at a time," he whispered.

She popped the first pill out with shaking fingers and tossed it in the sink. Stephen rewarded her with a smooth withdrawal and filled her again. Gabby gasped and met his eyes in the mirror, pleading with him and fevered in her need.

"Another," he prodded, knowing that he couldn't play this game indefinitely.

Another pill landed in the sink, and Stephen repeated the long, slow slide inside her. Gabby's legs shook under her. Two pills rolled down the porcelain, and Stephen smiled.

"So impatient," he chided her.

He didn't execute his slow slide in her again. Instead, he massaged her nipples, pulling her shirt from her waistband and undoing the last two buttons. Stephen guided it off her shoulders so it gaped open over her chest, displaying the hard peaks of her nipples for him.

"I'm going to suck them, Gabby."

She made an inarticulate sound of longing.

"Not now. After we've come, I'm going to suck them. Pills," he reminded her.

Another pill hit the sink.

"Better." He performed his long, slow slide, paused and did it again, groaning at how close he was. This teasing was driving him as mad as it was driving her. "How many are left, Gabby?"

"Three."

"All of them." His voice was rough now.

They hit the sink in quick succession, and Stephen kept time with them. Beyond control, he continued the pace, one hand playing at her breasts while the other held her hips still for his thrusts.

Stephen looked at their reflection, grimacing at his loss of control. He was wild-eyed, in a frenzy to claim his mate. He'd waited too long to ask. He should have asked before he was this crazed. Gabby was so slight and helpless in comparison to his height and strength that Stephen cursed himself. He could hurt her so easily, without meaning to. He had so little control left, he feared he would hurt her.

Gabby pushed back on his length, and Stephen growled, closing his eyes as he tried to rein in his reaction.

"No." Gabby gasped. "Don't hold back."

Stephen snapped, lunging into her again and again while Gabby urged him on. She shattered, her muscles contracting around him as her hands slid from the edge of the sink. Stephen threw out his hand instinctively, cushioning her body as he thrust one final time. He roared as he emptied his seed into her. She was his to love and protect forever now, his mind and body at peace as it hadn't been for days.

He stood, panting as he regained control. Stephen opened his eyes fearfully, taking in the sight of Gabby, still impaled on him. Her clothing was half off her body. He had torn her blouse in those final frenzied moments.

Stephen cursed softly as he eased her blouse off and lifted her off his length and onto the edge of the sink. His hands shaking, he wet a washcloth in hot water and stroked it over her core. She wasn't bleeding. Of that, he was grateful. Stephen could have done irreparable damage.

Gabby winced, and Stephen set his jaw angrily. He'd hurt her. Could he ever trust himself again? Stephen considered having Colin take her to Michael while Corwyn ended his threat.

"Stephen, you need to stop," Gabby groaned.

He closed his eyes, dropping to his knees with his shoulders slumped in defeat. "I'm sorry," he croaked. "I won't hurt you again. You have my vow."

Her hand trailed through his hair, firing his body for her. He cursed himself for the reaction. He had no right to touch her if he hurt her.

"Is that what you think?" she whispered. "You think that you hurt me?"

Stephen looked up at her uncertainly. "You said— You winced. I didn't—"

Gabby took his hand, still resting on her knee, and lifted it to her core. As his fingertips brushed over her, a fresh wave of her lubricant mixed with his seed leaked from her. Her engorged nether lips trembled against his hand. She threw her head back and arched to him with a moan.

"Stephen," she pleaded.

He pushed to his feet, kicking his jeans and shoes away impatiently. Stephen kissed her, savoring her arousal as Gabby wrapped her legs around his waist and drew him closer. He nuzzled her lips.

"I haven't hurt you?" he asked quietly.

Gabby shook her head.

Stephen slid his fingers inside her, and her eyes dilated. Her responses didn't indicate that she was in pain. Stephen had never seen her so aroused. He massaged her inner muscles, watching as Gabby's breathing hitched and her lower lip trembled.

"Why did you tell me to stop? Why did you wince when I touched you?"

"I'm...sensitive. Your touch—" She gasped. "Oh...Stephen."

His cock throbbed at his name on her lips. "Do you want me to stop, Gabby?"

She shook her head frantically.

Stephen lifted her slightly and eased inside her again, his knees weak at the pleasure riding his nerves. He walked to the bed, Gabby's light bounce in his hands nearly undoing his resolve. Stephen laid her beneath him, taking her in slow, smooth strokes. Gabby arched her breasts to him, reminding him of his promise.

* * * *

Corwyn smiled as Stephen and Gabrielle came down to dinner. "I told you a week," he teased his impetuous youngest brother.

Gabrielle darkened and looked away.

Stephen grinned and wrapped his arm around her. "I couldn't last that long," he admitted. "If you don't mind, we'd like to finish that week off as a honeymoon."

Corwyn nodded. "Take your time." Hunter could support the loss of a roving Night Warrior for quite some time if it meant heirs to the house. His gaze flicked to the open vee of Gabrielle's blouse. Corwyn raised a questioning brow at Stephen, demanding with his eyes to know what madness his brother was playing at by not protecting his mate properly.

Stephen's smile disappeared. He held his wife's chair for her, attending to her comfort as he hadn't her protection. "Things being as they are, Corwyn..."

Corwyn nodded in understanding. "You want her to wear the Lord's seal."

Stephen nodded.

"I think you're right. Gabrielle—"

"Gabby," she corrected him.

"Gabby. I don't know why Stephen hasn't done this yet."

"She's never been away from me after dark," he protested.

Corwyn shot him a quelling look. "And, you know better than to trust to that."

Stephen grimaced, his face darkening. "Yes. I do."

Gabby looked from one brother to the other in confusion. "Done what?" she asked nervously.

Stephen sat beside her, taking her hand. "There is an amulet we'll give you. It will protect you. With it on, the beasts can't touch you. If one does, the amulet will push it away, cause it pain, and call us to kill it. You need to wear it all the time. Never take it off, or you may forget to put it back on."

Gabby nodded. "And the down side to this is what, precisely?"

Corwyn laughed heartily. "There isn't one. Well, except that the amulet isn't very stylish."

"I can live with that."

"Good." Corwyn rose and collected a Lord's seal from the inside pocket of his coat, hung on the rack near the kitchen door. He returned to them and tossed it to Stephen. "If you would."

Stephen looked to him uncertainly. "It's the Lord's seal," he pointed out.

"You have my permission. She's your mate, Stephen. You should see to her protection."

Stephen nodded, averting his gaze in understanding. Corwyn bit back tears as Stephen gave Gabby his blessing. Stephen understood. Corwyn couldn't give a Hunter mate the Lord's seal and speak the blessing. The memories of Anna were too new, too raw.

Stephen sealed the blessing with a passionate kiss. Corwyn nodded. It was good that they had passion. Stephen would sire the Hunter heir, the heir that should have been Corwyn's son.

Gabby blushed. "I'm glad you did that," she commented to Stephen.

Corwyn howled in laughter at that, then laughed even harder as Stephen shot him a dirty look.

"Corwyn wouldn't have kissed you like that," he protested. "Tell her."

Corwyn stifled his laughter, suddenly acutely aware of the edge of *Blutjagd* burning in Stephen's hide. "Down, boy. She's your mate. I couldn't have feelings for her even if I wanted to. You know that."

Stephen sobered, his bloodlust melting away. "I'm sorry, Corwyn."

"Don't worry. I'm stable. I promise." He lied, but it helped to say it. "I would have kissed your forehead, Gabby. You have my word on that."

She nodded, then turned to the doorway as Colin breezed into the room.

Colin smiled widely, then crossed the room to plant a quick kiss on Gabby's forehead. He handed her a gift and took his seat. "Welcome to the family," he intoned, a smug smile and raised eyebrow announcing his happiness that it was Stephen who fell and not himself.

Gabby looked to Stephen uncertainly. Corwyn bit back a laugh at that. It was obvious that the couple hadn't spent a lot of time talking while he was away from the manor.

Stephen cleared his throat. "Corwyn is my oldest brother, the Lord Hunter. He's the head of our family. Colin is the next oldest. Then me."

Gabby nodded. "Are you the baby or are there more brothers around here?"

Colin snorted in laughter. "Oh, she'll do. Calling Stephen a baby. I'll have to remember to share that one with Kord on his next call."

Corwyn shot him a hard look. "Just because Stephen gave you a scar the last time you were foolish enough to say it—"

Stephen sighed. "No. There are only three of us. Thank Ani for that favor!"

Gabby furrowed her brow. "Is Ani your mother?"

"No. We have a set of gods. Ani is the mother, the goddess of life...of birth."

She fingered the amulet. "Oh."

Corwyn shook his head. "They're our gods. Worship your own, Gabby. We'll celebrate the usual holidays. We're not offended by our wives' beliefs."

Gabby smiled, her eyes lighting. "So, are there other wives?" she asked. Her smile disappeared, as Corwyn bit back a painful lump in his chest and Colin's jaw tightened. She sank closer to Stephen, looking from one older brother to the other.

"Gabby," Stephen began.

"No," Corwyn decided. "We'll tell our own stories."

"As you wish."

"You know we mate for life, Gabby?" Corwyn tried to keep his voice matter of fact.

She nodded. "Stephen told me that."

"I had a wife. Her name was Anna. She's been dead for four years."

"I'm sorry, Corwyn," she choked out.

"Don't be."

Gabby looked at Colin. "You don't have to—"

Colin shook his head. "I broke printing," he offered simply.

She looked at Stephen in confusion, no doubt unfamiliar with the terminology Colin had used.

Stephen sighed. "If you would have refused me, it would have been very painful. I might have gone insane. I think I almost did that anyway." He darkened.

Gabby touched his cheek. "Is that why you were worried about hurting me?"

Stephen kissed her hand, closing his eyes as if some memory tortured him. "When I thought I had..." He cast a miserable look at Corwyn.

Corwyn winced as his meaning became clear. "You considered having me destroy you. Didn't you?" He didn't really need to ask the question, but something told him that it would be better for Gabby to know what lengths Stephen would go to in order to protect her, even from himself.

Gabby gasped. "You didn't," she demanded.

Stephen nodded and lowered his face to her shoulder. "I'll never lose control again. You have my vow on that."

"You will never consider deserting me like that again. Do you understand me, Stephen?" Her eyes were fierce, and her voice shook in anger.

"Only if I'm a danger to you. I swear it."

"You won't be."

Stephen nodded, and Gabby's expression softened. She smiled and planted a kiss on his cheek as he raised his head.

Gabby draped her hand over his shoulder and met her husband's gaze. "So, which one of them told you that you wanted to marry me?" she asked.

Corwyn laughed. "That would have been me."

She glanced at Colin. "How did you know to buy us a gift? Did Corwyn tell you?"

Colin grinned. "Based on the racket from the general direction of your room, I guessed."

Gabby blushed at that.

Chapter Four

August 1st, 1982

Colin smiled at the sight of Gabby wrapped in Stephen's arms. She was practically crushed to his chest in the midst of a passionate kiss. Colin could smell her arousal plainly.

When Stephen set her away from him, Gabby gave him a look of stark invitation. Stephen faltered, then turned to Colin, seemingly disconcerted. Colin had only a moment to wonder if Stephen would be more a danger to himself in the face of a beast than the trained Warrior he was before Stephen regained his composure.

"Keep her safe for me," he ordered gruffly.

Colin hesitated. It would be an insult to hint that Stephen might not be up to hunting, but Colin considered saying it. If Stephen died without producing heirs, it all fell to Colin. He steeled himself. It would be too much of an insult, and Colin would never dream of worrying Gabby by making her think her husband might not come home to her. He nodded stiffly. "You know I will."

Stephen touched Gabby's face with a look of indecision and pain. He glanced at Colin and nodded grimly, resigned to his duty. Stephen turned and walked briskly to the stairs to the garage.

Gabby watched him in concern. "He will be okay, won't he, Colin?"

Colin sighed and steered her toward the kitchen with a hand on her elbow. "You know what we do, but I promise that Stephen is one of the best there is."

She nodded and played with her amulet nervously. "He seems so—not unhappy exactly. It's like he's in pain, and I don't know what to do about it."

He nodded. "He hasn't left you before. Corwyn only left Anna once, and it was disastrous." Colin motioned her to a chair and started making a tray of fruit, cheese, and fresh-baked bread for them.

"What happened to Anna?"

Colin faltered in slicing an apple, moving his hand to avoid a deep cut with the sharp blade he wielded. He sucked in his breath in surprise. "An elder named Veriel fixated on her. He—wanted to take her from Corwyn."

"He killed Anna because he couldn't have her? How could he with the amulet on?"

"She... Anna killed herself rather than—She gave her amulet to Erin."

"To who?"

Colin looked at her in disbelief. "Stephen hasn't told you?"

Gabby shook her head. "No. Corwyn said he'd tell his own story. I guess Stephen took him literally."

Colin brought the platter to the table and started slicing cheese. He tried to organize his thoughts while Gabby chewed on a slice of apple.

"Erin is their daughter—Corwyn and Anna's daughter."

Gabby choked on the apple. "Oh God! That elder—"

He shook his head. "It was Veriel's intent to take them both. He didn't want her dead—either of them dead."

"What happened? Is she? Did he take—Oh, Colin." Gabby looked hopelessly unhappy.

"Erin is missing. Lost to both sides. Anna didn't want Veriel to find Erin. All we know is that Anna hid her somehow, then gave her life to keep Erin hidden." Colin flicked a glance at her. "We won't give up. We can't give up—ever."

"Of course not. Do you have any clues? A picture? Anything at all?"

Colin bit back his pain at that. "She was newborn. Stephen and I—We never saw her."

Gabby tried to blink back tears. Failing that, she wiped them away and stared at the platter.

"It won't happen again. I doubt Veriel will fixate like that again. Even if he did, we'd close ranks. When you decide to have children, you will never be left alone. You have my vow on that."

She nodded.

Colin cursed the pain he was causing her. Worse, he hoped he wasn't giving her incentives not to bear children. If she decided that, Colin would be forced to print. The thought of it made ice floes of his blood. Printing again was more frightening to Colin than Veriel, by far.

At least Veriel could only kill him. Veriel couldn't drive Colin mad, though losing Erin nearly had. His oath scar ached at the memory of his vow, taken over Anna's still form.

The alley was icy cold. Colin wept when he found her, the shattered glass around her hand. He dropped to his knees, touching her lifeless skin as if there was some hope that he was mistaken, some hope that she might have a spark of life left in her body. Colin wrapped Anna in his jacket and ghosted her to his car, determined to allow Corwyn to grieve his loss and bury his wife properly.

He stood over her, shaking in his own loss. Colin had come to think of Erin as the child he would never have. He had planned to offer an oath of personal protection at her birth.

Colin pulled his sacred weapon, drawing his blood and painting the blood seal over Anna's heart and his own. "My blood for her, Anna," he whispered. "My life for Erin's. I am her servant. I swear it by Ani, by Syth, and by Dobler. And by Jee, I swear Erin will have justice."

Colin looked at Gabby, smiling weakly. The sooner she and Stephen produced children, the better. "Have you and Stephen discussed children at all?"

Gabby smiled. "We want them right away. Stephen took me to Michael to start me on vitamins and run some tests before we start trying."

"Smart man." Stephen had always been mindful of careful planning.

"I can't wait, Colin." She blushed and bit into a slice of cheese, looking thoroughly excited by the concept of children.

Colin smiled widely. His sanity was safe with that attitude. "Did Stephen say when you'd be fertile?"

She looked at him in confusion. "He can do that? Tell when, I mean?"

"Of course. He has to check. It's part of Warrior law. Hasn't he?"

Gabby shrugged. "Does he have to tell me when he checks it?"

"No, but he is supposed to check." *And ask when it's time. What is Stephen playing at? In a month, he hasn't asked? She hasn't been fertile?* If Gabby wasn't capable of producing, Colin was in the hot seat again. What had Michael's tests shown?

Gabby's innocent question drew him back to the conversation. "Then how would I know?"

"I guess you wouldn't."

Colin replayed the scene in the hall in his mind, his unease growing with each repetition. There was something seriously wrong here. Stephen hadn't been himself. He had been unsettled, skirting the edges of some nameless panic. Something wasn't right.

He nodded and gripped Gabby's hand as if in comfort, sensing her. Colin hid his shock carefully, offering her a smile to match her own. "I'm sure it won't be long. Stephen wants a son. I know he does." *Then why did he leave her?*

Gabby sighed. "I know. I guess I'm not very patient."

Neither am I! What game is Stephen playing? "I'll be right back, Gabby. I need a file from my office."

She smiled and nodded, then took a bite of bread.

Colin strode to the stairs, his confusion and anger growing with each step he took. He turned toward Corwyn's office instead of his own, knocking briskly and entering without waiting for an invitation.

Corwyn raised an eyebrow over the file in his hand. "Is there a problem, Colin?"

"Call him back."

"Stephen?"

"Call him back, Corwyn. Now."

Corwyn sighed. "He has to go."

"Send me. Whatever it is, send me." Colin fought back desperation at the idea of Stephen wasting this chance.

"I'm sending Stephen. I have to."

"She's cusp. She's fertile. Call him back. He—"

Corwyn grimaced. "You didn't tell her, did you?"

"No. Why?"

"Don't."

Colin stared at him in disbelief. That was an order. "Stephen—"

"Knows. That's why he asked to go."

"What?" Colin demanded, keeping his voice low so as not to project beyond the thick wood door.

"If he stayed, he couldn't guarantee his control."

"And what will change next month? She wants a child, Corwyn."

"I know she does."

"Then why—"

"Michael ordered Stephen to wait a month."

Colin sucked in his breath in surprise. "Why? What's wrong?"

"Birth control pills. It's standard practice to allow the body protection for the first cycle after you stop them."

"And?" he prodded.

"At the office, all Gabby could talk about was having a baby. Michael knows our drives well. He pulled Stephen aside and ordered him to give her that month to allow her body to prepare properly."

"Stephen thought Gabby would refuse to wait." He didn't question it. Colin's mind worked at that. What would a choice like that have done to Stephen?

Corwyn sighed. "If she did, Stephen knew he wouldn't be able to deny her. They both want this too much."

Colin sobered. "Where is he, Corwyn?"

Corwyn dropped his gaze. "You know where."

He shuddered, an involuntary motion as his mind rebelled. "It's that bad?"

"Yes. It is. He wants this desperately. Too desperately."

Colin nodded and left the office, his mind spinning. Stephen went to the mad cabin. They only used it when it was absolutely necessary. Colin had used it when he went through his printing madness. Corwyn had used it to howl out his grief for Anna. Her grave was on the grounds, dug with Corwyn's blade and bare hands in the frozen clay and slush, his blood staining the snow red. Now Stephen would make use of it, and another Hunter Warrior would scream his mad rage at a dark, uncaring sky.

Chapter Five

August 30th, 1982

Gabby smiled at the sound of the shower. Stephen was back early and showering. That meant he'd had a productive night. Gabby stretched in the bed. The rush of the kill would leave him sexually aroused. Gabby loved nights like this.

She smelled the fresh scent of Stephen's scrubbed body just before he lowered himself to the bed.

On that one point, Stephen was adamant. His soiled clothing and gear were taken care of and his body scrubbed of all trace of what he did before he approached her. Having seen Gabby fairly bathed in Polero's blood at their meeting, Stephen had sworn to do everything within his power to keep her from the harsh realities of beasts in the future. He'd literally gone down on one knee and taken an oath on it.

As she expected, Stephen gathered her to his body, his lips seeking hers. Gabby sank into his passion, pressing her hips to him in invitation.

When Stephen broke off the kiss, she giggled. "What if I had been asleep?"

"You weren't. I could see your eyes."

"Ah, that lovely night vision you have." It was true. He could see her clearly, no matter how dark the room was, but she could barely make out his features in the dim light he'd left on in the bathroom.

"I could hear your breathing."

"Is this where I say, 'What big ears you have?'" she teased.

He nipped at her throat, his teeth pulling gently, toying with the idea of leaving another love bite, no doubt. "I could smell your arousal. You knew I would want you, and it excited you. Am I wrong?"

Gabby shifted her chin to give her blessing for the bite he was itching to give her. "You know you're not."

She bit her lower lip, as he suckled at her, marking her as his again. There was something inherently sensual about that move, about knowing she was his, knowing Stephen would never take another woman while she lived.

Stephen kissed the mark he'd left tenderly, then kissed her brow.

There was something hesitant about his touch. "Stephen? What is it?"

"I have to ask you something."

Something he thinks I might say no to — or be upset about. "What is it?"

"Did you — You said you wanted a baby right away, and you stopped taking your birth control pills about seven weeks ago, and —"

"I'm pregnant?" A thrill passed through her at the thought of it.

"No," he assured her hurriedly.

"Oh." Her heart sank at that. Seven weeks was more than enough time.

"I would never —"

"Stephen, please explain. I've never seen you like this." No. That wasn't quite true. He'd been like this when he'd thought he hurt her, when they'd sealed printing. What could possibly be wrong now?

"Even though you said you wanted a baby right away, I have to be sure. Our laws say you have to want this. I can't take the chance of one, if I'm not absolutely sure you want a baby."

"I'm ovulating?" Colin said Stephen would know when she was fertile.

"In a few more days, but you could conceive even if we took the chance tonight and then started using protection." He tucked a small box into her hands.

Gabby didn't need to ask what it held. She fisted it, fighting back tears. "You don't want a baby?" she whispered.

"More than anything," he assured her, "but if you're not ready —"

"I am." She tossed the box in the general direction of the nightstand.

Stephen seemed speechless. He pressed her into the mattress, his knees urging her thighs apart silently. He kissed her, a slow, thorough kiss that made promises of loving her completely. Gabby arched up to him as Stephen slid a fraction of an inch into her.

He pulled back again. "Tell me you're sure, Gabby."

She groaned, her body in a fever for him. "I'm sure. Please —"

Stephen slid to the hilt in her, filling her in one leisurely glide. Gabby expected him to be fevered, but he took her solemnly, every stroke smooth and slow. Even when she urged him on, Stephen kept a torturous pace that sent her into one climax after another. He cupped her face, exploring her mouth while he pushed her steadily higher.

She shattered again, her short nails holding to Stephen's back her only anchor to reality. As if that one stimulation was too much for him, Stephen followed her over with a hoarse shout.

He hardly faltered, resuming his pace as he turned to his back and surged into her. Gabby groaned as she arched and took the last of him into her body.

"Stephen?" she gasped, needing to understand what he was doing to her and unable to ask.

He curled his upper body, taking one turgid nipple in his mouth. "Tell me if it's too much, Gabby. I'll rein it in when you want me to."

Gabby shivered, as he took the other nipple in his mouth. "Will you always be this..." She couldn't come up with an adequate word for it.

"You're giving me a tremendous gift." He planted a kiss on the aching nipple. "I want hours of fond memories, not a few rushed moments." Stephen rolled his tongue around the nipple and sucked it in gently. "Let me have you for hours."

Gabby gasped as he repeated the slow torture on her other breast. She moved against him, feeling the pressure build in her breasts and womb.

"God, Stephen. You can have anything you want. Just don't stop."

"All I want is you." His voice was laced with a longing, as if he was starving and she was all he needed to be sated.

She smiled. "And our son."

Stephen tensed inside her, wave after wave of hot cum swirling through her. Gabby screamed, her mind and body heavy and heated as Stephen withdrew long enough to lift and turn her, easing back inside Gabby's throbbing core again. She moaned at that, at the feeling of completeness that gave her.

He pulled her back slowly, until Gabby lay over him, her legs spread wide over his upper thighs and her head over his heart, his breath stirring the curls on her head. His hands circled her body, one massaging her clit in time with his thrusts while the other stroked her breast, making her entire body pick up the rhythm of his possession until it felt as if her heart beat in time with his lovemaking.

His voice was a harsh whisper. "Tell me about our son, Gabby."

She smiled, the image filling her mind. "He'll be tall like you and have your charm. He'll have your coloring and my curls. He'll forever be in trouble, but we'll love him despite it."

"What's his name?" His thrusts speeded at that. Stephen was getting off on hearing her predictions.

"You want me to name him? Now?"

"Now. The first name that comes to mind. Your fondest wish for him."

Gabby moaned, as his hand slid lower, massaging the sensitive flesh around his thrusting cock.

"What's his name, Gabby? Tell me, please."

She shook her head, her mind refusing to grasp on a name despite all the time she'd spent with baby name books in preparation for the day they discovered she was carrying. *Any name,* she argued. She had to be able to remember one name from those books. "Brandon," she gasped. "Brandon Alexander Hunter."

"Yes. By Ani, yes." His breathing was harsh. The hand on her breast massaged the nipple to a painful peak she wanted him to suck. "Will you nurse him, Gabby?"

"Yes."

"Oh, gods." The hand at her core moved to her curls, pressing her hard against him as Stephen's thrusts started coming faster and deeper. "Tell me again, Gabby," he begged.

"Stephen?" What was he asking? She couldn't seem to keep track of the conversation.

"Tell me you want my son growing in your womb, that you'll nurture him there and feed him your sweet milk."

"Yes. Stephen —" She groaned as his hips jerked, her body on the edges of release again. How many times could she survive in a night?

"Tell me you'll deliver my son into my hands for me to protect and teach."

"Deliver?"

"I want to touch him at birth, hear his first cries — " Stephen was fevered, his movements bordering on the fierce need of their printing seal.

"Give me your son, and you can catch him as he leaves my body," she promised.

Stephen roared, climaxing again. For several long minutes, he held to her, panting as her body spasmed around his length. He rubbed a shaking hand over her womb, pressing his lips to her temple and murmuring promises to her of all the things he would do for her while she carried.

When the shaking stopped and she lay spent over him, Stephen eased her to the bed and kissed her forehead. "I'm sorry," he breathed. "Lie here. I'll get a cloth."

Gabby grasped at his arm, confused by the abrupt change in him. "Why? I don't understand."

Stephen sighed and stroked his knuckles over her mouth. "I promised I wouldn't lose control again. You deserve better than that."

"I don't under —"

"I knew last month when I left here that it would be impossible, but I —"

"Last month? When you went on trail for ten days?" This wasn't making sense.

He grimaced. "I didn't go on trail. I went — away," he admitted miserably.

"You knew I was fertile, and you left on purpose?"

"Michael said your first cycle was off-limits, because of the hormones clearing your system. I was afraid — If you asked me for a baby, I knew I'd ignore his orders and take one from you, no matter the risks. I wanted it too much not to." His eyes pleaded with her for forgiveness.

"So, you left without discussing it with me?"

"I nearly went mad, knowing you were high cycle and I couldn't even ask. If I'd asked and you refused, I could cope. Not being able to ask... I knew then that when I had the chance, I wouldn't be able to —"

Gabby pressed her cheek to his smooth chest. She smiled as his still-insistent erection brushed by her hip.

Stephen shuddered and pulled away. "I'm a dog, Gabby. I have no control over my body where you're concerned. I'm sorry. I'll go —"

Gabby kissed his chest, putting the pieces together at last. "No you won't." Stephen wanted to shield her from what he felt were the failings of his curse. As he insulated her from the sight and smell of his hunting, he wanted to insulate her from the times when he was most fully a Warrior, the times when his control was strained, even when that strain was a pleasurable one.

His hand touched her cheek. "Gabby, you don't understand. I could hurt you. I don't want to, but I could without meaning to."

"You won't. You'll be chivalrous." She kissed at his throat, smiling at his gasp of surprise.

His lips pressed to her forehead, and his muscles tensed, as if he were fighting back his arousal. "I don't understand," he managed.

"You'll take me to the shower and help me bathe."

Stephen groaned, laying back into the pillows. "Gabby, I don't know how much self-control —"

"Shut up." Gabby pressed her lips to the edge of his jaw, nipping at him as he did at her throat.

"What?" he asked, his mouth feathering over hers.

"You have phenomenal control, Stephen. Besides that, we're not done with our discussion yet."

"What discussion?" She could barely tell that he was paying attention to the conversation. His hands stroked down her spine and drew her closer to him as his lips traced her ear.

"We can start off with how I intend to decorate the nursery."

Stephen's fingers drew circles in her curls, moving lower until he traced her swollen clit.

"Then we can discuss our rules for raising children."

He groaned, his fingers parting her and stroking inside her. "Gabby, if you continue this conversation..." he growled.

She circled her fingers around his cock. "You see?" she breathed. "You have incredible control. I expected you back inside me two statements ago — Daddy."

Stephen scooped her up and headed for the bathroom, turning up the dimmer slightly on the way. He reached for the shower controls, turning his head for a searing kiss. "I don't have much control left," he warned her over the pounding shower spray.

Gabby grinned at that. "I should hope not."

* * * *

September 8th, 1982

Gabby nodded her thanks as Stephen set a plate of food in front of her. She knew he was bursting to tell his brothers their news. Gabby could hardly believe that Stephen's senses could tell him she was pregnant when a home pregnancy test wouldn't be able to tell her for weeks.

Stephen cleared his throat. "I need to make a change in our routine," he announced.

Corwyn raised an eyebrow. "And what change would that be?"

"From now on, one of us will be picking Gabby up at work and escorting her home."

Gabby dropped her fork in surprise. "Stephen, we never —"

"It gets dark before your workday ends," he argued.

"I am not helpless, Stephen. You, better than anyone, should know that."

Stephen set down his fork and leaned toward her. "I warned you what I would be like."

"And I told you I would let you know when you got overbearing. Guess what? That moment has arrived."

Corwyn darkened in anger. "Enough," he shouted over the end of her protest. "Now... Stephen, it does seem that you're out of line. Justify yourself, or I will have to judge for Gabby in this matter."

Stephen motioned to her. "I will not allow *my* son, the Hunter heir I might add, to come to any harm."

Colin froze with his fork halfway to his mouth, a laugh bubbling out of his shaking chest. "Damn you. Do any of you know how to announce a baby in some normal fashion?" He launched to his feet and planted a kiss on Gabby's cheek. "Congratulations, Mama."

Gabby blushed. "Thanks, Colin."

She stared in wonder as a pained expression flitted onto, then off of his face. Colin nodded and sank bank into his chair. Colin said he didn't want to print, didn't want the responsibility of children. From the haunted look in his eyes, Gabby had to wonder what he really wanted and what he'd convinced himself he didn't want.

Corwyn nodded. "Congratulations. Now that this matter is settled —"

Gabby smiled in victory.

Stephen shook his head. "It's not settled. I was serious about the escort."

Gabby gaped at him. "Stephen, this isn't necessary."

Colin looked from her to Stephen. "It is the Hunter heir we're talking about, Corwyn. Unless Gabby has another —"

Corwyn shot Colin a quelling look. "I have no idea why all of you assume I've taken Gabby's side in this."

He met her gaze. "I'm sorry, Gabby. They're right. The survival of our house depends on that baby. He is heir. I have to judge for Stephen."

Gabby rubbed her forehead. "Heir? What about —" She blanched at the sadness in Corwyn's eyes. "I'm sorry," she mumbled.

Colin shook his head. "Even if Erin isn't found early enough to free her, she will never be Hunter's lord — er — lady. She will be of whatever house she marries into, if she marries a Warrior. If not... I suppose she'd still be a Warrior of Hunter? At any rate, the lord is always the oldest male —"

"That's sexist," she decided.

Corwyn sighed. "Maybe so, but it is our law, and your son is heir."

Gabby sent Stephen a pained look. "You could have warned me."

Stephen shrugged. "I thought it would be obvious. Even if Colin married today, our son would be the oldest of the new generation. Heir."

Gabby nodded. "Okay. You win. I'll have an escort."

Chapter Six

November 30th, 1982

Gabby glanced at her watch again, tapping her foot impatiently. The men had never been late before. If Stephen wasn't waiting for her by the inner doors at five o'clock, it was one of his brothers, without fail. It was almost five-thirty, and there was still no sign of a Hunter man, though she should have left fifteen minutes earlier.

"Are you sure you'll be all right?" Evelyn asked, pulling on her coat.

She forced a smile to her face, waving the gray-haired department head away. "I'll be fine. I'm sure Stephen just got stuck in traffic."

"He's usually early," she noted, still looking uncertain.

"Go on. I'm sure your daughter is waiting for you with that grandson of yours in tow. Even if Stephen is late, the security guards are still here."

Evelyn nodded and let herself out, locking the door behind her.

Gabby glanced at her watch again, noting that only another three minutes had passed. She grumbled a curse. Three months ago, she would have been miles away by now. In any other circumstances, she would have waited outside for Stephen or taken the bus home. Tonight, she was three months pregnant with the Hunter heir, and the Warriors' displeasure at her taking chances would not be pretty.

"Brandon, you will *never* treat your mate this way," she ordered under her breath. "I'll teach you better than this, if I have to employ my own form of trial."

Gabby startled at a sound from the back room. Was that the printer? It couldn't be. No one was in the office to run it. Still, it sounded like the dot matrix clattering through page after page of computer paper.

For an agonizing moment, she considered leaving, walking away without checking. *To hell with waiting for Stephen.* Gabby grimaced. She was the same woman who'd stabbed a maniac with a knife a little more than five months ago.

Gabby pushed off the counter and headed for the computer room. Vampires didn't ring doorbells, they didn't make good dates, and why would a vampire bother with a computer?

She opened the door and stared at the printer in confusion. It was printing page after page of reports, just as she'd thought.

Gabby sat at the terminal and read from the screen. She shook her head and read it again. What she was seeing made no sense. The printouts would take half the night. Who would ask for this? Especially when the dot matrix would have to be restocked with paper several times to complete it and there was no one here to do that?

"It must be a glitch of some sort," she decided. "I'll have to call the rep in the morning."

In the meantime, Gabby started shutting down the system. This should have been done before Evelyn left. Why hadn't she done it as she usually would? As the computer powered down, the printer ground to a halt.

The silence was like a living thing in the room with her. Gabby looked around, searching every dark corner for some sign of another person, but there was nothing. It was almost too quiet. Gabby shivered and pulled her jacket close around her shoulders. She glanced at the darkness outside the window, then at her watch. Where was Stephen?

A heavy-handed knock made her jump. Gabby launched out of the chair and sprinted through the main office, pulling open the door without asking who was on the other side.

Corwyn brushed past her, his sacred weapon drawn and his face tense. He ran a hand over her cheek. "Are you okay?"

Gabby nodded, her breathing still strained. "Where is Stephen?" she demanded, her voice shaking.

"Flat tire." He guided her to his back, pressing her hand to his ribs. "Stay with me. Here at my back, so I know where you are."

Corwyn eased back to the computer room, picking up her pocketbook from where she'd dropped it as she bolted. Gabby shivered at the blast of cold air that coursed through the now-open window. Corwyn left her at the doorway and closed the window, examining the room.

She glanced at the printer in confusion. The printouts were gone. Gabby manually turned up the last page and ripped it off, trying to make some sense of what she was seeing.

Corwyn returned to her side, took her by the arm, and guided her out of the office, hitting the light switches and locking the door behind them. They didn't speak on the drive back to the manor house.

Corwyn was shaking in rage. Gabby, meanwhile, had finally worked out what was going on.

* * * *

Corwyn nodded his assurances as Stephen swept Gabby into a shaky hug. "She's fine," he calmed his youngest brother's still-rising *Blutjagd*. He motioned them to the library.

Gabby sank into the couch, looking less pale and shaky than when she'd opened the door at her office. She accepted a glass of milk from Colin and started drinking it.

Corwyn settled into one of the matching chairs and leaned forward, his elbows braced on his knees. "Why were you so nervous when I showed up?" he asked calmly, reminding himself not to upset her further while she carried.

She shrugged. "I don't really know. I think I'm getting used to being surrounded by Warriors. I was shutting down the computer and it was too quiet and —"

"You were in that room when I arrived?" he asked urgently. "When I came to the door?"

Gabby nodded and sipped her milk again.

Stephen tensed beside her. "The beast was there? In the room with her?"

Corwyn nodded, and Gabby grimaced, putting her glass down on the table beside her.

Colin paced the length of the room slowly, turning back to them at the far end. "She can't go back," he decided.

Gabby darkened. "No. You have no —"

Stephen put up a calming hand and talked over her. "Gabby, our son —"

"You promised," she shouted. "You promised I could keep my job. Your honor —"

Corwyn groaned. "Did you?" he asked.

Stephen darkened and nodded, dropping his gaze in embarrassment. "I did. Before I sealed my printing, I told her that she could keep her job if it was her choice to."

Colin shook his head angrily. "Her safety is more important. She agreed to follow orders when it came to her safety."

Gabby faced Corwyn, no doubt realizing that he would be the final judge. "On the condition that I could continue to work if I chose to."

Colin growled in frustration. "Somewhere else. You can work somewhere else."

"Until a beast comes within a block of me there. This will never end."

"He wasn't a block away. He was in the room with you, at your back," Colin insisted.

Corwyn looked from one face to the next. No matter what he decided, he was about to alienate someone in his family. "Gabby, we do have to consider your safety," he began.

She stood, her hands on her hips. "They weren't after me. I guarantee it."

"What?" Colin stormed.

"Use your head instead of your bloodlust for a minute, Colin. Most of the beasts in this area are Veriel's turned."

Corwyn nodded. "What does that have to do with anything?"

"He can only die by the hand of a Warrior Hunter born."

Colin snorted. "So, he never dies. I'm sure he'll be crushed."

"Use your head. He could have killed off the Hunter line in the first two centuries, before you perfected ghosting and new fighting styles. He didn't. He always left a few alive to carry on the line. Why? He wants to die someday. He just doesn't want to die today."

Stephen nodded. "She's right about that. It makes sense when you think about it. He doesn't dare kill the next generation."

Colin shook his head. "Why not? There's one more Warrior that could print," he noted bitterly.

Corwyn winced at the panic in his eyes at that idea. He raised a hand to still Gabby's coming outburst before it could start. "Veriel won't take that chance if he wants to be sure that Hunter continues. You could be killed without producing heirs. He wants an heir. He wants more than one, so there will always be a Warrior and a lord."

"Then what was the point of tonight?" Stephen asked quietly. "Why come for Gabby like this?"

"He didn't," she said. "He couldn't see me."

"What do you mean?" Corwyn asked.

"My amulet. Most of the lights were off. I was in the main office with the door closed. I wasn't moving around and making noise. He thought he was alone when he fired up the printer."

"And?" Corwyn prodded, anxious to hear her theory. She seemed certain that this wasn't about her; he had to know what she was basing her belief on.

"He didn't want me. He wanted computer files in the office."

"What kind of files?" Colin asked, his anger dissipating in light of this new information.

Gabby pulled a printout from her coat pocket and handed it to Corwyn.

He scanned his gaze over it without comprehension. "What is this?"

"Adoptions. Names of adoptive parents, children's names and ages, dates of adoption, and cities from the database. Those are from Alabama in 1979."

"Why would a beast want these?"

Gabby sighed and glanced at Colin before turning back to Corwyn. "Erin is four, Corwyn. She was an infant when she disappeared. She's been adopted by someone by now. There's no way she hasn't been."

Stephen sucked in his breath. "She's in Alabama?"

She rolled her eyes. "No. Well... I mean, I don't know, but neither do they."

Corwyn rubbed his aching neck, feeling a sick headache coming on. "Explain."

"There was a whole set of orders for the printer when I shut down the computer. Printouts for every available state for every year from 1979 through the present. Look at the list." She came to sit on the arm of his chair and pulled a pen from her pocket. Gabby crossed off the first three names.

"What are you doing?" Corwyn asked.

"What they will. Look. Matthew and George are male. Not Erin. Susan is eight years old when Erin would have been a baby." She crossed off fifteen more names until only one was left.

Corwyn nodded. "Out of nineteen, only Eve Price is left on the list."

"You understand what they intend?"

"How do we stop them?"

"We can't. They failed here. They might come back, but they probably won't. The database hooks most states now. They can do this anywhere."

Colin paled. "We have to find her first."

Gabby nodded. "My thought precisely. There's only one way to do that." She stood and started buttoning her jacket.

"What do you think you're doing?" Stephen asked, his eyes wide.

"Requesting the same information he did. He only got thirty pages tonight. We could have them all if we hurry."

"What do you mean?" Colin asked.

Gabby nodded to the page in Corwyn's hand. "Page thirty-one, right?"

He nodded uncertainly.

"How high a level does a beast have to be to dematerialize objects with him?"

Corwyn barked a short laugh at that, remembering the open window. "The highest of the high or elder. The open window. He took what he had and ran."

"That's my guess."

Corwyn stood and grasped her hand, a smile on his face. "Let's go. Oh, and Colin? She keeps the job."

Gabby gave him a quick hug and headed for the door.

* * * *

January 2nd, 1983

Corwyn scrubbed his hands over his face, grumbling at his lack of sleep. It had been a month of pure hell, and they were no closer to Erin than they had ever been.

The adoptions for 1979 were the worst since there were so many babies listed. Luckily, there was a notation when the baby involved was a neonate adoption that allowed the Warriors to pare their list down to five hundred older female babies. Even that was nearly unmanageable. Only eight of them were Caucasian with the Warrior coloring. Checks with the adoptive parents or with protected in government service ruled out all of them as possibilities.

Unfortunately, the beasts were searching the same information. There had been two altercations where Warriors rebuffed beasts who seemed to want to snatch any child matching the general Warrior description to allow Veriel to weed them out later. Those two girls were placed under protection, much to the relief of their adoptive parents.

The adoptions from 1980 netted only eighty babies to check, three of whom fit the profile. There were only two each in 1981 and 1982. None of them were Erin. After those failures, they'd moved onto the states that had individual databases not hooked to the main bundle, but even those had turned up nothing of use.

Stephen nodded stiffly as he sank into a chair across the desk from Corwyn. "The Armens have checked the last two in California from their database listing."

"Neither of them is Erin," Corwyn stated, certain that he didn't need to make it a question.

Stephen didn't answer. "We've exhausted the states with searchable databases. The rest are individual paper files. Those will be impossible to search."

Corwyn nodded, fighting to release the tension in his chest causing the burning pain around his heart. "Which states?" he whispered.

"Texas, Mississippi, Alaska, New Hampshire, Rhode Island, Maine, and Vermont."

"Yeah."

"We'll find her, Corwyn. We'll find her someday."

"Only if the Stone wishes it."

"What did you say?"

"The Stone won't let her be found until it's too late. I know it in my soul, Stephen. Even if she's in one of the states we've searched, the file has fallen behind a drawer or was lost in a freak fire. The Stone would have seen to that. If it is there, it has been conveniently left out of the database somehow."

"At least the beasts can't find her. Wherever she is, Erin is safe."

"Yes. Safe."

Stephen nodded and left the room, looking as weary as Corwyn felt.

Corwyn stifled the urge to scream out his frustration. She was safe, but every day Erin was gone, he became more of a stranger to his own daughter.

Section Two

Colin's Challenge

Chapter Seven

June 15th, 1985

Jannelle Evans winced as the ER doctor put butterfly strips on the cut across her forehead.

"We'll keep you tonight for observation, but I expect you'll be out of here before noon tomorrow."

"Great," she grumbled.

"Is there anyone we should call? Someone who can drive you home?"

She stopped short of shaking her head. "No. I'll take a cab."

Thankfully, the doctor didn't press the issue. Even if Jan wanted to call someone, there was no one to call. Well, there was Uncle Devin, if she didn't mind him hiring a bodyguard for her. As it was, it would be hard enough to hide the bruise and cut under her bangs and makeup for a few days.

Oh, who am I kidding? Unless she bribed Paulings to keep her name out of his column, Devin would know about this by noon tomorrow.

But who else would she call? Her mother had died when Jan was a baby, and her father, AP photojournalist Scott Patrick Evans, had been a casualty of a terrorist uprising he was covering in Central America two years earlier.

Dragged on photo shoots or left with a nanny and tutors while Dad was hot-spotting the globe, Jan had never developed the talent of forming close relationships. Dad meant well. No boarding schools for his little girl, but a home without friends, a sporadic parent, servants, and security that had her labeled as the most protected little girl besides Christina Onassis wasn't much of a way to grow up, in Jan's opinion. Of course, no one ever asked Jan's opinion, and when she gave it, she was always assured it was all done for her protection.

The nurse settled Jan in her room and left. Jan sighed, knowing they would wake her several times to gauge her concussion. She snorted. Her head injury wasn't nearly as bad as the doctors believed. Jan didn't have a concussion. *At least not a serious one.* What she had was a lead on a story that would make her famous.

The police had dismissed her account as the disjoined imaginings of a woman suffering a concussion. Jan knew better. She knew what she saw before she got knocked for a loop, and she knew what she saw after.

The police had the dead body of the man who'd attacked her...if he was a man. The fact that his blood smelled like month-old garbage didn't faze them. In fact, one of them commented that he'd seen it before.

Seen that before? Damn!

Jan knew, before the bastard ended up dead, that he wasn't human. Her first clue had been when he'd appeared in her path out of thin air. Her second had been when pepper spray barely slowed him. Her third and fourth clues had been the fangs and glowing red eyes he had. The blood was just icing on the cake.

Of course, Jan had only mentioned his reaction to pepper spray to the cops. Any more than that and they'd think she was cracked.

No, the cops might have bought her story if she'd stopped there. What had cooked her was their opinion of her mysterious rescuer.

After her attacker knocked her around, Jan had lay on the ground, knowing she was about to become a deranged vampire worshiper's midnight snack. She had watched as the man was sliced and diced.

The problem was that she hadn't been able see her hero. It wasn't too dark to see him. He wasn't wearing a mask. He simply wasn't visible.

Not that she'd shared that with the cops. She'd told them that she hadn't gotten a good look at him at that time. *That much was certainly true,* she thought ruefully.

She had gotten one decent look at him. He'd knelt over her and checked her for injuries, most notably bites.

She'd surveyed him through her eyelashes. Her hero had been only a few inches taller than her five feet ten if she was gauging correctly. He'd looked incredibly strong, with a barrel chest, broad shoulders, and muscular arms and thighs.

His face had held her the longest. Serious and intense, it had been all sharp angles, from his furrowed brow to the tight-lipped expression over his chiseled jaw. His hair was black as the darkest shadows and clipped close to his head. His eyes were like onyx warmed near a campfire, black and shiny but somehow far from cold and hard.

Dressed all in black from his collared shirt and leather jacket to his jeans and armored boots, he'd blended into the night as if born to it. She'd caught a glint of his weapon, a knife more than a foot long, before he'd stood and walked away.

He'd smiled back at her and made one comment: "Balls of steel, baby." His smile had lit his eyes, making him heart-stoppingly beautiful.

Her hero had stepped aside as the cops rushed past him, grinning at them and giving a jaunty salute as they reached her side. That was the part that had branded her an unreliable witness. The two officers swore there was no one at the scene but her and the dead man.

There was a mystery here. Either the cops were in on this and allowed her hero his vigilante tactics or they really couldn't see him. If they couldn't, why could she? Who was her hero? What was he? And what was the man who'd attacked her?

Jan sank to the pillow and closed her eyes. *Strange.* She felt safe. Jan never felt this safe, not even in her own apartment with the security system Uncle Devin had insisted on.

* * * *

Colin Hunter stood in the corner of Jannelle Evans' room, ghosted and watching her carefully.

He scowled. Of all the people to get a glimpse of him, she had to be a reporter. Not just any reporter, but the hard-as-nails daughter of Scott Patrick Evans.

He had been sure she'd been out cold when he examined her. He was certain right up until Rachael Carson, a protected on the force, called him. Locker room talk was all about the reporter with a concussion who saw a dark Warrior savior who wasn't there.

Colin considered talking to her, but Jannelle Evans was dangerous. For one thing, she was a ballsy reporter with a name to make. At the moment, she had nothing but a rough description. She had no way to trace him, and they hardly moved in the same circles.

The other reason he kept his distance was more complex. Colin adjusted his jeans over his semi-erect length. If he spent time with Jannelle Evans, the raw need to see if her brass extended beyond self-defense into the bedroom would overcome his common sense.

Jannelle Evans was the type of woman who would warrant more than a single night of release, and that was dangerous. Seeing Corwyn lose Anna and Erin had steeled Colin's resolve never to print again. He'd barely survived Cass.

Stephen was mated with a son and another on the way. There was no need for Colin to risk his sanity and life, and any woman that made him think of exploring night after night of heated passion was a distraction he didn't need.

Janelle had spirit and fire that would never be reined. She wasn't the type of woman to take orders from Warriors. Becoming mate to a Warrior would stifle something free and beautiful in her, and Colin would never risk that, even if he was stupid enough to risk himself.

It was time to go home. Janelle Evans had nothing to go on. He would have to trust that was protection enough.

* * * *

June 30th, 1985

Jan sat at her desk, glancing over the file she was amassing. Research had always been one of her strong points, but she was finding a frustrating lack of evidence in this case. It had taken her two weeks to track down autopsy reports on half a dozen murders where the victims had matched her attacker's blood anomalies.

Tests on the blood had yielded confusing results. The chemistry was so badly skewed, the patient should have been dead. An acidic pH far beyond human tolerances, practically non-existent blood sugar and calcium levels, high levels of fat and sodium, high in several heavy metals, iron levels ten times normal, no white blood cells — How could a person live with a chemistry like that?

Three of the autopsies had mentioned abnormal musculature in the upper jaw. Two had mentioned a before-unseen form of radiation present in the body.

All had been killed by blades. Some had multiple wounds. Some had a single killing blow. All had a killing blow that took the heart. All were unsolved.

The killer or killers had never been seen...until now. Jan grinned at that thought. There was no physical evidence to suggest a killer. There were simply no clues.

She'd done a search for wanted men who fit her vigilante's description. There was nothing. Was she the only person who'd ever seen him? That hardly seemed possible, but what other options did she have? Surely, every person who had seen him hadn't kept silent for some reason.

"What are you working on?"

Jan jumped at the voice so close to her. She rolled her eyes at Jeremy Brand, one of the new night beat reporters. "Nothing much, Jeremy. Just a little after-hours research on a pet project."

"Don't you have a life, Evans? Why the hell are you still here at," he glanced at his watch, "nine o'clock?"

Jan scanned her gaze over Jeremy's six feet even, sandy blonde, blue-eyed, lean good looks. She'd much rather find her mystery man, but Jeremy could be fun if she was bored enough. "Is that an offer, Jeremy?"

He chuckled. "I'd probably get slapped with harassment if it was. Seriously, what's so interesting?"

Jan closed the file and locked it in her top desk drawer, suddenly self-conscious for no good reason. "Just a few homicides."

"Not your usual beat," he noted, leaning against the wall and crossing his arms over his chest.

She shrugged. "We all have inquisitive minds. If we didn't, we'd all be tax accountants instead of journalists."

Jeremy laughed. "Just be careful. There are dangerous beings out there who don't necessarily want to be found out."

"What did you say?"

His smile faltered. "What? Dangerous people don't like to be interfered with."

"But you didn't say dangerous people. You said dangerous beings."

Jeremy shrugged. "Did I? Well, I never really considered serial killers people."

"Who said —"

"You said homicides. Plural, Evans. What else would link them if not the killer?"

Jan nodded, unwilling to discuss what really linked them. "I'll be careful."

Jeremy shook his head and studied the ceiling. "Don't let Pierce catch you. You know how he feels."

"I know."

Jan did know. She had spent years building her own name, distancing herself from her father's shadow. She'd chosen editors and papers he'd never dealt with, trusting that Evans was a common enough name to allow her to escape notice. She'd cut her own niche here.

Then the paper had imported a new editor, Devin Pierce, Uncle Devin to her since she'd been five years old. Devin had seemed determined to follow her since the Dallas incident, and Devin Pierce was well-known enough to get a job in the industry anywhere he wanted to with a snap of his fingers if he lowered his typical price a bit.

So much for anonymity.

Chapter Eight

July 28th, 1985

Jan froze, a shiver of anticipation racing up her spine. She scanned the crowd on the street. *Pennies from Heaven come at the most unexpected moments,* Jan decided ruefully. She caught sight of her mystery man across the street.

It had to be him. At over six feet tall and wearing the same jeans and black button-down shirt with the sleeves rolled up he had on that night, he was exactly as she remembered. If he was wearing those high black boots instead of the tennis shoes he had on now, the black leather jacket, and that short sword wannabe of his, he'd be the image of that night.

She started following him, trying to decide how to approach him. It wasn't until she followed him into a baby store that Jan saw her true godsend. Not him, but the woman he was meeting.

The petite blonde who was showing about six or seven months pregnant was Gabby Farris. Jan hadn't seen Gabby since the younger woman quit her job at the courthouse. If she could just get her alone, Gabby could be a font of information. One of the reasons Jan liked talking to Gabby was that the woman was incapable of lying effectively.

It was a full ten minutes of following them, pretending to be interested in a crib mobile or a bassinet design, before the man kissed her cheek and disappeared with an indulgent smile.

Jan moved quickly. She waved to Gabby and made her way over with a wide smile. "I can't believe it's you. How are you, Gabby?"

"Wonderful. How are you, Jan? Still pounding the city beat?"

"Among other things. You look great. When are you due?" Small talk always helped put people at ease, Jan noticed.

"Not until New Years," she groaned. Gabby smiled at Jan's stricken look. "Small babies for small mothers be damned," she exclaimed good-naturedly. "Brandon was nine and a half pounds and twenty-three and a half inches. This one looks to be following suit, big like Daddy."

"Was that giant hunk your husband?" Jan gushed, cringing inwardly at the love struck act.

"Yes. That's Stephen." She practically glowed as she said it.

"What does he do?"

"He invests. His family has money. They're not rich precisely, but they have enough to be comfortable."

Jan glanced over Gabby's shoulder at the man. She was closer to him, and the picture wasn't perfect anymore. The man with Gabby was thinner, much thinner and maybe taller. There couldn't be two of them, could there?

She pasted on a coy smile. "I don't suppose tall, dark, and handsome has brothers?" Jan ventured wistfully.

Gabby laughed heartily. "Actually, he does, but they're not on the market."

"Married?" She feigned disappointment.

"No, just not looking. Actually, they are adamantly not looking."

"Do they look like yours?" Jan wagged her eyebrows.

Gabby's eyes narrowed, and Jan realized that she'd overplayed her hand.

"Why would you ask that?" Gabby asked suspiciously.

"Well, if they have your husband's looks, I'd give it a try anyway. After all, you never know until you try, right?"

"I know. I know them well enough to know they are not interested. Sorry, Jan." Gabby was nervous. She picked at the tie on her maternity dress and looked for her husband to return.

"Oh, well. Yours is a little tall and wiry for my tastes anyway. I always preferred broader and right about six feet, personally. And with my abrasive personality, I like a guy with lots of attitude."

Gabby's face paled.

Pay dirt. There is my connection. Mr. Mystery Man wasn't Gabby's husband, but one of his brothers.

Stephen came back to his wife, his smile fading into concern at the sight of her. "Gabby?" he asked quietly.

"I don't feel well. I need to go home. Now, please, Stephen."

"Yes, of course." He took the crib linens from her hand and placed them on the nearest shelf.

"Well, it was good seeing you again, Gabby," Jan cut in, angling for an introduction. "I hope you feel better."

Gabby nodded weakly, and Stephen raised a questioning brow.

"Sorry," Jan gushed, putting out her hand to him. "Jan Evans. I used to do research in Gabby's office."

Stephen took her hand in a firm handshake, and Jan saw Gabby grip his arm. *A warning?*

If it was, her husband missed it. "Stephen Hunter. Sorry we can't talk longer, but Gabby does need to lie down now. Maybe we'll see you again."

"I'm sure we will meet again, Mr. Hunter."

Gabby grimaced, and Stephen looked at her in confusion. He swept her away under his arm.

* * * *

Colin heard Stephen and Gabby coming in clearly. With their voices raised to an uncharacteristic high, it was hard to miss them.

"Calm down," his brother was urging her. "This is not good for you. I'm sure it will be fine."

"Fine? Stephen, I *know* her. She's a bulldog. She smells a story, and she's not going to let us go until she gets it. Why didn't I find a way to warn you?" she moaned.

"You can't know for sure —"

"She was blunt. I don't really think she's mastered more than Mack truck subtlety in her life. I'm telling you, she's met Colin. She described him to a T, and she's looking for him."

Colin launched for the entryway. "Who?" he demanded.

Gabby groaned and buried her face in Stephen's chest.

77

Stephen shot him a scathing look. "We'll discuss this later. Gabby is making herself sick over it."

"No," Gabby interjected. "She has enough information to find us now." She met Colin's eyes miserably. "Her name is Jan Evans, and she's —"

Colin felt his temper coming uncorked. "That damned reporter. I knew that one was going to bite me in the ass someday."

Stephen's jaw dropped. "What did she see?"

"Not much. She had a concussion when I got there. She wasn't bait. She has balls of steel. The beast was a low level, easy kill, but it was pissed off proper. She used mace on it. Maybe pepper spray."

"Okay. So, she can't be sure what she saw was accurate." Stephen's relief was palpable.

Gabby smacked his arm ineffectually. "Does it matter? She saw Colin kill a beast, and she can ID him now that she has tacked a name on. Consider this. Does she even realize what Colin killed was an honest to goodness vampire? What if she thinks he's a murderer?"

Stephen circled her with his arms and looked at Colin miserably. "See what I mean? She's making herself sick."

Colin nodded. "Get her settled with a cold drink and come to Corwyn's office. She shouldn't be this upset. It's not healthy."

Stephen nodded and led his wife away while Colin sprinted off in the direction of Corwyn's room.

A grumbled, "What?" greeted his knock.

Colin stuck his head in. "You'll want to get up for this."

Corwyn groaned. "I just got off trail. Is it that important?"

"Very."

The covers whipped back in irritation, and Corwyn dragged his jeans on. He muttered his way to the bathroom, obviously foregoing the idea of a shirt and shoes.

"I'll meet you in your office," Colin called out toward the half-closed bathroom door.

He didn't wait for an answer before going to his own office and rifling through his top drawer for the fact sheet he'd amassed on Jannelle Evans. Colin beat Corwyn to his office by almost five minutes.

When his older brother showed up, he had a forty-ounce mug of coffee in his hand. Corwyn settled into his chair with it. "Spill it."

"I'll wait for Stephen. No need to do this twice."

"I just saw him leaving the kitchen, looking rattled. Maybe you should fill me in," he suggested, taking a swallow of the hot liquid.

Stephen pushed through the doorway, looking intensely irritated. "Sorry I took so long. Where are we?"

"Waiting for you," Colin assured him. "How is Gabby?"

His jaw tightened. "Distraught. How do you think she is?"

"Down, boy. If anyone has to handle this, let me. It's my mess."

Stephen nodded slowly. "That's probably best," he agreed.

Corwyn looked at them in surprise over his mug. "Handle what?"

Colin sighed. "I have a reporter on my trail." He handed the fact sheet to Corwyn. "For the last five and a half weeks, she's had no leads."

Corwyn glanced up at him but left the question unasked.

Colin shrugged. "The fact that we all look so much alike has distinct disadvantages."

Corwyn groaned and looked at Stephen. "Tell me."

"The reporter came up to Gabby in the store to catch up on old times. Ms. Evans did the city beat when Gabby worked in the court clerk's office. At first, it was all innocent stuff. How are you? How far along are you? Oh, is that your husband? What a catch," he grumbled.

"And?" Corwyn prodded.

Stephen blushed. "She made a good show of playing love struck and asked if I had brothers. It seemed innocent enough, so Gabby confirmed that I did but assured Ms. Evans that you guys weren't in the market for wives. That's when she started asking if my brothers looked like me. Gabby has good instincts, and she knows this woman is a bulldog. She sidestepped it as neatly as she could." He took a deep breath.

"There's more," Corwyn guessed.

Stephen nodded. "The woman furnished a perfect description of Colin, right down to his sparkling personality traits, and labeled it her dream man. Gabby is expressive. Even without saying a word, her upset was written all over her face."

"That it?" Corwyn asked hopefully.

Stephen sighed. "No. Evans is good. She got me. I came back and found Gabby shaky and pale with no idea why. She tried to hurry me out of there, but she had no way to warn me off."

"And?"

"I introduced myself."

Colin groaned. "That's what Gabby meant about her having a way to track us."

"I'm afraid so. Gabby was smart enough not to mention our last name, and neither of us mentioned your given names, but I said too much. She's got me cold."

Corwyn rubbed his forehead roughly. "Okay. So, we have a bulldog reporter looking for a Hunter man, and she will obviously be able to tell which one of us is the right brother. Anyone have suggestions besides clearing out for a year or two?"

Colin shrugged. "Leaving now is risky. You know it's heating up again."

"I know. You have a better plan?"

"Yeah. I think I do. I'm going to talk to her."

Stephen choked. "You're kidding, right?"

Colin smiled. "No, I'm not."

Corwyn gave him a weary look. "And your plan is what?"

"Well, I'm not offering her an exclusive, if that's what you mean. I'll wing it."

Corwyn studied him. "You're looking forward to this, aren't you?"

"A woman who takes on beasts with her bare hands and pepper spray? Oh, yeah. I love a challenge."

* * * *

Jan knew something was wrong. She locked the file in her top drawer and listened for movement in the stillness of the floor. Jan peeked left and right down the hallway. There was nothing. Her mind was playing tricks on her. She turned and slung her purse over her shoulder. If she was this noided out, as the kids in the file room would say, it was time to leave.

"Hello, Ms. Evans."

The voice was deep, sure, and strangely familiar. Jan whipped around.

He was standing in her office, dressed as he had been that night. His eyes glittered in amusement, though his face was a study in calm indifference. He leaned against the wall beside the door, his arms crossed over his broad chest.

"I understand you've been looking for me. While I'm flattered, I don't believe for an instant that I'm your dream man."

Jan shook her head. At that instant in time, she could imagine him as her dream man. Wet dreams of hot, mindless sex to be precise. He was so undeniably masculine. He radiated control and confidence.

Oh, this is bad. I do not need to be thinking these thoughts.

She shook herself mentally. "How did you get in here, Mr. Hunter?"

"I have my ways. You've seen them."

Jan nodded and sat on the edge of her desk, swinging her leg. Mr. Hunter locked on the motion, his expression fierce.

"Why did I see you if the cops couldn't?"

"How do you know I'm real?" His grin was mocking.

"Don't play games with me."

"That is a little difficult to explain."

"Try me. I can follow pretty technical stuff."

Hunter chuckled. "I imagine so. You took enough science, math, and statistics classes to have them called minors officially."

Jan felt her face drain in shock.

He continued smoothly. "Typically As in your science classes, too. Of course, your computer grades were excellent. Not many people get an A-plus in COBOL. You're well known for your research skills.

"Don't look so shocked, Ms. Evans. You do your research. I do mine. It always pays to know your adversary. Don't you think?"

"Is that what I am? An adversary?"

"You don't have to be, but — Yes. You upset my sister-in-law in an effort to find me. I don't take that lightly."

"Protective of Gabby?"

"She's family. If someone said something against your father, you'd react." He shrugged.

Jan nodded. "Point well taken. I didn't set out to upset Gabby, you know."

His eyes hardened. "Then she's right. You have no subtlety. I'd add that you have no concept of empathy and grace to that."

Jan gasped for breath. "What the hell do you know about it?"

"I can watch you, remember?"

She blushed. In other words, he was judging her on isolated incidents without any concept of her past. "You've been watching me?"

Hunter shrugged.

"That stops right now."

He smiled rows of perfect teeth. "You stop investigating me, and I'll stop watching you."

"Why?"

"What do you think I destroyed?"

"Killed," she countered.

"Put out of the misery of its continued existence."

Jan hesitated. "I don't know. It appears to have once been human or humanoid in nature, but no human could survive the body chemistry it exhibited. Do you know what the radiation is? Is it some strange new isotope? Where did they contact it? Is that what destroyed their systems?"

His eyes narrowed. "Their? They?"

"Surely, you know the man you killed wasn't the first. I'd love to find out what they have in common, but they are all John Does that don't seem to match any known missing on file."

"You're trying to get yourself killed," he muttered. "You write about them, and they will kill you."

"They who? Fill in the blanks for me." A knot of nervous energy coursed through her.

"So you can get your story and get yourself killed? No way, lady." His eyes reflected the fury in his clenched jaw. "Let this go for your own good."

"Because you say so?" She'd always hated that reason. All her life, people had been ordering her around for her own good. How many times had she heard that litany? When Devin had her drummed out of Dallas and her life there, it was for her own good.

Hunter didn't answer.

"I will get my answers one way or the other."

She waited for Hunter to answer, but he gave her a stony look.

"There are answers here somewhere."

"I'm sure there are."

Jan startled at the sound of Jeremy's voice; she looked from one man to the other several times.

Jeremy scanned his gaze in the direction she did and shook his head in confusion. "Are you feeling all right?"

Hunter grinned widely, looking smug.

"Are you all right?" Jeremy asked again.

"Yeah. Just considering something."

She made a move toward the window, plotting a collision course with Hunter. He moved aside smoothly and guided her with a single hand on her hip to her destination. He felt solid enough. He looked solid to her, but she was sure Jeremy couldn't see him.

Jan pulled the shade down. Hunter's shadow fell across her chest from the light behind him. He shook his head, and his Adam's apple bobbed in suppressed laughter. Jan surged toward him, but he was a blur of motion ending to her left with a smooth bow and silent invitation to pass.

Jeremy stared at her. "Evans?" He put a hand to her flushed forehead. "Have you had dinner yet?"

She shook her head, focusing fully on Jeremy for the first time. "I'm okay, Jeremy. Just a little shaky."

"Well, it's my dinner break. Let me buy you something better than a burger."

Jan glanced around, but Hunter was gone, completely disappeared. "Yeah. I think that would be a good idea."

"I'll get my pack and meet you at the doors."

She nodded. "Yeah. At the doors."

His eyes darkened in concern. "Sure you're okay?"

"Fine. Close the door on your way."

His eyes narrowed.

Jan swiveled her foot with a painted-on smile. "Gotta straighten the pantyhose."

He smiled a slow, sexy smile and headed for the door. "Tease."

"Me?" she replied innocently.

At six feet, he met her eyes evenly in her heels. Jan raised an eyebrow at his hungry look.

The door closed, and Jan was all business again. She swept her arms in wide arcs as she stepped around her office. After three arcs, she growled in frustration.

"I just know you're still here, but you'll move before I touch you. You're not convincing me to back off unless you give me a damn good reason to. Copy or steal my file, if it makes you feel better. I can replace everything in it by this time tomorrow."

Jan slipped her purse over her shoulder again and headed for the door. She stilled with her hand on the knob, tensing as she felt someone behind her.

Hunter's voice was low, and his hot breath puffed on her neck. "I'll see you again, Ms. Evans. It seems you have other things to attend to at the moment."

"Is that a threat or a promise?"

"I don't make threats."

"That's good to know, Mr. Hunter."

"Oh, Ms. Evans. One more thing. I wouldn't sleep with Jeremy if I were you."

Jan stiffened. "Jealousy, Mr. Hunter?"

"Friendly concern. It's not an experience you would enjoy. I guarantee it." His fingers traced her arm.

"And what would I enjoy?"

His fingers stilled and moved away. "I'm sure I wouldn't know, but his tastes wouldn't be to your liking."

"You read minds, Mr. Hunter?"

"Sort of. I'll be making copies of your file, Ms. Evans, but it will be back in your locked drawer by morning."

"Should I leave the key for you?"

"That won't be necessary."

He backed away. How Jan knew that was a mystery to her, but she knew it.

"What are you, Mr. Hunter?"

"I'm just a man."

His voice was further away. He had moved.

"You should go." His voice dropped to a growl at that statement.

Jan shivered, suddenly aroused. "I won't sleep with him, Hunter. Jeremy really isn't my style." She didn't add that her style lately seemed to be Hunters, especially this dark Hunter.

There was a sound like a soft sigh. "I'm glad."

"Why?"

He moved. Jan felt his approach a split second before his breath was on her neck again, his lips a fraction of an inch from her.

"I don't want to see you get hurt," he whispered.

Jan moved back. Hunter didn't try to evade her. His lips brushed her neck, and the hard lines of his body pressed against her. His fingers skated down her hip. He moved away abruptly, his breathing harsh.

"You should go. Now."

Jan nodded and headed down the hallway, feeling more off-balance than she had in her entire life.

* * * *

Corwyn stopped in the doorway to Colin's office, watching his brother in concern. Colin stared off into space, a variety of paperwork strewn across his desk. Corwyn cleared his throat, and Colin startled.

"You didn't realize I was here. That's a bad sign, brother."

Colin scowled. "Take me to trial," he grumbled.

Corwyn's eyes widened. "Okay. You will explain." He dropped into a chair across the desk from Colin and motioned to the paperwork. "What's all this?"

"Beast autopsies."

"Really? Anything interesting?"

Colin scrubbed his face with his hands. "Tons."

"Then what's bothering you?"

Colin didn't answer immediately. He turned to stare out the window. "The beasts aren't happy with her."

"Jannelle Evans?"

"Yeah."

"You're sure about this?"

"There's a human minion sniffing around her."

Corwyn grimaced. "How serious is this?"

"I'm going on trail."

"Using Evans for your bait?"

Colin nodded, and his hand fisted. "I have to get her to back off. If I don't, they will silence her in the usual fashion."

Corwyn sighed. "We are sworn to protect her like we would anyone, but it would be so much easier —"

Colin's head snapped around. Corwyn sucked in his breath in surprise as Colin lit. His brother was in a barely controlled fury.

"I will never allow that. I will give my life if need be."

"You're offering her protection? Don't you think you ought to discuss this with me?"

Colin paled, his *Blutjagd* fading. "I didn't say —"

"Then what are you saying? Be very specific. You want her, don't you?"

"I won't deny that. I am male, and she is..."

"Female?" Corwyn smirked at Colin's discomfort.

"Beautiful, determined, and spirited."

"Sleeping with her under these circumstances is dangerous. You know —"

"I'm not going to sleep with her." He said it too quickly, too definitively, and he didn't meet Corwyn's eyes when he said it. Coming to his senses, Colin met his eyes fully. "I'm not."

Corwyn groaned. "I'll send Stephen. He's mated."

"Which is why he can't go near her."

"Excuse me?"

"Stephen sees her as a threat to his mate and children," Colin reminded him.

Corwyn groaned again. "You're right. If he was inattentive, it would be unconscious, but it would be a tarnish on his honor, and he would suffer for it. I can't ask him to make this choice."

"I know."

"Can you handle this?"

Colin nodded. "I can."

"Be sure, Colin."

"I'll survive this. I have to."

Chapter Nine

July 31st, 1985

"I'll survive this," Colin grumbled. "What the hell was I thinking?" He washed his hands in the sink, glancing at his reflection and wishing he hadn't. He'd been watching her for three days, sleeping little and subsisting largely on coffee. His reflection showed it, from the dark circles under his eyes to the strain lines around his mouth.

He returned to Jannelle's office, dodging workers oblivious to his presence and slipping silently through her ever open door. Her back was to him, her fingers flying over the keyboard as she composed an exposé on government graft in the Department of Public Works.

She stopped abruptly, stood, and crossed the room, chewing on the edge of her pinky finger, her red lipstick leaving a smudge on her unpainted fingernail. She closed her office door and locked it, then leaned back on the wood.

"I know you're here, Hunter. You've been in and out of here for days. What do you want from me?"

Colin held his breath. Did she really sense him while he was ghosted or was she making a lucky guess that he was here? Was she a sensitive?

Janelle closed her eyes and laid her head back. "I'm not crazy," she whispered. She pulled her head forward and pushed off the door with her eyes still closed.

Colin stood transfixed while she walked to him. His body responded urgently. Her hips swayed, and her arms swung at her sides. Jannelle glided toward him, and Colin knew he should move, but he waited for her.

When Janelle was less than a foot from him, she stopped. Her hands came up and traced his chest to his shoulders. "There you are." Her eyes were still closed, and her voice was low and sexy. "Will you show me your pretty face now?" Her fingers found and traced the line of his jaw.

Colin let out a shuddering groan, aching to make use of the locked door. "How did you know I was here?"

Her fingers moved to his mouth, exploring his lips. Colin nipped at her fingertips, and Jannelle moved against him, brushing her gathering heat against the hardening proof of his inattention to duty.

Colin cupped her face, desperate for some distraction from what she was doing. "Jannelle, look at me," he ordered roughly.

She opened her dark eyes, and her smile spread. "I can see you."

"Because you know what you will see and where you will see it." *Gods, why did I tell her that?* Colin shook himself mentally. "Tell me how you know when I am near."

"I feel it. It's silly. I can't explain it. I just know —"

"Did you feel the beast that attacked you? Before he became visible to you?"

She furrowed her brow, looking confused.

Colin brought his hands up to her shoulders. "This is important, Jannelle. Did you feel the beast, too?"

"I —"

"You did." His mind reeled.

"I don't know. I felt — I felt like I was being watched." Jannelle shook her head. "I felt like I should run the other direction."

Colin pulled her to his chest, his arousal forgotten in light of this news. "You're a sensitive." *Not a powerful one.* She couldn't see the ghosted beasts and Warriors, but she felt them. He had never hoped to find a sensitive, even one as weak as Jannelle. The gods granted few such a gift.

"I'm what?" Her question was muffled by his chest.

Colin released her, remembering himself. He knelt at her feet, cradling her hands to his lips. "I have to protect you, Jannelle. Please, let me do that."

She stammered through half an answer, pulled her hands back to her chest, and retreated to the edge of her desk. Jannelle regained her composure quickly. "I don't seem to have a choice. You are here anyway."

Colin rose, placing his hands on her shoulders, kneading her back through her thin blouse. Jannelle relaxed under his hands. Colin stepped into her personal space.

"I wasn't protecting you, Jannelle. I would have protected you when the time came, but —"

Her eyes widened. "You were spying on me."

Colin sighed. "Not really. I was waiting to destroy the beasts coming for you."

"I'm bait?" She wasn't angry at that. Her eyes were sad.

"Not anymore. You're a sensitive. Your protection is my highest priority."

"What is a sensitive?"

"You feel them...the beasts, even when they are gh — invisible. And you feel us."

Her eyes were suddenly wary. "Wouldn't that make me dangerous to you?"

"No, that makes you precious to me." *And dangerous. So very dangerous.* "Let me protect you."

"No, I —"

"I won't force you, but I will be close by, in case you need me. You will need me, Jannelle."

A brisk knock came at the door, and Colin backed away. Jannelle watched him, suddenly uncertain.

"Come in," she called.

The knob rattled, and a male voice answered in irritation. "I would, but the door is locked."

Jannelle shook her head as she went to the door and unlocked it. "Sorry, Uncle Devin. I must have hit the button by accident."

She waved Devin Pierce in. The gray-haired man with the green eyes that very much matched his name watched in amazement as Jannelle swung the door shut behind him. "Something wrong?"

"No. The noise level is just a little over the top today."

His eyes narrowed, but he nodded. "How's the DPW story coming?"

"Almost done." Jannelle walked around her desk, sliding a glance at Colin as if to assure herself that he was still there.

A smile curved Colin's lips. She didn't want him to disappear on her again.

For the next few minutes, she and Pierce discussed the story. Needing to move, Colin paced the rug silently. He realized his mistake when Jannelle glanced at his previous location. She looked at the screen, hiding the tears misting her eyes from Pierce.

Colin moved to her other side, kneeling on the edges of her personal space. Jannelle closed her eyes. She felt him. She knew he was near. Colin placed his fingers an inch away from the skin of her knee, watching her face as Pierce scrolled down her story, clueless to what was happening beside him.

Her eyes opened, and she met Colin's gaze. Her hand moved to his under the desk, pushing his palm to her leg. Colin watched her expressive eyes as he massaged her thigh just above her knee. He could feel her raging arousal at his touch...smell it...nearly taste it.

Careful not to disturb her skirt, Colin shifted and moved his massage higher, passing the top of her thigh-high stockings. Her skin was like silk, and his control was slipping dangerously. He wanted to tease her to climax with Pierce standing at her shoulder.

"Jan? Jan."

She snapped her head around to Pierce and their discussion. "Sorry. My mind was elsewhere."

Colin smiled, knowing where her full attention lay. He inched his fingers higher, her heat searing him and her moisture shattering his calm. Another fraction of an inch, and he would be at the gates of heaven.

Jannelle's thighs snapped shut in silent warning, and Colin pulled his hand back. She glanced at him out of the corner of her eye, and Colin made a show of licking her essence off of his fingertips.

Colin bit back a chuckle, as she swung her gaze back to the screen. She ran a nervous hand through her hair while her thigh muscles tightened under her skirt. Jannelle looked at him again, her pupils dilating as the unmistakable perfume of her climax teased his senses. She ground her teeth for a moment and shuddered, taking her pleasure in absolute silence.

"Are you all right, Jan?" Pierce asked, putting a hand on her neck to test her for a fever as if she were a child.

She cleared her throat, flushing down her neck and chest. "Fine, Uncle Devin. I just need a drink of water."

"Stay there. I'll get it for you."

As Pierce disappeared from view, Jannelle rubbed her forehead roughly. "I can't believe I just did that," she grumbled.

Colin chuckled. "You were incredible." He brushed his fingers over her trembling hand. "Did you enjoy it?"

She groaned, moving her legs restlessly. "I can't believe I did that," she repeated.

"Sh... Uncle Devin is coming back," he warned her.

Jannelle looked at him in disbelief, then snapped her gaze to Pierce as he breezed in the door. She blanked her expression as Pierce looked at her and then accepted the cup from his hand.

"Now, back to work," she announced.

Colin was sure that announcement was meant for him. He caught her attention and kept it as he lowered himself against the wall. When he was settled, she nodded in understanding. He'd keep a steady position, so she'd be able to see him, and he wouldn't touch her.

He smiled. He wouldn't touch her while she worked. Seeing her come, so controlled but so hot, shook him. She'd come to his hand or mouth very soon.

Colin bit back a groan. Corwyn was going to kill him for starting something, sensitive or no.

* * * *

Jan tried to keep her mind on work, but Hunter kicked back, with his smug satisfaction and obviously still aroused, drew her eyes often.

Damn him! If he hadn't licked his fingers, she would have found her lost control.

Oh, who am I kidding? She'd been out of control for days. She had always been attracted to Hunter, and his touch the first time he visited her office had left her scattered for hours and dreaming of his mouth on her ever since.

Having him watch her was disconcerting but exciting, and Jan found herself more attuned to his presence with every moment she spent in his company.

She wasn't sure exactly when he'd entered her office that first morning. She had been reeling from the rose she'd found atop her file in the locked drawer, his sign that he had made his copies. Everything was there, just as she'd left it. Hunter was a considerate thief.

Visions of him danced in her mind all day and invaded her dreams at night. She dreamed of urgent, tireless sex with him. At least twice she'd woken, unfulfilled and hungry for him, convinced he was in the room with her. It had taken all the restraint she could muster not to invite him to her bed.

Jan looked at Devin again. "The DPW story will be on Carter's desk in an hour or two."

"Sounds good. Do me a favor. Don't work late tonight. I think you need the extra sleep."

She smiled. "Not too late. I want to finish up the precinct reorganization story, and then I'm out of here."

Devin nodded. "I understand you're working on a homicide case." His eyes were suddenly very hard.

Jan swallowed, feeling six years old again. "It's not what you think. I'm not chasing a killer this time."

"Then what are you doing?"

"I'm investigating the victims, not the killer."

Hunter's grin faltered a bit, but he recovered quickly.

"Come again?"

So much for putting Devin at ease.

Hunter's chest shook in silent laughter. Jan's face burned at Devin's unintended double meaning, and she crossed her legs smoothly. If Devin wasn't watching, she'd shoot Hunter a dirty look. Instead, she answered the question posed.

"There's no evidence pointing to a killer, but all the victims are young, clean-cut John Does with weird blood chemistry caused by some sort of radiation poisoning, I think. It's intriguing. I smell a story."

Hunter's smile disappeared, and his eyes went cold.

"If you write about them, they will kill you."

She shuddered as she remembered his words. Hunter didn't want her to write the story. She knew that.

"I promised —"

"Don't bring Dad into this. You got me fired in Dallas for taking on a killer. I'm not doing that this time."

Devin shook his head. "I don't like it. I want you to hand this off. Brand is —"

"No. This is my baby. You are not handing it off to that wet-behind-the-ears pup."

Jan watched as Hunter came to his feet, motioning her to back off. She looked back at Devin, fuming at the men ganging up on her.

"This is non-negotiable, Jan."

"You're right about that. Read my contract. No one assigned me to this story, and I've done my research in my free time. The story is mine. The documentation is mine. If you choose not to run it with your first run option, I can freelance it out. If you fire me..." She honed a hard look on him. "...the story walks with me."

"Be reasonable, Jan."

"I've grown up, Devin. I'm twenty-seven, not six. I'll take care of myself."

"If you stir this up, the killer is going to come gunning for you."

"I don't think so."

"Why not?"

"For one thing, there is no forensic evidence to connect anyone to the dead men. And..." She smiled. "The killer uses a knife, not a gun."

* * * *

Jan glanced at her watch. "Eight o'clock. I'm knocking off."

Hunter nodded. He hadn't spoken to her since the argument with Devin.

She sighed and turned toward him. "What has you so upset?" She had to know. His sulking had had her on edge all evening.

He shrugged. "We should go."

"Typical male. Give orders with no explanations and expect the good little girl to go along with you."

Hunter went rigid, his jaw tight. "When they come for you, you'll have to follow my orders. You won't accept my full protection. It will be difficult enough without that step."

"Why are you so sure they're coming for me now? How would they know before it hits print?"

"They have eyes here, influence here. You don't think Pierce tried to get you off of this without a push, do you?"

Jan snorted. "Devin doesn't need pressure. Two words in his ear, Jan and murder, would be enough to send him off half-cocked."

"He was pushed. Trust me."

"Are you saying Devin Pierce is part of this? If you are, you can leave right now. I know Devin, and I trust him a lot more than I trust you."

Hunter sighed. "I didn't say he was a conspirator. I said he was pushed. He was duped, and by now they know you will not be dissuaded."

His meaning sank in slowly. "So they'll be coming for me directly."

"I tried to warn you."

Jan felt weak and shaky. "Damn it. What do I do now?" She closed her eyes in sick resignation. He had tried to warn her, had done everything but shake it into her, but her pride was running high.

She hadn't realized Hunter had moved until she was pressed to him, one arm around her lower back and the other hand cupping her head, so her cheek rested on his shoulder. His heart beat steadily, calming her while his musk teased her sensitized libido.

Jan raised her face, his hand moving back with it as if he was loath to let go of her. She pressed her lips to his lower lip, nipping at it in invitation. Hunter didn't hesitate. His face lowered a fraction of an inch, and his lips were hard and hungry against hers. She opened for him as his mouth slanted over hers, his tongue alternating hard and demanding, then slow and sweet.

Hunter groaned as he pulled his mouth from hers. Jan watched him in dazed wonder as he reined in the urge to take her where they stood. How she knew that was what he wanted was a mystery, but she knew it was. Some part of her wanted it, too.

"Like my dreams," she murmured.

He smiled, still shaking and panting. "You dream of me?"

"Hot, urgent, endless sex."

Hunter groaned. "We have to leave. This is the worst place for us to explore this."

Jan nodded. "We should definitely go somewhere else. Quickly."

"Will you let me protect you?"

"I'll let you stay the night, if that's what you mean."

"Gods alive, yes! But that's not —"

"For now, and on one condition."

He looked at her expectantly.

Jan brushed her lips over his jaw. "I don't sleep with a man if I don't at least know his name. I do have my limits."

Hunter looked at her in surprise and dropped a quick, fierce kiss to her lips. "Colin. Colin Hunter."

Jan smiled, but her smile faded with his. "What is it?"

* * * *

Colin froze, his arousal taking a back seat to the sense of beasts. There wasn't just one but several closing in on their position. "Shit."

"Why do I —" Jannelle's voice had gone panicked. She backed off, running her hands through her hair. "Oh, no."

"Four that I can see," Colin confirmed for her. "Calm down. This is what I do."

Jannelle slung her purse over her shoulder. "I've changed my mind."

"About what?" Colin drew his weapon.

"No story. I don't want to know what that is. I don't want to know how widespread this is. I don't want to know anything about them."

"Stay at my back."

"You're going to protect me?"

"Not fully. There's no time, but I will keep you safe." He swept her behind him. "They're here."

Jannelle's hand closed on his shoulder. "I know. I'm sorry, Colin. I should have listened to you."

He nodded, focusing on the four beasts. "Back off a few steps," he breathed to her. Jannelle complied without question, and he nodded to the beasts. "Name yourselves."

A red-haired beast stepped forward, identifying itself as the highest ranked. "Flarehty and me boys are Datante, Penn, and Belloch." He twitched his head toward the others in turn.

Colin pasted on a cold smile. "Who's your master, beast?" Few Warriors asked that, but he wanted to know which elder was calling the shots, though he had his suspicions that it was Veriel.

"I have no master."

"Ah, one of Veriel's turned. You'll be entertaining." Veriel demanded well-trained turned, which meant a decent fight, something Colin had missed on trail.

Flarehty darkened but didn't answer.

"Thought so. Well, come for me. I have other things to attend to tonight."

Datante laughed and leered at Jannelle. "Yes, but we will meet your engagement for you, Colin of Hunter. I can smell her sweet fragrance from here."

Jannelle let out a frightened squeak.

Colin felt his *Blutjagd* step up another notch at that. "I guarantee you will never taste any of her delights." He said it to calm Jannelle, but it was a solemn vow to the beasts at the same time.

Datante shrugged and launched toward him. Colin aimed his first slice as a bleeder to his throat while he kicked the beast back. Penn and Belloch came at him together. Colin took Penn's heart while he landed a bone-jarring punch to Belloch's chin. Datante was back, and Flarehty ghosted. Colin took Datante's heart and spun to land a bleeder on Belloch's abdomen as the beast jumped back.

Colin didn't speak. He didn't use the active portion of his mind to analyze. He didn't battle like Corwyn and Stephen did. Colin didn't believe in amusing anecdotes in battle. He was all Warrior at times like this.

Jannelle's scream and dodge away answered Colin's unasked question of where Flarehty was. Colin turned and sliced, feeling his blade catch flesh and bone. He turned back to take Belloch's heart as Flarehty dematerialized and sped away.

Jannelle's muffled cry made his blood burn hotter. Colin turned and stalked toward the sound of her voice, knowing the pathetic creature he faced now.

* * * *

When the thing brushed into Jan's personal space, she fled her spot behind Colin despite his orders. She stopped at the doorway.

Jan watched him in stunned, and slightly ill, fascination. Colin was deadly force personified. His face was set in stone. He moved almost faster than she could follow, every motion a blur of economical death. The smell of beast blood was thick, and Jan choked on it.

When the crushing arm locked on her chest, Jan was too stunned to scream. A moment later, realizing that her attacker was carrying her away from Colin, she was unable to scream for a totally different reason. The hand clamped over her mouth kept her from breathing, let alone screaming.

Jan kicked at him as he turned into the darkened corridors near Devin's office. It was largely ineffective;

she lost one of her heels and felt a spike of pain in her opposite ankle without so much as a grunt of pain from the man who held her. He dropped her, and she sent an awkward blow in the general direction of his chin, wishing she could see him in the blackness around them.

A hand closed around her wrist before her blow connected. He could apparently see better than she could. Jan heard the click of a lock in the darkness. Her unseen attacker pushed her into a bank of shelves. Jan stumbled and lost her other shoe.

I have to do something. She grabbed a handful of the man's balls.

A hand locked on hers, prying her fingers open with amazing strength before she could twist and have him at her mercy. Her attacker groaned and shuddered, but the sound seemed to be one of pleasure rather than pain. He shoved her hand away, but a knife pressed into her throat before she could strike again.

Jan stilled, her heart pounding and her mouth dry as her other hand was released. The knife moved, making a cut under her jawbone. A thin trail of blood ran toward her throat. Just as she pulled in her breath to scream, his hand covered her mouth, and her scream was little more than a strangled whisper. The knife pressed into her throat in warning, and the hand moved away.

"Shhh." The voice came from inches away from her chin.

Lips pressed to her chin further up. He ran his tongue down her jawline to the cut he'd made. He sucked the stream of blood on her throat, then licked her skin clean up to the cut where he sucked at the continuing flow with a groan deep in his chest. Jan shuddered.

He pressed his hips to her, his erection growing as he licked at the cut again, his tongue enticing the flow to continue for him. His pants were open, and Jan felt a drop rub off the head of his cock through the silk of her blouse just above her waist. He was getting off on tasting her blood. Jan whimpered, her mind and stomach rebelling against this form of kink.

The man's hand skated up beneath her skirt, and Jan tried to lock her legs together. His fingers tightened on her thigh, and she grunted in pain, acutely aware of the knife at her throat.

"Let's play, Jan." Jeremy's voice was a whisper next to her ear. "A little pain and blood makes it sweeter, you know." The hand under her skirt snagged the edge of her panties. "Enough foreplay."

Colin's presence closed on her, moving silently. She swallowed down the urge to beg for his help. That would be warning Jeremy that he was there.

Jan screamed as the knife was ripped away from her throat, and Jeremy crushed her against the shelves. Her panties tore, but not all the way through. His fisted fingers tightened...then loosened. At the warm, wet sensation on her chest and stomach, she thought he'd climaxed, but there was far too much area covered for that to be the case.

Jeremy moved away from her so abruptly that Jan collapsed to the floor, smoothing her skirt as she scrambled for the doorway. She screamed as arms circled her, bringing her to a halt.

"It's okay. It's me."

Jan sank to Colin's chest, feeling his familiar body pressed to hers. She shook with sobs. "No story," she whispered. "I swear it, Colin."

"Shhh." Colin smoothed her hair and held her for several long minutes. "We have to leave. More are coming."

She nodded, letting Colin lift her onto quaking legs.

"Stand here for just a second. I have to get his weapon."

"Why?"

"It was stolen from a Warrior. I have to return it."

"A Warrior?"

Colin grumbled a curse. "Someone like me." His jacket dropped around her shoulders. "Wear this."

"My shoes and purse?" How could she be inconspicuous with no shoes?

She pulled the oversized jacket around her and cinched the belt. It reached her knees, even though Colin wasn't much more than her five feet ten.

Her purse settled into her hand. Colin grabbed her free hand and led her through the darkness.

"How can you see?"

"Shhh."

Jan stumbled, and Colin swept her up into his arms. "Colin —"

"Quiet, until we're outside." Gone was the passionate, playful man. Colin was cold and controlled — or maybe controlling.

Jan shivered and pulled his jacket closer around her despite the pungent smell of the beast blood that clung to it. Controlling, overprotective men were the bane of her life.

Colin paused, and Jan felt a warm caress surround her. He whispered against her hair. "Magic, Jannelle. Be very quiet for me."

She nodded against his chest, as Colin stepped out of the shadows and walked silently between the two guards in the lobby. Jan held her breath, meeting the bored gaze of one of the guards head on. There was no reaction from him.

Colin hit the door and kept moving. Behind them, Jan could hear the guards scrambling.

"What the hell was that, Pete?"

"Wind, I guess. Must not have been closed tight."

"Phew. What is that? A skunk get hit out there?"

"Doesn't smell like skunk. Smells like a sewer backed up."

Jan sank into Colin's arms, too numb to think. Whatever Colin Hunter was, he wasn't human. She gave in to exhaustion before Colin reached his chosen destination.

* * * *

Colin laid Jannelle on the bed in the small cabin, brushing his fingertips over her forehead as he headed to the bathroom for the first aid kit. He pushed his *Blutjagd* back. He'd almost lost her. It wouldn't happen again.

He grabbed one of his button-down shirts from the closet and headed back to the bed. Colin dropped his jacket in the garbage bag. It was stained with beast blood, and the leather would carry the smell forever and be eaten away slowly.

Colin hesitated. He should clean himself before caring for her. He handled that as quickly as possible; stripping off his boots and belt, putting his clothing in the washer, and scrubbing the beast blood from his body before pulling on a fresh pair of jeans.

Jannelle was pale and still, her heart rate depressed. He cleaned the cut under her chin carefully. It didn't need more than a butterfly strip and antibiotic cream. That was good, since his hands were shaking too badly to set stitches.

Colin took a deep breath and started stripping off her ruined clothing. He dropped the blouse and bra into the garbage bag and washed the minion's blood from her chest and abdomen, then slipped his shirt on her. Her skirt and ripped thigh-high stockings followed the rest of her clothing into the bag.

Colin grimaced at the sight of the fingertip bruises on her thigh. Shaking, he pushed the shirt up to clean the blood from her lower abdomen. Colin bit back a scream of fury and pulled off her ripped panties, fisting them, wishing he could put his fist through the minion's face. He tossed them in the trash bag, cleaned her, and smoothed the shirt over her thighs.

He covered her with a quilt and stormed outside, ditching the bag on the porch. He'd burn the contents later. For now, he needed the space to calm down. The damned minion almost had her. Colin had promised Jannelle he'd keep her safe. He'd given her his word.

The minion knew it was over when he attacked. Jeremy knew he'd die either way, by Colin's hand or his master's. It was his idea of revenge, Colin was sure.

Minions were chosen for their sick, twisted minds and souls. With the promise of being turned for their loyalty, rewarded for their brutality, the minion would have raped and killed Jannelle as much for the perverse pleasure it gave him as for revenge.

He came too damned close for Colin's comfort. Colin vented his scream of rage to the night sky. Another minute or two and it would have been too late for her. The bastard had been out of his pants and ready, tearing off her clothes. A minute at the most would have been too long.

Colin whirled and stalked back to Jannelle. Suddenly exhausted, he crawled onto the bed with her and wrapped his arm over her waist. He couldn't lose her. She'd have to agree to let him place her under his protection.

Chapter Ten

August 1st, 1985

Jan shifted under the blanket, and her eyes opened in shock. She wore nothing but some sort of nightshirt. At a movement behind her, she bit back a cry of alarm and tried to jump from the bed.

Arms closed around her, and Colin's voice rasped in her ear, half-asleep. "It's okay. You're safe here."

Somehow the idea of being safe in Colin's arms in a bed seemed like an oxymoron. She pulled at his arms, and Colin moved them with a sigh. Jan distanced herself from him, curling the blanket around her as she turned to face him.

"Where are my clothes?" she asked.

"Ruined. I'm sorry. I'll buy you more. We can probably cut off a pair of Stephen's jeans for you, in the meantime."

"You — uh...ch-changed my —"

"Yes."

Jan darkened. "Oh." She looked away in embarrassment. "I want to go home."

Colin shook his head. "Not until you're fully protected. Maybe not even then, for a little while."

"You can't keep me here."

"I can." Something dark and fierce burned in his eyes.

Jan's mouth went dry, remembering her final thoughts of Colin the night before. "What are you, Colin?"

"I — Well, that's not so easy to —" His expression was suddenly vulnerable.

"You're not human, are you? Are you one of those — beast things?"

He launched off the bed, his back muscles bunching as he crossed the room. Even in his anger, his movements passed without a sound. Jan held her breath as he turned with his knife in hand and headed back to the bed. Her gaze locked on the knife, and she backed to the far edge of the mattress.

Colin's voice was as tense as his muscles. "Look at me, Jannelle."

She met his gaze. Colin raised his empty hand until his palm faced her and cut a long slice with the knife. Jan flinched. He didn't. Colin tossed the knife back on the dresser and stood, his eyes locked on hers as blood ran down his hand and wrist.

"I am not a beast," he informed her.

"Colin, your hand. That wasn't —"

"I am not wholly human, either."

Tears stung her eyes. "What?"

"I am a Warrior, from a long line of Warriors." He dropped his gaze. "I won't lie to you, Jannelle."

"But you wanted —" Her voice choked off.

"We're very close to human. Our wives are human women."

"You're an alien?"

Colin swallowed what was probably a harsh laugh, his throat bobbing. "No. We're more like a different subspecies of human or a mutation of human, close enough to cross-breed and produce fully-functional, fertile children together like wolves and dogs do. Homo nocturnus? Homo badassus, maybe." It was a weak joke.

Jan shook her head. She winced at the sight of the blood coursing off his hand. "Shouldn't you take care of that?"

"It will heal quicker than you can imagine. My body will take care of itself." His voice was bitter, and he sank to the edge of the bed, looking tired.

Jan wanted to touch him, but she talked herself out of it. He wasn't human. She wasn't sure what Colin was. Encouraging him sexually was a bad move. She startled as he touched her jaw, launching to her feet with the blanket wrapped around her.

Colin nodded with sad eyes. "I only wanted to check your cut."

She ran her fingers over it. "No. Please, don't."

"I understand."

Jan looked at him in disbelief. "No, you don't. That freak was — He was drinking my blood, Colin, and doing it turned him on." She shuddered at the memory.

Colin fisted his hand, and his jaw tightened. "He what?" he demanded.

"He — Oh, I don't want to discuss it." She ran a hand over her churning stomach.

Colin nodded. "I'll make you breakfast. Then we'll discuss your protection." Colin tossed a pair of jeans from the bottom drawer onto the bed. "Scissors are in the bathroom on the other side of the living room. They shouldn't be too big if you take five or six inches off of the legs." He left without a backward glance.

* * * *

Colin slammed the cast iron pan down on the stove burner and reached into the refrigerator for the supplies he'd taken from the freezer in the wee hours of the morning. One of the few cabins that was connected to a town power supply, it was stocked with a variety of foods besides dried and canned staples.

Staring at the smear of blood on the pitcher of reconstituted dry milk, Colin sighed and turned to the sink. He scrubbed his arm and hand, grinding his teeth in pain. It wasn't physical pain. Colin wasn't sure he was capable of feeling physical pain anymore. He was too busy blocking out the pain in his heart.

Jannelle had rejected him, not in words but in her actions. She couldn't accept a man that wasn't quite human. She didn't want this life. Jannelle wasn't the first woman to make that decision. She wouldn't be the last.

She wasn't even Colin's first. He'd only been twenty-one the first time.

Colin had saved a woman named Cass, and they'd had a brief but torrid affair. His only salvation had been that he'd been young and impetuous. He'd asked for her choice early, long before *Endspiel*.

Cass had cooled immediately. She'd been blunt. Colin was good for an affair. He fucked like an animal in rut. He wasn't someone she would tie herself to.

Colin had gone through withdrawal alone in a cabin an hour away from this one. Corwyn and his father had known his problem and had given him the time and space he needed to vent his madness.

His healing had come as he'd repaired the damage he'd caused at the cabin. Colin shuddered as he remembered standing naked in the swirling snow, screaming his rage to the night sky at the height of his madness, much as he had the night before.

He hadn't wanted to start printing again. He had reminded himself that first night at the hospital that Jannelle wasn't suited to the life. Then why had he been stupid enough to let his guard down?

Colin growled. That was a useless question. No matter why he did it, it was over. Jannelle was a duty now and nothing more, by her own choice. If her proximity grated on the edges of printing, he'd destroy another cabin when she left. If it went too far, he'd hand Corwyn the blade to destroy him himself, before it was too late to make that rational choice.

* * * *

Colin felt Corwyn coming long before he neared the cabin. He slipped out and met the car down the access road. There was no mistaking the mixture of concern and anger in Corwyn as he stepped from his car.

"She's here?"

Colin nodded.

"We discussed this."

"No, we didn't."

"Have you given her an amulet?"

"She hasn't accepted one, yet."

Corwyn pushed back his fury. "Then you can't do this."

"I can."

"By whose authority? As Lord Hunter and Stone lord —"

"Ghost up to the house with me. I want to show you something."

"I'll humor you, but you'll face me if I'm not convinced that you have a damn good reason for what you're doing."

"You'll be convinced."

They walked back to the cabin and slid in the door Colin had left open. Colin motioned to the bedroom.

* * * *

Jan sat at the mirror, brushing her hair. She felt the energy coming behind her and glanced up. No one was in the mirror, but it was definitely not one of those things. She closed her eyes and spun with a curse, stopping when her fist hit solid mass.

She opened her eyes. "Damn it, Colin —" Jan ended on a hoarse cry, hitting the mirror as she jumped back from the strange man towering over her. "Who are you?" she demanded in a shaky voice.

Colin appeared in the doorway, his hands up in a calming gesture. "He's okay. Calm down."

"What are you doing?" She shot the stunned man a dirty look, then marched to Colin and cuffed him in the chest. "Are you trying to give me a heart attack? What is wrong with you people?"

Colin reached for her, but she pushed him away with a look of warning.

The man behind her sat in the chair she'd vacated, looking pale. "She's a full sensitive?"

Colin nodded. "Convinced?"

"You're sure she senses the beasts, too?"

"Positive. I've seen it in action."

Jan ground her teeth. "*She* has a name. *She* wants to know who the hell that is." Jan motioned to the new arrival.

Colin sighed. "My older brother."

Jan rolled her eyes. "Lovely. Another Hunter man. Just what I need. One isn't trouble enough."

The man in the chair laughed heartily. "The Hunter man has a name."

"Well, it took me four days to learn Colin's. Four days of calling him Mr. Hunter or Hunter for lack of anything better — strike that — more ladylike to call him. Sure you don't want to go for the record?"

"I'll pass. I'm Corwyn."

Jan eyed him warily. "I don't think Gabby said how many brothers there were. Have I seen the full roll call or are there more surprises in store for me?"

"I hope not," Colin muttered.

* * * *

Corwyn surveyed Jannelle Evans across the dinner table. The Stone was amusing itself as usual. Why would She place such an obvious adversary in possession of the power to see the combatants?

Colin cleared his throat. "I need to ask two favors of you," he hedged.

Corwyn raised a brow in surprise. "For instance?"

Colin went to the cabinet above the freezer and pulled out a sacred weapon reverently. Jannelle glanced at it and shuddered, averting her eyes as it moved closer to the table. Corwyn watched her in amazement. For the last hour, she'd been flanked by both Warriors and their blades without difficulty.

Corwyn turned his attention back to Colin as the weapon met his outstretched hand. The seal in the hilt was the Lord Maher seal. "Jason's?" he asked quietly.

Jason Lord Maher had been killed by one of Veriel's turned three years earlier. The turned had had the audacity to steal the Lord's blade from his body though he couldn't kill with it.

Colin nodded. "It will have to be reconsecrated before you return it to Calvin."

Corwyn nodded fiercely. "Carried by a beast for three years." The thought made him ill. "Maybe the blade should be reforged before it's reconsecrated."

Colin's next statement solidified that opinion. His brother darkened in fury. "It was gifted to a minion. It's been used to draw human blood. Maybe to kill. I can't be sure."

Corwyn felt the blood drain from his face. The blade clattered to the tabletop in his surprise. Janelle dropped her fork at the sound of the blade striking wood and edged away from it. Corwyn snapped a look at her, finally working to the truth that it was this blade, in particular, she feared.

Colin snatched the blade up and returned it to the cabinet more forcefully than he should have, slamming the door shut behind it. He paused with his hand on the door, regaining his calm. "You won't see it again, Jannelle. You have my vow."

She nodded shakily. "Thank you, Colin."

"My honor." He returned to his chair, giving her shoulder a squeeze on the way.

Corwyn looked at the cut under her chin. Switching to German, he glanced at Colin. "*The minion did that to her?*"

Colin's eyes burned. *"That and more. He was playing beast with her."*

"Did he succeed?"

"In drinking her blood, but not in taking her. She barely escaped that much."

Corwyn nodded and offered a strained smile in response to Jannelle's confusion. He switched back to English. "I apologize. That was rude of me. I won't do it again." It was hard to think of Jannelle Evans as one of their most prized, but she was, and she deserved his respect.

She nodded mutely, looking vulnerable. She knew they were discussing her.

Colin sighed. "The other favor is highly irregular."

"How so?"

Colin pushed a folded letter across the table to him. "I promised Jannelle that we'd deliver this to Devin Pierce."

Corwyn's eyes widened. "Why?"

Jannelle looked down, pushing her food around her plate with the newly-retrieved fork. "He'll be crazy when he finds the — It's too much like..."

"Like what, Jannelle?" Corwyn prompted her.

"My mother." She raised her head to face him, her eyes glossy with unshed tears. "She was killed when I was a baby."

Colin motioned to get his attention. Corwyn watched his brother's eyes shift in a signal. Then he started speaking. "Sharon was at home with Jannelle and a servant. Her mother and the servant were both killed. When Scott returned home, he discovered it. Jannelle was asleep in her crib, cried herself back to sleep apparently."

Jannelle broke in. "They were killed in the nursery, and one of their attackers was dead with them."

Corwyn nodded. "So, one of the women killed him?" he asked, knowing Colin wouldn't bother with this if they had.

Colin shook his head. "The police theorized that he was killed by his partners, that they'd intended to kidnap Sharon and Jannelle together and weren't prepared to care for a nursing infant without her mother."

"Why did they think that?" Corwyn led Colin to what he needed with the ease of years of practice.

"No weapons were found at the scene. Someone had to take them away." Colin rubbed his knuckles slowly and shifted his eyes again. "He died of two stab wounds." Colin scratched his chest over his heart.

Corwyn nodded. Colin's true favor was a little investigative work. "I don't remember hearing about that. Was it in Colorado?"

Jannelle shook her head. "Dad sold that house. He couldn't bear to live there after my mother died. We lived outside Seattle then."

Corwyn nodded. He had a place to start now. "I'll make sure Pierce gets this."

"Thank you."

* * * *

Corwyn went to Pierce's office first. The note was safe. He'd checked it before giving Colin his solemn vow to deliver it.

Ghosting in was easy enough. Guards were coming and going through the open doorway.

Devin Pierce gave orders in a crisp voice, addressing a guard that almost matched Corwyn's height and bulk. "I want her found and I mean found now."

"We're working on it. None of the cameras show any sign of her after Brand dragged her from her office. Once we figure out how she left the building —"

"Do it. I have no intention of losing Jan. Not this way."

The guard left, realizing he had been dismissed. Pierce scrubbed his hands over his deeply lined and strained face. He closed his eyes, looking wholly exhausted.

Corwyn slid the letter onto the desk where it would be visible out of his hands, then waited to confirm that the older man understood and accepted its content. Pierce froze as his gaze settled on the folded sheet of paper. He scanned the room, and his jaw tightened.

His voice was low and full of malice. "Damn you, Armen. Scott told me we'd never be rid of you. Scott told you to stuff your protection. Now I'm warning you. I'm telling you, if you don't return Jan to me, I'll hunt you down personally. I made Scott a promise to keep Jan out of your games."

Corwyn tried to think through his shock. Maybe Colin was right. Maybe there had been a beast involved in Sharon's death. But if beasts knew Jannelle was a sensitive, why hadn't they killed her years ago? No amount of human protection that Scott Evans and Devin Pierce could offer would protect her from even a low-level beast.

Pierce grabbed the letter with a muttered curse. He read it and folded it again, his expression pained.

His voice was a whisper. "I want to see her, Armen. I know enough of your rules. She's not one of your females. You have no right to this one."

Corwyn's eyes widened. What did Pierce know?

"I'll be waiting. You have a week to return her to me. I know you'll protect her, but you don't own this one. A week, Armen. After that, my men will be looking for you with every piece of information I have to give them."

Corwyn left, knowing he had to speak to Todd Lord Armen immediately.

* * * *

Corwyn hated using his rank to force compliance of the other lords, but being Stone lord did have a few perks. He demanded that Todd Lord Armen return his call within the hour. It took forty-five minutes.

Todd Armen wasn't happy when he phoned in. "What is it, Hunter?" he growled irreverently.

"Tell me about Scott, Sharon, and Jannelle Evans."

Todd's voice didn't change. "Has the girl asked for Armen protection?"

"No."

"Then she's no concern of mine. I am only obligated to honor that which was offered if she requests it of me."

"Not so fast. It may not be your problem, but it is mine, and I will have the information I need to solve this. A week from now, it ceases to be my problem as much as it is yours."

"Why is that?"

"Do you know Devin Pierce?"

Todd grumbled a series of curses.

"I'll take that as a yes. What exactly does Pierce know and how does he know it?"

He sighed, a sound that communicated a Warrior weary from long nights. "You know Carrick had a sister?"

"Yes. I met Grace once."

"When you were a teen in the pit matches, I'll wager."

"Of course. When else would I have met her?"

Todd grunted. "Then you know she came back to Armen when her human husband died. She couldn't bear to remarry after she lost him."

"I remember that she hadn't remarried when I was fifteen."

"She came back to us carrying her husband's child. Carrick doted on Grace. Her child was a girl. Carrick insisted Sharon be protected, given Carrick's Lord's seal."

"Oh, hell."

"It gets worse," Todd warned.

"Can it get worse?"

"Much. Carrick regarded Sharon much as we do our freed females. Sharon balked at that. For Sharon, it was a matter of Warrior law. No one had accepted her curse back in the *Zeremonie der Freiheit*. Armen didn't *own* her. Carrick viewed it as an act of love for Grace and Sharon. Out of love, he would see to her protection as if she was his own daughter."

"Sharon left angry." Corwyn didn't make it a question. There was little question in his mind that it was the truth.

"Sharon called Grace from her dorm room the night she finished graduate school. She announced that she wasn't coming back. She was marrying. Carrick calmly informed her he'd interview her young man and start the background checks immediately. Sharon hung up on him. By the time Carrick reached her dormitory, Sharon was gone. Her amulet lay on her pillow as her final act of defiance."

"Continue."

"It took Carrick almost two months to find Sharon, when a marriage license was filed for her and he finally had a name to track her husband by. She left us, because she would not submit to our ways. She ran..." Todd grumbled a series of choice curses. "...because she was pregnant."

"She was afraid of Carrick's reaction? Even though her husband was human and ignorant of our laws?"

"So much so that she made excuses not to come home between Christmas and graduation. By spring break, she was pregnant. She knew if any of the men sensed her for any reason, they would know. When Carrick found her, Sharon was already entering her third trimester. She backed from him as if she expected him to harm her."

"Or her husband," Corwyn grumbled.

"Yes. Most likely. Carrick left them in peace, but he left her amulet with her. He begged her to take it to put Grace at ease."

"Sharon accepted it?"

"Yes, but she didn't accept his protection for her baby. Carrick offered it. He told Sharon to call, and he would give Jannelle his blessing and an amulet, but she believed he meant to own Jannelle. Sharon never could get past that idea. The Warriors owning our women. She never called."

"Tell me about Sharon's death. Was it a beast?"

"An old adversary of Carrick's. The Stone sent Carrick to them. Jannelle was nine months old at the time."

"Sharon wasn't wearing her amulet?"

"No. The beast killed the nanny first. Sharon could have saved herself by putting her amulet on. She had a blessing."

Corwyn felt a cold certainty settle in his chest. "She gave the amulet to Jannelle without a blessing." Just as Anna had.

"Yes, she did."

"But the amulet is useless alone."

"Not if the Stone wishes it to do a job."

"It worked?"

"Limited protection. The Stone told Carrick that Sharon spent those few moments begging the Stone to protect Jannelle, trying desperately to recite the words of protection, even biting her thumb to draw a shaky blood symbol on Jannelle in hopes that it would give her some measure of protection."

"But, she's not —"

"According to Carrick, the power of the blessing doesn't come from a Warrior. We channel the Stone's blessing, and we are good at it because we are cursed and so intimately linked to it. Sharon was known to the Stone, protected by it. She also had a mother's love for her child. You know the Stone respects that bond."

Corwyn felt hope for the first time in years. Anna had been protected. Anna had a mother's love for her child. Anna had loved Erin so much that she'd given up her own life as Sharon had done for her child. If Anna asked the Stone to protect Erin, would the Stone protect her without a blessing?

"What protection did it grant Jannelle?" He had to know.

"When Carrick arrived, the beast had Jannelle in his hands, but he couldn't feed or use his claws. He could hold her, but only just. Jannelle was screaming as if she knew what she faced. That rattled Carrick most of all."

Corwyn shuddered, sure that Jannelle knew, even then, what she faced. A sensitive...an infant in such a situation, sent chills up his spine.

"The amulet would not call a Warrior, since her blessing was not of a Warrior. It wouldn't keep her from being touched." Todd sighed. "Carrick took the beast's heart and scooped her to his chest as Jannelle fell. He wanted to give her a proper blessing, but —"

"She couldn't accept his protection. Her father would have to permit it, and he didn't."

"Scott Evans returned home soon after." Todd's voice was bitter. "It only took him a moment to realize the full import of what had happened."

"He knew?"

"Sharon had told him long before, but he took it as a joke, a harmless aberrant behavior in an otherwise sane young woman. Seeing a Warrior cradling his sleeping child, both of them covered in blood in the midst of — Carrick took the brunt of everything Scott Evans threw at him, from the verbal accusations to the physical blows Evans threw after he returned Jannelle to her crib.

"Carrick offered protection for both of them with no strings attached. No control. Complete autonomy and more. Evans threw Sharon's amulet at Carrick and threatened to expose all he knew if we came near Jannelle again.

"When Evans died, we tried to reopen communication lines with Jannelle, but he left a guard dog to keep his threat alive."

"Pierce."

"Yes. Tell me. Why is Pierce up in arms? Why now?"

"Jannelle stumbled onto this whole mess accidentally. She's in my temporary custody."

"Stumbled onto the Warriors?" His disbelief was impossible to miss.

"In a round-about way. She stumbled onto the beasts."

"How? I mean, humans have survived attack, but they have no concrete proof."

"She does. Colin saved her from a beast. She's uncovered medical proof of a half dozen of our kills."

Todd groaned. "What now?"

"We'll figure it out, but at least I know why Pierce assumes the Armens have her. It's the only Warrior family he knows."

"We hope. It may be the only family he expects to be involved." Todd hesitated. "Will you protect her?"

"If Jannelle allows it. You have my word."

"Thank you, Corwyn. Armen appreciates it."

Chapter Eleven

August 2nd, 1985

Jan swung her legs off the bed, trying to figure out what woke her. The sun was still a gray line on the horizon. A careful inner check showed no energy signatures besides Colin's to distract from the peace. She padded on bare feet toward the kitchen but stopped in the doorway, her breath catching in her throat.

A soft sound from Colin was her first indication of what woke her. He lay on his stomach, one hand tucked between his hips and the couch beneath him. His other hand gripped the arm of the couch, white knuckled. Colin rolled his forehead against his pillow as he stroked himself, his entire body rippling with the motions from his powerful thighs and butt, clearly visible through his jeans, to the nude expanse of his back, shoulders, and arms.

Jan leaned against the wall, unable to look away. She licked her lips, imagining herself under him, Colin's thrusts filling her. Her nipples beaded against the shirt she wore, Colin's shirt, and moisture gathered between her thighs. She wanted to be under him, running her hands over the rippling muscles in his shoulders and chest.

She bit back a groan, images filling her mind as they had in her office when Colin kissed her. He wanted her there. He was fantasizing about her, about filling her with his length and feeling her slick walls gripping him as she screamed out her climax.

Oh, God.

Colin's motions speeded, a groan rumbling from his lips and through her like a caress. Jan's hand moved down her stomach, and she pressed the heel hard against the tightness winding above her womb.

"Oh, Gods, yes," Colin breathed.

Jan's eyes widened as his head turned to her, his eyes glassy in need.

"You smell so good. You look —"

Jan's gaze panned over his body, and she licked her lips. She locked on the motion of his hips, feeling light headed as what he wanted assaulted her mind again. "Colin, I —"

"Yes. Tell me, Jannelle."

Tell him? How could she tell him that the visions in his mind were driving her insane?

When she didn't answer, his eyes closed. "I want you, Jannelle. You drive me crazy," he admitted.

I know. Oh, do I ever know. Jan felt like she was on fire. She slid her hand down, stroking herself through the split at the bottom of the shirt.

Colin opened his eyes, and Jan spread her thighs further, stroking her fingers through her labia and deep inside as she laid her head back against the wall and bit her lip. She watched Colin through heavy lidded eyes.

"I want to touch you." His voice was hoarse.

Jan groaned at the stamina he obviously had. "Colin." *Oh, this is a bad idea.* Still, she wanted him to touch her.

"No sex, Jannelle. You have my word."

She whimpered, wanting to feel his body. Her fingers moved to her clit.

"Imagine my fingers there, Jannelle. Let me touch you." Colin turned to his back, his hand stroking the length of him through his jeans.

Jan moaned at the sight of the telltale wet spot at the head of his cock near the waistband of his jeans. He had to be close to nine inches of thick, aroused, tireless sex waiting to happen. Better, or maybe worse, he wanted that sex to happen with her.

Colin rose from the couch, every muscle outlined in the dim light through the windows as he moved to her. He placed his hands on the wall on either side of her head, his breath hot on her lips. "What do you want, Jannelle?"

Jan kissed him, running her free hand up his chest. Colin cupped her head, his kiss fierce as he lifted her with his other hand and moved. Jan gripped his shoulder, though he had no need of her assistance. Her head sank into his pillow, and his scent surrounded her.

Colin pulled her hand up to his mouth, sucking in her fingers while Jan watched. His tongue caressed her, his eyes closed in pleasure. Jan tried to close her thighs, needing to feel pressure as she started to throb for him. Colin braced them open, releasing her hand with one last lick.

"I love how you taste."

But he didn't taste. His hand slid up her thigh, learning the contours of her body by Braille. He circled her clit, swallowing her scream in a kiss as he brushed the rough pad of his thumb over it slowly. His mouth was demanding while his hand traced every inch of her lazily. His thumb massaged her clit while one finger ran the length inside her labia. Jan arched to him, her hand rubbing at the growing wet spot at the head of his cock.

Colin pulled back from the kiss, plunging two fingers deep inside her. He massaged the walls clenching him. Jan moved against him restlessly, her fingers working open the first two buttons on his jeans.

He stilled her, his hand shaking. "No. I don't have that much control."

Jan nodded, not at all sure that control was something she wanted him to have. She massaged the head, groaning as more moisture beaded up to her touch. Colin's hand speeded as she massaged the drop into the sensitive skin stretched tight over the head and underside of his cock.

Jan met Colin's slumberous eyes. "What do you want, Colin?" She'd offer him anything at that moment.

The vision of himself plunging into her was strong and immediate. Colin shook his head, trying to dislodge it. "I promised," he bit out.

"Colin —"

"I won't convince you into anything."

Too late. Jan stroked him more urgently. Her fingers picked at the remaining buttons that separated them. "Colin, please."

"Come for me."

Colin sucked in one rigid nipple, and Jan cried out. His hands and mouth were everywhere, smoothing here, nipping there, licking and sucking, leaving little love bites. Colin played at her body until Jan shattered in his arms. Her scream of release echoed off the rafters, and she arched against him.

His hand left her and the hard ridge encased in his jeans replaced it as she opened her mouth to protest the emptiness. Jan moaned, meeting his gaze as Colin stroked himself against her sensitive core, her juices soaking through the fabric and coating the thick veins she'd uncovered. Jan wrapped her legs around his thighs, urging Colin on. She licked and kissed at the rippling muscles of his chest, her fingers still playing at the engorged head hovering over her abdomen.

As her tongue teased at his nipple, Colin fisted the pillow above her shoulder and roared, hot cum splashing over the backs of her fingers and the shirt she wore. Colin dropped his head to the pillow, keeping her pinned by his hips and lightly caged by his arms. Jan laid her head back and watched him as he shivered. His eyes opened slowly, and Colin seemed to be at a loss for words.

Turnabout is fair play, she decided. Jan brought her hand up between their bodies and sucked in her coated fingers, sending Colin a heated look.

His eyes widened, and his breathing was harsh. He pushed off of her abruptly, turning his back and running his hand through his hair.

Jan stared at him in concern. "Colin?"

"I lost my head," he whispered. "I had no right to —
"

Tears gathered in her eyes. "Don't apologize, please. I walked into your space. If anyone is to blame —"

He turned, his face a mask of surprise and his cock still standing at full attention. "I don't blame you. I want you, but I won't touch you again."

"Why?"

"If I touch you again, I won't be stopping. I won't try to convince you. I know how you feel. If we proceed, it will be your choice." A muscle tightened in his jaw. "I don't count on it." He left the cabin, barefoot and bare-chested.

Jan watched his retreating back. She stood on shaking legs and made her way to the shower. The water was hot, but it didn't make a dent in the chill in her soul. She'd lost her mind somewhere along the way. She'd wanted him. She still wanted him, but his words sent a deeper chill through her.

Colin wasn't human, by his own admission. He wanted her intensely, but he wouldn't touch her. She took away his careful control, he said.

That concept stunned her. He feared he'd become exactly what she dreamed him to be.

What I want him to be.

Jan groaned at the visions from her dreams. She wanted Colin that way, wanted it more than she'd imagined possible, enough that she wasn't sure she ever wanted to return to the city and her job.

But he isn't human. Jan wasn't sure that she was ready to enter into any sort of relationship, even a purely sexual one, with someone who wasn't even her subspecies. Better to get back to the city soon, before she lost her head again.

* * * *

Colin stripped off his jeans and plunged into the icy water of the lake. He growled as he surfaced.

Images of Jannelle sucking fingers coated with his still-warm seed taunted him. His unruly body was rock hard and pulsing for her even in the chill of the water. "So much for cold showers," he grumbled.

He was going insane. Printing was moving much faster this time. He'd never lost control with Cass. His body and mind had been his own despite the burn for her, until she'd rejected him and he'd set out to break printing.

Colin had started off to relieve his tension with self-release, but the sound of Jannelle's hitching breaths, the smell of her arousal, and the sight of her wide eyes had taken away any urge to stop or turn away. Colin had been driven from that moment on.

He hadn't intended to tell her how much he wanted her, but he had. After that, it had all been a delicious game. His arousal had fed her arousal and vice versa.

When she'd started to pleasure herself, it was all Colin could do to stamp down his climax. The last of his control had snapped. He'd had to taste her and touch her to complete the circuit of his senses.

His cock twitched at the memory of that need.

He still needed it. He needed to lose himself in every sensory input he could steal of her. He'd like to believe he would have stopped if she had asked, that he wouldn't have tried to convince her to willingness, but Colin couldn't swear an oath to that in good conscience.

She'd tasted so good. Colin groaned, sorry that he hadn't dropped to his knees and taken her sweet nectar directly from her body.

He stroked himself unconsciously as he considered what he might have enjoyed with her had he not been in such a mindless rush. If she came to him and gifted him with her body again, that would be the first thing he would do. He would lick and suck at her until her musk flooded his mouth and her muscles gripped his tongue.

He'd had to stop her from removing his jeans. The urge to surge into her had been too strong. Colin couldn't swear that he would have been able to deny himself that despite his promises to her. If she took him again, he would take her fully, her warmth pulsing around him as she screamed for him again.

Colin exploded, his hand tightening as wave after wave of cum were washed away by the gentle lake current. He groaned as his erection, at last, lessened.

Taking that as his cue, Colin pulled his stained jeans on, trying to ignore the perfume of Jannelle's climax that teased his battered mind. He headed back to the cabin, reasoning with himself that there was no chance Jannelle would go further.

He slipped in and headed for the bathroom. Jannelle came out of it as he reached for the handle. She was wrapped in a bath sheet and smelled of the honeysuckle bath gel of Anna's she'd found under the sink.

His erection returned with that little provocation. Colin was far gone. If he didn't break printing soon, he was a dead man.

Chapter Twelve

August 4ᵗʰ, 1985

Jan stared at Colin across the dinner table. It had been two full days of hell. Ever since their encounter in the living room, Colin had been completely unreachable. He rarely looked at her. He spent the days outside chopping wood, running to town to bring her clothing and buy supplies, or staring at the scenery. He spent the evenings sulking around the cabin.

He hadn't touched her, though he'd come close that first morning. She had come out of the bedroom dressed in one of his button-down shirts, motioning for him to take his turn at dressing.

Jan had tried to ignore the sight of Colin's bare chest above the tented bath sheet. *Was the man in a constant state of arousal?*

Colin had stopped before her, and she'd met his gaze in confusion. *Oh, what a mistake that was.* His eyes had been darkened and intense. His fingers had plucked at the collar of the shirt she wore, uncovering the love bite on the top swell of her left breast. His fingers had hovered a fraction of an inch from the discoloration, making Jan acutely aware of him. Colin had met her gaze again, pulled his hand back, and fisted it at his side.

"Go," he had told her gruffly. "Please."

Jan had ducked away with a nod, trying to ignore her body's insistent signals telling her to head the other direction.

Colin hadn't come close to touching her again; he'd stayed well out of reach of her after that. It wasn't far enough for her peace of mind. Maybe the clothing he'd brought her later that morning had been enough for his peace of mind, but it had done little for hers. Between being a sensitive and the raw sensuality Colin radiated, not wearing his clothing was the least of her worries.

Not taking midnight runs through his fevered mind might have been more helpful. Jan still felt the energy of his presence anywhere within the confines of the cabin. She still caught glimpses of his erection far too often. Clothing was no cure for those conditions.

Jan rinsed her plate in the sink. She sighed as she glanced out at the treeline.

"Something wrong?" Colin asked.

"No. Just a little stir crazy."

"Missing those long nights at the office?" His voice was cynical.

"A little." Jan shook her head. "There's nothing wrong with my job, Colin. I don't work for some gossip rag."

"What you do isn't safe, Jannelle. Not for you."

"Because I'm a woman? You sound like Devin and my father. Typical male."

"Because you're a sensitive."

She turned to him. "Tell me about sensitives. Why am I one? Is it some accident of birth?"

"Maybe. In your case... I don't think so."

That surprised her. It was probably the only thing he could have said that would have. "Why am I special?"

"Your grandmother was a Warrior's daughter. She and your mother were both protected."

She sat across from him. "Like you want to protect me?"

He nodded.

"What is this protection?" She should have asked the specifics long ago. If her mother was protected, it couldn't be that bad.

Colin pulled a necklace from his pocket and placed it in her hand.

Jan examined it. It was a metal disc, like dark pewter but not quite. There was an etching of two crossed arrows superimposed over a bow. The word *Jäger* graced the top. *Jäger* was the German word for Hunter, wasn't it?

"What is this?" she asked.

"An amulet consecrated in —" He looked uncertain. "Consecrated in our beliefs."

"I take it you're not talking Catholic holy water here."

Colin grimaced. "Hardly."

She tried to hand the amulet back. "Then I don't suppose this will help me much."

Colin didn't take it from her. "Why?"

"I don't believe in it."

"And?"

"Well... Why would a god protect someone who doesn't even believe in him?"

"Because, it's not you asking. It's me, and I do believe in it." His face was deadly serious.

"What's in it for you?"

"Knowing you're safe."

Jan shifted uncomfortably. "What do I owe you in return?" *No such thing as a free lunch. He has to be getting something from me.*

Colin shrugged. "If trouble comes, and a Warrior gives you an order, you follow it. If you travel, you let us know so we can see to your safety. Once you accept this amulet, you never take it off."

"Why?"

"You are only protected while the amulet touches on or very close to your skin. It can lie over your shirt instead of beneath it, but close is the key.

"If you take it off, you may forget to put it back on. Or you may take it off at a time when trouble is headed your way and not be able to reach it again in time."

She hesitated. "You believe this?"

"Of course."

"My mother believed this?"

Colin darkened and didn't meet her eyes.

"Colin? My mother believed this?" Her heart pounded at his refusal to answer her. What was he hiding? She sensed there was something.

"Yes," he whispered. "She believed it."

There was still something he was hiding. "Colin?"

"Come with me. I want to show you something." He stood and headed for the door.

Jan looked at the amulet in confusion and stuffed it in her pocket. She followed him out of the cabin and up the mountainside.

Colin squatted in the grass, staring out across the lake. It shimmered a beautiful rose gold in the setting sun.

"Colin?"

"Shhh. Just watch."

"I don't —"

He grasped her waist and pulled her down beside him. Jan stared at him, her heart hammering against her ribs as she searched his face.

His eyes darkened to smoky black. "Shhh." He turned her face to the lake. "Watch."

Jan nodded. Colin lowered the hand from her chin to the ground though he left the other on her hip.

The sun sank further behind the mountains. A strata of rainbow colors decorated the sky and reflected in the still water. Just as Jan gasped at its beauty, the scene changed. The sinking sun sent its rays across the surface of the lake, setting the water on fire with a red-gold glow that reflected off its surface like a mirror to bathe the surrounding woods in a shimmering midday glow. The leaves and flowers erupted in startling color richer than Jan had ever seen before. It lasted a few precious moments before it was gone.

Jan pressed to Colin's side, his breath making currents in her hair. Her awareness of him sent her mind in new directions. It was a lovers' sunset, made to be watched while making love. Colin would make love to her during one of those sunsets if she asked, Jan was sure. She pushed the thought away.

The sight was fantastic, a true marvel. Photojournalists waited a lifetime for the chance to capture such images on film. Most never got the gift.

Colin whispered next to her ear. "What are you thinking?"

"It's beautiful. My Dad would have killed for a photo spread like that. I wish he could have —"

She stopped in shock as Colin moved away from her and stood, pausing only long enough to make sure she didn't fall from the loss of his body supporting hers. His eyes were hard and his hands fisted at his side.

Jan shrank back. "What? What did I say?"

"Nothing. I'll see you inside." He turned on his heel and stormed away.

* * * *

Colin stomped back down the slope to the cabin, cursing himself for his stupidity. It had been a tactic to get her mind off her mother before she asked questions he didn't want to answer, but it had turned into something else.

At least, it had for him. He'd thought it had for her, too. Colin saw Jannelle's wonder. She was beyond beautiful. He'd thought she saw the raw power and sensuality inherent in that sunset.

Jannelle saw only a story. Everything was a story to her. Everything would always be a story to Jannelle Evans. She would never be anything but Scott Patrick Evans' daughter.

Colin slammed his fist into one of the porch uprights, then rubbed the cracked bones of his knuckles in sheepish regret. "Stupid," he growled. "That'll take a week to heal." Then again, maybe the pain would remind him how hopeless this whole situation was.

He went to the sink and cleaned the blood from his abraded hand, groaning at the erection that refused to fade. Ever since Jannelle had leaned into him, his body had reacted in a fierce need for her that seemed to get worse with every touch of her body. Knowing she didn't share his wish did nothing to cool his arousal.

Colin glanced at the gathering darkness, then around at the cabin in surprise. "Jannelle?" She hadn't followed him in. Colin was sure of it.

He headed for the door with a muttered curse. It had been a boneheaded move to leave her. She was probably scouting for a photo shoot and oblivious to the coming night. He had convinced himself into a righteous anger with her when Jannelle screamed.

* * * *

Jan watched Colin's retreating back in confusion. She had said something that angered him, but she couldn't imagine what it was.

Maybe he'd hoped she'd invite him to make love to her. She shivered at the thought. She almost had.

Maybe if she let him protect her, Colin would take her home. If she didn't go home soon, she'd end up in bed with him. Worse, Jan was sure she'd want more than an affair with Colin, and she couldn't go there if she risked a broken heart. Colin Hunter wasn't the type of man you walked away and forgot.

Jan pushed to her feet and brushed the dirt off her hand. It was getting dark. It was time to get under cover.

Three steps toward her goal, the urge to run the other direction assaulted her.

"Oh, no." She shifted from foot to foot. She couldn't run the other way, but the thing was between her and the cabin.

A sudden thought occurred to her. Jan dug the amulet out of her pocket and settled it around her neck. "What can it hurt?" she grumbled. "Now to figure out how this thing works." *Why didn't I ask Colin while I had the chance?*

She started down the slope again, feeling the danger getting closer. Jan tried desperately to calm her pounding heart. Colin had promised this would work. She had to trust that it would.

A man appeared before her, his dark hair hanging in long waves to his shoulders and his ice blue eyes glittering in amusement. His smile revealed lengthened canines.

"Great," Jan breathed. "Another guy who thinks he's Dracula. Just what I need."

The man laughed. "Oh, I'm the real thing, baby." He took a step closer, giving her a leering once over. "Nice try with the amulet, but you can't fool me that easily."

Jan's mouth went dry. "What do you mean?" she stammered. "The amulet is real. A Warrior —"

"Ah, yes. The infamous Colin of Hunter gave you the amulet."

He moved into her personal space, and Jan shuffled back several steps, cursing the loss of ground. She needed to reach the cabin, not be forced back from it, but the feeling of him so close made her physically ill.

He kept coming. "He didn't give you his personal touch, I'll wager."

She darkened and backed off further.

The man raised an eyebrow in surprise. "Maybe not, but he has...touched, hasn't he?" His hands feathered just shy of touching her shoulder.

Jan recoiled from the near touch as his brow furrowed. Her legs were shaking. She had no idea what the amulet was supposed to do. How could she know if he was telling the truth? How could she tell if it really wasn't working as it should?

His hand came out again, that time toward her neck. Jan leapt back, and rough bark scraped her back.

His eyes narrowed. "You're not protected. What are you?"

Jan's head spun. Not protected? What kind of touch — Her face burned. Surely, she didn't have to sleep with Colin to be protected.

"What are you?" he demanded, his breath hot and sour on her face.

Her thoughts scattered. What was she? What was he asking?

"Sensitives are precious." Colin had said that, hadn't he?

"I'm a sensitive," Jan blurted out, hoping for the best.

His face hardened. His eyes flashed red.

Jan realized that telling him what she was had been a serious mistake, but she didn't know why. Frightened, she continued. "My grandmother was a Warrior's daughter. My mother was protected. I —"

His hands closed on her arms roughly. "All excellent reasons to kill you. I don't know what does protect you, but it's not the Warriors. That means I can kill you before he reaches you." His face flashed down toward her throat.

Jan screamed, but his teeth didn't sink into her. He stilled, his breath on her skin and his fingertips digging into her arms while his teeth brushed over her throat without so much as scratching off a layer of epidermis. He raised his head, his blue eyes glowing solid red, shaking as if under a great strain. He started to drag her toward his body.

"Stop," Colin demanded.

* * * *

Colin's entire body burned in *Blutjagd*. He held his breath until the beast turned from her. Her neck was clean. No blood and no sealed marks marred her creamy skin. The beast hadn't managed to feed from her.

Colin knew it was silly to worry. He should have felt it if the beast had fed, but this was Jan, and Colin never believed in taking chances with that.

The amulet lay over Jannelle's chest, and Colin sighed in relief. Once blessed, always blessed. Her mother's plea still held some power as long as she wore the amulet, but how much?

The beast pulled her to his chest with his arm locked around her hips to keep her from escape, both of them facing Colin. Jannelle stomped his instep, but the beast ignored the move. His other hand came up to cup one of her breasts. Jannelle darkened and looked to Colin hopelessly.

In that moment, Colin knew he couldn't let her go and live. The urge to tear the beast limb from limb with his bare hands was overwhelming. Jannelle was his mate in his heart, whether she accepted him or not.

Colin forced out the formal demand. "Name yourself, beast."

"Tyner," he breathed into Jannelle's ear. The beast glanced at Colin as his hand moved south, baiting Colin with his ability to touch her. The beast knew that Colin didn't dare move against him while there was any chance of Tyner killing her before Colin killed him. "The little sensitive knows your touch, Colin of Hunter. Now she'll know mine."

Colin looked at Jannelle in surprise.

She shook her head. "You said sensitives were precious," she managed in a choked whisper.

Colin grimaced. "To us," he explained.

Jannelle nodded, then jerked as the beast touched the button on her jeans. She elbowed him in the ribs.

Tyner jerked the hand from her jeans up and clamped it around her chin. He pulled her face up until she winced. "Nothing you are capable of doing to me will stop me."

"I'll shove this amulet so far up your ass you'll taste it," she promised.

The beast laughed.

Jannelle glanced at Colin out of the corner of her eye. "What are you planning on doing? You can't use your fangs on me. You couldn't do what you wanted to with your hand when you reached for me."

Colin bit back a smile. No feeding and no claws, just as Armen said. All the beast had was his strength and speed. Now that Colin was sure, he could move.

Jannelle continued, pushing the beast to his limits and beyond. "You probably can't even get it up," she accused.

Colin laughed outright at that one. "Balls of steel, baby," he whispered under his breath. *That's right, Jannelle. Bait him into a stupid move for me.*

With a growl, Tyner captured her mouth.

Jannelle squirmed against him and clawed at his hands, trying to escape his touch.

Colin pushed past his shock and fury. He ghosted and sped to the beast's back just as Tyner realized his mistake and lifted his head to search for Colin. His blade was planted in the beast's heart before Tyner could react. Colin dragged Tyner's dying body off of Jannelle while she sputtered and wiped her mouth on the back of her hand. He wiped his blade on Tyner and sheathed it, reaching for Jannelle.

She pushed him away and pulled off the amulet, shoving it at him with wild eyes. "I don't want it. It doesn't do what I need." Jannelle turned and started walking to the cabin.

Colin followed on her heels. "It's not just the amulet. There's more to it."

Jannelle turned on him, her eyes blazing in anger. "So I heard. *How* do you have to touch me, Colin? No. Don't answer that. I don't want to know. It's probably not worth it." Jannelle started toward the cabin again, her arms locked over her chest.

"It's not what you think," Colin protested. "It's not sexual. It doesn't have to be —"

"Sure. Take me home."

"Not until you're protected." Colin knew he had no right to say that. Even a sensitive had the right to turn down his protection. He couldn't force it on her. There was only so far he could go.

"Why?"

"You told him you're a sensitive." *And you're my mate, damn it! I can't let you go without protecting you.*

"So? He's dead." She faltered. "He is dead, isn't he?"

"He is, but he's also connected to the hive mind. What he knew, they all know."

"Lovely. You could tell me these things. Half information is hurting me."

"Do you know the meaning of 'off the record'?"

"That's low."

Colin didn't answer. It was low, but it was also true. The last thing he needed was to be responsible for the "I Am A Warrior Princess Pursued by Vampires" exposé she could write if she was fully armed with information. Everything was a story to her, and he couldn't forget that.

"This is my life, Colin. You're keeping secrets that can get me killed."

"Let me protect you, and you won't have to worry about a beast handling you again. That's what you need to know."

"And have you hovering over me for the rest of my life?"

Colin bit back the image of him hovering over her in bed. "It wouldn't be like that," he snapped as he followed her into the cabin. *No matter how much I wish it could.*

"You're right it won't. I'm leaving."

"You're half right. We're leaving together, and we're leaving now. Use the bathroom if you need to. I'll get your clothes."

"What? Where are you taking me now?"

"Someplace safe. One dead beast will bring more in the area."

"Will it always?"

"No." *Not usually when they know the Warrior is strong, unless they are coming in force.* "But they will for you."

Jannelle looked at him with frightened eyes. "Why am I special? Why did the amulet — Why couldn't he — Colin?" She shook in the delayed reaction.

The lost look on her face made Colin's heart ache. He pulled her to his chest. "When your mother died, she gave you her amulet. She asked our gods to protect you. Our... Our gods have a great deal of respect for a mother's love for her child."

She went still in his arms. "The man who killed my mother —"

"He was a beast. Your grandmother's brother killed him to save you, but he wasn't in time to save your mother. His name was Carrick Armen."

"You knew this and didn't tell me?"

"I suspected, but I found out for sure when I called Corwyn yesterday. He called the Armens and got the information for me."

Jannelle pushed away from him. He reached for her again, but she spun out of his reach with tears in her eyes. "No. You're telling me my life is a lie."

Colin hesitated. "Your father wanted to protect you. He thought being with us was more dangerous than —"

She stalked to the bathroom and slammed the door behind her.

Colin rubbed his neck roughly. "Five minutes, Jannelle. We have to leave."

She didn't answer him. The water turned on behind the closed door. Jannelle was probably washing the beast's touch and kiss off of her. He couldn't blame her for that reaction.

Colin tossed the clothes he'd bought her in a gym bag from the closet.

He pulled on his jacket, scowling at his reflection in the mirror. He was at the edges of restraint and courtesy. He wanted her desperately, and it was about to get worse. The closest cabin was the one he'd used for his printing madness after Cass. He was at a second turning point, but there was no question this time. If he didn't have her, he would die. The cabin would be the site of his grave, if Jannelle turned from him.

"Colin?"

He furrowed his brow at the confusion in Jannelle's voice. "Yeah?"

"Colin," she screamed, her panic a living thing.

He turned, his weapon in hand. His blade sliced unseen flesh, and he felt an answering cut through the leather of his jacket as the beast lost its ghosting. Colin pulled back and struck again before the shock of his first blow wore off.

Jannelle stood in the doorway, her hands pressed to her stomach.

Colin grabbed the gym bag and sprinted to her. "Are there more?"

She stared at the downed beast.

He pulled her face gently back to his. "Are there more?"

Jannelle shook her head. Colin grabbed her hand and led her toward the car.

Chapter Thirteen

Jan's breathing was harsh in her own ears. She glanced back toward the cabin disappearing into the dark woods as they sped away. She looked back to Colin, noting the tension in his face as he drove.

Her anger was quickly overwhelming her fear. She just saved his life in there. The least he could do was thank her.

She sobered. Of course, without him, she was helpless.

Damn it! She couldn't even be mad at him for not thanking her. She certainly hadn't thanked him for saving her nearly enough.

"What the hell was that?" she demanded. "I want to know this time."

Colin shot her a look of disbelief. "You are unbelievable, Jannelle. That's your fourth time, and you're still asking me that?" He shifted his eyes back to the road and shook his head angrily.

"Vampires don't exist," she stormed at him. Whatever these things were, they were a natural phenomenon or man made, not some dime store book monster.

"Oh, really? You know many people who appear and disappear without smoke, trap doors, and mirrors? That have a cross between sulfur, battery acid, and tar for blood? Get real, lady."

"Jan! At least if you're going to yell at me, use my name."

He scowled at the windshield. "Jan... What do I have to do to prove this to you?" The irritation left his voice. Colin seemed resigned. It was disconcerting to see him resigned to anything. It was too much like defeat.

"I — I don't know. I'm sorry, Colin. I'm used to dealing with facts."

He met her gaze, looking tortured. "The beasts are a fact, Jannelle. At some point, you have to either accept that fact or become a casualty of war."

"You'd let..." It was suddenly hard to breathe.

"Why would I save you four times if I intended to let them harm you? It certainly would have made my life easier, but I don't believe in sacrifices."

"What will you do?"

"Protect you. That's what I do." His hands tightened on the steering wheel.

"You don't want to," she guessed.

"Yes. Yes, I do want to."

"Then, why —"

"It's nothing. Really, it's nothing."

He didn't have to say that he wanted more. Jan caught on, but she couldn't comment on that. She twisted her fingers in her lap. "All right."

Colin shot her a narrow-eyed glance. "You'll let me protect you? You trust me that much?"

"I've got nothing to lose. They know who and what I am now. I don't even know where I can hide. With you, I'm safe."

A strained smile pulled at his lips. "I wouldn't bet on that."

"Because they could win someday?"

"No. Not that."

She nodded. Colin didn't fear losing. He feared losing control, and she was the icebreaker poised over that control. "Colin?"

He sighed. "I'm just tired, I guess. Don't listen to me."

Jan nodded and reached a hand out to touch his shoulder. The cold, tacky fluid on his arm startled her, and she drew her hand back in shock. She reached to flick the overhead light on with her other hand and stared at the blood on her fingers in horror.

Colin snapped the light off. "What are you doing?" he demanded.

"You're hurt."

"Calm down. It's just a scratch," he dismissed her.

"No. Pull over. Let me check it."

He shook his head. "We'll be at the other cabin in thirty or forty minutes. I'll take care of it when we get there."

"I'll take care of it," she insisted.

"All right, but it's minor. I got worse fooling around with my first training blade."

"We'll see."

She fidgeted in her seat until he pulled into a cabin and stopped him as he tried to disappear into the back room. "Oh, no. Get me the first aid kit and sit down."

She could barely see Colin's raised eyebrow in the light from his flashlight. "Generator first, so we have light to see by?"

She brought out her best hard-ass reporter look for him. "Agreed. No tricks, Mr. Hunter."

Colin smiled and turned away. "Yes, ma'am," he replied smartly. "Anything you say, ma'am."

Jan sighed. "Would that that were true."

He laughed lightly as he filled the reservoir and started the generator. He moved to the breaker box and reset the board. Lights blazed on, and Jan switched the flashlight off.

Colin turned to her and closed the door to the utility room with a wide smile. He surveyed the cabin. "Little dusting and a few light bulbs and we're in business," he decided.

Jan stepped in front of him to block his retreat. "Your arm first," she ordered.

"As you wish."

"Saying things like that will get you into trouble with me," she warned him.

Colin's smile disappeared. "Will it? Maybe I should say it more often then."

Jan felt her heart skip. Was he flirting with her? After his cold demeanor the last few days, the change surprised her. Part of her hoped he was flirting. Whatever else Colin Hunter was, he was a fine figure of a man.

She swallowed slowly. "Maybe you should. Now, where is the first aid kit?"

"Bathroom."

"Good. We'll need water anyway. Lead the way."

Colin met her eyes for a moment, and she was locked in the intensity of his gaze. His hands circled her shoulders, and she was suddenly sure he intended to kiss her. At the last possible second, he guided her aside and stepped around her.

"This way," he whispered as he turned away from her again.

Jan followed him, sure that the close quarters in this cabin would be measured even less in square footage than it was in the last cabin.

* * * *

Colin sat on the toilet, peeling off his shirt while Jan set out the supplies she'd need on the sink. He scanned her body while she worked, and a raging hunger pooled in his groin.

This cabin alone would drive him insane. In the morning, he would have to move her to another. If he didn't, the end would come for him all too quickly.

It didn't help that she was flirting with him in the living room. Jan wanted him. Her arousal was sweet perfume to him when he touched her. Given half a chance, he knew he'd bed her. But how far did her flirting extend?

Jan looked at him, and her breathing went ragged. Her gaze roamed the bare expanse of his chest and settled on the half-erect length of him, rising at her perusal and the smell of her heightening pheromone level. She snapped her attention back to the cut on his upper arm. Her hand shook lightly as she ran a soap and water cloth over his arm to remove the dried blood.

Her chest was even with his face, and Colin found himself wondering what she would do if he brushed his lips over the rigid peaks pressed to the fabric. Would she cry out as she had at the other cabin?

He gave himself a mental shake. It was his printing talking, and it was speaking out of turn. He gave his vow that he wouldn't touch her. He was honor-bound not to convince her to willingness.

Jan groaned as she set the cloth aside and reached for the alcohol swabs.

Colin looked away from her tempting body. "Problem?"

"It's not as deep as I thought. That's good. I'm still going to clean it and bandage it."

She accomplished her task quickly and efficiently and packed the soiled shirt and supplies in a small trash bag. Colin stood as she backed away, crowding her in the tiny bathroom, needing to feel her warmth.

"What are you doing?" Jan asked nervously.

"Do you trust me, Jan?"

She took a step further into his body. "Implicitly," she breathed.

"Good." He pulled the amulet she'd shoved back at him earlier from his front pocket. "There is a ceremony."

"What kind of ceremony?"

"You wear this amulet from now on. As long as you have it, you are protected by the Hunter family. I bless you. The amulet is useless without the blessing. Then I seal the blessing."

"Seal?"

"A kiss. That's all I need." Colin grimaced at the Freudian slip. "That's all that's needed to seal the blessing. Do you trust me?" She would have to. It would be difficult for him to restrain himself to a chaste kiss and let her go.

"Absolutely."

She shouldn't trust him that much. "Good."

He looped the amulet around her neck, cupped the back of her head with his hand, and — knowing that Jan would demand to know what he said later —

pronounced the blessing in English for the first time in his life. "By the gods who forged us all, I grant you the protection of the House Hunter. Any and all of our kind and kin shall lay down life to preserve yours from the evil that walks among us. Walked blessed among us now."

Colin leaned to kiss her. Jan wrapped her arms around his neck, running her fingers through his hair while she slanted her mouth to his. Nothing more than a chaste kiss was required, but she was offering more. Colin knew he should tell her it wasn't necessary. His honor required that he only take what was necessary.

Fuck my honor. I have to know if she's as explosive as I remember.

He parted her lips, groaning as she met him passionately. Jan molded herself to him, and Colin guided her back until her hips were trapped between the countertop and his body. She gasped as he pressed to her, her eyes opening wide for a moment before she pulled his face closer to hers, seeking more from him.

Colin sensed her, groaning in the knowledge that she was high cycle. He slid the medicine cabinet behind her open, searching the contents with his eyes. *Thank the gods.* There was a box of condoms.

He broke off the kiss, holding to her hips lightly. "Anything you say. Anything you wish. Is this what you want?"

Colin pulled back his arousal and waited for her answer. If she said no, he would force himself to walk away somehow. If she said yes, he would be hard pressed to do more than take her here on the sink in his frenzy.

Jan shook her head, and his heart sank. He started to back away, but she molded herself to him again.

Her voice was rough in his ear. "A bed, Colin. I want you to take me to a bed."

He kissed her, his need fierce and hot. Colin gripped the box of condoms blindly and knocked toiletries into the sink in his haste. He pushed the bathroom door wide and swung her out toward the bed. Colin set her on her feet as he pulled the dust cover back.

"Last chance, Jan. Tell me."

She moved her hands to his belt and captured his groan in her mouth. By the time his belt slid to the floor and she had unbuttoned his jeans, Colin was easing her hands from his body to pull her t-shirt over her head and slide her now-unclasped bra off of her.

Colin's uncertainty gelled into a mindless demand from his body. When he lowered his mouth to her breast, his movements weren't gentle, slow, or controlled. He expected Jan to protest, to demand that he not be so rough with her. She didn't. She cried out in satisfaction and tugged him down with her to the bed.

Jan arched to him, and Colin realized that the move was intended to slide her jeans off her hips as much as to feel him pressed to her again. He moved down her body, running his hands and mouth over her. Colin pulled her jeans down her legs, stripping her shoes and clothes off quickly before settling his mouth at her core, as hungry and driven as he had been at her breasts.

Jan rose up under him, screaming out a release that had her contracting against his tongue. Colin teased at her with a satisfied smile. She'd take him in a few minutes, and he'd make her come again and again. There'd be no more frustrating nights dreaming of what her body might feel like under his.

Colin slid up her body, teasing the head of his erection into the waiting fluid heat of her. If only she weren't high cycle, he'd know the joy of her body encasing him with no delays. Jan bucked, sheathing him in her warmth. Colin cried out, pushing deeper into her in his need.

"Yes, Colin. Don't stop now," she pleaded, settling around him again as he started to back away.

Colin locked her hips to him, stilling her movements while he gritted back his arousal and talked himself out of the release pressing at him. "No," he panted out. "You're fertile. If I finish without a condom — Oh, gods." He found a hidden well of his control to tap as his balls drew up to his body in preparation to finish that last thought in the flesh.

Jan nodded and let him back out of her. Colin lay weakly beside her, trying to make his body heed his mind's decree that finishing in the depths of her was not for that night.

Her hand ran down his stomach. "You want to, don't you?"

"More than anything," he admitted. "But I won't."

"The idea of a baby?"

Colin ground his teeth at the spike of pleasure the idea of his son growing in Jan caused in him. *Gods, I am far gone.* "Only until I'm married," he assured her.

"Old fashioned?" she teased.

"Fond of my head. We live by a strict set of laws. We do not ever chance babies outside of marriage."

"Why?"

"We can't train and protect them if they're spread all over creation."

"That makes sense." Jan rolled toward him, circling her hand around his length. "So, which drive makes you want to?"

"What?" His mind seemed incapable of following her logic.

"Is it the wish for a baby?"

Colin groaned and pulled her to him, enjoying the feel of her curls on either side of her stroking hand.

"Is it a wish to marry me?"

He kissed her in a hopeless need, moving with her stroking. *What I wouldn't give if you would agree to that.*

Her eyes glittered knowingly. "Is it the feeling of being inside me while I'm so hot and wet for you?"

Colin closed his eyes, knowing the end was near. Jan massaged a drop of his precum into the engorged head.

"Or maybe —"

He met her gaze, holding to the last glimmer of his self-control.

"Maybe it's all three," she suggested.

Colin dragged her tight against him, tensing as he roared out his release. His seed left him in spasm after spasm, leaving a warm slick between their bodies that sensitized him as he heaved deep breaths in and out, still searching for his shattered control.

"Definitely all three," Jan breathed, seemingly stunned by the concept. "This is something I think we should discuss."

"Do you?" he managed, burying his face in her throat as he shuddered to aftershocks.

"How long have you wanted me?"

"Wanted you or wanted to marry you?" Colin asked for clarification.

"Both. Either."

"I wanted you when I realized you fought a beast with pepper spray. I wanted to marry you — I don't know. I know I finally admitted it to myself earlier this evening."

"When you kissed me?"

"No. When Tyner had you cornered. The bloodlust to protect you was more than I could attribute to anything else."

"The baby?" she asked quietly.

He trailed his lips down to her pulse point. "We don't just marry. We mate for life. Even if our wives don't give us permission to create life, the drive is there. It's beyond a drive. I want you as my wife. The idea of my baby in you is erotic to me. But that is another of our laws. Even if we marry, until our wives give us permission to produce a child, we will not do it."

"You won't have a baby unless she wants to?"

"Never. That's why our numbers don't increase overmuch. The women are always mindful of the fact that they may lose their husbands in battle and have to raise their children alone, with the help of the other males of the household to mete out punishment and handle training the young Warriors. It is her choice to add to her burden. A Warrior cannot consign her to that fate."

"You find a baby erotic?"

Colin groaned. "Everything about it. It's not just the lovemaking to start one. It's knowing my baby is inside you, feeling him move, you feeding him, holding him — It's all a rush."

"An experience that you want?"

Colin pushed back and met her gaze. "Not until you. Only with you." Even with Cass, it hadn't gone that far. *I'll have to hand Corwyn my blade, for sure.*

"You mate for life. What if you — grow apart?"

"We don't. In fifteen hundred years, it's never happened. You've seen Gabby. Does she look unhappy?"

Jan bit her lip and seemed to consider it. "There are concessions. There have to be in a relationship like that."

"Not many. More for the men than the women."

"How so?"

"Well, the women agree to obey the Warriors in matters of their safety, and they accept that we will be protective. The men find ourselves willing to do almost anything for our wives."

Jan's smile spread. "Anything?"

Colin sobered, angry with himself for breaking his own council and telling her anything she could use against them. He'd die and be a traitor fool to printing at the same time. "Except exposés," he growled.

Jan looked as if he had wounded her. "Is that all you think of me?"

He found it difficult to answer that. His heart ached at the pain in her eyes. *And I caused it.* "No. I mean, I'm sure there's more to you than a story."

"Is that why you think I slept with you?"

"I sure's hell hope not," he grumbled.

"Well, it's not." Jan pulled back tears even as she pushed away from him.

"You're angry again."

"You're damn right I'm angry." She fumbled with the amulet, trying to pull it over her head.

Colin closed his hand over hers, enclosing the amulet in her fist. When she favored him with a fierce look, he lowered his face to capture her mouth.

Jan broke off the kiss, backing away from him with a suspicious look. She moved her neck uncomfortably when she came to the limit of the leather thong that held the amulet. "What are you doing?" she whispered.

"What can I do, Jan? I want you to trust me. I want to protect you. Don't take the amulet off. Trust me, please."

"Then trust me. This story has almost gotten me killed twice. Do you really think I could ever trust anyone to publish it? Either they would rent me a rubber room or sic more vampires on me."

"You're saying the story holds no interest for you?"

She darkened slightly. "Of course, it still interests me. I'd be lying if I said it didn't, but it interests me in the same way a black widow spider interests me. It's great to look at as long as it's safely caged and can't bite back." Jan hesitated.

"It's more than that, Colin. I don't want to see you hurt. I'm sure the vampires already know who and what you are, but humans don't. There'll be an unruly mob trying to stamp out their one chance, if I tell the story." Her fingers played at the curls on his chest while she talked.

Colin felt himself hardening again at that light touch and her claims that she didn't want him for a story, that she didn't want him hurt.

Jan looked down at him with stark hunger in her eyes. "So, this job of yours — It's a family thing?"

"I shouldn't —"

"Tell me. You want to marry me and give me children. Would they have to fight vampires?"

"Yes. Our sons would hunt."

"And our daughters?"

"Probably —" Colin groaned as she stroked him. "It's unlikely that we'd have one. If we did, she wouldn't have to hunt."

Jan nodded. "How do I make you trust me?"

Colin's mind was scattered. He moved against her hand restlessly, wishing he could finish inside her for once but already soaring to another release in her hand. His blood burned for her.

She brushed a kiss on his chest. "If I marry you — If I am willing to tie my fate to yours because I trust you that much, would you trust me?" Her voice purred against his ear.

"We mate for life," he reminded her. "It's not all me. You'd feel it, too." Colin wasn't sure that was true, but Corwyn had theorized it, and the warning was a valid one.

"Is there a ceremony or do we just go find a JP?"

Colin groaned. "I ask you to be mine forever and you agree. Then I make love to you. We can use protection, but I make love to you properly." Gods, how he wanted to be inside her. How he wanted to seal his printing and have her forever.

Jan pushed at his shoulder and straddled him smoothly, locking Colin inside her body. He cried out. Colin tried to lift her off, but Jan locked her legs around his thighs and anchored herself to him.

"Jan, I'll come. I swear you're fertile. You can't —"

"Ask me. You said you want to."

"Jan! Please." It started as a demand but ended on a plea.

Jan rocked against him, and Colin fisted his hands in the sheets. "Ask," she crooned. "No babies before you mate." She moved over him again.

Colin cried out again, willing his body to his tenuous control. "Gods, please don't." He tensed, unwilling to injure her but unable to conceive of another way to force her compliance.

She rocked back and forth over him several times, smiling as he ground his teeth. "You'll have to come soon, Colin. Do you trust me enough to marry me? I trust you enough to marry you and have your children.

"It may be too late, you know. Precum has a high concentration of sperm. Have you lost that much control yet? You were coated in sperm before I trapped you in me. Do you think one of them —"

Colin pulled her down to capture her mouth, his balls pulled up tight in preparation to climax in her. "Tell me," he growled. "Tell me what you want from me."

Her breathing quickened and her heat increased. Gods, she was so excited. "Ask me. Ask me to marry you and complete the ceremony."

"Do you want forever, complete with a little Warrior? If you don't stop now, that's what you'll get, Jan. Be sure before you agree." *I was coated in my seed. It may already be too late.*

"Is that an offer? Ask me."

"I want forever, Jan. I want you as my wife, my mate, and I want my son in you. Will you give me that? Will you marry me?"

"Yes, I will. Find me a JP tomorrow."

Colin grinned and ran a hand over her breast. "The day after," he corrected. "If you think I'm willingly leaving this bed in the near future for more than a shower or food —"

"Why is that?"

"Tell me again. Tell me you want my son in you."

Jan moved against him restlessly, but Colin locked her hips to him.

"Tell me."

"God, yes. Colin please. I need you to come in me."

"Why?" He stroked deep inside her and froze again, enjoying the torture of it now that he was controlling her need. "Tell me."

"I want your son. Colin, please."

He flipped her beneath him, surging into her over and over while Jan cried out in time with his possession and climaxed around him. Having come once gave Colin the control he needed to hold off, driving her to another release before he roared and spent his seed in her in violent explosions of his need.

Colin sealed his mouth to her, feeling the shift that made her his and needing her again, needing to make his son a solid reality. He groaned as he sat up, lifting Jan into his lap as he soared toward another release.

Jan nestled her breasts to the solid wall of his chest. "Colin. Oh, God! I don't know if I can." She groaned into his shoulder as she nipped at him lightly.

Colin felt a momentary qualm. "If I hurt you — If it's too much, let me know, Jan. I will never hurt you."

She smiled. "Hurt me? Oh, Colin. I may die of pleasure."

He laughed weakly. "I want you to live in pleasure, not die in it. Although —" He groaned as he climaxed again. *I may die. No wonder Corwyn and Stephen lost their minds. It's nothing like I imagined.*

Chapter Fourteen

August 7th, 1985

Jan looked around the entryway of the manor house in awe. The name was well deserved. "So, why is this called the manor house?" she asked, distracted by the hand-turned wood and carved mirror.

Colin looked around and darkened. "That's a little hard to explain."

"Try me. I mean, I associate manors with lords and ladies and —" She swallowed hard as his eyes narrowed. "This is America, Colin. We don't have nobility."

"It's not nobility. It's a job, a chain of command. It's like calling someone a CEO."

"So, if one of you is lord —"

"Corwyn. He's Lord Hunter."

She nodded slowly. "What is your title?"

Colin sighed. "I'm a Warrior. Unless Corwyn dies, that's all I am."

"Good." She meant that sincerely.

A smile pulled at his lips. "You don't want to be Lady Hunter?" he teased.

"Me? A lady? Are you nuts?"

"Well, Corwyn is the best, so I wouldn't worry about that for a long, long time."

"Better than you?"

"You have no idea." Amusement was written on his face.

"I find that hard to believe."

He laughed heartily. "Would you like anything before I go?"

"Go?"

"I assume you'd like some of your own clothes. I'll take care of that."

"I'll come with you."

"Not until you contact Uncle Devin and explain your disappearance." He grimaced. "Maybe in terms of your whirlwind marriage and honeymoon."

"There are people watching my apartment?"

Colin shrugged. "Maybe. Knowing Pierce, probably."

"Then you can't go there."

He smiled in boyish glee. "What's life without a little adventure?"

"You want to get caught?"

"You've seen me appear and disappear. Do you honestly think someone will see me if I don't want them to?"

Jan argued with herself. Why she would worry about Colin in broad daylight was beyond her, but she did. She nodded, unable to form a gracious response.

"Do you want anything before I go?"

"No. I'll be fine."

"If you're sure — The kitchen is through there." He pointed to an immense dining room to their right. "The library is there, and the living room there." He pointed to the further and closer doors on the left. Colin's smile widened as he pulled her into his arms. "If you'd like to go to bed," he teased, his eyes glittering, "our bedroom is up the stairs to the right, second door on the left. Got it?"

"Sure. So, what would I find if I went left and second door on the right?"

"A half bath. The door just past our room is a full bath. Planning on exploring?"

"I'll wait for you."

"Good idea." Colin kissed her solemnly. "I'll be back soon."

Jan watched as he exited stage right, striding back to the lower stairwell below the main staircase and his car in the garage. There was no one here, Colin had assured her. He thought Gabby might be when her car was in the garage, but no one answered his call. Colin had assured Jan she was safe from even human minions at the manor house. The security system would bring their own security men if there was any problem.

She sighed and decided to look around the library. There were novels, but she gravitated toward the leather-bound volumes on one long wall. They were invariably penned in foreign languages that she could sometimes identify but not read. Still, Jan took a stack to the table by the leather couch and settled in to look at the illumination.

The work was stunning, quality she'd expect to see in museum pieces, and they were very old. Jan had a momentary qualm. What if they weren't meant to be handled? Surely, Colin would have warned her if that were true, and she couldn't pass up the chance to look at something so precious.

Even without reading the text, the paintings were evocative. The illuminations depicting the vampires' depravity were suitably dark and sinister. The battle scenes were fierce, bold, and bloody. There were whimsical scenes of Warriors with fat, happy babies playing on their laps and at their feet and a touching print of a Warrior running his hands over his wife's pregnant womb.

"At least they know what's really important in life." Jan sighed as she switched the volume in her hand for the next one on the stack.

It was a thin volume, and the illuminations were very detailed, less stylized and more like portraits. The first half-dozen or so seemed to center around a huge red jewel with a blue halo surrounding it. She wondered what it was. It was obviously important to them, whatever it was.

The next portrait took her breath away. It showed a Warrior and the shadowy form that represented a vampire facing off over the jewel. In the stone base the jewel sat on was the face of a woman.

Did they fight over the jewel? Was that what started the whole thing? And who was the woman? She was beautiful and haunting. From the portrait, it would seem that she was linked to the jewel somehow.

Jan looked up at a soft gasp from the doorway. Gabby stood, her face pale and one hand gripping the hand of a child Jan knew was a toddler though he was easily the size of a first grader. Gabby backed off a step in shock and disbelief.

"It's okay, Gabby. Colin knows I'm here. I understand now. I won't —"

"Stephen." Her voice was tremulous, and her eyes were locked on the book in Jan's hand.

"I didn't hurt it. I was very careful. Colin didn't —"

"Stephen!"

Jan winced at the panic in Gabby's voice. She had done something unthinkable, though Jan couldn't imagine what it was. It had to be something about the book. Jan held her breath as Stephen stepped around his wife. His face darkened in fury, and Jan swallowed a knot of fear.

"I was careful," she whispered, unsure of her exact crime.

Stephen stalked to her and pulled the book from her hand. Jan winced. His treatment had a much higher probability of hurting the antique than hers. What had she done wrong?

Stephen waved his hand toward the door. "Gabby, take Brandon up for his nap."

Gabby nodded. "Good idea."

Jan sank back into the cushions behind her as Stephen crouched to her eye level. He waved the book between them.

"Getting information for your story?" His voice was cold, and he radiated anger from every inch of his body.

"No, I — There is no story."

"How did you get in here?"

"Colin said I'd be safe here."

Stephen's eyes narrowed. "Really?"

"Yes. He — He'll be back soon."

Stephen drew her to her feet and started patting down her pockets.

Jan pulled away. "What are you doing?"

"Where is Colin's passkey?"

"With him, I'd guess." Jan dodged as Stephen reached for her again. "What the hell is wrong with you?"

The muscles in Stephen's arms bunched beneath his shirt. "You come here, a threat to my family. You upset my wife at a time it is unhealthy for her to be upset, and you ask what my problem is?"

Jan backed off, putting as much furniture between them as she could. "I didn't mean to upset Gabby. I tried to explain."

Stephen growled in irritation as he rounded the couch and started toward her.

Jan shuddered. "Protecting his mate," she breathed, frightened by the intensity in Stephen.

He launched toward her, his hands closing on her upper arms roughly. "You will not print that," he ordered. "You will not endanger my family that way."

She shook her head. "I won't. You have my word. I know —"

"You know nothing," he roared at her.

Jan pulled out her reporter face. "If you don't mind, Mr. Hunter." It wasn't a question.

Stephen looked at his hands and pushed her away, shoving his fists deep in his pockets. "My brother may or may not have brought you here. If he did, I think he's insane."

Jan nodded, watching the muscle at the back of his jaw twitch. "I can see you don't want me here."

His hard gaze settled on her face, and she backed off another step.

"In that case, I guess I should leave."

Stephen raised an eyebrow, and all the muscles in his upper body tensed as if he was about to pounce. "That's a good idea."

Jan turned and forced herself to walk through the entryway and out the front door. She didn't slow, didn't even consider what she was doing and where she was going until she was blocks away.

She stopped, running a shaking hand through her hair. Jan couldn't go home or to work. She wasn't safe anywhere, and night would be falling in just a few more hours. Jan shuddered. She had to get out of town. She'd take a cab to the train station and leave. Resolved, Jan started walking again.

What about Colin? He took you as his mate. He can't choose another woman.

"And his family won't accept me." Jan stifled a sob. She'd contact Colin from wherever she ended up. She owed him that much. She wanted him that much, but would he balk his family for her?

Jan pushed the thought away until she was at the train station with a ticket in hand. The first train leaving that wasn't a local didn't depart until after nightfall, but she had to chance it.

She washed her tear-stained cheeks in the restroom and twisted her wedding ring. What would Colin think when he found her gone? She shook her head, feeling the amulet shift against her breast.

Jan pulled the amulet out of her shirt, fingering the design. A Hunter amulet. Colin had explained the amulet. The ring was from Colin, but the amulet was from his family, and the Hunter family didn't want her. Jan pulled the amulet off with a grimace and buried it deep in one of the zippered pockets of the vest Colin had bought her.

* * * *

Colin felt the tension in the manor house before he parked and wound his way up the stairs to the foyer. He followed the waves of unease to the library. Stephen and Corwyn sat back in the two deep, leather chairs.

Colin shook his head. "What is wrong with you two?"

Corwyn locked a hand on Stephen's arm to keep him seated. "Let me."

Colin hadn't seen Corwyn this battle-ready in months. He pushed his hands down in his pockets, feeling the duffel of Jan's belongings brushing his hip. "What —"

Corwyn scowled. "You brought Jannelle Evans here to the manor house?"

Colin bit back a smile. "Yes, I did."

Stephen uttered a string of curses in three languages. "Are you insane? Bringing a reporter looking for a story —"

"She's not writing a story."

"You believe that?"

"Yes, I do."

Corwyn tightened his grip and wrenched Stephen down again as their younger brother vaulted toward his feet.

"Why would you trust her?" Corwyn asked.

"Have you talked to Jan?"

Stephen ground his teeth. "You mean after I caught her rifling through the ancient texts, and she scared Gabby half to death? Yeah, I talked to her all right. Did you have to give her so much ammunition?"

Colin tried to control his temper. "What did you do, Stephen?"

"What did I do? I tried to find out what she was doing, and I warned her not to write about my mate or family. That's what she called Gabby — my mate. What is wrong with you, Colin?"

"Where is Jan?"

"She left."

Colin dropped her bag in shock. "You let her leave?"

"Was I supposed to let her gather more information to sink us?"

"She's not trying to sink us," Colin raged. "She wants to know more —"

"Why? For what reason? Do we ever invite humans, even protected humans, in to read our texts?"

"No, but we're awful damn open with our mates, aren't we?"

Stephen froze, his breathing strangled as Colin's words sank in. "You want to —"

"I don't want to, Stephen. I *have*. The ring and amulet escaped your notice? Jan is my mate, and you chased her away from our sanctuary."

Corwyn shuddered. "A reporter, Colin?"

"Don't give me that. You took a woman from Veriel. Stephen mated with a woman who stabbed him, and you two think you have the right to question my choice?

"The last time I checked, a first-nighted and blood sealed Warrior chooses mate and wife without any hindrance. Jan is my mate and legally my wife. She probably carries my son by now. If it comes to a choice, my allegiance to *Jäger* be damned! I'm going to find my mate and my son. I don't care what you do."

Colin paused with his back to his brothers. "Jan is not going to sink us, because she's one of us. In case you've forgotten, she's also a sensitive." He added that as a dig at Stephen for so obviously disregarding it in his protection of Gabby. "Believe it or don't. I don't care."

He strode to the garage stairwell, giving Gabby a sour look as she watched, stunned, from the upper stairs. He was halfway down the stairs when Colin felt his brothers behind him.

Stephen spoke first. "Will she run or hide?"

"Run." Colin's heart ached as he said it. Jan would run from him, and he knew it.

Corwyn started issuing orders. "We split up. I'll take the airport. Colin, bus depot. Stephen, you take the train station."

Stephen passed Colin and yanked open his car door. "On my way. We'll get her back, Colin. You have my vow."

"You'll accept her?"

Stephen blushed. "I'm not killing you. You mated with her. If you don't have her —"

"Thank you, Stephen."

"Colin?"

Colin met his younger brother's eyes.

Stephen struggled, and his expression was tortured. "I'm sorry. If she had told me she was your mate —"

"I know, Stephen. I just want her back."

* * * *

Jan stared at the darkness outside and shuddered. She looked at the bank of pay phones. If she called Colin now, would he come for her? He told her he'd do almost anything for her, but this was his family, his life.

Her train would board in five minutes. There was enough time for a call. The number was unlisted, but Colin had given it to her. Jan punched the number with shaking fingers, praying Colin would answer.

It wasn't Colin. It was Gabby. "Hello?"

Jan bit back a sob. She couldn't ask Gabby for Colin. She wasn't sure Gabby would get him if she did ask.

"Hello."

Jan reached to hang up the phone.

"Jan? Jan, wait. I need —"

She hung the phone back on the cradle and fingered the ticket in the inside pocket of her vest. Jan didn't want to get on that train. She didn't want to leave Colin this way, but what choice did she have?

The wash of awareness struck her, and Jan scanned the crowd for the familiar man in black, hoping against all hope that it was Colin. For one heart-stopping second, her gaze locked with Stephen's. Jan turned and ran.

She chanced one look back and saw Stephen wading through the crowd heading for the tracks, for her train. Jan turned the opposite direction. Even if she got on the train now, where would she be able to hide for the fifteen minutes until it departed? She hit the emergency doors at a full run, wincing at the alarm as she hit the pavement and started sprinting from alley to alley.

Her knees shaking, Jan hid in the shadows behind a row of shops. She held her breath as she heard boots on the pavement. They slowed, and she prayed Stephen couldn't track her. His footsteps started moving away, and Jan let out her breath slowly. From far away, she could hear Stephen yelling her name, begging her to answer him.

Jan listened to him, suddenly torn. Stephen sounded desperate. Colin said the Warriors wouldn't hurt her, that they couldn't hurt her, despite Stephen's actions at the manor. She started moving toward the sound of his retreating voice. If she showed Stephen the amulet, he'd have to take her to Colin. Stephen was honor-bound by their code to do that much.

Jan turned a corner and saw a tall, dark figure. She wanted to run and hide, but she wanted Colin more. Stephen was honor-bound to take her to Colin. Then why did he scare her to death? She took a deep breath to steady herself.

"Stephen?"

The man turned, a strange man. He looked her up and down, and his smile spread.

Jan took a step back. "Sorry, I thought —"

"That I was Stephen of Hunter? I pride myself in that I look like a Warrior without illusion."

"Who are you?"

"Only Warriors ask that question." He stepped toward her, and Jan scurried back several steps. "The question is, who are you?"

He moved quickly, so quickly that he had Jan by the arms before she registered that he was moving. He lowered his face and sniffed at her cheek. Jan shuddered and pulled her face away from him. Beast.

She didn't question her panic now that he'd touched her.

"Colin of Hunter. You're his woman? I smell his sex on you."

Jan tried to push him away, and the man shoved her into a row of plastic garbage cans. She grunted as she landed, opening the zippered compartment that held her amulet with shaking fingers from her place on the ground.

His hand locked around her wrist, bringing her hand up to his mouth. He licked at it with a tongue that was abruptly long, snakelike, and hot. "Took off your amulet? Now why would you do that? No matter. I'll enjoy having a Hunter woman, however she came to me."

Jan bit back a sob as his teeth lengthened into fangs and he lowered his face toward her wrist, pulling her arm out painfully. Seeing his distraction, she eased her other hand into the unzipped pocket. His teeth pierced her skin, and Jan screamed, her hand groping for and then closing reflexively on the metal disc.

The vampire flew away from her as if thrown by an invisible hand at the scruff of his neck. Jan looped the amulet around her neck and tucked it under her shirt as he launched back to his feet. His eyes glowed red, and her blood stained his teeth and chin.

Jan locked her hand around the free-flowing source of her blood, pushing up the wall and easing away. The vampire followed her. He squatted where she'd originally fallen, dragging his fingertips through the small pool of blood she'd left while she got the amulet on.

He met her eyes as he licked the blood from his hand. "You taste sweet, Jan. I've heard sensitives do. I am honored to be the first to take your blood."

"How —"

"You're mine now. Wherever you go, I can track you. I've tasted your mind, your soul."

"No. I don't believe you."

He stood and faced her, a dark outline with the fires of hell in his eyes. "Believe it. Your favorite color is red. Your birthday is January the twelfth. You have an erogenous zone that Colin of Hunter discovered —"

"Stop!" Her heart pounded against her ribs.

He chuckled. "You're mine."

"Never." *I'll die first.*

The vampire bowed back. He roared at the sky. Jan shuddered as he met her eyes, then fell. A familiar foul smell filled the air. Stephen appeared from the shadows, his face hard as he wiped his knife on the vampire.

Jan recoiled as he reached for her. What was she now? Would he kill her next?

His eyes softened. "Please, Jan. Let me help."

"No. I don't want —"

"Jan, what's wrong? I need to see the bite. Please."

She raised her injured arm hopelessly. "I don't want to be like that thing."

Stephen dragged her hand off the bite, cursing under his breath as he pulled out alcohol pads from his pocket and started cleaning it to check the damage. "Damn it. It's ripped. I was afraid of this."

Jan sobbed. "It's too late, isn't it?"

He looked at her in confusion, then touched her cheek. "It's not passed in the bite, Jan. You'll be fine."

"He said —"

"They can track you now. Never take off your amulet. Never."

She nodded weakly.

Stephen clamped a gauze pad over the bite and returned her hand to it. "Hold this. We'll get you help."

* * * *

Colin stormed through the halls of the semi-deserted medical center, barely maintaining his ghosting. He knew before he called home. Everything happened at once. The victim who was fed on had to be Jan.

He pushed past Corwyn and pulled the treatment drape back. Stephen nodded and placed her hand on the table, leaving to join Corwyn in the hall.

Colin took a deep breath and nodded to Michael on his way to the table. Jan's eyes were closed, but her color was good. Michael was stitching up the second tear on her wrist.

The doctor met his eyes. "She'll be fine, Colin. I gave her something to help her rest, but the damage is minimal."

"Thank you, Michael."

"My pleasure. You know it is."

Colin brushed a kiss over Jan's forehead, pushing her dark hair from her face. She stirred and her eyes opened. Jan touched his cheek and sobbed his name.

"It's me." Colin wound his fingers in her hand and kissed it.

"He —"

"I know."

"They can —"

"Yes, but only if you take off your amulet."

"I'm sorry. You told me."

"Don't be. You were right. I didn't give you enough information."

Michael started winding gauze around her wrist. "You know what to do. I'll give her antibiotics. Ibuprofen for pain. Call me for fever. Extra rest. I don't think she'll need vitamins."

"Give us some, anyway."

"Why?"

Colin smiled. "She's my mate."

"Is she —" Michael paled and swallowed hard.

"Too early for even me to be sure, but the vitamins won't hurt."

Jan groaned. "If I am, will it hurt the baby?" Tears ran down her cheeks.

Colin brushed his lips over hers. "Shhh. The beast didn't take enough to harm our baby."

"You're sure?"

"I'm sure."

Jan snuggled her face into his chest. Michael nodded to him, and Colin cradled her into his arms and headed away. Michael opened the curtain for him and motioned to Corwyn to come collect the prescriptions.

Stephen gave Colin a shaky nod. "I'm sorry, Colin. This is my fault. First, I chased her away. Then, I lost her in the confusion."

"And you killed the beast that laid his hands on her. I owe you my thanks."

Chapter Fifteen

August 9th, 1985

Colin held his breath as Devin Pierce brushed through the door with Corwyn on his heels. He favored Stephen with a hard look before his gaze settled on Jan.

The change that came over Pierce stunned Colin. The older man blinked back tears as he gathered Jan to his chest. His fingers traced the thick bandage on her wrist.

Colin noted, making an inventory of Pierce. This man would be either a formidable enemy or a strong ally, depending on how the next few minutes played out.

"You're okay?" Pierce asked Jan in little more than a whisper.

She nodded. "I'm fine, Uncle Devin."

He glanced at the three men suspiciously. "The Armens? Did they treat you all right?"

Jan blushed. "They're not the Armens. I — Uncle Devin, let me introduce you." She pulled herself from his arms and walked to Colin, taking his hand. "This is my husband, Colin Hunter. We were married three days ago."

Pierce weaved on his feet, and Stephen guided him to a chair.

"Sit here," Stephen soothed him.

"You married one of these —" Pierce blanched and shot a venomous look at Colin.

"Warriors," Jan offered. "I love him, Devin. Please, understand."

"I promised —"

Jan released Colin's hand and moved to Pierce's side, sinking to her knees with her arms crossed over his knees. "How much did Dad tell you?"

"I don't —" He shook his head and glanced at the ring of Warriors nervously.

"I'm hunted. That's why Dad never let me go to school. That's why I was always guarded, why you were afraid to let me investigate murders. Right?"

Pierce nodded and touched her cheek. "Yes."

"My father took one of these," she pulled the amulet from under her blouse, "from my neck that day."

Pierce paled. "You don't know what this means, Jan. If you accept this —"

"No. You don't understand. Carrick didn't put the one on me that Dad threw at him. My mother did. She knew this was my only chance."

"You don't have to do this. I can get more protection for you. Scott left money."

"I love him, Devin. I want this life. If you'll still have me, I'd like to come back to work."

His eyes narrowed. "But?"

Jan took a deep breath. "This is my family. You have to accept that. You can be part of my family, too...but if you can't accept the rest..."

"In other words?"

Jan returned to Colin and pulled his offered hand around her hip. "If you hurt them, you hurt me. No more threats of exposing them for what they do. If people rise up, they'll be coming after me now."

Pierce's jaw tightened. "How long have you known these people, Jan?"

"A little less than two months."

"The night you were attacked?"

Her face darkened, and she looked at Colin helplessly.

Colin nodded. "I saved her that night. A beast attacked her."

"He's saved me countless times. They all have. Please, Devin."

Colin tightened his arm around Jan, and she sank to his chest.

Pierce sighed. "I know a little about their laws. If you choose this, it's forever."

Jan smiled. "I hope so."

"Then I hope you're very happy. Will I see you back at work soon?"

"Soon. We have a honeymoon to finish."

Colin chuckled. "Do we?"

"We have a lake to visit."

Colin shook his head. "With a camera?"

Jan turned into his arms. "Why would I want to share that view with anyone but you?"

Chapter Sixteen

April 2nd, 1986

Jan kicked her low shoes off her swollen feet and rubbed her hands over her son. She smiled despite the discomfort inherent in being so close to term. She could beg off work and go home to her husband. Colin would delight in massaging her aches and pains away, making love to her until it was time to go hunting for the evening.

He was never far from her now. He even took a pager with him so Jan could reach him instantly if she went into labor. It was sweet, and she loved every minute of his pampering.

Devin stuck his head in and smiled at her. "Need anything?" he offered. Devin was solicitous, too. Any little ache or craving was paramount to front-page news in Devin's book.

"Yes. An end to this pregnancy."

He laughed heartily. "I can't give you that. Sorry. Oh, something came for you." Devin came to the desk with a large manila envelope in his hand.

Jan took it from him. "What is it?"

"Something from Melanie Cook."

"Oh, thank you." Jan had been waiting for the information from her old college friend for two days. She could barely contain her excitement as she tore the envelope open and pulled out the file on the little girl.

Devin crossed behind her and looked at the file in confusion. "What is it?"

"Just a file." Jan cringed inwardly at the half-truth. This was Hunter business. Outsiders weren't permitted to know about this. Even Devin, who could help with his almost limitless resources.

"You're not doing dangerous research again, are you? You know Colin gave me a firm warning about that."

"I know." She bristled at these overbearing men. In truth, Jan knew that Colin would be upset if he knew she was investigating anything having to do with Veriel. "It's nothing, Devin."

"If you're sure —"

"I am," she lied.

"Then I'll leave you in peace."

Jan nodded, already distracted by the file she was reading. Melanie had warned Jan that she couldn't get the complete file. Much of it had been sealed when the girl was adopted. Melanie couldn't access that information or the details of the adoption, but what was left should be enough to give her a clue.

She scanned the scant information. The infant had been abandoned in a car along the interstate in New England and went unclaimed. If it was Erin, how would she get so far away? Colin was certain that the beasts wouldn't carry her away only to abandon her. Veriel had been prepared to take Erin and keep her for his own. He wouldn't risk losing her.

If someone else — someone human — had taken her that far, would they abandon her out of fear or desperation? If they had, why would they have taken her at all?

Jan shook her head and moved on. The baby was only six and a half pounds. That was unusual for a

Warrior-born child, even a girl. She did have dark curls and dark eyes, even as a neonate. That was typical of them. But, the baby was jaundiced. Jan's heart sank. Warrior babies were disgustingly healthy. It had to be the wrong baby.

Her eyes locked on the last medical notation. The baby had a birthmark on the back of her right shoulder. It was the only possible concrete proof not expunged from the file. The details of her abandonment, including what she wore and whether or not she had an amulet, were state secrets now.

Jan stared at the two photos in the file in wonder.

The first had been taken in the hospital isolette. The crib card pronounced her "Baby Girl New York." Jan grimaced at any baby being named that way.

The second photo was of a smiling toddler, shortly before the adoption was finalized. The little girl clutched a teddy bear more than half her size.

"My God," Jan breathed.

The girl was petite, with fine features and bone structure. Still, her coloring was right, and her age was right. Her dark hair hung in ringlets around her face, and her dark eyes glittered in carefree glee.

Jan chewed on her lip. She picked up the phone. Gabby answered, as Jan knew she would.

"Gabby, I have a question."

"Why are you so nervous?"

Jan sighed. Gabby knew her too well. "I'm not. Sort of. I don't know."

"Spill it. I won't tell on you, unless it's really dangerous. Cross my heart."

"Okay. Did Erin have a birthmark?"

Gabby sucked in her breath. "A blood mark?"

"I don't know. It's called a small, oddly-shaped, dark port wine malformation in the file."

"File?" Gabby replied in a choked whisper. "This is dangerous, Jan. Colin is going to —"

"I know," Jan said hopelessly. "I can't help it. The idea of that baby — I want to earn my keep. This is what I do."

"Look down."

"What?"

"Look down," Gabby instructed.

Jan glanced down at the file, then at what little she could see of her body. "And?"

"You see that beach ball of active son who's been torturing you?"

"Who could miss it?"

"That is you contributing. That is the future of ending those beasts."

"But —"

"Leave Erin to the men."

"Did she have a birthmark?"

"We don't know, but the doctor who delivered her didn't see one."

Jan sighed. "Then this can't be the right child. I was hoping — It couldn't have been anyway. She was too tiny and she was jaundiced. I just —"

"I know. It's the pregnancy talking. Destroy what you have, Jan. Don't let the beasts think you're useful or dangerous. Either way, they won't hesitate to hurt you."

"I know, Gabby. Thanks." She hung up slowly and wiped away a tear.

Jan collected up the file and headed for the shredder. As an afterthought, she pulled out the picture with the bear. She'd destroy the rest, but there was something compelling about the little girl's face, something hauntingly familiar. Jan pinned the photo on her smaller bulletin board. Somehow, it calmed her just to look at it.

Section Three

Laura's Luck

Chapter Seventeen

October 14th, 1986

Laura Briony glanced at the man next to her nervously. "Why the hell am I doing this?" she exploded, knowing the man wasn't conscious to answer her and cursing herself for the fact.

She surveyed him again. He was well over six feet tall and was easily one of the most fit, strong men she had ever seen; and as a doctor, she had seen a lot of male bodies for comparison.

His black hair was cropped a little longer than military, and wisps fell across his forehead over eyes she knew were sinfully dark and expressive. His face was akin to that which she would have granted Apollo, a warrior's face but beautiful enough to grace a god with his strong chin, a slightly-imperfect nose that had been broken and set badly, and long dark lashes that made him look like a child in sleep...or an angel.

There were just a few little problems with tall, dark, and sinfully godlike. First would be that he was bleeding all over himself in the interior of the car...his car, thankfully, but bleeding all the same. He had a deep bruise on his face that wasn't helping the situation, but the stab wounds in his shoulder were the worst of it.

Second, he refused to go to a hospital. He was unconscious. She could take him to the ER without his consent now, but there were more than a few problems with that idea. Besides the fact that she owed him her life, she'd be hard pressed to explain his injuries, his arsenal, or the black blood that stained his hands and his leather jacket.

Third, she had a few thousand dollars worth of stolen equipment from the clinic in the trunk. She could go to jail for that. She could go to jail for any number of things up to and including the charges that would be filed if he died in her care.

Fourth... *Ah, hell!* She could hardly think about that part. She owed him her life. That thing that called itself Niko Evulsson would have killed her if it weren't for this selfless man.

She could leave it at that, right? She should leave it at that, but she knew it wasn't that simple when you find out the man you're on a date with is a vampire. Worse, when you learn it after you accidentally get your would-be savior damn near killed because you didn't realize he was the good guy in time to stop yourself from making the wrong choice.

She glanced at him again, aching at what she'd cost him. No matter what the cost to her, she had to repay the debt she owed him. He'd saved her. She had to try to save him in return.

Never mind that the likelihood of that was depressingly slim. Even if she figured out how the hell she was going to get an unconscious man that was twice her hundred plus small change up the flight of steps to her condo, she couldn't be sure he'd survive the night. In fact, it was a hedged bet that he wouldn't survive it.

What surprised her the most, well besides the whole idea of real vampires, was how understanding Corwyn was about her mistake. Even wounded, he'd kept himself between her and that thing. When he'd killed it, his first concern had been for her.

Getting me the hell out of there and making sure I was all right.

He'd run his hand over the cut on her throat, apologizing that "the beast" had harmed her.

In the frantic moments that followed, half-dragging him to his car, she'd learned the sum total of what she knew about him. Corwyn Hunter was a vampire hunter, one of many all over the world. The other hunters could track him wherever she took him, and it was imperative that she treat him herself. None of his doctors were in this area. None of the other hunters were close enough to reach him tonight to treat him themselves.

Doctors, she learned, were prized and protected. If she were willing to tend to an injured hunter whenever there was need, she would enjoy immunity from the vampires. That was an offer she hadn't taken time to think about. Rendering aid was a small price to pay for not becoming some vampire's dinner.

So, while she'd packed gauze from his first aid kit in the worst of his wounds, Corwyn had hooked an etched metal disk on a leather thong over her head, gasped out something in a language that sounded faintly like German, and wrapped his hand around her neck to pull her lips to his own.

She'd startled at that, not because he'd kissed her but because of the warm burst of energy that seemed to accompany the kiss. Maybe that was how he passed the magic that protected her, she decided. The problem was that it was sinfully arousing.

Laura pulled Corwyn's car into her usual parking space and thanked God, probably for the first time, that the light outside the stairwell was out. She lived on the second floor. With any luck, she could get Corwyn into her condo without anyone seeing him.

She circled the car to his door and pulled it open. Squatting next to him, she patted his cheeks.

Laura winced at how cold he was. He was losing blood, way too much blood. She checked his pulse and sighed in relief. It wasn't great, but it was there and stronger than she'd expected it would be.

Getting him upstairs was imperative. She slapped his cheeks harder. "Corwyn, snap out of it," she ordered. "I need you to help me now."

She cursed solidly and slapped him as hard as she could across his uninjured cheek, giving in to her frantic need to move him. The only alternative would be risking a hospital, and the higher chance of prison didn't sound all that hot to her.

"Corwyn, we need to move," she pleaded, biting back a sob. God, if she had to take him to the hospital, what would she do? Dump as much of his gear and her equipment as she could and hope for the best? "Corwyn, please help me for a minute."

His eyes fluttered open, and he fought to focus on her. His voice was slurred. "Doc?"

"Yes, it's Laura. Get up, Corwyn. I can't care for you here. I'll help you, but you have to meet me halfway."

He shook his head, and she was afraid he was giving up. He gripped her shoulder with one powerful hand and dragged himself out of the car, grinding his

teeth in pain as his injured arm and shoulder left the
support of the seat.

Laura braced him up as he half-fell over her,
panting and sweating. "Okay, big boy. It's going to be a
rough flight of stairs, but there is a warm, soft bed
waiting at the top."

Corwyn groaned and tried to hold up more of his
own weight, but his knees threatened to buckle under
him with every step. He muttered in another language.
She couldn't understand the actual words, but she
could guess that he was swearing profusely.

"It's all right, Corwyn. Lean on me, and we'll get
you upstairs."

She drew his uninjured arm over her shoulder and
got him moving. Twice, he lost his footing on the stairs
and stumbled, almost pulling Laura down with him.
Both times, she managed to stabilize him a riser or two
down from where they started.

By the time she got him to the bed, they were both
exhausted, and he was little better than out on his
feet. Lowering his bulk being a physical impossibility,
she let him collapse to the bed, wincing as she
calculated how much worse that would make his
injuries.

Laura muscled his legs up onto bed with him and
dropped down beside him for a moment, her hand
splayed on his chest, shaking in the aftermath of her
exertion. "God help me, I will never yell at a nurse
again," she vowed.

Reality intruded, and she pushed to her feet,
trudging back to the stairs. Her first priority was
getting the supplies up the stairs and doing her best to

save him; she couldn't waste time sitting down on the job.

She paused, letting go of the box of surgical supplies and running her hand over a duffle beside it in the trunk. Laura opened it, cursing herself for invading his privacy. As she'd hoped, it contained clean clothing.

"Wonder how often he finds himself stuck this way," she wondered aloud.

Maybe this is a business trip for him. The other hunters are far away, after all. Maybe he expected to be here anyway.

Sighing, she shouldered the bag and settled the box on her hip, slamming the trunk with her free hand. She had almost cleared the front of his car when his cell phone started ringing from somewhere inside the car. Her brain kicked in when she was halfway to the door, and she abandoned the car for the stairs.

Who knew who might be on that phone. It might be the other hunters, but it might not. Did vampire hunters have day jobs? Even if they didn't, would everyone who knew him know what Corwyn was? There was no way Laura could hope to explain who she was, why she had Corwyn's phone, and why he couldn't possibly come to that phone right now. Better that they get his voice mail than go through that.

And I don't have time for silly games. How much time would I waste trying to explain it while Corwyn is bleeding out?

Besides, he'd said the other trackers could track him wherever he went. She wondered if he had some sort of homing beacon on him...or maybe it was more of his magic.

She sighed as she made her way upstairs. There wouldn't be anything left of him but that near-perfect body if she didn't kick it in gear.

Laura worked for hours: cutting off his coat and shirts, inserting an IV, medicating him for pain, and cleaning the work site before she started stitching muscle and skin. Surgery wasn't her specialty, but she was all he had. She didn't take note of the other scars until much later. Obviously, Corwyn took his job very seriously.

He wasn't what she'd consider a safe man in any way, shape, or form. His job was hazardous. He was most likely wanted for some crime, even if the police didn't realize who they were looking for, which meant they probably didn't have a physical description to work from. After all, there couldn't be another man like Corwyn Hunter in all of creation.

In that respect, he was less safe than any other.

She glanced at her watch. Disbelieving, she swept the curtain back from the bedroom window. It was daylight. If the myths were right, they should be safe until nightfall. She just hoped the other hunters would arrive by then.

Laura stretched her back and stumbled onto the bed. She grimaced at the sight of his armored boots. Her fingers were stiff, but she managed to undo the buckles and slid them off of his feet. Her hand hovered over his jeans. She pulled it away slowly and drew the blanket over him. "Sorry, big boy," she whispered. "The doctor is only human, after all."

Her next objective was changing her clothes, cleaning those that could be cleaned, and bagging up anything that couldn't. Laura looked at the bed in longing, then headed to the couch. *Only human...*

Chapter Eighteen

October 15th, 1986

Laura startled awake at the sound of the knock at her door. The hand was heavy and impatient, and she said a prayer that it was the help that Corwyn told her was coming and not the police or other unwelcome company.

It was getting dark outside, and she had expected to see the other hunters much earlier. Maybe they had finally arrived.

Or maybe, it's the police...or a vampire.

She shuddered, then rolled her eyes at that ridiculous thought. The police would have announced themselves by now, and a vampire... Would a vampire bother to knock? She'd seen one turn into smoke, after all. Then again, the myths said they had to be invited into a home.

The person on the other side of the door pounded louder, and she shook her head. It had to be his friends. Why would a vampire knock? Still, she couldn't take the chance. She unsheathed Corwyn's knife and hid it behind her back, then made her way out to the door.

The man outside looked at her across the security chain, and her breathing hitched. She caught sight of yet another behind him. It had to be a trick. She'd seen the vampire change his looks. These ones were obviously trying to put her at ease by using Corwyn's face.

"What do you want?" she demanded.

"We're looking for Corwyn Hunter," the closer one replied simply. He was the shorter of the two, stockier than either Corwyn or the one behind him.

Her mouth went dry. "Look somewhere else."

Laura started to close the door, but he braced it open with his hand. She sucked in her breath at the look of malice he shot her.

"We know he's here, miss. I don't want to break in, but we have to see him, and we will do that however we have to."

"Who are you, and what gives you the right to threaten me?"

"Corwyn is our brother." He unsheathed a knife, and she backed off a step in fear, releasing the door, though that would give him the opportunity to unfasten the chain...or batter it in without her body braced against it.

"Calm down," he soothed her. He turned it to show her the badge in the hilt. "His has a wolf's head at the top...but you know that already. Let us in, please."

Laura paused for just a moment before unlocking the chain and waving them in. "I'm sorry. He didn't mention you were his brothers. I thought..."

"You've seen an illusion," the second man said, offering his hand. "I'm Stephen, and this is Colin."

"Laura." Her hand came out, and she stopped short in the realization that she still held the knife. She blushed. "Sorry," she grumbled.

Colin took it from her hand. "Don't be," he grumbled. "I should be used to Corwyn handing women blades by now."

Laura sighed. Maybe he did find himself in these situations often. He certainly had enough scars to have done so.

Stephen's voice drew her back to reality. "Which room?"

"This way." She started down the hall, the two men at her heels.

Stephen brushed past her as she opened the bedroom door. To her surprise, he started assessing her patient. "He's weak, but he'll make it. Lost a lot of blood." He looked at the IV in disgust. "Who did this?"

"I did." She silently challenged him to find fault with it. "I stitched him up as well. He wouldn't let me put him in the hospital where he belongs, so I did my best here."

"You're a nurse?" he asked. Stephen didn't look at her as he asked it. He peeled back the bandage on Corwyn's shoulder to inspect her work.

"Doctor, actually."

Colin nodded, sighing in seeming relief. "Good. Then I trust your work. Corwyn always did have more luck than seemed possible."

Stephen huffed at that one. "Don't suggest that to him," he noted. "No sign of infection, but you never know."

"We'll call ahead and have Jewel and Michael come up with antibiotics to be sure."

Laura set her jaw angrily. "You're not taking him out of here until he stabilizes," she ordered.

Colin looked at her in surprise. "He'll be fine. He could probably use a transfusion from one of us, but he'd survive without it. We need to get back."

"Why?" she demanded. "You've got a doctor right here. I can call a prescription in around the corner. I can even jury rig a transfusion before you leave; it's probably a good idea if I do, since you know you're compatible. Like it or not, he's my patient, and I can't let you risk him."

Stephen motioned to Corwyn. "I hate to admit it, but this might be the better option...at least for a few days, until he gets his strength back. We can take his car and get it detailed, and he can drive mine back when he's up to it. We'll have to leave an amulet to protect him, which he won't care for, but —"

Laura stared at him. Corwyn was strong, but no one was that strong. Though the chances of his survival seemed better by the hour, there was no way he'd be driving that quickly. "Days? Are you insane? He'll be lucky to be up and around in a week."

Colin snorted rudely and motioned to her. "You see? We can't leave him here. She has no idea what she's getting into. She'd probably take off his amulet to give him a sponge bath."

"Excuse me? I may not have known what Niko Evulsson was at first, but damned if I didn't figure out how to plant one of your magic blades in him well enough when push came to shove," she replied hotly.

Colin groaned. "Dear Fih and Ani! Not another one."

Stephen snickered. "At least he's already printed. We don't have to worry about that again, but we also know she'll protect him with her life. They always do."

Laura felt her face burn. *They always do.* A spike of unreasonable jealousy coursed through her. "What is that supposed to mean?" she demanded, planting her fists on her hips, prepared to take the first one who laughed at her down any way she had to.

Colin grinned and raised an eyebrow at her. "Oh, yeah. She'll do nicely."

Stephen nodded. "Just Corwyn's type. Maybe she'll get him to release some of that pent-up stress he's carrying around."

Colin sighed. "Don't count on that." He raked his gaze over her and smiled. "Still, it is a nice thought."

Laura eyed his wedding band and gave him a bland look. "If you're done evaluating whether or not I'll abandon my ethics and sleep with a patient just north of the critical list, I'd thank you to make your decision. Then one of you can pick up the prescriptions I'll call in while the other rolls up a sleeve, and I will get back to the business of saving your brother's life."

Stephen chuckled. "I vote for leaving him here."

Colin nodded his approval. "Spunky women, the bane of Hunter men," he mused. "At least she'll keep him on his toes." He pointed a finger to Stephen. "And just because you're so *fond* of needles, you get to be the blood donor."

Laura knew just enough French to pick out the many names Stephen called Colin in return for that.

Chapter Nineteen

October 17th, 1986

Laura knew before she touched him that Corwyn was fevering again. For the last two days, he had drifted in and out of consciousness, his fever rising and breaking, borderline coherent, then incoherent, managing only liquids and the occasional assisted bathroom trip. Now a sweat covered his flushed skin, and he burned at the touch.

She administered a shot of ibuprofen and pulled the blankets off of him. "Time to cool you off, Corwyn." She applied a wet cloth in swipes over his face and chest.

Corwyn groaned as she tended to him. "Oh, honey," he mused. "Thank you."

Laura smiled, certain that he had no idea what he was saying. "Just lay back and let me work, big boy," she teased.

She moved her hand in long arcs over the strata of muscles on his bare chest and arms, admiring the cut of his body. The rough stubble on his chin scratched at her fingers, bringing memories of Bill's stubble against her lips, but Bill's beard had been softer than this. Touching Corwyn was addictive.

Laura freshened the rag and moved on, disconcerted by how he was affecting her. *So much for professionalism.* It hadn't been *that* long since she'd had a man in her bed, and this one was injured, sick. *My patient.* Still, he was too good-looking for her peace of mind.

A jarring revelation pulled her out of her internal argument. Laura leaned over him, staring at his cheek in confusion. There had been a deep bruise there only yesterday; she was sure of it. It was gone, completely healed overnight.

"What the hell is going on here?" she wondered aloud.

Corwyn's eyes snapped open, and his gaze locked on her with a fierce intensity that frightened her. "Anna," he whispered. His hand cupped her chin.

She shook her head. "It's Laura, Corwyn. You're sick. You have a fever, and you're still healing from your injury."

His expression softened, and he drew her to the heat of his body. "Anna." His voice was tender, nearly choked with emotion.

She tried to push away gently, hoping not to jar his injuries. "Corwyn, it's not Anna."

He held her closer, his grip like iron. "Don't leave me again," he pleaded, turning to trap her body beneath his.

Laura tipped her face up to his. "Corwyn —"

He silenced her with a tender kiss. She cursed herself for allowing it, but she couldn't deny that she wanted him to kiss her. She'd wanted it since he gave her the amulet. She'd wanted it even more since his brothers had left Corwyn with her in the anticipation that he would give her a lot more than a kiss.

For a long moment, she allowed herself to forget that he didn't know what he was doing, that he was her patient, and that he thought he was kissing another woman. *Anna.* Whoever Anna was, she was lucky to have Corwyn this way. Laura realized, with some surprise, that she was jealous of a woman she didn't even know.

Some selfish part of her mind pushed away the thought that Anna might be a wife or girlfriend. It reasoned that Corwyn didn't wear a wedding band. It argued that she could assume he was single, because his brothers intimated that he was footloose and cavalier in his dealings with women.

Corwyn broke off the kiss and traced his lips down her throat to the vee of her shirt. Laura arched beneath him as his hand cupped her breast.

Stop him. My God! Corwyn is in no condition to follow through. He'll hurt himself.

But she couldn't seem to convince herself to stop him. Laura wanted what he was doing too badly to call a halt. She groaned as his fingers worked the buttons on her shirt open.

His mouth burned torturous trails over her breasts as his hands continued their quest to divest her of clothing. She ran her fingers through his hair and cradled his head to her, inviting his exploration of her chest.

Her body seemed to be radiating the same heat as his. As her shirt slid off over her hands, some rational part of her mind screamed at her to stop, but just as quickly, she seemed to forget that there was any reason not to let Corwyn do exactly what he was doing. Instead, Laura guided his mouth back to her own and demanded more. She lowered her hands, working the button on his jeans.

Corwyn did the same, pulling her jeans open in a few decisive tugs. "It's been so long." He pulled his jeans away impatiently, kicking them off the bed.

Laura tried to force herself to think...or to breathe. He was hard and pulsing in her hand. Then he slid from her grip, moving down the bed to suck in a nipple roughly. He nipped at it, sending a wave of pleasure through her that was heart stopping. His cock brushed her thigh as he shifted over her.

That lone rational part of her mind spoke up again, urging her to say something in the negative before he finished that move, but his mouth returned to hers so hot and needing that she couldn't bear the thought of not letting him continue. She sucked in her breath as he filled her, quenching some need she hadn't even realized she harbored.

Corwyn groaned, pausing, his chest rumbling against hers. He laid kisses over her face, making tender love to her.

No...not me. He's making love to some lucky woman named Anna, who he obviously dotes on.

She pushed that thought away and decided to enjoy what was happening without analyzing it too closely.

Corwyn grasped her hips and pulled her to fit his body more closely. Laura arched with the motion, crying out in unison with him as he surged further into her and buried himself fully. He went still again, and she opened her eyes, touching his cheek, struck by his desperate longing.

His pace quickened, sending her over into a shattering release. She screamed out his name as his heat exploded into her, warming her entire body in the process, her nerves buzzing in awareness of how good he felt.

He buried his face in her neck, shuddering as his cock pulsed inside her, most likely in aftershocks. It took her several moments to realize that he was weeping softly.

Laura tried to lever him up, but Corwyn wasn't helping and she couldn't move his bulk without his participation. "God, Corwyn! What is it? Did you rip your stitches open again?" A pang of guilt assaulted her at the thought that he probably had.

His voice was a broken whisper. "I'm sorry, Anna. All my fault... I'll find her for you. I swear I will."

Her heart pounded at this insight into his life. "Find who, Corwyn?" she whispered.

"I'll bring Erin home, Anna. I swear I will...before it's too late."

She cradled his head to her gently, at a loss to soothe whatever personal demons haunted him. "I know you will," she crooned. "Get some sleep now."

Chapter Twenty

October 18th, 1986

Corwyn groaned, rolling his shoulder and wincing at the pull of stitches. The healing was well under way, at least. He wondered how long he'd been out. The stitches felt nearly healed. That should have taken two to three days.

Awareness of his surroundings came slowly. He was sleeping in the nude; that wasn't unusual, in and of itself. The warm, soft body brushing against him and causing him to stiffen in preparation for sex was, however, new and disconcerting. Corwyn forced his eyes open and looked at the woman beside him in shock and dismay.

While awareness came slowly, realization came in a flash. She was the woman he'd saved...the doctor. What was her name? *Laurel? Laura? Lauren? Lori, maybe?*

Damn! If the signs were right, he took her, and he couldn't even remember her name. How could he do it?

The completely outrageous thought that he probably did it well had him swallowing a groan. He shook his head in disgust. He must have been out of his mind to do this.

Corwyn looked at the sunlight streaming around the drapes in confusion. He wasn't even sure how long he'd been here. Where were Colin and Stephen? Why hadn't they taken him home? None of this made sense.

He took a deep breath, looking down at his chest in annoyance at the feel of metal shifting against his skin.

They wouldn't dare!

Oh, they had dared. An amulet lay on his chest, a lord's amulet. Corwyn pulled it off, fisting it in his hand. *When I get my hands on those two...*

It was bad enough that they'd left him unprotected with a new inductee to their ranks, but putting an amulet on him like a trainee was going too far. If his brothers thought for one minute they were getting off with less than trial for this, they were in for a big surprise.

Corwyn started at the woman beside him, cataloging the lush lines of her outline beneath the sheet hungrily. His need was sudden, hot, demanding. He took a deep breath and closed his eyes. It must have been good. *Very good.*

Some irrational part of him demanded to have her again. *Now.* He wanted to wake her just to touch her. That nagging voice argued that he deserved to remember how good it had been.

"No," he breathed. He couldn't do this. Did he have this little control over his curse? What was wrong with him? He'd never been this out of control, even as a trainee.

Well, he had, but that had been with Anna, so it had been a completely different situation. There was no excuse for it this time.

She stirred, stretching, then opening her eyes to stare back at him.

Corwyn searched frantically for something to say, anything at all. In the end, a rather hoarse "What's up, Doc?" was what he managed.

"You, and that's a good sign," she commented. "Your fever is down. Can you take some oral meds for me now?"

"Sure." Taking them orally was probably preferable to whatever she'd been doing to get them into him so far.

He watched in awe as she nodded and leapt from the bed, striding naked across the room and into the hall. The need to pull her back into bed would have floored him had he been standing.

"Why is she so calm about this whole thing?" he grumbled.

The answer to that was obvious, really. She had the benefit of remembering what they did together, and she must have enjoyed it, or she wouldn't be so quick to parade around unclothed in front of him.

That thought sent a new wave of desire through him. Corwyn pushed it away insistently, reeling from his uncertain grip on his drives.

He stared at his hand, noting that he was imprinting the amulet on his palm with his death grip on it. He dropped it to the carpet beside the bed.

Corwyn thanked whatever gods were favoring him that she came back clothed in a robe. It didn't leave much to the imagination, and he knew very well what lay beneath it, but it allowed him to leash in his arousal a bit...until she leaned forward to hand him the pills and water and his eyes feasted on the open neckline.

Her voice brought sense back to him. "Here you go, big boy. Before you ask, amoxicillin for infection, ferrous sulfate for your lingering anemia, and ibuprofen for pain...unless you'd rather have Tylox?"

"No. I'd rather have a clear head. Thanks, though."
A clear head was essential. Any edge he could get in
this fight with himself was essential. He swallowed the
offered meds, then hazarded a look at her. "What
happened... I was out of line, Doc. It won't happen
again," he promised.

His body protested the comment, testing his
resolve. Corwyn wished he felt more certain that he'd
win this fight.

"You remember what happened?" she asked in
surprise, imperfectly masking something he'd identify
as embarrassment.

"No," he admitted, "but everything I'm seeing points
to some pretty enjoyable sex with you. That tells me I
went too far. I'm sorry."

"I'm not," she answered coolly. "Don't sweat it,
Corwyn. We both needed it. I can't say I'm happy that
it's over already, but I guess I knew it would be."

"What did I do?" he asked suspiciously.

"You said it already," she answered, avoiding his
eyes. She started to stand.

Corwyn captured her wrist gently and drew her
back. "Not so fast. Answer me first."

She blushed. "Look, it's my fault. You didn't even
know who I was."

Still don't, he fumed.

"I knew that, and I still let things happen between
us that I probably shouldn't have. Okay...definitely
shouldn't have. I needed it, and I figured some part of
you needed it, too. It was selfish, I know. You were
delirious, so..." She looked away from him. "So, if Anna
is upset, tell her that you thought..." She faltered.

Corwyn groaned, putting the pieces together. "I called you Anna?" Why didn't that thought hurt as much as it should have? He was being unfaithful to his mate's memory, and that should have made him feel bad for Anna's sake, but he didn't. He felt like shit for it, but he felt that way because of how it had made *this* woman feel.

She tried to pull her arm away, but he held her in place. The irrational, needy thing inside of him took root again, and he guided her face down to his and kissed her. She groaned, meeting his advances avidly.

Corwyn's control slipped, and he pulled away, pressing a kiss to her forehead, reining in the wild urge to be inside her. "That wasn't Anna. That was you, Doc."

"But —"

He pressed his thumb to her lips, moving his gaze from her mouth to her eyes with a pang of loss. "Anna was my wife. She's been dead for a long time," he explained, amazed that it didn't hurt him to say it. His body reacted to her look of concern. "I'm sorry you thought of yourself as a replacement. You're not."

She nodded, brushing her lips over the pad of his thumb.

Corwyn lost the battle. He dragged her mouth back to his, drowning himself in her heated responses. Gods, but she felt good in his arms. He had to know what he couldn't remember. He had to know how good she felt around his length.

"Did you mean what you said about not wanting it to be over?" he managed, preparing himself for her refusal. He'd called her by his dead wife's name. She would likely refuse him.

The doctor answered by stretching out beside him, leaning over him, her lips coming down on his. He untied her robe by feel and bared her body again. Corwyn kicked away the blankets separating them, his need searing him, his hands tangling in her hair and pulling her flush with his body but not directly aligned as he wanted to be. He needed to take her with an intensity he hadn't felt since...

Anna.

The thought stuck with him, but instead of repelling Corwyn, it herded him on. He knew he wasn't printing again. That state was forever, but he allowed himself to wonder if a Warrior was capable of something akin to human love.

He supposed it was possible. Warriors still retained their human emotions. Love was usually funneled into printing for them, the animal urge to mate for life. But what happened when that tie was cut short abruptly? Could they achieve a more balanced sort of human love? Part of him hoped that was what he was feeling. Part of him was afraid it was.

Whatever the case was, Corwyn recognized that he felt something deeper than a serious case of lust. He groaned, his thoughts scattering as her mouth left his and she straddled him, encasing him in instant ecstasy.

"Was this what it was like last night?" he teased, fighting for clarity.

She started moving over him, drawing Corwyn into the rhythm of her body as her muscles milked him in a torturous motion. She watched his expression, smiling smugly. "No. It isn't. You were the aggressor last night.

You swept me along for the ride, and what a ride it was," she assured him.

Corwyn gasped as the image of him pounding into her nearly sent him over. "You enjoyed that?" he asked. *Ani, let her say yes!*

"Immensely."

He flipped her beneath him without warning, taking her in swift strokes as she cried out in surprise. "I do, too," he grumbled, pulling her hips up to his. Corwyn was more than enjoying it. If this was what last night was, he was surprised he wasn't still inside her this morning.

Her hands brushed over his chest, her stunned pleasure disappearing into a look of carnal determination. She settled her hands on the meat of his buttocks, arching her hips and pulling the last of him inside. She smiled in satisfaction as he groaned in need.

"Now it's like last night," she crooned.

Corwyn shuddered, taking her faster, aching to feel her climax for him. She cried out her release almost precisely as he achieved his own, and the effect shook him to his core. Wave after wave of his cum flooded her, intensifying just when he thought it would end, thanks to her aftershocks massaging him.

She gasped out his name, reminding him that he was sharing nearly the most intimate moment he could with this woman, and he still didn't know what name to use in return. Corwyn cursed himself silently as beyond contempt for this, but his body still disagreed with him, sated in a way women hadn't sated him since...

No. I am not going to rehash this again.

He sank over her, laying a gentle kiss on her temple, wrapping his body around hers protectively. "You are fantastic, Doc," he breathed.

"Laura." Her smile was slightly strained at that. "If we're going to keep doing this, you should probably know my name."

"I'll never forget it, but I like calling you Doc."

Laura scowled. "It's not very sexy," she complained.

"I don't know," he teased. "I don't think I'll ever be able to look at a doctor the same way again." He shivered in pleasure as his softening cock slid from her body. "Talk about natural healing."

She smiled, an honest smile that lit her eyes. "Well, as your doctor, I should probably note that this isn't good for your shoulder."

"That'll be healed in no time," he assured her.

Laura shook her head, and he could almost read the condescending comment forming behind her lips.

"Check it," he offered.

She raised an eyebrow dubiously, but she grasped the edge of the bandage. "Brace yourself," she warned him, ripping it back. Laura winced as if she expected him to do the same, staring at him in confusion when he didn't.

"Go on. Check it."

Laura looked at it, her brow furrowing. She brushed her fingertips over the pink skin around the stitches, gasping as the last of the scabs pulled away from the wounds.

Corwyn smiled at her shock. "Told you. Our healing is faster than you're accustomed to. You can pull those out now. Aside from the knitting muscle inside, it's pretty well healed." In fact, the only thing that would impede his performance for the next week would be the dissolving stitches inside his shoulder. Unfortunately, his healing didn't make them dissolve as fast as he healed.

"I wasn't dreaming," she decided.

"About what?" Corwyn turned to his back, pulling her along to straddle his hips again.

"You had a bruise that disappeared overnight." She laid over him, resting her head on his uninjured shoulder.

"Probably. You should see how fast broken bones heal."

"I hope I never have to." She was suddenly very still and quiet.

"What's up, Doc?" Corwyn teased.

She didn't answer.

His heart pounded in terror that he'd pushed her away already. *Damn it! Why is she affecting me this way?* "Laura?" he prodded.

"I just... It's none of my business."

"What isn't? You can ask me anything. What could be more personal to me than Anna? I'll tell you about her, if you really want to know." He wanted to tell Laura about Anna, and that was more disconcerting than the rest combined.

"Did a vampire kill her?" she managed in a tentative voice.

Corwyn sighed. "Yes. An elder named Veriel. He's still out there somewhere." The urge to protect Laura rose up hard, and he wrapped his arms around her, his jaw tightening reflexively.

"That the only time you've been married?"

"Yes. I'll never marry again. It's too risky. Not to mention that we...mate for life, more or less." He raised his head a bit to look at her. Would knowing he wouldn't marry her make her turn him away?

Why the hell does that thought bother me so much?

She chewed at her lower lip lightly, and her eyes were focused on a spot on the wall.

"Ask what's really on your mind," he invited.

"Was...Erin your daughter, then?"

A sick swirl assaulted him. Of all the questions he'd expected, that wasn't one of them.

"I'm sorry, Corwyn. It's none of my business."

"Yes." He forced the word out, his throat tightening even as he managed speech.

She nodded. "I'm sorry. I won't ask any more."

Corwyn sighed, stroking one hand along the line of her spine. "Yes, Erin was...is my daughter."

"The vampire who killed your wife?" she asked in surprise. "What does he want with your daughter?"

"No... I mean, I don't really know." He growled in frustration. "He doesn't have her, but he wants her. I...don't really know that, either. He might know where she is. It's possible that he does. It would be the perfect plan. Leave her where she is, so I can't track him to her until it's too late."

"You keep saying that. Too late for what?"

"She must be... I have to make her fully human before she turns sixteen."

"If she isn't? What, then?"

He reasoned his way out of the *Blutjagd* that gripped him every time he thought of the chance of failure. "If that happens, she'll never be free. She'll be a slave to whoever claims her first. I promised Anna I wouldn't allow that."

Laura furrowed her brow. "So... Why didn't you?"

"Free her?"

"Is it time dependent? Why didn't you?"

"I was ambushed...twice actually. By the time my brothers got to me, my wife was dead and my daughter was missing. Warriors all over the world have been looking for her since, but we still don't know how Anna managed to hide her, so we don't know where to look. She simply disappeared." His frustration came through in that speech, the years of searching without return, the unwillingness of the Stone to tell him whether his daughter was alive or dead, whether she was taken or unharmed.

"How old was she?" Her voice was hushed, as if his anger frightened her.

Corwyn calmed himself; he didn't want Laura to fear what he was capable of. Too many people already did. "Hours..." He swallowed painfully at the memories of the few moments he'd had with her. "I only held her once." His voice held firm, though he wasn't certain how he'd managed that feat.

Laura pressed a kiss to his chest. "Corwyn, I am so... How do you survive something like that?"

He laughed harshly, at the edges of tears he didn't want to shed. "I'm still trying to figure that out, actually."

"How old is Erin now?"

Corwyn hesitated. He'd always tried not to consider that question carefully. He realized that fact as he completed the mental math. "Nine," he replied solemnly, his heart aching. "She'll be nine in a few months."

Laura went still, then her head came up, her eyes wide and wild. "Nine? She's been missing for nine years?"

He nodded, the crushing loss pulling him down again. "I have to find her, Laura. I can't give up."

"Of course not," she replied hurriedly. "What do you know about her?"

He shrugged uncomfortably. "She'll have my coloring, black hair and dark eyes. She would have been found with an amulet like the one I gave you...only hers will have a howling wolf head at the top."

"Like the one Colin left with you." She glanced at his chest, her brow furrowing again, probably noting for the first time that he'd removed the amulet.

Corwyn scowled. "Thank you for the reminder. I have to kick his —"

"So, she at least has your protection," she interrupted him. "They can't touch her, if she does."

"She doesn't have my protection. She has her mother's amulet. Or...she *had* her mother's amulet. I pray to Ani every night that she still has it."

"Is that how the vampires killed your wife? She took off her amulet?"

"Yes. Anna would do anything for Erin, even sacrifice herself."

"I can understand that," she decided.

A chill assaulted him as the full force of what Corwyn had done struck him. *I didn't check her cycle this morning. I probably didn't check it when I was fevering, either.* He scanned her fearfully and... groaned at the results.

"What is it?" Laura asked urgently, touching the stitches as if afraid that he'd injured himself again. "What's wrong?"

Corwyn covered his eyes with his hands, gritting his teeth. "You're fertile. Damn it! I should have checked first." He lowered his hands and met her eyes miserably. "This has just gotten much more complicated."

Laura shook her head. "Corwyn, if you're worried about a baby, don't be."

He bit back the first snapping response that came to his mind. *He* was the one who had screwed up, not Laura. There was no way she could have known what was at risk.

And Colin and Stephen left me here. I am going to kill them when I see them. It's a good thing they've produced heirs already. That thought brought him back to the possibility of another new heir to Hunter.

"Corwyn, really —"

"You're not on the Pill."

Her mouth opened in a little O of surprise.

"I'd know it if you were. You're cycling. You don't have a diaphragm in...or a sponge, and I didn't use anything to prevent it." He knew his voice took on a sharp edge, and he hated himself for it, but he seemed incapable of stopping himself.

"I can't have children," she informed him, apparently recovering her wits enough to be offended by his treatment.

"Why not? Are your tubes tied or something? You *do* cycle. Trust me. If they told you that you don't, they're wrong."

"It's an extreme case of endometriosis. It's chronic. My body is unable to hold a fertilized egg. I'd be surprised if one could even pass the tubes. Everything we've tried failed to correct it. Surgery, hormone therapy... I've even tried herbal cures. I can't have a child, Corwyn."

"Ah..." He winced, torn.

"What now?"

"Now I don't know which would be worse," he admitted. This was insane. Now he was weighing her happiness against his future as a Warrior and his life? When had life gotten so mixed up?

"Whether or not I'm lying?" she countered. Her cheeks darkened in a flush of anger and her eyes hardened in warning. Laura started to push off of him.

Corwyn pulled her back to his chest. "Oh, I believe you," he assured her. "I believe every word you're saying."

"But?" she grumbled.

Her proximity scattered his senses. Corwyn stroked his fingertip along her chin, watching her eyes soften, trapped in her gaze.

"What would be worse, Corwyn?" she whispered.

"Giving you hope and you not conceiving or the consequences if you do conceive."

"What consequences?"

"I won't lie to you. It would be a boy. I've already had a girl. No Warrior has ever had two daughters."

"So?" Her voice regained an edge of irritation.

"I told you I could free a daughter, that I could make her wholly human. I can't do that with a son."

Laura seemed to consider that carefully. "Then he would have your attributes. He'd be fast and strong. He'd heal quickly. Those are useful gifts."

"They're not gifts. It's a curse."

"I don't understand. He would be a wonderful police officer or fireman."

"From the time he turned fifteen, he would start to exhibit all of the qualities you mentioned, but his curse would surface with it. He would sense the beasts, and they would sense him. He would experience *Blutjagd*, the bloodlust that drives us to hunt them. His anger, even at humans, who would be helpless when compared to him, would be fierce and, without training, uncontrollable. He would need the constant release of training and hunting. He would..." Corwyn sighed; he hated admitting this to a woman he'd just had sex with. "He would need sexual release often, and when he chose a wife, the bond would be intense. He could kill for her easily."

"But, the training you go through would make him safe. Right?"

"Safe is a strong term. We're kind of like pups. We can be trained, but in the right circumstances, we still turn feral. Not to mention, we do go hunting beasts. I imagine you'd find that rather nerve wracking."

"Well, I guess it's a good thing that I can't have children," she stated, as if the subject were closed.

"You don't understand." Corwyn grasped at any way to explain this to her. "Look... I assume the fertility experts gave you odds?"

"Ridiculous odds. Bill, my ex-husband, knew how impossible those odds were. Notice that he is my *ex-husband*," she growled.

"Yeah. Okay... Let me put it this way. How many people do you know who can knit bones in a week or have lacerations that require stitches heal in a few days?"

She started to speak, then closed her mouth, looking disconcerted.

"Warrior babies are beyond what you'd call hearty. In fifteen hundred years, there's never been a miscarriage. A single sexual encounter long before high cycle will produce a child. We're the height of fertile. If there's an egg to be reached, our sperm will reach it. If there's a zygote formed, it will plant and survive to adulthood, barring accident or murder."

"You're saying this curse of yours can overcome my condition?"

"It's entirely possible."

"You're entirely crazy," she countered, touching his temple lightly. "I think you took a blow to the head."

"My head is fine. If I had taken a blow to it, it would have healed by now, anyway. I guess... Only time will tell. If it does happen, what will you do?"

"You mean...about the baby?"

Corwyn held his breath, nodding stiffly. Gods, he wanted this chance, even with the problems involved for him. Maybe that was why he hadn't checked. Maybe he'd finally gone over the edge of propriety and sanity to grasp one thing for himself.

"After all the trouble I've gone through to have a baby of my own, nothing is too great a price to pay for one."

He let out his breath in a rush, chuckling in relief. He'd hoped she wouldn't want to abort. That would be the final straw for his tenuous control, he was sure.

Her face broke into an impish grin. "But he'd need training, so... I guess Daddy comes with the package?" she teased.

Corwyn hardened at the thought of another child, at the fact that she was offering him that child. He had given up all hope of that when Anna died, and he'd given up all hope of raising his child when they'd failed to find Erin's adoption records.

He teased the tip of his erection over her slick core, smiling at her sharply-indrawn breath. "Would that be so bad, Doc?" he crooned.

That rational corner of his mind was working overtime again, reasoning that the damage was already done. If a child was going to be conceived, it was likely already accomplished, Warrior potency being what it was. Why shouldn't he enjoy every minute inside Laura that he could.

She lifted herself onto her knees and guided him in, taking all of him in one slow movement. Corwyn grasped her hips, meeting her in fierce thrusts, feeling the familiar burn of the drive to produce a child. It had been so long since he'd experienced the seemingly endless arousal the permission to do it caused. Laura gasped as he drew her down to his mouth, exploring her neck, jaw, then ear, nipping and kissing, showing his tenderness that way when his body insisted on showing her no mercy.

"Keep this up and you can stay forever," she promised breathlessly.

"Do you want a baby, Laura?" he asked, needing to hear it again, needing to know he wasn't hallucinating.

"Yes. God, yes! Corwyn, if you could do that for me —"

He sealed his mouth to hers, silencing her as he pulled her hips to him and filled her with his seed again.

Laura was still gasping in her release when Corwyn's mind started to numbly work out the details of a match like this. It was slow moving, because his body wanted to shut down the higher functions in favor of maximizing their chances of a child with frequent lovemaking.

She was a doctor. Laura couldn't just pick up and follow him around. Either he would have to base himself here in St. Louis, or Laura would have to relocate with him to the manor in Denver.

More importantly, he'd have to face the Council of Lords for having a child outside of printing. He would have to relinquish his place as Lord Hunter to Colin...at a minimum. The only saving grace was that the lords probably wouldn't exact the ultimate punishment on him for this lack of control. If the new Stone lord had made his first kill, Corwyn hadn't heard it yet, and that was something Kord was likely to proclaim to the stars. Until Lewis had relinquished his amulet, there was no one to take Corwyn's place at the Stone.

The Stone had to have a lord. In that, he was safe...for now.

Chapter Twenty-one

October 20th, 1986

"Do you have to go?" Laura asked, her eyes pleading with him, though the rest of her expression didn't show it.

"I wish I didn't have to, but no one would believe I'm not healed by now. As it is, my brothers are going to know I've been slacking off."

Already, he was planning his return, though how he'd justify leaving the manor for an extended period of time was still unresolved. Leaving the Stone wasn't a problem, since he was typically separated from it by at least a hundred miles.

She sighed and laid back to watch him dress. "I suppose that's better. If you stayed, I'd be tempted to use more sick days."

Corwyn laughed heartily. Though he had been capable of fending for himself for the previous two days, Laura had taken sick days. As she pointed out, when a doctor calls in and claims stomach flu, no one argues the point. At least she hadn't lied about spending time in bed, though her claim that she was resting had been stretching the truth.

He pulled on his weapons belt, and Laura scowled.

"What's up —"

"Don't you ever worry about being caught with that?" she asked, pointing to the sacred weapon hung at his hip.

Corwyn glanced at the belt and shrugged. "No one sees me...or my weapons, unless I want them to." He started pulling on his boots.

Her scowl deepened.

"Honestly," he protested.

"Show me."

"You'll have to take off your amulet."

She fingered it, undecided.

"The amulet helps you recognize Warriors in case you need one."

Still, Laura hesitated.

"You weren't fed from. Beasts can't track you unless you were."

She nodded and removed her amulet to the pillow beside her. "Show me."

"Close your eyes for a moment."

Laura complied, and Corwyn moved to confuse her tracking. He ghosted, then touched her knee and pulled back to her side as she opened her eyes.

"Christ," she exploded, her eyes widening. Laura looking around the room, running a shaking hand through her hair. "You're still here? You haven't left?"

Corwyn smiled, touching her hair, then moving again as she whipped around to the feeling. She launched toward his previous location, her hands outstretched. Corwyn scooped her up as she overbalanced off of the bed. She laughed nervously as she encountered the solid mass of him, and he released his ghosting.

It took her a moment to recover enough to speak. "Wow. That was incredible. I have to know. Do people...walk into you? What do you see?"

"I still see myself. I'm projecting the impression of empty space to others...and that is full ghosting. We usually reserve that for humans...and for getting out of tight places with humans, ducking the police and things like that."

"What do humans usually see?"

"That won't work on you. I tried it once with Anna. You know I'm here, what I look like, and what I'm wearing already. I can't fool your mind into seeing me as an indistinct face in the crowd, even without your amulet."

She laughed heartily. "You? Indistinct?"

Her appraising eyes nearly convinced him out of his clothes and back into bed with her. Corwyn forced his mind to function along lines that would get him out of her condo, home, and back in her bed the fastest. "Hard to believe? Yeah, I've heard that before."

"I can spot you guys a mile away. How is it that no one else does? It's not like you're inconspicuous. You're a rather striking group of men, you know."

I do not need to be thinking this. "People don't notice me if I choose that they don't. I register to them as average all the way around, unremarkable in looks and clothing, not carrying weapons..."

"I don't buy it. I didn't know what you were in that diner, but I sure noticed you, even before you opened your mouth. Did you want me to see you?"

Please, stop this. But, he could hear Anna. He could see her.

Why was it that Laura and Anna were so much alike at times? Why did thoughts of one bring thoughts of the other?

Laura nodded uncertainly. "That would almost be worth testing someday."

It was Corwyn's turn to stare in confusion. All thoughts of Anna fled momentarily.

"I mean...ask someone if they see someone of your true description...or point you out and have them describe you to find out what they really see. It might yield interesting results."

"It might," he mused, then shook his head. "We like to keep a low profile, so we're not accustomed to drawing attention to ourselves that way."

He returned to the buckles on his boots, noticing Laura reach for her amulet. A sudden surety struck him, and Corwyn swept it into his hand before she could close her fist around it.

Her eyes widened. "Corwyn? The amulet... You're taking it away?"

He shook his head, reaching into the front pocket of his duffel for the amulet Colin had left around his neck. "No. I'm changing it."

"I don't understand."

"There are two types of protection. Your original amulet marks you as Hunter protected. That means any Warrior would give his life to protect you from beasts."

"What else is there? Sounds like a serious commitment to me."

He hung the Lord's seal around her neck. "This means you have my personal protection. You're considered part of my immediate family, and any Warrior you encounter will treat you that way.

"They'll protect you as they would any other person with an amulet, but they'll notify me immediately if they do and pass you into my custody as soon as possible. It also means they know they may not...offend you without personal retribution dished out by me."

"So, uh... How would they offend me?"

"There are laws for how any human is treated by a Warrior, protected or not. Those laws are much stricter when you have the personal protection of a Warrior." He ran the backs of his fingers over her cheek. "This amulet means that any Warrior who breaks those rules answers to me for it."

Laura blushed, a shy smile curving her lips ever so slightly. "Is this your way of proclaiming me as your woman?" She asked it in a low, serious voice.

"Yes. In this case, it does...if that's all right with you." His entire body tensed. He needed her to say yes. That shook him. It wasn't possible to print twice, but damned if this didn't feel like printing. It was maddening, thrilling, heart-wrenching.

Laura's smile widened, a clear invitation. "I've already told you that you can stay forever."

Corwyn felt a burn that he hadn't thought he'd feel again in his lifetime. "If you use that word, mean it," he grumbled. The need to seal beat at him.

It's not possible!

Her smile dimmed. "What word? Stay?"

"No. Forever. I didn't think this was possible, but I'm feeling... Tell me forever right now, and I'll give you forever. I won't be able to give you less."

"Are you asking me to marry you?"

"If you wish. What I'm asking for is beyond a piece of paper and a priest. If I give you forever, there's no such thing as divorce for me. I'll be bound to you."

"But," she gasped out, "if you mate for life..."

"Anna. I know. I can't explain it. That's why I didn't think it was."

How is this possible? He sent his question to the Stone without forethought.

{Amusement. Finally! You've allowed yourself to find your true mate.}

True mate? But Anna —

{Was chosen to bear an heir for me. It was necessary. She was of the right line; you were of the right line, but I knew you couldn't have a lifetime with her. The loves of my chosen up until now never have. Hopefully, that will change now.}

You gave Anna to me, knowing I'd lose her? A spike of anger coursed through him.

{You will not forgive that. I know. I needed an heir, and you were chosen to provide her. You were the only one fit to the task.}

Heir? What heir? Anna hadn't borne an heir. She'd borne a daughter, and daughters were never heir.

{The ones who will end the curse. Children of Raga and her true mate are my heirs.}

Anna was Raga.

{Silence.}

No. Erin was Raga. Anna was right about that. It was Erin.

{Silence.}

Erin is alive?

{Silence.}

Damn you! Why won't you tell me this one thing? I won't ask you where she is. I know you won't tell me that. Why won't you tell me if she's alive?

{What help I will not give one, I cannot give the other.}

Damn you. You enjoy playing with people's lives.

{I give you what you must to steer your course. No more and no less. You wouldn't choose your true course if I told you what you ask of me.}

I printed on Anna. I know I did. You cannot demean what I had with her!

{I wouldn't dream of it. You made each other very happy in the short span you had together. Your souls called to each other, the realization of a prophecy. You were meant to mate, but that much was merely a pleasant duty you were born to. Yes, you printed...and now you will print again.}

This is crazy. A Warrior can only print once. The traditions —

{Exasperation. Corwyn, when will you learn that there is little I cannot control?}

Why would you do this?

{Why did you allow Evulsson to wound you? Why when you are the better fighter? You have forgotten your reasons for living.}

Because you won't tell me if I have a reason for living! Is Erin alive?

{A printed man is more stable,} the Stone continued as if he hadn't addressed it. *{Your duties will not be completed for some time to come. You need a reason to survive that long. You need to remember what makes life worth living.}*

But —

{You take no joy in your own family. Your brothers' happiness brings you only pain. You cannot continue to

seek your end, even if you don't acknowledge that it is your aim. You need printing, Corwyn.}

Did you plan this, too? Is Laura just another pawn to you like Anna and Erin are?

{I feel for all those I choose.}

That you use, he accused.

{Only when I must.}

Laura? It was a demand now.

{You chose each other. I only gave you the capacity to have another, because you need a stabilizing force. There is no plot involving your Laura, and I have no plans that would take her from you. You must be Lord Hunter and Stone lord in the years to come. Only printed can you accomplish that.}

But, I won't be Lord Hunter. Even if I tell the Council of Lords that this is your will, they won't believe me. They'll accuse me of breaking the rules of sanction. My position will be passed to Colin. Nothing will stop that.

{Only if you let it be. This need be only known to Hunter. I wish it to be internal to Hunter.} The command in the Stone's tone was impossible to miss. She was playing mother again, and that always annoyed him.

But, if we have a child... A Warrior isn't something I can hide from the other houses.

{There is little I cannot control.}

You would deny us children? The realization hurt. He'd been hoping for a child, praying to Ani for one.

Worse, Laura had been praying for one. After assuring her that his curse could overcome anything, it would crush her if she couldn't have a child. Would she leave him if he couldn't? If she did, the Stone's plan for making him stable was up in smoke. The madness of losing her would be the end for him, but maybe it would be time enough for the Stone's purpose.

{You will remain Lord Hunter as long as it serves my purpose to have you remain.}

Are you going to deny us children?

{I will do nothing that makes you less stable.}

"Corwyn!" Laura was face to face with him, her hand on his cheek and her eyes wide.

How long had she been trying to talk to him? He cupped his hand over hers, turning his face to kiss her palm. "I'm sorry. As Stone lord..." He sighed. "Business sometimes calls at inopportune moments."

She smiled tentatively. "And I thought phones were disruptive. Are you sure?"

"That I want you?"

Laura nodded.

"More than just about anything in my life, but do you?"

"You know I do. I keep telling you I do."

He ran his fingertips along her cheek. "What if... What If I'm wrong about being able to give you children? Am I enough?"

She blinked in seeming surprise. For a long moment, she didn't speak. "I think so."

"But you're not sure." His heart sank. If he sealed printing with her, and she changed her mind, it would kill him.

Laura seemed to withdraw in confusion. "I...I didn't mean that, Corwyn. I got my hopes up, but I know what my odds are. I'm not deluded, and I do want you...no matter what."

He nodded grimly. "I need you to be sure before you commit yourself to this."

"Don't leave like this, please." The lost expression almost undid him.

Corwyn captured her in a searing kiss, reminding himself firmly that taking her at that moment would be disastrous if he wasn't enough, in the long run. "I want this, but I won't take the final step until I know you're sure."

"How?"

"You said you'd relocate to Colorado if you get pregnant."

"And...if I don't? How will you know I'm sincere?"

"I'll trust you." He pulled a pen from his duffel and a notepad from the nightstand next to the phone, then started writing. "I will arrange to stay at this house for three weeks, starting two weeks from now. Come to me or call me to come to you, and I'll know I'm enough. If you don't —"

"I will."

He nodded. "I would have to come to you anyway. I would have to be sure you weren't... I could never force myself to let you go unless I was sure."

"I'll come to you," she repeated. "Will you still be there for me when I do?"

"Absolutely." If there was a chance of printing, how could he turn away? Corwyn pressed the address and phone number into her palm and kissed her forehead. "I'll be waiting for your call."

"My visit," Laura corrected. "You're not getting rid of me that easily."

He nodded slowly. "I'm not trying to get rid of you. I will see you soon...whatever your decision."

* * * *

Colin looked up from the desk in surprise as the door opened. His smile at the sight of Corwyn faded in light of the look of pure menace on his brother's face.

"What's wrong?" he demanded.

"Nothing," Corwyn grumbled.

Colin shot him a scathing look as he vacated the chair behind the desk. "Here I was, hoping you were taking a vacation in the lady doctor, and you come back more pissed off and uptight than ever," he muttered.

He tensed as Corwyn's hand closed around his throat, exerting pressure. *A lot of pressure.* Shock alone kept him from fighting for his life.

His brother's eyes were set angrily, and *Blutjagd* flared in his skin. "Never," he growled. "Never talk about Laura that way. She is no one's plaything." His hand loosened just enough to allow Colin's breathing to ease.

Colin nodded, his face burning. For the first time since the year he'd lost Anna and Erin, he was afraid of Corwyn. "I apologize."

Corwyn's hand retreated, but he stayed face to face with Colin, as if daring him to speak flippantly about Laura Briony again.

"Gods damn it. What is wrong with you, Corwyn?"

He turned, ambling to the chair Colin had so recently vacated. Corwyn sank into it and planted his face in his hands, rubbing at his temples roughly.

"Corwyn?" Something was wrong here. Very wrong, but Colin couldn't imagine what it could be.

"Maybe..." He stared at the far wall of the office, his eyes bloodshot. "The rest of you should leave for a little while. I'm not fit company right now. The women and children shouldn't be...exposed to this."

"For how long?"

"Weeks... Maybe a month. Maybe more."

Colin startled. "Is it Erin? Has the Stone finally told you something?" His heart pounded in trepidation. If the Stone told Corwyn that his daughter was dead or taken by Veriel, no one would be safe: humans, Warriors, or beasts.

Corwyn barked in laughter. "Oh, the Stone is full of surprises, but it won't tell me a damned thing about Erin. You know it won't until it's too late for me to make things right, as I promised Anna I would."

"Then what is the Stone saying?" Whatever it was had pushed Corwyn over the edge of reason.

He sobered so abruptly Colin was afraid he would erupt into some form of violent or hysterical outburst. "It brought Anna to me, knowing I would lose her. It...planned for me to lose my wife."

Colin sucked in his breath in shock. "Why would it admit that to you? Why now?"

"Because it tampered with my future to make me father Erin with Anna. The Stone wanted her born, and it derailed my entire life to get it. It made me print and suffer the loss of my mate and my child for its damned plans."

"Why tell you?" he repeated.

Corwyn met his eyes and managed a weak smile. "I'm printing. True printing. As I should have done in the first place."

"You left her?" he exploded. "How could you leave her? I'm not losing you to madness, brother, so you get your ass back —"

"I have to make sure this is her choice, and I needed to speak to you. If the Council of Lords finds out I'm printing again... Their list of possible reasons won't include the truth. They won't believe the truth."

"You're prepared for that eventuality." It wasn't a question.

Corwyn nodded solemnly. "The Stone assures me it will never come to that, but I am prepared for judgment."

"You're giving the doctor...Laura, I mean...time to consider it?"

"Five weeks. If I haven't heard from her in five weeks, I'm going to visit her."

Something in that didn't sound right. "Why?"

"If she carries my son, I cannot let her go, no matter what decision she makes. She knows that."

"Your..." Colin reined in his anger and lowered his voice. "You took her high cycle without even completing printing first?"

Corwyn rubbed the pads of his fingers and thumb to his eyes, sinking into the leather further. "I could give you all the excuses in the world, but I won't bother. When I was capable of coherent thought, I really didn't care that I was breaking the rules of sanction to take her again."

"Again?" Colin dropped into the chair opposite Corwyn's, but he didn't look at his brother. "What other laws did you break?" *And will I have to kill you after this discussion?*

Who will be Stone lord then?

"If the first time had been all there was, I would have been judged innocent. I was fevering...incoherent." He winced. "I am sure I probably convinced Laura willingness that time, but I have no memory of the act. Apparently, I was so far gone, I thought she was Anna."

It was Colin's turn to wince. It was amazing the little spitfire hadn't given Corwyn a new set of stitches right then and there. He nodded Corwyn on.

"Maybe it was my mind's way of dealing with the sensation of printing. It recognized it and identified printing as being Anna? I don't know.

"But I do know Laura was willing...every time." He smiled a wistful smile. "By the third time, she told me she wanted my baby and that I could stay, with or without one. After that pronouncement, the lords could have asked any price and had me submit willingly."

"How many times, Corwyn?"

His smile widened, but he didn't answer.

"Surely not worse than you and Anna."

"I wouldn't place bets on that." He sobered. "Which is precisely why I'm going to be intolerable. On the off chance that she doesn't conceive and doesn't choose me —"

"Doesn't conceive. You are insane. Of *course*, she'll conceive."

Corwyn darkened. "There are...factors. There is a possibility that Laura will be unable to carry even a Warrior's child."

"And?" he asked suspiciously.

"The Stone doesn't want this second printing to be public knowledge. Since I can't hide a young Warrior..."

"It would deny you children?" The thought was chilling.

Corwyn shrugged, looking uncomfortable at the thought. "Can you think what else it has in mind?

After all, Laura already believes herself infertile. It would be the perfect answer. Wouldn't it?"

"Not for you. You want to be able to, don't you?"

"Of course, I do," he groused. "What Warrior doesn't, for a woman he's printing on? Especially one that wants children?"

Colin searched for words to answer that for a moment. Finally he growled out a few choice curses on the Stone. "I'll send the others away. I'm staying."

"It's not a good idea. I won't be pleasant."

"I'm not staying for the pleasure of your company, brother. I'm staying for duty."

* * * *

October 30th, 1986

Laura stared at Evelyn in disbelief. "You have got to be kidding! We haven't seen a case of measles in years."

"Well, it's an outbreak, and we know you saw at least two of them while they were incubating. Reynolds' orders. Everyone in the office has to have a current titer check in the files or get inoculated."

"They did mine when I started working here," she dismissed the head nurse.

"I said the same thing. They can't find mine, either. I think that's why I got this duty. People are less likely to yell at a fellow sufferer."

Laura groaned. "Okay. Draw the blood, but it's a waste of time." *My time and my blood.*

Evelyn prepped the vial and needle, while Laura rolled her shirt sleeve.

"Oh, yeah. Have to ask." Evelyn didn't look up from the tray. "Any chance you might be pregnant?"

Laura paused in her flip answer and stared at the papers on her desk without really seeing her notes. "Yes," she blurted out. "Yes, there is."

Evelyn chuckled. "Really? You have been holding out on me, Doctor."

Her cheeks burned in embarrassment.

"Was it that sweet little number that picked you up at Rich's a few weeks ago?"

Laura almost gagged in response. "Niko? Puh-leeze." She could see Evelyn charging up to ask what went wrong. "Don't...please. Let's just chalk that one up to the worst date I've ever had. The man was a psycho." Well, at least she wasn't lying about that. It was the worst date she'd ever been on, bar none, and a vampire cannot, by definition, be sane.

"Okay, then... Spill."

She sighed in contentment at the memories of the days following the demise of Mr. Evulsson. "His name is Corwyn, and he's..." She smiled. "He's like no man I've met before."

"Sounds like love. Are you hearing wedding bells?"

"Gladly. I just hope he is."

Evelyn wrapped the rubber band around her arm and secured it. "So, will a baby be good news or bad?"

Laura pumped her fist open and closed. "Good. He lost his first wife and daughter years ago. I think he'd welcome a baby as much as I would."

The isopropyl alcohol was cold enough to make Laura shiver.

"Well, looks like you get a free test on us. Just in case you're susceptible, I have to run it. When would you be due for a period?"

"You know me. With my condition? Who knows?"

Evelyn slipped the needle in with practiced ease. "Any clue how far along you might or might not be?"

She did the mental math. Corwyn had been gone for ten days. They'd been sleeping together for three days before he left. He'd pronounced her "fertile" on the first day, but where in her cycle would he have made that proclamation? She decided to go for late rather than early.

"Not far...three to four weeks since last cycle maybe."

"Good enough. Serum should give us an indication then."

Moments later, Evelyn was out the door and headed to her next unpleasant discussion over Reynolds' orders. Within heartbeats, Laura had put the possibility out of her mind and settled into her work again.

It was Monday before Evelyn showed up in her cubicle with a smile on her face and a slip of paper in her hand. Laura's titer was positive for antibodies, just as she knew it would be. The serum hCG was likewise positive.

Chapter Twenty-two

November 5th, 1986

Laura paid the cab driver and stepped away from the curb with her backpack and a small suitcase in hand. She pulled her collar tighter against the late-October chill and looked up at the house behind the wrought iron gates.

One glance was all she needed to double-check the address against the sheet of paper Corwyn had written it on. *It's a joke. It has to be a joke.*

Please, tell me it's not some sort of sick joke.

Corwyn had called this place "the manor house," and the description fit. The huge red-brick structure had two long wings off the front edifice. The wings were two stories each, and the centerpiece was a high three, she'd guess, based on the windows at the top.

All the windows were trimmed in pure white that indicated at least yearly painting to keep it looking fresh and new. Heavy drapes of Hunter green gave just a hint of color.

The entire estate — *what else could you possibly call this place?* — was surrounded by a six-foot stone wall, complete with camera surveillance. The final straw came in the form of the control panel outside the gate.

She sighed and squared her shoulders. Standing outside was not going to answer if this was a con or not. Only buzzing the intercom would. Laura walked to the control panel and searched out the buzzer.

"Yes?" a male voice answered. "May I help you, ma'am?"

Laura sucked in her breath, flicking her gaze to the nearest camera. It wasn't Corwyn's voice. It wasn't either of his brothers, either.

Come on, Laura. Anyone that lives in a place like this isn't answering his own door. Here goes nothing. "I'm here to see Corwyn Hunter."

"I'm sorry. Mr. Hunter isn't seeing anyone right now."

"He's expecting me. He told me to come in the next few weeks."

"I'm sorry. My orders are that he's seeing no one. If I could —"

Laura felt her temper spike. "What is your name?" *Corwyn isn't getting rid of me that easily.*

"Excuse me?"

"Your name? I want to know who I'm reporting to Corwyn when this is cleared up," she snapped, feigning confidence she didn't feel in the least. "I'm sure Corwyn didn't mean me when he gave orders that he wasn't seeing anyone."

"The orders didn't come from him, ma'am. They came from his brother. If I could have —"

"Which one? Colin or Stephen? Colin, I'll bet," she muttered.

A low chuckling came over the speaker, shocking her out of her anger.

"You know them well enough. Hold on. I'll wake Colin for you."

"Oh...joy..." she grumbled.

The chuckling turned to outright laughing. "I can't let you on the property without permission, but I can wake Colin and get that permission. What's your name, ma'am?"

She wasn't certain how much Corwyn had told his brothers about her. *Better safe than sorry.* "Tell him it's Doctor Laura Briony of Saint Louis, the bane of the Hunter men. He'll figure it out."

"Hold tight. I'll be right back."

The minutes until the guard returned were the longest since the uncertain moments while she was treating Corwyn.

"Welcome to the manor, Doctor Briony. Drive your car to the gates and bring it to the garage entrance at the right, when the gates open."

"Uh...I don't have a car. I flew in and took a cab from the airport."

"All right. I'll buzz open the smaller gate. Walk to the front porch, and I'll meet you there."

"Thank you."

The smaller inset gate buzzed, and Laura pushed through, making sure it latched behind her before she moved away. The walk to the porch wasn't quite as far as it had seemed from the curb. All in all, it was maybe forty yards of paved drive.

The man that met her at the stairs smiled broadly. His hair was steel gray, and his blue eyes twinkled in a ruddy face. His uniform proclaimed him a supervisor for Atlas Security.

He put his hand out for her suitcase. "Welcome to Hunter Manor, Doctor Briony."

She let him have the load gratefully. "Call me Laura, please, Mister...?"

"Just Joseph. Colin is itching to talk to you. I'll just show you into the library."

"I'm really not here to see Colin. I'm supposed to see Corwyn."

"Ma'am, if you know the Hunters, you know no one gets to the Lord Hunter but through his brothers...especially Colin."

"Oh, I know them." Laura stuffed her hands in her pockets, her mind dissecting what Joseph had just said to her. Something was decidedly not right about it, but she couldn't put her finger on —

Lord? She stopped short, her breath coming in sharp gasps that she would find alarming in a patient, let alone herself.

Joseph looked back at her in concern. "Are you all right?"

"*Lord* Hunter?"

His smile returned. "Don't worry. His protected and Colin take it much more seriously than he does. I dare say, if you called Corwyn that to his face, he'd screw up his face in disgust. He doesn't use his own titles unless he has to."

Titles? This was getting worse by the second. *I'm pregnant to some sort of European noble. My God!* The sudden urge to bolt hit her full force.

Joseph must have seen it, because he took her elbow gently and drew her up the wide front stairs. "Come on. If you know the Lord... If you know Corwyn, you know his titles don't mean a damned thing to him, unless he needs to throw his weight around with other Warriors."

"The only thing I know is that I fell through the looking glass somewhere back there." She looked at the gate longingly. "Where's the door home?"

"Not so fast. I have orders to deliver you. You get delivered."

Laura nodded, but her mind was working on plans for escape. She was so busy trying to decide what would give her the best odds for success that she almost missed the polished wood floors, the antique brass coat rack, and the fine Persian rug in the entry hall.

When she caught sight of the etched eight-foot mirror...and her own reflection in it, against the backdrop of the house, her heart sank. *I don't belong here.*

Somehow, she couldn't picture Corwyn here, either, but she assumed he looked different when he wasn't chasing vampires around the country. Maybe he wore silk shirts and Armani suits when he wasn't covered in that awful black blood.

Joseph waved her into a library twice the size of most formal dining rooms. Three of the walls were covered in shelves of books, floor to ceiling. One was full of leather-bound editions, charts and scrolls, and antiques that would fetch thousands or tens of thousands in any upscale shop.

"Colin will be down in a minute," Joseph informed her. "Make yourself at home." He left her, dwarfed by the room.

She glanced at the fireplace that took up a full third of the last wall, noting the worn stone that attested this house had seen generations of Hunters. The leather sofa drew her gaze and her hand. She stroked the butter soft material, biting back a sigh.

It was a showplace, but here and there, there were signs that people lived in it. There were faint glass

rings on the mahogany table next to the sofa. A
leather-bound book lay on one arm, a brass marker
tucked between the pages, an almost palpable feel that
someone was coming back to read it in the air.

"It's Italian."

Colin's voice startled her, and Laura pulled her
hand back.

"My father had a fondness for Italian leather," he
continued.

"Why the interview, Colin? If Corwyn doesn't want
to see me, I can turn right around and leave now." Her
heart ached at the idea, but she managed a steady
voice to deliver it.

He didn't answer immediately, but she heard the
hallway door close. "Sit down, Laura. I just want to talk
to you before you see Corwyn. Trust me, if he knew
you were down here, he'd be here already."

Laura turned to face him. Trying to guess his game
was impossible. His face starkly serious, Colin was all
business.

At least the business of vampire hunting. He was
dressed in the same jeans and black he'd been wearing
the first time she'd met him, right down to the armored
boots and the short-sword in training.

"Laura?"

"If Corwyn wants to see me, why the interview?" *If
he thinks he's going to talk me out of accepting Corwyn
somehow, he better make his reasons good.*

"I need to know what you've decided," he said
simply.

Her cheeks heated, and Laura cleared her throat.
"That is between me and Corwyn."

Colin shook his head, his jaw tightening. "I'm walking a fine line, Laura. It will crush Corwyn if you turn him away, but there's damage control if you accept him. Either way, I have to protect him from himself. Can you understand that?"

Her anger started coming unglued. "I'm sorry that I present such a problem to you. I didn't know I was cavorting with a titled man."

"His title has nothing to do with this!"

She raised an eyebrow at him. "Oh...really?" Every ounce of sarcasm she possessed was poured into those two words, but Laura suspected her body was busy coming up with more.

Colin blushed. "All right. It does...but not in the way you think it does."

Laura crossed her arms over her chest and waited to hear the rest.

"He doesn't need to marry some sort of nobility. The problem is that he's printing...marrying *anyone* after losing his first wife." Colin sighed deeply. "But if he doesn't print on you, he's toast anyway.

"He could be forced to relinquish his title to me, if the other lords find he's married you. The Stone doesn't want that. He doesn't want it. Believe it or not, I don't want it.

"Now, I need to know. Are you here to make him a happy but secretive man or to leave him with nothing?"

"That is between Corwyn and me," she repeated.

"You have no concept of the condition he's in, do you? He is in agony...physical pain. If you turn him away, I'm not sure he will pull out of this. You must tell me what you intend to do."

Laura started tapping her feet. She could feel her eyes narrowing. "I owe Corwyn the right to speak to me directly." *And he owes me the right to hear me out.*

"Do you carry his son?"

She felt as if she was standing on sand, and it was sifting from beneath her feet. "What?"

"Are you?" It was a demand now.

"Colin, I don't know what you're accustomed to, but Corwyn and I forged our own understanding, away from you. I do not intend to discuss this situation with anyone but Corwyn."

"Laura, you have no idea what you're doing," he pleaded.

"I think I do. I'm handling my life without your interference. Now, if you would be so kind as to let Corwyn know I'm here —"

The door swung open. "Corwyn knows."

The color drained from Colin's face, and he winced.

"Get lost, Colin. You owe me satisfaction for this later."

Colin nodded stiffly and rounded his brother. He closed the door carefully behind him, as if he felt anything more dangerous ground.

Corwyn watched him go before turning back to her. His scowl melted into a nervous expression that was decidedly at odds with his physical presence. "Hi, Doc. Welcome to the manor house."

"It's beautiful."

"It's cavernous. I prefer the training house and cabins, personally...but every range has a manor house."

She smiled, shaking her head in relief that he didn't like the pomp and circumstance of the house.

"What is it?" he asked.

"I'm glad it isn't your idea of home. I rather thought it didn't seem like you. A cabin matches your jeans and tennis shoes much better."

"Yes, but the manor house is easy to find. The other places are in the middle of nowhere."

She nodded again, abruptly unsure of herself.

"Can I get you anything? I've been told I make a mean omelet."

"No thanks. I don't do breakfast very often."

There was an awkward silence, during which they regarded each other across the empty room.

At last, Corwyn spoke. "How are you?"

"Great. No blood sucking visitors. Work is fine. We have an outbreak of measles."

"Measles?" She could read the concern on his face.

"My titer came up fine. I'm immune." *Why are we talking about this? Why can't I say what I came to say?*

The chilling possibility that Joseph and Colin had somehow changed her mind made her mouth go dry.

"Good. That's good." Corwyn fidgeted, averting his eyes. "Laura, I don't know what Colin was telling you, but —"

"It's okay. He's just worried about you. I guess this is all more complicated than I realized."

"No. It's not complicated at all. You just give me an answer." He met her eyes fully. "And...and I abide by it. You know what I want. It's all or nothing for me, but the choice is yours."

"It think it's a little late for nothing, Corwyn. I won't lie to you. This..." She waved a hand around at the opulence of the house. "This whole Lord Hunter thing has thrown me for a loop, but I'm miserable without you.

"I have a lot to learn about your lifestyle. I'm sure I'll screw up a lot before I get the hang of it." She shrugged, at a loss to explain her concerns fully.

"Are you saying 'yes' or 'maybe'?"

"I'm saying... Help me rent a moving van, while I put in for a transfer to Sentcare Denver...if you're still interested."

"You're sure. You'll give me forever?" There was a note of disbelief in that.

Laura crossed the room to him, digging for the lab sheet she'd stuffed in her front jeans pocket. She handed it to Corwyn.

He didn't open it. "What is this?"

"Read it."

He started to unfold it.

Laura waited until he was reading it to continue. "I was smiling when they asked me if there was any chance I was. I couldn't stop thinking about our time together. They checked it when they did my titer. Standard procedure with measles."

Stop rambling.

Corwyn stared at the lab results as if he was in shock.

"You were right, Corwyn."

He looked up at her, his mouth quirking up in a smile. "Please tell me you're as happy about this as I am."

"Are you?"

Corwyn trailed his fingers along her lower abdomen slowly. "Say you'll give me forever," he

256

breathed. He covered her mouth with his hand before she could answer. "Not here."

"Why? Are you planning on consummating immediately?" she teased.

The hungry look he shot her made Laura weak in the knees.

"It's one of those lifestyle things you have to learn. That is part of printing. Once you tell me you'll give me forever, I seal my printing to you."

"With sex?"

"Has it ever been just sex?" he countered.

"No. I guess not."

"Good. Then let me take you to my bed and do this properly."

"I think that piece of paper proves you don't know how to do it improperly."

His smile widened. "You ain't seen nothing yet, Doc."

"Do me a favor." Egging him on seemed more natural than breathing.

"What is that?" he asked, suddenly serious again.

Laura wrapped her arms around his shoulders, rising on tiptoe to accomplish it. "Ask me in bed?"

Corwyn growled and scooped her into his arms, making tracks to the door. Once he had it open, he vaulted to the stairs and took them two at a time, Laura giggling at the response.

* * * *

Corwyn hadn't spent two and a half more maddening weeks since just after he lost Anna and Erin.

He couldn't blame Colin for being concerned. In many ways, he had been more animal than man while he'd waited for her answer. He'd paced, snapped, growled...

In retrospect, Corwyn was glad he'd ordered Stephen and the other family members away. He wouldn't have harmed them. He was sure of that, but he wouldn't have been pleasant, and none of them deserved that. Not even Colin deserved it, but the stubborn idiot had refused to leave.

Corwyn had been at the edges of madness by the time two weeks had passed, and had started actively cursing himself for not simply promising to be at the manor house for five weeks. He'd set her a waiting period without meaning to do so, and there'd been no way to correct the oversight without contacting her. Since he'd given his vow to leave her in peace to decide, he'd had to live to the vow...no matter how uncomfortably he'd done so.

He'd been in a fitful sleep when he'd heard Colin's headlong rush down the hall. Frustrated by his own lack of sleep and burning with the need to know what would drag Colin out of bed after only four hours down, he'd dressed and headed downstairs.

His hand had been on the knob when he heard her voice.

Laura. She came. Probably on the first day off she had after the waiting period I set.

Reining in his excitement and dousing it with the cold fact that she'd said she'd come in person either way had stretched his control to the breaking point.

Nearly to the breaking point.

The sound of Colin arguing with her had accomplished that. Corwyn had opened the doors with every intention of taking it out of Colin's hide immediately, but the sight of Laura had soothed the bloodlust enough to let him send Colin away. He'd been enchanted by her windblown honey-brown hair and her startling blue eyes.

Memories of her straightening, bringing her five-feet-two to challenge his brother's six feet even caused the still-raw printing to chafe. Laura shouldn't have had to square off against Colin. There was no excuse for it.

For weeks, Corwyn would have made Laura Lady Hunter by day's end, if he'd had his way.

He had his wish now...or would in a few minutes. Corwyn kicked the door to the lord's chambers shut behind him and set Laura on her feet beside the bed.

Corwyn started to ask his question, but she kissed him and moved her hands to tug his black t-shirt from his jeans. "Uh uh, big boy. I said to ask me *in* bed."

A smile twitched the edges of his lips up. "What did you have in mind?" He bent his knees slightly so she could draw the shirt over his head and groaned as she pressed her lips to the longest of the wounds she'd tended.

Laura cast him a coy look as he unzipped her jacket and slid it off her shoulders. "I just want to show respect for your lifestyle, Corwyn. If making love to me completes this printing of yours and should immediately follow your asking, it will. You are not allowed to ask until we are on the verge of consummating. Agreed?"

The idea of it heated his blood. Corwyn nodded as he tugged her sweater up her body and over her head. There was no bra beneath, and Corwyn groaned, cupping breast one up. "You tease," he breathed.

She chuckled at that. "Though I do admit to a certain impatience for this, it's a fortuitous circumstance."

"Impatient? For this?" he teased, lifting her by the waist and taking the peak of one nipple in his mouth.

Laura moved against him restlessly, seeking to anchor herself to him in invitation.

Corwyn moved to the wall, lifted his knee between her thighs, and lowered her astride it. He touched and tasted, teasing while she rocked against him.

He moved his hands from her hips to the button and zipper of her jeans. He lowered his knee, letting her slide to the floor with his knee stroking at her.

Laura kicked her shoes away. "Oh, I missed you."

Her clothing loosened, Corwyn looked down between their bodies.

"What now?" she teased.

He smiled and sank to his knees. Corwyn laid kisses along the smooth skin of her abdomen, swirling his tongue in the indentation of her belly button, all the time stripping away her clothing. Once she was nude, he sank lower to run his tongue through her folds.

Laura cried out softly, her hands closing on his shoulders. Her knees started shaking, and she slipped down the wall. Corwyn lifted her into his arms and turned for the bed.

"Now who's the tease?" she managed to gasp.

"I don't tease, Doc. I always pay off." He laid her on the mattress and stood to remove the rest of his clothing.

She surveyed the length of him as he eased down next to her. "So...what's the pay-off?"

Corwyn ran a fingertip down her nose to the full lips he intended to spend a lifetime tasting. "Let's see... You are carrying my son. I guess that means I owe you sixteen years of shattering orgasms for that...plus nine months for carrying him and a few years for the pain of childbirth. How am I doing so far, Doc?"

"Hmmm... I'd offer two thoughts."

He swallowed back a chuckle. "I'm listening."

"First... You know any other way to make love than giving me shattering orgasms?"

Corwyn gave up the serious act and chuckled darkly at the compliment. He ran his fingertips up her seam and into her, moving them in a slow, pumping rhythm. Laura whimpered and rose to meet him.

"And?" he prodded.

"I don't remember, but I think it had something to do with negotiation."

"I'm always open to negotiation."

Corwyn replaced his hand with his mouth. Tasting wasn't enough. At the edges of control, he rolled to his knees between her ankles, spread her legs, and angled Laura to tease his cock at her ready body.

She strained to lower herself around him, but he held her so they barely touched, torturing himself with what he wanted. But there was something even more important he had to accomplish first.

"How is this for negotiation? Promise me you'll be mine forever, and all time limits are off. As long as I live, you'll have my love, protection, and as many orgasms as I can give you."

"I'll hold you to that."

A smile caused a tic in the side of his mouth. "Is that a yes?"

"God, yes! Give me forever, Corwyn. You have my word I'll give you that long."

Groaning, he eased inside her. Laura opened to him, engulfing Corwyn in the only peace he would ever know.

He slid his hands from her thighs, up the back of her buttocks and back, and to her shoulders. He lifted her, positioning Laura over him. She straddled him, her head laid back and her hair tangling in his hands as he thrust into her, tasting her skin at every pass of her body against his.

Her hands roamed his arms and chest, and she met his eyes with a heavy lidded gaze before she cried out his name wildly and contracted around him. Corwyn seated himself fully as he filled her with his hopes, his dreams, and his seed.

His cry of release seemed to rip him apart. He shivered in delight at the feeling of closure and completeness. Anna was no longer a ragged tear in his soul. Laura held his soul as she should have all along. There would be no ghosts between them.

Corwyn tested the belief gingerly. He remembered his love for Anna, felt warm stirrings in his heart at the memories. He loved her still, but not in the heart wrenching manner that had weighed on him so grievously for the last nine years.

Erin was another matter. She was still an empty ache in him and would be until he reclaimed her or mourned her properly. Even the child Laura carried couldn't change that, and he didn't want it to. To his surprise, he craved both of his children more than life itself.

And still not more than I crave Laura.

Corwyn pulled the lady in question to his chest, burying his face in her throat. "I am yours," he breathed into her skin. "You can't get rid of me now."

"Oh, yes... I traveled all this way to get rid of you," she offered in seeming disbelief.

"You did promise to come here either way." Just the thought that she could have turned him down made him distinctly uncomfortable.

"Who says I want to get rid of you?" Her voice softened at that. "The day you left, I wanted to follow you."

"You may want to. I'm going to be very protective of you and our son."

Laura hesitated. "How protective?"

He shrugged. "I'll be pushing you to make an attempt at three meals and eight hours of sleep a day. Knowing Warrior babies, you'll want to do that soon anyway.

"Printed men are protective. When we perceive a threat, we take a defensive posture and do whatever needs done to protect our families."

"I reserve the right to tell you when you're being overbearing," she informed him.

"Good. You may have to, from time to time."

"Well, I guess I have a few weeks of freedom anyway."

Corwyn pulled his head back, straightened, and looked down at her. "Who says?"

"I can't stay this time, Corwyn. I have two days here. After that, I have to go home and put in for my transfer, pack the condo, arrange to sell it, arrange for the movers or a truck to drive here... This could take eight or ten weeks to settle."

"Then I'll be with you until it's settled. That's the way this works. But having handled relocations before... It's not going to take us that long. I have contacts that will expedite more than a few things we need to accomplish."

Though she seemed stunned by the concept, Laura nodded her agreement.

* * * *

Corwyn looked at the crowd around the table in surprise. Colin and Jan sat at far side of the table, Nicky in the playpen behind them. Stephen and Gabby bracketed a fidgeting Brandon, and Joel was in his highchair at Stephen's side. Everyone went silent and looked at Laura as they entered.

Corwyn squeezed Laura's hand in comfort and turned to Colin. "Isn't this a little overwhelming?"

Colin shrugged. "Based on the sounds from your room, I assumed we were celebrating."

Laura blushed and rubbed her cheek on Corwyn's bicep. "The family?" she guessed.

Corwyn nodded. "This is the whole lively bunch."

Jan laughed heartily. "We have names, Corwyn. Don't worry, Laura. Hunter men aren't very forthcoming with information. I'm Jan, by the way."

Laura cracked a smile. "Hi, Jan. I know the men...unfortunately."

"I'm Gabby." She looked from one younger brother to the other, settling on her husband. "Which one is in trouble?"

"Hi, Gabby. Don't worry. I fight my own battles."

Corwyn scowled at Colin. "Some battles, I fight for you. You will meet me in the training room after dinner."

Colin sighed, looking heavenward. "I figured that was coming."

Jan rolled her eyes. "I take it I'm not getting any tonight?"

Her husband gifted her an unholy smile. "I promise to protect all necessary portions of my anatomy."

She huffed. "Uh huh. Likely story. It will be ice packs."

Laura stifled a laugh and ambled over to the playpen to peek in on Nicky. The baby stared up at her, a wooden teething toy crammed in his mouth, clutched in a chubby fist.

"Oh, the babies are absolutely gorgeous," she crooned.

Colin sent Corwyn a pained look.

Corwyn chuckled. "I assume Colin has explained that Laura is my mate, the new Lady Hunter?"

Stephen nodded. "Yeah. We understand how it happened. We'll do whatever we have to."

"We have a finite timetable."

His brothers shared a wary look. "How finite?" Colin asked.

"We'll be training a new young Warrior in just shy of sixteen years."

Colin paled.

Stephen swallowed hard. "Oh, hell... This... This is much harder to hide."

Chapter Twenty-three

December 15th, 1986

"Well, whose idea was it to have another so soon?" Laura teased Jan.

Gabby howled in laughter.

Jan blushed deeply and shot a warning look at the tiny blonde. "Oh, do shut up," she snapped.

Gabby hefted Joel from the changing table. "Of course, if he convinced you into it, you could have Corwyn take him to trial under the rules of sanction," she suggested sweetly.

"You know he didn't."

Laura bit back her smile. "So...knowing Nicky was only eight months old, you *asked* for another?"

Gabby settled Joel in the playpen, smoothed the amulet pinned under his footed pajamas, and straightened. "Yes, Laura. That is exactly what Jan did."

The other woman smiled smugly. "Shall we list your lapses in judgment, Gabrielle?"

Gabby shook out her curls and sighed. "Yeah, I know. Stab my husband, offer my body in payment, jump him when he gallantly lets me off the hook, and tie him up and decide to keep him. All old news."

Laura gaped at her. "You didn't!"

Jan snorted in laughter. "Yes, she did. It's quite the story. Get her to tell it to you someday. Better yet, get Colin to. The bit about Stephen staggering in here, half-dead from her blade, passing out on the garage floor... It's a hoot."

Gabby grimaced. "Over the top, Jan."

"Sorry. Mack truck subtlety, remember?"

Gabby nodded. "Of course, you're probably the first woman in history to force an unwilling Warrior to take you as his mate."

Jan laughed so hard she doubled around the arm she had planted at her abdomen. "He loved every minute of it."

"You tortured him," Gabby protested.

"He still loved it."

Laura settled in the rocking chair, rubbing the heel of her hand over her still-flat womb. "Colin — Mr. Sex Fiend for His Wife — was unwilling? Now that is one I'd pay to see."

Jan smiled and pulled herself up on the low bureau. "He was far gone in printing."

"So? Shouldn't that make him *more* willing?" The more Laura learned about the Warriors, the more she felt she'd never learn it all.

"He was terrified of convincing me to willingness. That's against their rules. He was afraid of losing all self-control with me."

"They have a thing about that," Gabby inserted. "Sometimes they forget that control can be overrated."

Jan nodded her agreement. "Anyway, Colin was so terrified of losing control that he refused to ask me to be his mate, so I forced him past self-control."

"How do you force a Warrior to do anything?" Laura asked. They were singularly the most stubborn men she'd ever met, and they had the physical prowess to back up their decisions.

Gabby started laughing, her head through the doorway to the adjoining playroom, where her older son, Brandon, was playing. She looked around, her eyes glittering in amusement. "She trapped him in her body with no protection when she was high cycle and used the rules of sanction against him."

Jan kicked her feet off the edge of the bureau. "The man did say he was fond of his head."

"Which one?" Gabby teased.

Jan darkened in a blush, something Laura had decided was atypical for her. "Both, and am I ever glad about that." She pushed off the bureau and went to check on Nicky, napping in one of the cribs.

Halfway there, she stopped and ran a hand over her forehead. Jan grasped at the edge of the playpen, weaving as if she was dizzy.

Laura reached her first, smoothing Jan's hair back from her sweat-soaked face. "Honey, sit down. Gabby, get my bag."

"No," Jan breathed. "Get Brandon. Get the babies together. He's coming."

Laura stared at her in confusion. "Who is, Jan?"

Gabby was already in motion. She hauled the complaining four-year-old from his toys. The spunky little woman hefted her older son into the playpen and handed him a wooden sacred weapon. It was a toy that had been given to every young Warrior Brandon's age by every Warrior father for more than fifteen centuries.

"It's your duty to protect Joel," Gabby told him solemnly. "Duty, Brandon."

Laura shook her head. "I don't —"

Jan launched away from the playpen and scooped Nicky to her chest. She patted the baby's amulet and nodded to Gabby, who had just performed the same test on Brandon. Jan settled Nicky in the playpen with his cousins.

Laura touched her own amulet in fear. She had no idea what was going on, but their reactions were enough to make the fuzz at the base of her skull stand on end.

Jan sucked in her breath and pointed a shaking finger toward the hallway door. "There."

A deep, amused laugh broke the stillness a moment before the beast took shape. Without thinking about it, the three woman closed ranks between him and the babies in the pen.

Laura scanned her gaze over the beast. He was almost as tall as Corwyn was though slightly leaner. His hair was a rich shade of brown and long enough to reach his shoulders, and his eyes were like liquid silver. She noted with distaste that he was clothed as a Warrior would be.

He bowed to Jan, a mocking movement at best. "I see Tyner's information was correct."

Tyner? Who is Tyner?

Jan shuddered.

Beast. Nothing else would make Jan react that way.

The beast made a tsking sound. "I don't blame you, Jan." There was a note of false condolence in his tone. "His sexual tastes would have been far too tame for you. Still, a sensitive like you would have been quite the prize."

Sensitive? I've heard Stephen call her that before. But Laura had no more clue what a sensitive was than she did who Tyner was or what he'd wanted from Jan.

He took a step toward them, and the women tightened their stance. Laura squeezed Jan's hand in comfort.

"No need for that," he stated. "I have no interest in your infant *Krieger*."

Laura stiffened her spine. She was Lady Hunter, the leader of this little pack. *The alpha female.* "What do you want, beast?"

Gabby grasped at her arm hard enough to send pinpoints of pain racing up and down from the grip. "Silver eyes, Laura. Don't do it."

What does that —?

The beast laughed heartily. "Corwyn Lord *Jäger* took everything from me. I intend to renegotiate."

"Veriel?" Laura choked the name out. *Silver eyes. Veriel. Oh, God.*

He took two more smooth steps toward the assembled group. "Call me Jörg. Anna did."

"Then I certainly won't."

"I thought that would be your answer."

Laura didn't see him move, not even a blur of motion. Veriel seemed to be two places at once.

She stumbled away from the other women, hauled out of line by his grip on her wrist. The pains shooting up her arm were excruciating, and Laura screamed. The pressure she'd barely noticed increased, and the amulet's backlash continued. Laura pulled back, trying futilely to free her arm, and his fist tightened in warning.

Veriel yanked her closer to his face, his expression fierce. The scent of wintergreen was a cloying cloud in her throat, and she choked.

Gabby and Jan launched at him, beating at Veriel and clawing at his hand, fighting the amulets as much as they were fighting the beast.

Veriel ignored their attempts to free her. He leaned closer, ratcheting down his grip another notch. Laura whimpered, going lightheaded in agony. She swallowed her scream, unwilling to give Veriel the satisfaction of hearing it.

"Now he will come for me. Now we will dance."

Veriel pushed Laura away. She collapsed against the wooden slats of the playpen and sank to the floor. The air seemed trapped in her lungs. Her thoughts were disjoined.

Gabby and Jan crouched over her, murmuring words she couldn't understand. One of them touched her arm, and Laura grunted through clenched teeth. She pulled the injured arm to her chest and shook her head. Forcing herself to sitting, one-handed and uncoordinated as she was, wasn't easy, but Laura managed it.

"The babies are crying," she breathed. "Take care of them."

Gabby and Jan nodded, then circled the playpen and scooped up the younger boys. Jan changed Nicky and quieted him against her shoulder while Gabby settled in the rocker to nurse Joel.

Veriel leaned against the bureau Jan had hoisted herself onto and viewed the scene in something resembling scorn. "Warrior women," he mused. "You fight. You nurse your young calmly in the face of your enemy. You even protect your men."

His cold gaze settled on Laura, and she pressed her back to the solid slats of the playpen.

"Do not be so foolish as to attempt that with me," he warned. "Anna was my wife. I forgave her everything from taking your husband to her bed to planting a blade in me in his defense. I do not care for you, Laura. Do you understand what I am telling you?"

She nodded. "Yeah. I understand."

"Good. This is between the great Lord *Jäger* and myself. Let it remain that way, and you may survive to lie in his arms again." He tilted his head to one side. "He is coming. Come to me now, and I promise to let him live."

Laura stared at him in shock, and Veriel pushed to his feet and stalked toward her.

Brandon! She scrambled away from the playpen before he could touch her again or injure the little boy watching the scene quietly from inside the pen. Out of the corner of her eye, she saw Brandon hoist himself over the top rail and back to his mother, his wooden weapon up.

When she turned back, the beast motioned to the far corner of the room. Laura flicked a glance at Jan and backed into the corner he'd indicated. He glared at her, and she sank to the floor. Like it or not, Veriel had her where he wanted her.

* * * *

Corwyn slammed on the breaks, letting the car skid the last few yards to the front stairs, jamming it into park when it was still rolling. There was no time to turn off the engine and secure the vehicle. He threw the car door open and sprinted to the manor door. It was standing open, which told him all he needed to know.

It doesn't tell me anything I need to know. Is Laura all right? Is our son? And the other women and children?

That thought driving him near mad in worry, Corwyn vaulted up the stairs, his sacred weapon out and ready for a fight.

Finding Veriel was no challenge. The beast wasn't trying to hide himself. Corwyn cursed fluently as he headed for the Warrior's nursery suite. Colin and Stephen would be here soon, but Corwyn was closest, and he wasn't about to wait around for them, considering the stakes.

He stopped in the doorway, taking stock of the scene. Jan sat in the far corner of the room, nursing Nicky. Gabby sat in the rocking chair with Joel curled to her shoulder and Brandon sitting at her feet with his wooden weapon in an attack position.

Good boy!

Veriel had placed Laura behind him. She was curled into the corner with her right arm drawn up to her chest. She managed a weak smile for him before she bit back what were probably sobs.

Veriel's voice was cold and laced with malice. "I broke her arm. I did it so you would know I do not hold her in the same regard I held Anna. Do not seek to play on those memories with me."

Corwyn forced back his fury. Veriel wanted him in a mindless rage. Laura deserved better that than from him. "This is between us."

Veriel inclined his head. "The other women and children may go. Your woman stays."

"Go."

Gabby and Jan stood. Gabby took Brandon's hand, and they headed out into the hall.

Corwyn dug out his keys and tossed them to Jan. "The van. Don't stop for anything."

She didn't nod. Jan pulled the double-sided key up and quickened her step.

Corwyn sighed in relief. Gabby would use the radio as soon as the boys were safely in their seats. Stephen would go to the women to protect them. Colin would come to Corwyn's aid.

If there is anything left of me to aid.

Corwyn waited for the sounds of them rounding the base of the stairs and starting down the stairs to the garage to continue. "What's your game this time, Veriel?"

"What is yours?" he countered.

"Protecting my mate, as you well know."

"Your mate." He sneered at that.

"Yes. My mate. What concern is it of yours?"

"What was Anna to you, *Jäger?* You stole my wife from me and turned her against me. For what purpose? Did you take her to wife only to keep her from me? Or perhaps to save your head? You wanted her. You had her. Why did you break with the rules of sanction and have a child with her if she wasn't your mate?"

"She was my mate," Corwyn insisted. But he understood Veriel's meaning. When he'd considered the repercussions of printing again, it was the Warriors he'd feared. Corwyn hadn't considered Veriel's rabid fixation on Anna.

Veriel's eyes burned a fierce red, and he motioned to Laura. "Then what madness is this? You defile Anna's memory by taking another woman to her bed and planting your seed?"

Corwyn swallowed down the fact that, for all his posturing, Veriel took countless women to bed, willing or not. Instead he focused on the question at hand.

"Laura *is* my mate. The Stone brought her to me. You stole my family from me. You know the perversity of the Stone better than just about anyone on Earth." *Except me.* Corwyn firmly believed he'd had the worst of it.

"You cannot take another," Veriel raged.

"You did. How many times have you fixated on your *wives*? Why do you? What sets you apart and makes you mad for these women? Regana? Caitrina? Anna? How many others, Veriel?"

Veriel roared and punched through the wall next to Laura's head. He turned back to Corwyn as she sank further from him, shaking and wide-eyed.

Corwyn swallowed hard. "Laura?"

She nodded and flicked a glance at Veriel. "Here."

Veriel growled in displeasure. "That woman is not of Regana's line. She is not of Regana's soul. You think I cannot tell the difference?"

Corwyn ground his teeth at the Mad Deceiver's delusions. "The soul is not the only measure of a woman."

"If you seek to find peace, it is."

"Were you printed on Regana?" How many years had he wondered that and never had the moment to ask it? *Since the afternoon at the Maher manor, when*

Anna was carrying Erin. He pushed the memories of his daughter away. His mate needed him now.

Veriel shot him an irritated look. "Do not seek to analyze me, *Jäger.*" He paced back and forth between Corwyn and Laura, growing more agitated. Veriel pushed a hand through his hair, and his movements were jerky and tense. "There are too many years and too many lies between the Warriors and myself to count today. To count in a decade," he grumbled.

"What do you want from me? Why are you here, Veriel? I won't permit you to take my mate in some form of revenge. *You* were responsible for Anna's death. Not me."

"You stole her from me. She was mine, the only woman alive who could be mine."

"Because of her soul?" The need to understand his fixation had never waned and probably never would.

Veriel glared at him. "You want to know my purpose here? I intend to negotiate with you."

"Negotiate what? We have nothing to offer each other."

"We do. Your dalliance with Anna bore the sweetest fruit."

"You took Erin from me, too." *Dalliance?* It took all of Corwyn's self-control not to seek vengeance for that insult.

"No. I did not take her, though she is mine to take."

Thank the gods! He doesn't have Erin. Corwyn didn't doubt she was safer hidden than with the beast. "What is your point?"

"When Erin is found, she is mine to take, as she was born to be mine. You will not interfere with that."

"What if she's dead?" Just saying the words made Corwyn want to scream in frustration. She couldn't be dead. He couldn't envision a world without hope of finding Erin and bringing her home.

"She is not," Veriel snapped. "I would know had she died. I would have felt her death."

Corwyn bit back a dozen curses on the damned beast. He envied Veriel the certainty that Erin was alive, though it was probably one more mad delusion.

"Well, *Jäger?*" he prompted.

"I cannot allow that. You know I can't." If Erin was alive, Corwyn had to do all he could to protect her. *To free her, if that is possible.*

"You will. I have no interest in this mate of yours or the child she carries, but I will have one of your daughters as my wife. If you deny me Erin, I will take the other, freed or not. If she cannot bear my children, I will take your mate as well...for my trouble." Veriel scowled at him. "What god tortures me by giving you two daughters?"

Laura sucked in her breath in shock, and Corwyn offered a reassuring nod.

Veriel pasted on a vindictive smile. "Erin is rightfully mine. The other two are not, but I will not hesitate to make good on my threats unless you give your sacred vow — on the damned Stone Herself — that you will leave Erin to me."

Corwyn faltered. He met Laura's eyes miserably. It was a vow he couldn't make. She might hate him for it, but Corwyn couldn't bargain with Veriel, even for her and their child together.

Laura nodded grimly. "No deal, Veriel," she informed him.

The Mad Elder turned to her in seeming surprise. "You addressed me?"

Her eyes narrowed. "He's not making that vow. Not tonight. Not ever. If Corwyn gave his daughter to you willingly, he wouldn't be the man I love and respect. We don't negotiate with beasts, even the king of beasts."

Veriel's shock would have been amusing in any other circumstances. *Almost any other,* Corwyn amended.

That shock melted into fury. The beast dragged Laura to her feet and released her against the wall. "You would choose to experience my body?" he asked.

Laura paled. "Never."

"Then your *mate* will agree. He will negotiate to save you. Or perhaps..." He shot a feral grin over his shoulder at Corwyn. "Perhaps he is not your mate at all and does not love you enough to make such a bargain."

Corwyn cringed at the escalating scene. The amulet was useless against Veriel. Even he couldn't be sure how useless it was, and the Stone wasn't offering that information.

"Leave her, Veriel. Face me." *Time to piss him off.* "Or do you prefer to fight unarmed women?"

The beast chuckled and placed his hand next to Laura's head. "You would not enjoy what I would do." He tilted his head to one side. "Or maybe you would. I could make you enjoy it. You would enjoy the most degrading acts; then I would release you to the truth at the height of your pleasure." He hummed in satisfaction. "I have done that before. The woman's horror at that moment is sweeter than her blood. Taking you while I feed —"

Laura flicked a startled look between their bodies, no doubt an indication that the beast's cock was rising. The look of pure panic she shot Corwyn confirmed it.

Veriel was either too absorbed in his fantasy to notice or acted as if he was to unnerve them. "I could take the form of your mate, letting you respond to him in your confusion. But it would be my eyes you meet at your climax.

"You know, a woman's climax quickens at that moment. What do you think that means, Laura? Do you think she screams in terror or in the realization that she enjoyed being in my arms, if only for that instant in time?"

His breathing went ragged. "Would you scream for me, Laura? Would your release quicken when you saw my face and knew it was my cock inside you?"

Her face darkened in fury. "No. And Corwyn will not make that deal with you, no matter what threats you make."

"Even this one?" Veriel lowered his face toward her neck, his teeth lengthening for a feed.

Corwyn snapped. No matter the danger, he couldn't allow Veriel to feed on Laura as he had on Anna. If Veriel could lay hands on her, there was no telling what he could do.

He crossed the distance between them in a single leap. Veriel dematerialized as Corwyn struck. He'd suspected the beast might do that, hoping Corwyn might injure Laura accidentally in his rage. He didn't. Corwyn's blade swung back into an arc as he spun.

This was Veriel. Corwyn had no doubts the beast meant to go for a shot at his back.

His blade bit soft tissue, and Corwyn smiled. "Your throat again, Veriel?"

The beast flickered, and Corwyn lunged to land a second bleeder. Too late, he gleaned Veriel's game. Just as his blade bit, Veriel disappeared.

Corwyn started his next arc a heartbeat too slow. His right leg crumpled as Veriel's claws sliced deep. Corwyn swung his weapon as he fell, hoping for another bleeder, but Veriel snagged the blade from his hand just as it would have ripped at the beast's thigh.

Veriel grasped Corwyn by the shoulder and flung him away as one would a child's doll. The air left his lungs in a rush as he hit the far wall. The sickening crunch and searing pain announced a fractured collarbone. Corwyn landed hard, and a shower of plaster dust followed him down.

He raised his head blearily, trying to shake off the disorientation. Somewhere in the distance, Laura screamed a protest at Veriel.

That brought back a semblance of focus, and the amulet's reaction to the beast touching Laura's skin finished the job. Corwyn forced himself to his feet and braced his good hand on his injured leg, cursing as Veriel returned to her throat to feed.

Laura pushed at him insistently, but neither her strength nor the amulet's moved the Mad Elder. She jerked as Veriel's face disappeared against her throat.

Corwyn reached for Veriel, releasing the gushing wounds and stumbling the yards that separated them. His hand passed through the wisp of air where the beast's collar had been a blink before, and Veriel raised his bare arm and buried Corwyn's weapon in the wall next to Laura's waist. The beast dematerialized, leaving Corwyn to fall through the spot he'd occupied instead of tackling him.

Corwyn looked up at Laura, taking stock of her condition. Veriel hadn't fed, but a deep bruise marred the skin at her pulse point, most likely where the Mad Deceiver had pressed his lips to her. Her eyes were wide and wild, and her gaze was locked on the hilt of the sacred weapon touching her hip.

Unable to stand the sight of her trauma, Corwyn vented a scream of rage. If his *Blutjagd* burned any hotter, the idea of it catching the wall on fire wouldn't seem impossible.

Laura shook violently and fought to normalize her breathing. She started to gag, and her eyes watered.

Corwyn focused on the beast blood staining her shirt. *Neck shot. One of these days, I will take the head completely off and kill that bastard.*

Veriel's voice came from the doorway to the play room. "You cannot protect her from me, *Jäger*. Consider my offer carefully. We will speak again."

Corwyn didn't watch him leave. He reached up and circled Laura's wrist with his fingers.

Veriel streamed away, not bothering to ghost himself.

"Laura."

She was hyperventilating and shaking her head at the blade planted beside her.

"Laura." Corwyn tried to push himself up again, groaning at his broken body.

Her gaze snapped to him, and Laura's eyes widened. She knelt at his side. "Corwyn, no."

He circled her head with his good — but bloodstained — hand and eased Laura to his chest.

"Corwyn, your leg," she protested.

"Later." All that mattered now was feeling Laura in his arms.

She nodded against his chest. "Why is he doing this?"

Corwyn sighed. "It is an obsession."

Laura settled her length against him, and Colin rushed through the door.

* * * *

Corwyn growled in frustration as Michael stitched the last of the lacerations on his thigh. "Colin?" he called out.

His brother sauntered into the room, looking peeved at the interruption. "She's fine, Corwyn. Laura is asleep in your bed, and we will move you to join her when Michael is finished."

"Now that you've given me an update I didn't need, I want Stephen to get the women and children relocated to the training house."

Colin leaned against the door frame and crossed his arms over his barrel-like chest. "All of the women?" he inquired with a tone that challenged the order.

"What?" Since when did Colin question Corwyn's orders?

"Laura, too?" he qualified.

"What? Hell, no. You know what I mean."

"Are you making this an order as Lord Hunter?"

Corwyn shook his head. "What drugs did Michael give me? Or you? You're not making sense, Colin. Are you saying I should make this an order?"

Colin's chuckle was his only immediate answer.

"Want to let me in on the joke? Why should I make this an order?"

"Well, it's the only way Gabby and Jan *might* obey you. Of course, they'll probably mutiny anyway. I think you're outmanned and outclassed in this situation, big brother."

It took Corwyn several seconds to form words to respond to that pronouncement. It was Michael's smirk that finally set him off.

"Excuse me? You might want to run the logic past me again. With Veriel involved, they have to be relocated. Or Laura and I do."

Colin sighed. "Jan and Gabby won't leave Laura. They are adamant about it."

"They want to face Veriel again? Colin, you felt —"

"Have you talked to them?"

"Of course not. You think I had time for pleasantries when the beast had Laura? I told them to move, and they moved." *So why isn't that a good enough order this time?*

"He didn't lay a hand on anyone but Laura. The rest of them aren't worth his trouble. Face it. The only bedmates he's ever cared enough to harass or threaten have been yours."

"I felt the attack. You had to have felt it, too."

"They attacked him. The other women were trying to pull Veriel off Laura. He didn't even bother to swat them away."

Corwyn bit back his anger at the mental movie reel that caused. In the end, he couldn't decide if the image of Veriel attacking Laura or the fact that the others chose to attack the elder heated his blood more. "They did what?" That came out a growl.

Colin shrugged, as if what he was saying didn't affect him at all. "The women are a tight little group."

"This is Veriel we're talking about," Corwyn stormed. "He broke Laura's arm for no better reason than to prove to me that he'd hurt her."

Colin darkened. "We've discussed it at length. I believe our wives understand our orders for any future encounters."

"You admit there will be future encounters, and you still think it's a good idea? You know, the rules of sanction say they follow our orders, when their safety is at risk."

"We do, and they will." There was no hesitation and no second-guessing on that one.

"May I remind you that your mate has already thrown caution to the wind once." Neither of his brother's mates were known for a cool head in a crisis.

Colin scowled at him. "Pregnant or not, I could easily have hurt Jan when Stephen told me." He muttered the rest. "Probably why he told me over the radio and not in person."

That stopped Corwyn cold. "Pregnant?"

His smile returned. "Yeah. I told her two days ago."

"She wanted this?" Nickie was only eight months old. What was she thinking? What was Colin thinking to do this?

"Unlike some brothers in this family, I don't take chances. Of course, she asked to carry again."

None of this made sense. "You and Stephen are willing to have your families in the middle of this?"

He offered a curt nod in response.

"Why? Why are you chancing this?" And how could Corwyn talk them out of it?

Colin favored him with an exasperated look. "There are several factors we had to consider. First, Jan will be upset if I force her to leave Laura. I don't need to tell you that I don't want her upset."

"Veriel attacking is going to upset her," he countered, at the edges of his limited supply of patience.

His brother continued, as if Corwyn hadn't spoken. "Laura will be upset, if she doesn't have the other women around. The last thing you want is Laura upset."

"I can't prevent that, either."

"She'll be less upset, if she has company. Third... Jan is a sensitive."

"Sensitives don't have to face beasts," Corwyn argued.

"We can't force them to. We can't stop them, either. Do you have any concept what stopping Jan from doing anything is like?"

Corwyn sighed. He could see that nothing he said would dissuade them. "Go on."

"We're not splitting our forces again. Stephen and I have discussed it. We lost Anna, because we didn't centralize. If we lose Laura, we lose you. That is unacceptable. One of us will always be with her. More than one, if possible."

"You discussed this without me?"

Colin darkened and nodded. He hunched his shoulders and shoved his fists in his pockets. "Should we meet you in trial, once you heal?" he asked in something that sounded like resignation.

Corwyn bit back a laugh at that. "Hell, no. I need you in top form to fight Veriel."

"It's decided? You're not going to fight us on this?"

"It's decided, but I hope you know what you're doing."

Chapter Twenty-four

February 4th, 1987

Laura sighed, shifting against Corwyn in a half-sleep. Though she knew she should, she was too warm and comfortable to consider getting out of bed. As if he agreed, Corwyn turned to her and pulled Laura into his arms. She smiled at the feeling of his hands roaming her body.

"Such a bad boy," she half-yawned.

"You have no idea."

She snuggled closer to him and pressed a kiss to his shoulder. "I think I have some clue."

He chuckled. It was not his typical sound of arousal; rather it was a dark laugh that made her heart rhythm falter.

"Corwyn?" she asked, forcing her breathing to even.

"Laura?" His voice was more a taunt than a tease.

Doc. He didn't call me Doc. Corwyn always called her Doc in bed. She was only Laura in company.

She levered her eyes open, bringing him into focus slowly. It was Corwyn, their bed, their room... But something felt wrong.

His hands closed on her hips, pulling her to the column of his cock. "You're not too tired, are you, Doc?"

"No. I — I mean yes. I'm tired, Corwyn."

What did Veriel say?

"I could take the form of your mate, letting you respond to him..."

288

This wasn't Corwyn.

"Now is that nice?" he grumbled. "You ruined my surprise."

Laura shook her head, pushing at his chest. How could he do this? How could he touch her with the amulet on? There wasn't even a reaction from it.

His eyes turned from Corwyn's deep brown to silver and his hair from close-cropped black to long brown, but Corwyn's face remained. "Nothing can save you from me."

"I don't believe you." There had to be a way out of this.

Laura searched everything Corwyn had told her about Veriel. *A dream. This is a dream. Anna had dreams like this, but —*

Oh, no. Her heart stuttered at the story she'd heard.

"That's right," Veriel crooned. "What I do here manifests on your physical form."

"No." Laura wrenched at his hold but with no success. "Corwyn!" She screamed for him, even as Laura reasoned that he couldn't hear her outside the dream.

Anna woke herself by punching him. She aimed a punch for his cheek. Maybe she could snap them both out of —

Veriel grasped her hands and forced them over her head, shaking his head as if correcting an errant child. He stroked his fingers up and down her recently-healed wrist, seemingly considering breaking it again.

Laura steeled her nerves for it, and Veriel laughed heartily.

"I never do repeat performances, Doc."

She didn't doubt that he used the nickname now to make her loathe it. It wouldn't work. Laura reminded herself that he might look like Corwyn, but he wasn't.

He rolled his hips against her, transforming slowly to his own countenance. "I can do whatever I wish," he breathed. Veriel lowered his head and nuzzled her cheek.

Laura jerked her face away from his, trembling, desperately trying to reason her way out of this living nightmare.

"I could take you, but my beast has played hard tonight, and I have no need of companionship. Perhaps on a night when I'm...more desperate for a woman," he suggested.

Laura bit back a series of curses.

"Tell him, Laura. Tell him you're not safe. You will never be safe, unless the great Lord *Jäger* agrees to my terms."

She nodded slowly, jerking her head away again as he drew in her scent.

"Oh, and one more thing," he murmured. Veriel waited patiently for her to acknowledge him.

"What?" she managed in a calm voice.

"A warning."

Laura screamed in shock and agony, as her shoulder exploded in sensation.

* * * *

Corwyn snapped awake at Laura's howl of pain. She arched up off the mattress, and the sharp tang of blood filled the air. He slammed the light switch on, slipped his sacred weapon from the sheath on the night stand, and reached for her.

"Dear gods." He cursed fluently, pulling the sheet away from the injury. He stared at the dual punctures for a moment in disbelief before he came to his senses and applied pressure to it.

Laura moaned, seeking out his eyes with a grimace and ragged breaths. He whispered soothing words through a clenched jaw.

Footsteps pounded down the hall from the opposite wing, and his brothers launched through the door, dressed in jeans and with their weapons in hand.

"Get the emergency kit," Corwyn ordered.

Colin turned and sprinted the other way.

Stephen came to the bed. "How bad is it?"

"Deep enough! Not...too deep," he amended in a lower voice.

"Let me see it."

"Do you think —"

"I think you're in *Blutjagd* and unable to think clearly. Hold her hand. Kiss her forehead, if you have to find your center again. Let me see the damage."

Corwyn nodded, pulled his hand away from the punctures, and pressed his forehead to hers. He forced his *Blutjagd* back, recognizing his near loss of control when Laura sobbed.

Stephen spoke in low tones, passing supplies back and forth with Colin. Laura's breathing calmed as the bleeding slowed. She burrowed her face into Corwyn's shoulder, and her unaffected arm gripped his hip in a shaking hold.

"Stephen?" Gabby called out.

"I told you to stay away," he growled.

"Good God!" That was closer. "How —"

"Gabby!"

"In my dream," Laura choked out.

Corwyn tensed, memories of the beast's nightly visits to Anna's dreams sending his *Blutjagd* off the charts again.

"Corwyn," Stephen warned him.

"What did he do?" he demanded. "Tell me everything."

"She's not ready for this," both brothers warned him at once.

"I have to know."

Colin leaned close to his ear. "She is carrying your child. Do you want to upset her further?" There was a challenge in that, a tone that said his brothers would tie him down and sedate him, if they had to, rather than see him push Laura any further.

Corwyn winced. "No. I don't." He kissed Laura's temple tenderly. "I'm sorry, Doc. I wasn't thinking."

Laura sighed as Stephen taped a gauze pad over the bite mark.

"She should sleep," Colin noted.

Laura's hand tightened, and her eyes opened wide. "No. Not a chance."

Stephen smoothed her hair. "Laura, you have —"

"No," Corwyn growled. Visions of the beast touching his mate had him near-feral. "If she doesn't want to sleep, she won't. Not yet. We'll talk." He looked down at Laura, his heart aching. "About whatever you want to." *And nothing more. No matter what I want to know.*

* * * *

Laura held to Corwyn's arm, though he didn't need her help in carrying her to the library. He'd been solicitous to the point of dressing her in a long, silk gown and robe. He treated her as if she'd been gravely injured and left unable to do it for herself.

It was touching. She'd never been pampered this way before him.

Gabby looked up at their entrance, offering a wan smile as she set out a tray of coffee and hot chocolate. Though no one had said it aloud, Laura knew Jan was helping Colin change the bloodied sheets before she joined them.

She'd like to believe they were washing the sheets, but she suspected they were burning them. Warriors were like that when it came to beasts.

Corwyn settled on the leather sofa and set Laura next to him. While he reached for a cup of hot chocolate for her, Gabby spread an antique quilt over her and tucked it lightly around her legs.

He offered the hot chocolate, and his gaze met hers, pleading, then moved away guiltily. Corwyn didn't ask what he wanted to, though she knew it ate at him not to. After the warning his brothers tendered upstairs, he wouldn't dare to.

Colin walked into the room and nodded to Stephen. Laura used the prompt to force herself to speak.

"The bite *was* the worst of it," she assured Corwyn, staring into her cup.

He let out an explosive breath, his shoulders sagging. "Then he didn't..."

She laughed harshly at that, and Corwyn raised his head, his eyes narrowing.

"He said he wasn't desperate enough for a woman to attempt that rather odious task tonight."

A growl issued from deep in Corwyn's throat.

"Corwyn," Stephen and Colin barked in unison.

Gabby retreated to the furthest chair in the room, her eyes wide.

"He will never," Corwyn barked.

Laura found it hard to speak. The hopelessness of their situation made putting her thoughts and feelings into words nearly impossible.

As if he understood perfectly, Corwyn touched her cheek, then eased her to his chest and wrapped his arms around her. He didn't offer false assurances, and neither did anyone else.

"Corwyn may not be able to stop him," Gabby offered quietly. "But maybe you can."

* * * *

February 12th, 1987

"Did you miss me, Laura?"

She forced herself not to scream in frustration, backing away from the sensation of body heat. An arm crossed over her hip, blocking her escape.

Laura opened her eyes, staring at the room in disbelief. The walls were stone blocks. A fire roared to her left, opposite Veriel's position. The bedding beneath her was something she couldn't identify, some sort of soft woven.

And *he* was half over her, bare-chested, his brown hair framing his face, only a pair of leather pants between them. "Your wound is healing well." A cruel smile twisted his features.

"Yes. It is." It hadn't been deep, but it was still healing more than a week later.

He didn't answer.

"What do you want?" she asked bluntly, testing the abilities Gabby had taught her behind the shield of thoughts Corwyn had. In truth, it was the only way Corwyn had permitted her to try this at all.

"How interesting," he mused. "The little doctor has learned a new trick."

More than one. To her surprise, Gabby's idea was working. She could feel the cold edge of steel under her fingertips.

"Only if he forces you to it."

Corwyn had made her swear not to take any action unless she had no other choice. Even now, Laura wasn't certain that Gabby's idea would work. If it failed, he might kill her for trying it.

Veriel touched her cheek, and Laura shuddered in response.

If he intends to rape me, I don't care if he kills me. I'll die trying to take him with me.

Her qualm at what her death would do to Corwyn was washed away by the certainty that she wouldn't die before the Stone was done with him. It wouldn't allow it.

Will it?

She hoped it wouldn't, anyway.

"Has he reconsidered accepting my offer?" Veriel asked.

"You know he hasn't. He can't." *Corwyn has more honor than that.*

"Then I suppose we will learn what lengths *Jäger* will go to in order to protect the woman he *loves.*" His snide tone said he didn't believe Corwyn loved her.

Laura forced her mind to function when she felt panic closing in. If she panicked, she could lose the ability to shield him.

He lowered his face toward hers. "Do not concern yourself. You are not the first woman we have shared."

She struck, praying to God and Corwyn's Stone that this would work. The sacred weapon was perfect, right down to the Hunter seal in the hilt...the Lord's seal, Corwyn's blade. Laura visualized it as she had with Gabby since the first night he'd attacked her in her dreams.

Veriel recoiled, bleeding profusely. He looked at the damage in shock, touching the wound that would have taken his left lung.

But will it hurt him like he hurt me? It was a gamble that the injuries would travel both ways. If they didn't, she'd just signed her death warrant...or as close as he wanted to come to it. The fact that she'd stabbed him and not snapped them both out of the dream didn't bode well.

Even if it worked, would it convince Veriel to stop? Corwyn had postulated that Veriel had fifteen hundred years of battle training. Having a weapon wasn't enough. She had to know how to use it, and without the speed and stealth of a Warrior, that would be problematic.

Laura visualized herself clothed and slid off the bed when she was, the sacred weapon still clutched in her hand. At the very least, if he attacked, she could cut herself to wake herself up...she hoped.

He met her eyes, seemingly confused.

And she snapped awake.

"Laura," Corwyn shouted, both hands cupping her face.

"Here," she breathed.

A collective sigh went up from all three Warriors, making her wonder how long Corwyn had been trying to wake her.

"He was here."

Laura nodded in response. She lifted the wooden weapon she'd used in her visualization exercises and had slept with every night. *Yes, he was here, and I did it.* But had she done him any real damage? There was no way to know.

As if arguing that point, the stench of beast blood assaulted her, and she gagged. Laura looked at the blade and her hands, but there was no sign of blood.

"Open the windows," Corwyn ordered. "Air it out."

"He was here?" she asked, her mind in a flat spin. "In the room with us?"

Corwyn nodded. "He probably has to be close. You — In the dream, you wounded him." It wasn't a question, but his eyes added the inflection for him.

"Yes. I did."

"A chest shot?"

Laura touched his ribs with her fingertip. She'd like to answer, but the smell set off a coughing fit, and her eyes started watering. She'd leave the room, but the foul odor was clearing slowly.

"Yes!" Stephen cheered, punching the air.

Corwyn kissed her brow. "Okay. It works. Prepare yourself every night, Doc."

She sighed. "He's coming back?"

"I don't know. Better to be prepared for it."

Corwyn didn't add that if he did come back, Veriel would come back prepared to fight her. It was easily the one thing neither of them wanted to think about, she was sure.

Chapter Twenty-five

Playing Games I: The Game Begins

May 1st, 1987

Denise Roberts shook her head at the report again, dropping it on the passenger seat of her car. It didn't make sense, and reading it a hundred times or a thousand times wouldn't help that situation.

The victims were primarily female, young and attractive. Only one of the ten was male, and only two were over the age of twenty-five. They had all been found at the doors of one of the four local hospitals, hypo-anemic and confused, unable to recall what had happened to them. They were in good health except for their condition when they were found, not using drugs or drinking on the night of the attacks. It was rare to find a mark on them save the one that baffled all the experts.

It was a single puncture over a major artery, too large to be even the largest medical-grade needle for drawing blood...by far. She could pick up the file and find the precise grade she was looking for, but until something led her to a suspect or crime scene, what was the point of that?

"It's not like I'd recognize a single gauge of needle, even if I did know which one I was looking for," she sighed. This was decidedly not her usual beat.

Moreover, the marks left were healed sites that the victims and their families all attested had not been there hours earlier. The wound had somehow been used to draw off blood, but how was the mystery Denise was ordered to discover.

How was the blood drawn off without leaving an open puncture anywhere on the body? The experts had been over every victim with a fine-toothed comb. There were no scabs, no evidence of a deliberate blood draw.

What caused the discoloration reminiscent of a childhood scar, the pale or silvery oval, smaller than a fingertip, that refused to fade over time?

What caused the memory lapse?

That bothered Denise most. No drugs were found in the blood they took, urine, saliva, or even in the spinal fluid. There were no signs of head injury, indicating that they had been rendered unconscious, and it was simply unbelievable that they would all choose to lie.

While Denise found it intriguing, the street cops were frustrated over the lack of evidence, the media was scared shitless, and the forensics specialists were ready to rip out someone's throat themselves. There had been ten victims in less than four months and not a shred of evidence to link them to an assailant or to each other. There was never evidence on the victim, and since they were all taken from popular sites, there was no hope of finding evidence at that end by the time the victim could state a location or the guys on the street found the victim's car.

Denise was their last line of defense.

She sighed and clicked off the overhead light in her car, cursing herself as a fool again. Denise had been on this case for two months and had made no more headway than anyone else. It was embarrassing, an insult to her professional track record.

What Denise did was hard to describe. Even her boss didn't care how she did it. She just found her way to results that no one else seemed able to. If they were desperate enough to assign her for no better reason than that, they were more desperate than she had seen them in years.

So what am I doing? Skulking around the alleyways where these people last recall being. Why? What am I going to find that no one else has and that I haven't up until now? What do I hope to accomplish by coming here at night?

Denise shifted nervously. She *needed* to catch a sicko who drained blood from unsuspecting victims, before someone else got hurt, but this was crazy.

If Adam knew she was doing this, her boss would handcuff her to her desk. As it was, Adam was nervous that Denise had been requested for this assignment. He'd called her into his office more than once to lecture her on all the rules she already knew, his green eyes showing moments of deep emotion while he spoke. Her night excursions without an escort would drive him batty. Worse, Adam would have her banned from the case for her blatant disregard of protocol.

The alley was between a restaurant and a dance club. It led from the main street to the parking lot where she'd left her car. The last victim had disappeared from this alley more than two weeks earlier, and another would go soon. There was never more than three weeks between attacks.

Denise turned on her flashlight and panned it over the ground and walls. There were no doors that opened onto the alley or hiding places large enough for an adult to use. The fire escapes and dumpsters were at the back of the buildings, nowhere near the mouth of the alley. Both ends were well lit and the alley not poorly lit either. There was no conceivable way to sneak up on a person. The victim hadn't been with anyone else when she entered the alley. *So how —*

"Lose something?" a deep voice inquired, a rich voice with a faint accent.

Denise turned with a yelp, losing her balance and landing on her ass with a grunt. She swung her flashlight up at the man standing over her.

He blinked stunning sky-blue eyes in the glare of her light, then shaded them with one large hand. His hair was a mass of bright blond curls spilling over his forehead almost into those beautiful eyes. "Are you all right?" he asked.

She felt her cheeks heat. Denise pushed to her feet awkwardly. "How did you do that?"

He furrowed his brow. "Do?"

"How did you sneak up on me?" she demanded. "Where did you come from?"

He rolled his eyes. "I didn't sneak up on you. I walked, and I came from the street."

Denise ground her teeth in frustration. He did sneak up on her, and she had to know how. Denise didn't get lost in her own mind. She was always aware of her surroundings.

He smiled. "Are you sure you're all right?" He reached a hand out as if to check the temperature at the back of her neck.

"Polero," a new voice barked. "Face me."

Denise swung toward the new arrival, taking in the tall, dark man dressed all in black. He pulled a wicked-looking dagger more than a foot long from a sheath at his waist; the metal was dark, some alloy that didn't reflect the light as a steel blade would, making it seem to appear from and disappear into the shadows.

When she could see it clearly, she wondered at the design; it was like nothing she'd seen before: flat on one edge, slightly curved on the other. The thing had to be heavy, and yet he was hefting it as if he held a butter knife. *Of course, he is six feet five, at least.* She backpedaled, expecting to hit the wall of the blonde's chest.

She didn't. Denise glanced over her shoulder and felt her breathing hitch. He was gone, disappeared without a sound, though he had to have traveled more than fifteen yards to leave the alley. Denise turned back to question tall, dark, and dangerous, but he had disappeared as well — silently. She ran a shaking hand over her forehead.

"People do not just disappear," she assured herself. Denise turned her light to the ground, scowling that the blond had been on the cobblestones. She spun back to the other man's position, sighing in relief at the boot prints in the dirt break. "Okay. They do exist," she decided.

The blond would be long gone. He'd been on the street side of the alley and could have turned any direction at the other end. The dark man was on the parking lot side. Unless he could run the hundred in ten flat while hauling that hardware, she'd see him.

Denise vaulted toward the lot, stilling and turning back at a sound behind her. Dust danced in the beam of her flashlight. Her hand shook. Denise sank to her knees and touched the cool soil where the boot prints had been.

* * * *

Polero smiled, watching the policewoman examining the alley feverishly. She was special in many ways: intuitive, determined, and intelligent. Her confusion and denial of the truth was the best part of the game so far.

When Jörg had ordered him to play this game with the Lord *Jäger* and his brothers, Polero hadn't been pleased. After the disaster of trying to take Lord *Jäger's* daughter and his near miss with Stephen's young bride, Polero didn't want to be within two states of those Warriors, but Jörg was his master, and Jörg's word was law.

Sometimes, Polero cursed his moments of weakness: the moment when he'd entered Jörg's service and the moment he'd accepted this damned half-life to escape death at the hands of Jörg's enemies. Polero hadn't realized how the loss of kind emotions would eat at him, as the centuries fell away.

He smiled at the policewoman again. *Denise.* There were only two things that made Polero feel truly alive now, and pretty Denise could provide him with both. And she would provide...willingly.

Polero dematerialized and drifted toward her. Denise wanted answers. Her thirst for that knowledge would be her undoing. In nearly three centuries walking the Earth, Polero hadn't found a woman who wasn't consumed by curiosity.

He took shape behind her, watching her sift the dirt through her fingers, listening to her internal list of possible explanations, none of them remotely close to the truth.

"I take it he didn't harm you," he noted quietly.

Denise jumped to her feet, laying a slap across his cheek, her heart pounding and her mind a riot of thoughts tumbling over each other. She blushed in the sudden realization that she had lost her composure. It wasn't something she was accustomed to doing.

"Y — You," she stammered. "Who t — the hell are you?"

Polero smiled. Being able to tell her was half the fun of this game. "Antoñio Pablo Polero, at your service." He executed a formal bow for show.

She took a step back, her eyes widening in surprise. Denise motioned toward the parking lot. "And Conan?" she asked lightly.

Ah yes. Stephen of Jäger. "An adversary."

Denise raised an eyebrow, regaining a bit of her composure. "You must be good at dodging."

"I have means of protecting myself."

"Where did you disappear to?" she demanded.

"I was leading him away from you. I knew he'd rather hurt me than you."

She didn't miss a beat. "Why would he want to hurt you?"

"Because I am a threat to his safety, and you are not."

Denise laughed harshly.

Polero started speaking before she could. "Don't laugh, Officer Roberts. The police cannot touch him. It isn't safe for you here. You should leave...*before* he comes back."

She paled.

He nodded. "Yes. I know exactly who you are, Denise."

Polero turned toward the street, counting the seconds it took her to recover enough to try and stop him. She moved on five, surging toward his back, her quick steps eating up the distance between them.

"You're withholding information in a police investigation, Mr. Polero," she growled. "You're not leaving here until you give me those answers. Or would you rather leave in cuffs?"

Polero stopped and shot her a look of amazement. Denise was a formidable woman. And a surprising one; even he hadn't expected her to consider arresting him without some sort of aid in the task.

He crossed his arms over his chest. "Your superiors won't believe what I have to say," he warned her.

"What I've seen so far defies logic. How much worse can it get?"

"Don't ask what you don't want to know."

Denise strode to him. "I do want to know. That's why I'm here."

Polero shivered. *Stephen is back.* The youngest of the *Jäger* brothers had always left a slight tremor in his wake when ghosting that his brothers weren't sloppy enough to leave. That tremor had saved Polero's life more than once.

He launched toward her, covering Denise's mouth before she could scream. He ghosted them both. "Shhh," he soothed her. Polero scooped his crucifix from beneath his t-shirt and held it between them, as if it had meaning.

She stilled, looking at the couple walking through the alley in confusion. Denise furrowed her brow, her mind desperately trying to analyze why they weren't reacting to her obvious distress.

He nuzzled against her ear, closing his eyes to the sweet smell of her fear. "Shhh," he reminded her, taking his hand away slowly. "He's back."

Denise's eyes darted back and forth, searching for some sign of Stephen. "I don't see him," she whispered.

"You will not, unless he wishes to be seen."

As Polero expected, Stephen heard at least part of their exchange, but still he didn't allow himself to be seen.

Stephen's challenge came from nothingness. "I know it's you Polero, you baby-stealing monster. Using the woman as a shield won't last long. Either you'll move or reveal yourself. I have all night."

Denise's eyes widened, and her fear intensified, but with it came her innate curiosity.

Polero pressed a kiss to her ear, speaking in a voice too low for Stephen to hear. "I will lead him away again, but you must promise to leave immediately."

She nodded slowly.

"If you wish to know the truth, meet me at the attack site preceding this one three nights from now."

She nodded again, her heart pounding in excitement.

He kissed her ear again, smiling at how easily she was falling into his trap. Polero pushed away from her and released his ghosting, relinquishing the game...for the moment. "Come for me, cursed one," he spat, as he turned and ran.

It was a chance. The Cursed Warrior could choose to stay behind, to educate the woman in what Polero was, but the odds were against it. Most Warriors would choose to leave an uninjured victim that had not been used for feeding behind for the possibility of making a kill.

Polero laughed aloud, laying on speed as he left Denise's line of sight. Stephen was close behind, as Polero knew he would be. Any Warrior would follow. To revenge themselves for the loss of the Lord *Jäger*'s wife and child, any Warrior of *Jäger* would pursue Polero to both their deaths.

Chapter Twenty-six

May 4th, 1987

Polero materialized behind Denise, running his fingertips down her arm slowly. Denise turned to him, her hand fisted on the grip of her handgun. She met his eyes, relaxing with a sigh.

"Mr. Polero," she greeted him stiffly.

He chuckled. "Antoñio will be fine," he assured her. "Shall we go, Denise?"

She backed off a step, her eyes narrowing. "Go? Where are we going?"

Why didn't I tell Adam and get backup?

Because, he would have had a cow about the first night out, let alone this one!

Well, what would he say to you going somewhere with —

"You want to know the truth?" he interrupted her internal argument, dizzy in the strength of her mind. It had been a long time since he'd encountered a human whose thoughts were projected so clearly. She would be all the more enjoyable because of it, though there was the risk that she would be able to fight his control, in the end. He bit back a smile at that; what challenge could be found in a game with no risk involved?

"Of course." *Adam is going to kill me.*

"Then come with me."

She hesitated. "Tell me why that man called you a baby stealer first."

Polero affected a sigh. "It's not what it sounds like."

"You took his child," she accused.

"No. His master took my brother's wife. He nearly killed Jörg to take her. I was trying to take Anna — I was trying to take her and her child back."

He paused for effect — and to push back the true anguish of his failure. Anguish wasn't a kind emotion; as such, he was more than capable of feeling it. Anguish and regret...would that men never knew them. No, there were too many beasts like that already, insane men who were without kind emotions in their human lives, so they didn't possess them as beasts.

He continued. "She's dead, and her daughter will never know her. I failed utterly."

"How utterly?" she asked suspiciously.

"There's a reason they want my brother and me dead. If I ever get the chance again..."

She shuddered.

"Do you want to know the truth?" he asked.

Denise nodded. She didn't pull away when he wrapped an arm around her hip and led her along the nearly-deserted streets. This was the most amusement Polero had gotten from the game thus far, giving Denise just enough of the truth and avoiding just enough lies to make it more interesting.

He'd chosen this site for a reason. One of his holes was close to this alley. Polero had surrounded himself with books and icons over the centuries, copying or stealing texts to keep a stable library, even on those rare occasions when Warriors discovered one of his holes. Tonight, Polero would sacrifice one to his pleasures.

She entered his hole, an apartment over an abandoned clothing store, willingly and looked around at some of his treasures. He'd collected both Christian and Warrior icons: artful recreations of the crucifix, religious robes, a few amulets stolen from dead Warriors, and even a sacred weapon. He'd copied religious texts from both religions, some calligraphed meticulously and some rewritten to suit his own needs.

Denise ran her fingers over a twentieth century Roman Catholic collar. "You mugged a priest?" she joked.

Polero chuckled, dragging off his sweatshirt in favor of the muscle shirt beneath. "I was a priest," he answered honestly. *Not in this time, but I was once of the order.*

She turned to him in surprise, running her eyes from his jean-clad legs to the ladder of muscles up his abdomen to the tattoo of the cross on the front of his right shoulder. "You?"

He nodded. "Surprised?"

"To say the least," she admitted. "What happened? You *were* a priest."

Polero shrugged. "The organized religions aren't into the hunting of evil, as they once were."

"Evil?" she asked dubiously.

He strode toward her, pressing lightly to her body as he reached for one of the volumes on the shelves at her back. Polero kept his gaze locked on hers as he brought the book down for her.

Denise gasped as he hardened, and she snapped a look down between their bodies.

Polero backed away, biting back a smile at her interest. "Natural reaction to a beautiful woman," he confided, opening the book and feigning interest.

Denise blushed. "But...you're a priest," she protested weakly.

"No, I *was* a priest. That was a long time ago, and even priests react to a beautiful woman."

Polero had certainly reacted to Yzabeau. Whether it was Jörg's possession of her or something nameless about her, Polero could never say. Regana's souls had always captured men, Warriors, and beasts alike.

"Beautiful?" she scoffed.

He moved his gaze over the bun of auburn hair and dark eyes to the ample breasts, half-disguised beneath her jacket, to the outline of her mound through her jeans. "Yes," he answered bluntly.

She blushed deeper and cleared her throat. "Answers," she reminded him.

Nevertheless, she was pleased that he thought her beautiful, and she wished another man thought so —

Adam.

The man must be a fool.

Polero looked back to the book. "Of course."

Denise was the type of woman Polero enjoyed. It wasn't so unusual that she didn't find herself attractive, though. Americans of the present day leaned toward willowy females, not a woman with lush curves and breasts a man could become lost in.

He sat on the couch, in the circle of light cast from the lamp he'd left burning, and waved for her to join him. She sat on the opposite end, and Polero scowled at her.

"You speak Latin?" he asked bluntly.

She shook her head, easing next to his body.

Denise took the book from his hands, gasping at the illumination on the first page. Polero swallowed a laugh. He'd chosen this volume purposefully. Long ago, Polero had designed this seduction piece for nights like this. When he surrendered this hole to the Warriors, it would be the one treasure he carried away with him.

Her breathing was ragged as she surveyed the illumination of two beasts sharing a woman while they fed from her, the victim's face a study in exquisite pleasure.

Polero remembered the night in question well. Every illumination in the book was a recreation of some sensual pleasure in the years since he'd abandoned the church to follow the more powerful gods of the beasts. Having the trappings of his former life around him served only two purposes. It was once a comfort, and it put humans at ease to associate him with the position he'd once believed in.

"They're..." Denise's eyes went wide in understanding. *He's cracked.* "But that's not —"

"Real? I assure you, the beasts are very real. What you see there is a new beast awakening after his change."

"A what?"

"A turned. A beast made by one of the elders, a master. Some of the elders would just fuck the new recruit while he fed, but that is not as striking a picture as them sharing the turned's first victim." *And Jörg is not like other elders.*

Polero hardened further at the memory of taking Jörg's blood, Polero's beast demanding other pleasures.

Jörg ordered him to close his feeding site, looking at Polero's engorged member in something resembling pity, then ordering him not to make a move. It was maddening, feeling the burn to climax and not having the leave of his master to seek it. For a long moment, Polero believed it was some sort of punishment Jörg was handing down, though he couldn't think clearly enough to reason why Jörg would want to punish him that night.

Polero watched as Jörg drew the woman between them, the elder's hands teasing the woman sexually as he began to take her blood. She cried out in ecstasy as Jörg pushed his cock into the depths of her ass.

Polero's fangs itched to taste the blood he smelled. He stroked his cock, needing to taste other depths. Perhaps Jörg would give the woman to Polero when he tired of her, but the waiting would drive him mad, seeing and smelling their blood and sex.

Jörg closed his feeding site and met Polero's eyes. "Join me," he invited. "Feed your beast, but feed it slowly. Feed it gently."

From that day to this, Polero had never felt anything as sublime as sharing that woman with Jörg: kissing her as they thrust inside her, sharing her blood, taking her body in every conceivable combination that night. He and Jörg had shared women on many occasions, but there was something unforgettable in that first time, a dark rush of power, the fellowship of blood...before it became jaded and forgotten as every other kind emotion had been.

Polero forced his mind back to the subject at hand.

Denise flipped the page, swallowing hard at the illumination of him taking a woman over a ship's railing.

Ah, yes. The captain's mistress had been luscious and willing. The captain had been a bought human. He'd had her himself after Polero was done with her, though for her comfort, she had no memory of anyone but her lover.

Polero forced his fangs back as Denise's body prepared for him. Given enough time with her, he could fully sate every one of the fantasies her fertile mind was concocting at the book's suggestion. But they wouldn't have that much time together.

She turned another page.

The minister's daughter he'd deflowered, his tongue taunting her spasming body as he drank from her engorged tissues.

She bit her lower lip, moving her thighs against each other restlessly. Denise turned another page, her breath hitching at the next scene.

Oh, yes. She likes that. Polero smiled, morphing his member larger as he had that night.

She'd been a streetwalker he'd picked up for his amusement. Polero had enjoyed watching her mouth spread wide around his increased size.

"No one is that big," Denise whispered.

Polero chuckled. "Really?" he drawled.

Denise glanced at his face, then panned her gaze down to his lap. She darkened and looked at the book again, running a hand through her hair nervously. *He was a priest? What a waste!*

"These beasts," she choked out. "Vampires — Tell me about them. What does all of this say? Besides their love for screwing anything that moves, of course."

She was sweating, shaking. Her body needed completion almost as much as his own did, but she directed him back to the subject at hand. *Self-preservation. She's afraid to take what she wants.*

He reached across her body, pointing to the text. Denise's eyes strayed to the inked drawing often.

Polero snuggled closer to her as he eased his fingertip across the page.

"It talks about the limitations of the beasts, the ways to kill them."

"How?" she asked urgently.

"There are icons."

"Crosses? Holy water?"

Polero laughed harshly. "No. I believed the old stories, too. Nothing so mundane works against them. I learned that the hard way."

Denise searched her eyes over him frantically, locking on the marks Jörg had left on him when Polero had entered into service with him. She touched the marks, rising to her knees. Her breath was hot on his skin. "Do you remember this?"

"Yes." Jörg had wanted him to remember every searing second of that feeding without the pleasure he typically gave his bought humans. It was a punishment, a warning of what cruelty he was capable of if Polero ever crossed him again.

"Why did they leave your memory? That is how they're taking away memories. Right?" She touched the marks gently, as if he would break.

"Yes. The beasts reorder or blank memories to hide their existence." He cupped her hip. "I imagine the one who did this was playing with me. I was a priest, after all."

"You tried to use the usual means to stop a vampire?"

"He walked into my church, killed a bishop, and nearly killed me. Nothing worked against him. It was years later when I found these texts, when I learned that my fellow clerics knew much more than they let on." *Ah, Jonrie. Working for the enemy all that time.*

"You confronted them?"

Polero rubbed her lower back. "Yes. It's amazing the things the church doesn't admit to."

"So you set out to do this on your own?" she asked in awe.

"Armed with some texts I'd liberated from the church and a few loyal men with the same beliefs."

"Your brother?" Denise asked, sitting down and meeting his gaze.

"Yes. Jörg and I have always been in this together." Polero smiled sadly at that. *Little comfort that is. I cannot even find comfort in our connection. I cannot find comfort in anything but what Denise can offer.*

"Why?" she mused, her mind abruptly elsewhere, on a track and moving so fast, Polero had trouble following her.

"Why what?" He ran his hands further up her back, easing the tension in her muscles.

Denise sighed.

So typical. My past always makes them feel so safe.

"Why is the vampire doing this? I mean, he has to eat, but it's more than that. He wants these victims found. What is his reason?"

"It's a game," he confided.

"A game? What kind of game?"

"Look at it from the culprit's mindset. This brings attention the pursuer does not want or need." *At a time when he needs the distraction least.* "It flaunts the ability of anyone to stop him. It sends pursuers scrambling to end it."

She nodded. "He's amusing himself."

Not yet. "They live to appease their hungers and still their longings. They want endlessly."

"Blood," she mused.

Polero picked up the book from where she dropped it between them and flipped another page, turning it for her to see. "And other pleasures."

Denise looked at the book for a long moment, barely breathing in her excitement. She blushed deeply.

"What is it?" he asked, though Polero knew well enough that she wanted him desperately. She'd resigned herself to the fact that she could never tell her co-workers about all of this. What Denise learned now was for her own avid thirst for knowledge.

"W — who wrote and illustrated this book?" she stammered.

"Priests," he offered in half-truth. "Working from the actual accounts of copulation of beasts with human women."

"They're drawn — They all seem to be enjoying themselves."

"That surprises you?" he asked.

"Yes," she practically shouted. "They... And they drink blood, and...and —"

He smiled at her unsettled mind. "Ah. I see. The beasts feed off of emotion almost as much as they feed off of blood. They don't feel kind emotions of their own."

"They want to make the woman happy to experience the rush of her emotions?"

"Absolutely."

And much more.

318

"The beast demands satisfaction sexually while it feeds, satisfaction for the beast. Any powerful emotions mollify the beast. A woman's terror in rape is enough. The stillness — The peace in feeling her pleasure is for the tattered remains of the man, not for the beast. One who forgets the pleasure and peace to be had for the man should be exterminated." Jörg had taught Polero that on the night he turned.

Denise fingered the illumination, staring at it again. "There was no sign of sexual assault," she noted.

Polero grimaced. "You're not listening. It wouldn't be an assault."

"You're saying the women willingly screwed a beast?"

"If you want a man badly enough, don't you?" he prodded.

She darkened further and cleared her throat. "How would he convince them so quickly?"

He smiled. "A being that reads minds? He knows exactly how to touch her, exactly what to say to her."

"It can't be that easy."

Polero rolled his eyes at that. It wasn't the easiest thing Jörg had ever charged him with doing. "He picks his victims carefully."

He dragged a finger up her arm. Yes, Polero had chosen Denise very carefully.

"And the man?" she asked slowly.

"He's not into men. That was a simple feeding."

"Why vary the typical plan?"

He scowled. "Irritation. Pure and simple. Days without finding a suitable woman. The beast got hungry."

She nodded and leaned back, flipping through the book. Polero counted the pages, mentally picturing each illumination as she went, gauging its effect on her. Gods, but her scent was driving him mad.

"What is it like?" she asked suddenly.

"Like?"

Polero traced the outer seam of her jeans from knee to hip. Though she pretended not to notice, he knew she was aware of every touch, reveling in it, wanting it.

"Tracking them. Dodging them."

"Lonely." Loneliness wasn't a kind emotion. Loneliness was something Polero felt every day of his life.

Denise turned the page again, and Polero bit back a chuckle. The illumination was so close to their current situation that Polero knew she would be affected. Her perusal of the book was giving him a very clear picture of what would excite her.

"You don't interact with other people much," she guessed. "Not even your brother."

"He's mourning," Polero excused Jörg immediately.

Until he claimed his mate, Jörg would always mourn them. *No. He mourns the lost souls even as he revels in the one he holds. There is no peace for Jörg.*

"You've never married?"

"No. I have never been blessed with something so precious," he decided bitterly. From priest to bought human to damned beast, there was never an appropriate time to marry.

Her hand touched his thigh and lingered, brushing over the muscles, taut in his restraint. She started to pull back, but Polero covered her hand with his.

Denise met his gaze and moved her hand beneath the cover of his, toward his inner thigh and up to his crotch. He matched her movements, encouraging her.

She wanted to seduce him. Denise wanted to be bold. That was the fun of this game. He'd known when he'd chosen her that Denise would pursue given the chance to do so.

He tensed as her hand covered his aching length. She stilled, uncertain.

"Don't stop," he gasped. Polero tipped his hips beneath her.

Denise traced the bulge breathlessly. "So big," she whispered.

Taste it, he begged silently, restraining the mad urge to coerce her. *Nothing the Warriors can see until it's too late,* he reminded himself.

Polero moved his free hand to the space between her slightly-parted legs, skating his fingertips over her damp jeans, over the heat he'd created in her. His hunger spiked at that, at her excitement and the blood rushing in her veins.

"The hungers of the beast are formidable. He who cannot order his beast doesn't deserve to live another day."

Denise pushed up on her knees and brought her lips to his, tentatively, questioning Polero silently. He captured her mouth, stroking her more purposefully, letting her feel his hunger.

She did feel it. Warriors believed there were few human sensitives, but Polero secretly believed that every woman was one, to some extent. They all felt the darkness of the beast. Some were drawn to it. Some were repelled by it. Those who were drawn to it required no coercion to make them hunger to taste the darkness.

Denise hungered for it, and the hunger made women behave in unbelievable ways. Denise pulled up at his shirt, and Polero released her long enough to allow her to pull it off.

Strictly speaking, clothing wasn't a necessity for Polero. He could project the illusion of clothing right down to the feel of the fabric against his own skin and the skin of anyone who touched him. He certainly didn't need them to shield his body from the elements. Even in a solid form, the elements didn't touch him, and dematerialized, he was impervious even to attack.

But Polero preferred clothing. He was one of the highest level turned there was. Elders and others like himself were capable of dematerializing solid, inanimate objects worn or carried on their bodies. The illusion of clothing was one of the few powers he possessed that Polero seldom used. He preferred the reality of true clothing, and he preferred feeling women remove them.

She kissed him, sinking into his hunger, matching his rising lust. Denise unbuttoned his jeans with a single pull. Polero groaned at the sensation. He loved the feel of the new jeans: acid-washed, relaxed fit, soft, and form fitting. Nothing, not even leather or silk, felt as good against his body.

Denise's mouth closed around the head of his aching cock. *Almost nothing feels better than jeans, but a woman's body tops the list.* She strained to take him in, and Polero wished he'd made himself smaller just to feel Denise take all of him. He smiled. She would take all of him very soon.

Polero dragged her shirt up her body and unhooked her bra, playing at the tips of her breasts. "I will be returning this favor," he promised her.

She met his eyes, peeling her jacket, shirt, and bra off as she drove him on, inviting Polero blatantly to use her body. He smiled, the predator raising its head and taking in her scent.

Polero wanted Denise more than he'd wanted a woman in years. She was a classic beauty. Her hips were made to carry sons that some lucky human man would give her. Her breasts were lush and full, capped with rose-colored nipples.

Only one thing was wrong. He reached out and pulled the clips from the bun, letting the heavy waves of auburn hair cascade over her shoulders.

"Now," he ordered. "I have to taste you."

Denise stood before him, unbuttoning her jeans and easing them down those wonderful hips. Polero took over as her curls appeared, sweeping her down onto the couch and stripping off her remaining clothing and shoes. Her gun thumped to the rug, forgotten by its owner.

He buried his tongue in the well of her honey, drawing her essence out and tasting her. Far from assuaging his hunger, it fueled him. Her musk and her cries made him ache for more.

The minister's daughter danced in his mind much as she had danced naked for Polero, begging him to possess her again. He could take Denise's blood now, drawing it from her as she shattered, her blood and climax mixing in his mouth, but the Warriors would be on him before he could find further pleasure with her.

Polero rose up over her, determined to feel his cock buried deep inside her.

Denise's eyes opened wide as the engorged head parted her. "No," she gasped.

He ground his teeth, tapping down his frustration. If she told him to stop now, he'd use coercion. He'd feed. Polero would taste her climax any way he had to. "Yes," he countered urgently.

Denise's hand circled him. "Let me get on top." She didn't plead for what she wanted. She ordered what she needed from him.

Polero smiled, visions of Denise stolen from her mind making him pulse in anticipation. He eased off of her and sat on the couch by her feet, stroking his length in invitation. "Yes," he growled his agreement.

She sat beside him, dropping to encase him in her mouth one last time and releasing him before Polero could protest. Denise placed a hand on his shoulder and swung her leg over him.

He guided his cock, still wet and tingling from her mouth, between the slick outer lips of her sex. Denise lowered herself, sheathing his increased size, inch by torturous inch.

"Yes," he hissed. "Take me. Take all of me." His hands tightened on her hips as Denise settled in his lap, taking him to the root.

She started moving over him, taking what she needed from him, her body and mind a riot. Polero teased at her breasts, guiding her over his length faster, pounding hard into her.

Denise was close, ready to plunge over the edge. It was time. Polero nuzzled her throat, allowing his fangs to extend as she threw her head back.

"Why?" she whispered.

"Why what?"

"Why one puncture? Why not two?"

He kissed at the artery, feeling the pulse of blood to her brain speed. "He's a turned. Long before his master turned him, they went head to head, and one of his eyeteeth was broken in the exchange. It extends, but it isn't sharp enough or long enough to pierce flesh."

Denise sighed as she wrapped her fingers in the waves of his hair. "How do you know?"

"I was there."

Polero sank his single good fang into her, shuddering as the pain drove her over. Denise screamed in ecstasy, her muddled mind trying to piece together what he was doing to her. Her hands fisted in his hair, and her body clenched rhythmically on his length.

He suckled at her, drinking deeply of both her blood and emotions, wrapping her at last in the pleasure he could give her while he fed. He was a master at this, at gauging how much pain a woman would bear in orgasm before he had to trick her mind into finding his feeding a joy.

Polero pulled back as he climaxed, filling Denise with his sterile fluids, the peace he came to associate with sex, blood, and death washing over him. His beast was sated, though the smell of her blood rushing over her chest called to him, and Polero resumed his feeding. The spilled slick teased at their bodies, as he took her in slow, sensuous strokes.

He spoke to her through their newly-forged link, needing to explain to her as he'd never explained to the others.

"Soon. I will clean you and dress you. I will leave you where you will get immediate medical care. I wish I could leave you this memory, but I cannot."

Denise moaned her protest, wanting to hold to this moment as they all did...until they weren't in the arms of the beast and wrapped in the alluring cloak of darkness. Few women pursued the game that far.

"You have earned a page in my book, Denise. You will forget this night, but I never will."

The game was all that was left to tickle his morbid sense of humor after all the centuries of living with his beast. Polero began his reordering of her memory with a heavy heart. Of all the women over the years, few made the game as amusing as Denise had.

Chapter Twenty-seven

Denise groaned, squeezing her eyes shut against the harsh light without opening them to it. She reached blindly for the light switch next to her bed with the other. The switch wasn't there. The wall was tile instead of wallpaper.

She opened her eyes a slit and furrowed her brow at the sight of the IV stand over her. The scent of antiseptic was heavy in the air. It was a hospital, but what the hell was she doing here? Denise fought for a clear memory, but her head ached in the effort — almost as much as her body ached.

"Finally," a voice growled at her.

Denise turned to it tenderly. "Adam?"

He nodded grimly. Her boss looked sleep-deprived. Dark circles shadowed his beautiful green eyes, and it looked like he hadn't had a shave recently.

"What the hell did you think you were doing?" he continued.

She closed her eyes, trying desperately to remember what she did to end up here. Denise wasn't a street cop. There was no reason that she should have been shot or beaten, though beaten didn't sound far from the truth by the feel of it.

"You didn't think to ask for backup? You didn't call me?"

"Backup?" she repeated.

"Backup. Something you were ordered to take along if you were going to do something this monumentally — You met a possible suspect alone," he hinted in irritation.

"What suspect? I would never —"

He held up her pocket brain, his eyes flashing in fury.

A pulse of sexual excitement coursed over her nerves. Denise pushed it away, disconcerted. "And?" she asked weakly.

"You tell me. It's your handwriting, and we retrieved it from your car."

"Adam, all I know is that my head hurts, my stomach is upset, every muscle and joint in my body aches, and you're yelling at me."

And all I can picture is you alone with me somewhere private. What the hell is wrong with me? She'd always fantasized about Adam, but it had never taken over her mind like this. Maybe her walls were down.

"You don't remember arranging to meet a Mr. Antoñio Pablo Polero?" he demanded, flipping the notebook open to a page three or four in.

"Who the hell is —"

"Six feet, two-ten, blond, curly, halfway down his neck, light blue eyes, slight accent, maybe Spanish...*with* a question mark," he snapped, his body trembling.

"Sounds cute," she quipped. "Sort of like you, except for the accent and your pretty green eyes. Where can I find this Adonis?"

Adam raised an eyebrow in surprise.

Denise ran a shaking hand over her forehead, swallowing down a wave of nausea. *Why did I say that? I am never going to live this one down.*

Adam shook his head, suddenly uncertain. "Denise... What day is it?"

She glanced at the sunlight streaming around the window blinds. "Daylight," she noted. "Saturday."

He paled. "What's the last thing you remember?"

Denise grimaced at the spike of pain thinking about it caused. "Punching out," she groaned. "I think. No. I had soft tacos for dinner," she continued hopefully. "Taco Bell... The one by —" She grimaced, the headache raging abruptly out of control.

"By? By where?"

"I don't know. I..." The pain spiked again. *Don't want to know.* She panted, waiting out the agony, praying it was over.

"Friday?" he asked urgently.

"Of course, Friday," she snapped. "Adam, what the hell is wrong with you?"

He sank into a chair next to the bed and extended his hand toward her, touching her cheek with a pained look. Adam turned his arm to offer his watch for her inspection. Denise looked at him in confusion.

"Read it," he ordered quietly.

She squinted at the digital numbers. "Eleven-twenty," she noted. "I don't —"

"The date."

"The — Have you lost your mind? I told you the date."

"The date," he insisted.

Denise shook her head, biting back a sick swirl. She locked her eyes on the watch again, her heart stuttering. "The fifth? Adam, please tell me your watch is fast," she managed weakly. "Otherwise, I've been unconscious a long damn time."

"You've been unconscious for thirteen hours, but you've lost four days."

"Then I did even worse than the civilians," she complained bitterly. *Oh, I will never live this down.*

"Not entirely."

"What do you mean?"

Adam took her hand, squeezing it and offering her a rakish smile. "You came back with two descriptions and a name for the clear description. At least we have somewhere to start. That's more than anyone else has given us."

Denise nodded. "If it does us any good."

He stroked her knuckles, an almost unconscious move. "What do you mean?"

"Just a feeling that someone is playing games with us."

His smile disappeared. "What makes you say that?"

"I have no idea." She blushed. "I just...know it."

Adam nodded grimly. "That was why you were requested. Wasn't it?"

"Yes," she admitted. "Yes, it was."

Chapter Twenty-eight

Playing Games II: Blackout

May 10th, 1987

Denise straightened her spine, forcing her breathing to remain slow and steady as the room fell silent around her. She wouldn't accept their pity. She'd meet their eyes steadily when they wanted the simplicity of looking away from her.

"You don't have to do this," Adam whispered. "You don't have to see this."

"I do. I have to know." Ten days earlier, her life had come to a screeching turn, one that she could neither remember nor explain. If the answers were here, she wouldn't leave until she had them.

"It's only been four days since you were released from the hospital. You can see the videos later and —"

"I'm fine...a little weak but strong enough for this."

He nodded and handed her a pair of latex gloves. Denise pulled them on and ambled along the shelves, touching antique books and religious icons, trying to fathom the mind that would surround itself with these things, a mind she supposedly touched in those four lost days.

"Some of these things are priceless," Det. Ross said, examining what appeared to be a jewel-encrusted, golden Celtic cross in awe.

She fingered an etched disc hung on a frayed loop of silk string. It was a strange design, not unlike and old bit of heraldry, crossed swords with a howling wolf head above. She brushed her fingertips over the faded word beneath. "*Schwertträger*," she read.

"Sword bearer," Sgt. Peters stated without looking up from the book in his hand.

She turned to him. "What did you say?"

Peters darkened and didn't quite meet her gaze. "That's what it means. I had someone check. I mean... It's one of those things that's not like the others, so — It will take us months or even years to translate all of this. We're dealing with at least ten languages here, some of them dead languages."

"Oh. I'll keep that in mind. What language is this?" She pointed to the disc.

"German."

"Thanks."

He nodded and turned back to the shelf, studying a green stole embroidered with black a little too intently.

Denise moved on, acting unaffected when she wanted to scream. When she'd woken in the hospital, she'd been afraid she'd never live down the laughter of the other officers. She'd been wrong, and the truth was worse.

The guys weren't laughing. They were terrified. Whoever their maniacs were, they weren't afraid to take down a cop.

Still, Denise had done the impossible, which only seemed to heighten their unease. She may have been found, blood weak and near death at the ER doors of Central, but she'd come away with descriptions on two suspects and a name for one scribbled in her pocket brain, though admittedly she had no memory of either of them. The information had netted them nothing so far, but it was more than any of the other victims had come away with.

Officially, Denise was still on medical leave. Unofficially... *Adam would have to handcuff me to the bed to keep me away.*

That was an image she didn't need. She pushed it away and resumed her personal tirade.

Memories or no, I have to see this.

She scrunched her nose at the rancid smell emanating from the far reaches of the room beyond the rows of shelves. That was what brought them here, the smell that convinced the building's owner to call the police in to investigate the supposedly-abandoned site. It hadn't taken her brothers in blue long to identify the blood as hers, and Denise had insisted on visiting the scene with Adam.

There's no time like the present. She turned and strode toward the back of the room.

Without missing a beat, Peters and Ross blocked her path. Abrams joined them, shaking his pale face.

"You don't want to do this," Abrams assured her.

"Don't, Roberts," Ross agreed. "It's not pretty."

She managed a cold smile. "I didn't expect it to be. Let me pass."

Adam stepped to her shoulder. "It's okay. I'll go with her."

Denise ground her teeth at that, swallowing her protest that she didn't need a babysitter. Adam had agreed to let her come here only because of her badgering. He could ban her from the scene just as easily.

The officers parted, resuming their disconcerting avoidance that simply.

She looked at the opening, her heart pounding and her mouth dry. Her feet felt nailed to the floor, and she was acutely aware of the empty space where her gun would have lain had she not been on leave.

"You don't have to do this," Adam breathed at her shoulder.

He was right. Denise planted her feet, stifling the mad urge to turn and run the other direction. She didn't *want* to do this. "I have to," she whispered, her voice wooden.

Ross winced.

Denise didn't give herself time to reconsider. If she did that, she'd manage to talk herself out of this, and she would never forgive herself — or win back the respect of these men. She strode past her coworkers, her head held high.

The space behind the shelves was set up as a living room. She panned her gaze over the touchier floor lamp, a stack of books at its base, freezing at the sight of the sofa. Blood was soaked heavily into the green cushions, dime to half-dollar-sized droplets dotting the floor and a bloody handprint on the back cushions of the couch. Bile rose in her throat, and she swallowed it down painfully.

She didn't question that the print was her own, but that raised more questions than it answered. There hadn't been a drop on her when she was found. Of course, she could only assume the clothing she'd been found in was what she wore out to meet Polero, since she had no memory of dressing and no witnesses to what she'd been wearing that night.

Adam's hand closed on her shoulder, and his breath was rough.

"He bled me," she choked out. She'd known that, of course, but there seemed to be more blood spilled on the sofa than she'd expected to see. *Blood weak... How much blood did I lose?*

As if he read her mind, Adam answered her. "It's not as much as it looks like...not even as much as you lost, according to Wilks from forensics. It's not precise yet, of course, but they're fairly sure of that."

Her mind fought the idea that finding the site was a good thing. They'd never had a site to dig into before. Surely, something would come of this.

Denise pressed a hand to her forehead, noting the sweat coating her body numbly. The air suddenly seemed thick and hard to draw into her lungs.

She stared at the sofa, arousal beating at her nerves, her nipples coming to uncomfortable points against her bra. Heat radiated from the wound on her throat outward, akin to the feeling of hot breath swirling against her neck. She braced herself, dizzy in the unexpected response.

Her mind rebelled. A maniac had bled her here and dumped her at the hospital in what she knew was some sadistic game. What was there to be aroused about?

Her body ignored her mind's protestations, a disconcerting heat pooling at the apex of her thighs.

"Denise?"

Adam's voice wrapped around her, stoking the embers of excitement into a roaring conflagration. Phantom hands skated over her body, and she swallowed a groan of pleasure.

A flash of a memory crackled in her mind, a book in her hands though she couldn't read the page, the lamp burning brightly in the dark room. There was someone beside her.

Not here. There!

Denise shook off Adam's hand and vaulted toward the sofa. The smell assaulted her, and she pushed it away, standing with her calves pressed against the unstained portion, unwilling to sit there even to acclimate herself. "I sat here," she whispered.

She vaguely noticed that the other officers had put down the objects they held and congregated at the mouth of the isle between the first two shelves, waiting to see what would happen next.

"He..."

She turned her head, barely breathing. At first, there was nothing, just the room in its state of disrepair.

"Denise," Adam rasped.

Denise... The ghostly voice whispered in her mind, rich in a thick accent and — excitement?

The face floated before her, insubstantial as smoke. The entire room changed, growing darker, the far corners lost to shadows, the single beacon of light at her side...and him.

"Antoñio."

She met his eyes, light blue eyes the color of a summer sky, eyes that pleaded for something — or did they demand it? It was hard to reconcile that point.

His blond hair was wind-ruffled, and he was smiling. The tattoo of an ornate Maltese cross peeked from behind a black muscle shirt. Muscles, he had in abundance: washboard abs, strong arms and thighs that strained the seams on his faded jeans.

Everything about him was sinfully decadent. He was eye candy, but something about him screamed that one taste of him would be addictive and dangerous.

He laughed, and her eyes locked on the one imperfection. His left eye tooth had been broken at some point in the past.

Pain sliced through her mind, and Denise clasped her hands to her temples, whimpering, her balance deserting her.

"Denise!" Adam caught her, swearing profusely and supporting her against his chest. "I shouldn't have let you come."

"No," she pleaded, stumbling along as he turned her toward the shelves. "Paper. I need paper."

"Denise —"

"Now, Adam. While I still remember —" A new spike of pain assaulted her, and her knees buckled.

Adam lowered her to the floor with her back to one of the shelves. "We have to get you some help and —"

She grabbed the pocket brain from his jacket pocket, then fished for the pen stuffed deeper in. Denise wrote everything she could remember about the man's physical appearance. *Antoñio...* Her hands shook wildly, and more than once, she had to stop because the pain made thinking impossible.

At last, she handed the notebook to Adam, her breathing labored. She met his green eyes, abruptly drained.

Adam took the notes from her hand, staring at them in disbelief. "Abrams," he managed. "Get this information added to the file." He met her gaze as the other three officers poured over the new description. "Can you work with an artist tomorrow?"

Denise rubbed her aching forehead, nodding. "I think...I can," she gasped.

"Good. Then let's get you home."

Chapter Twenty-nine

Home. Denise looked at Adam out of the corner of her eye, watching guiltily as he washed their dinner dishes. Since she'd been released from the hospital, her home had been his, and he rarely let her lift a finger.

The first night, he'd claimed concern for her medical condition. After that, he'd argued that her attacker or attackers might come back for her while she was so weak, knowing she might remember more than she already had.

Adam wrapped his hand around the back of her neck as if checking for a fever. "Your headache gone?" he asked.

She nodded, her gaze straying to his bare chest.

"I still think we should have someone check you over."

"No. I'll be fine," she lied. In truth, every time she focused on the black hole that encompassed four days of her life, it felt as if her head would split in two. Dealing with the artist was likely to make her puke. Worse, nothing more had come of her attempts to remember the lost time.

"What is it?" he asked.

Denise shook her head hopelessly, stepping toward him and letting him pull her to his chest. She closed her eyes, greedily breathing in his scent. These moments were the calm in the howling hurricane of her life.

Adam massaged her neck, his breath stirring her hair. "What did he do?" he murmured. "Why does it hurt you to —"

"No," she pleaded, tipping her head back. "Please, don't talk about it anymore today."

For one agonizing minute, they stared at each other. Then his mouth closed over hers. Denise closed her eyes, giving herself up to the cascade of feeling that submarined her every time Adam touched her, nearly every time he looked at her.

It was like no first kiss she'd ever experienced. There was no hesitation, no exploration. It was purely carnal, dark and rich as Godiva chocolate, and all-consuming.

Adam pulled back, his breathing coming in sharp gasps. "Oh, God. What are we doing?"

"Do it again." She wrapped her hands around his neck and guided his mouth back down to hers.

The second kiss was no less involved. He pulled her against his body, nestling her to the rigid proof that he wanted her, despite his protestations.

Denise sighed into his mouth. She could have taken the time to argue with him that it wasn't what he thought. He wasn't taking advantage of her in a heightened state of emotion. She'd wanted him for at least the last year they'd worked together, moreso since she'd awoken in the hospital with Adam hovering over her. She didn't waste her breath explaining it when he wasn't actively refusing.

He pulled back again, every muscle in his body rigid. She opened her eyes, staring into the intense green of his. It couldn't stop here. Denise couldn't let it.

She started unbuttoning her shirt, and his gaze followed, his tongue darting out to wet his lips.

"This is going to complicate things at work," he grumbled, not taking his eyes off of her bra.

Denise shucked the shirt off of her shoulders. "Do you really care?"

Adam shook his head slowly, trailing his hands up her spine and unhooking her bra.

She peeled it away, feeling a wanton thrill at standing topless with him in her kitchen. "Adam?" she purred, her voice strange in her own ears.

He held her lightly to his body so that the tips of her breasts brushed his chest, still staring between them. "Yes?"

"I think we should go to bed."

"Definitely." But, he made no move to accomplish it. Adam pulled her closer to him, rolling his hips against her as if in amazement. "Now," he breathed. "Right now."

He turned Denise and crowded against her back all the way to her bedroom. His hands cupped her breasts, pinching and kneading the ample globes lightly until she ached for more. "Take off your jeans."

His voice was a growl that made her shiver in need. Denise spread her feet slightly, pressing back into his hips and forward into his hands as she opened the jeans and peeled them down onto her thighs. She paused, unable to go further while he held her this way.

She gasped as he slid his hands down the soft expanse of her stomach. One pushed her jeans further while the other skated down between her thighs, teasing at her seam, then dipping inside. Denise murmured protests as his fingers retreated.

Adam circled her, scanning her body slowly. "Take them off," he ordered again.

Denise considered her move for only a second, pushing away the nagging voice asking when she'd become so sexually bold. True, it wasn't at all like her. She'd always found her slightly-plump form an embarrassment, but Adam's blatant perusal made her feel sexy.

Adam was more than she'd ever hoped for in a man. He was worth seducing, if needs be, and she didn't believe in seducing men as a rule.

Moreover, Denise wanted him at the edges of control. *Out of control.* She wanted him to shed the careful patience he showed in the precinct house and show her the man beneath.

She released the knot of hair at the back of her head, letting the auburn tresses tumble down. Denise arched her back, pushing her breasts up and forward, her hair fanning over the back of her buttocks and thighs. At Adam's groan, she turned her back to him, folding herself and pushing the material to her ankles, exposing herself to him.

"Oh, yeah." The unmistakable sound of a zipper spurred her on.

Denise pulled one foot free of the denim and spread her legs further, kicking it free of her other foot. She placed her hands flat on the floor and cast a sly smile at Adam from between her legs. She'd always been flexible, and it was time she used it to her advantage.

His jaw was taut and his eyes slightly manic. One hand circled his length while the other rolled a condom down. His jeans lay crumpled at his feet.

Then he moved, stepping to her, grasping her hips in his hands, and thrusting inside her with a primal growl. Denise cried out, scrambling for balance and sighing in relief that his grip held her upright.

Adam slid his hands down, gripping her inner thighs and lifting slightly. He turned toward the bed, holding her off the floor, impaled on him. "Kneel," he gasped, though she didn't doubt that he gasped in pleasure and not in the exertion of lifting her.

He leaned forward, and she folded her legs onto the edge of the mattress, laying her cheek on her folded arms and opening herself to his resumed thrusts.

"Oh, yeah," he repeated, a sound of complete satisfaction.

Denise panted back her release, memorizing the sensations of every slide he made within her. Adam was fierce, driven; and she could almost taste his lust.

Disturbing images flirted at her consciousness and were shoved away. She didn't want to remember anything now. Adam was what she wanted...and she'd have him again. She'd taste him and seduce him into her body again.

She pushed back onto Adam, determined to force him over just so she could tease him up again. He growled a series of curses, his hands tightening on her hips and his length pistoning in and out of her.

Waves of delight lapped like an incoming warm tide up her body, taking more of her with each thrust. Denise screamed at the sensation of those waves crashing into foam and disbursing along her nerves.

Adam forced himself deep and flattened her beneath him across the mattress. His heat teased her through the latex, and he buried his face in her shoulder.

He laid a kiss on the join of her neck and shoulder. "He'll never touch you again," he vowed.

And, the memory exploded in her mind, nearly blinding her in its intensity.

The room she'd been attacked in loomed around her, dark and forbidding, as she'd seen it that afternoon. Antoñio was under her on the sofa...naked. She was riding him, enjoying the exquisite pleasure and pain of her orgasm.

Denise squeezed her lids shut at the spike of pain behind her eyes. Her climax quickening, she squirmed against Adam.

Some corner of her mind argued it. Not that it was true! Somehow... For some mad reason, she'd obviously screwed Antoñio Polero — and screwed her life completely in the bargain. But taking pleasure in it while she was having sex with Adam was too much.

He nuzzled her jaw aside, oblivious to her inner struggle. His next kiss was placed over the faint scar on her throat. "Never," he breathed.

Antoñio pulled back, his eye teeth lengthened into fangs, one flattened where the tooth was broken. Blood stained them, running in thick rivulets down his chin and splashing onto his chest as he exploded into her. The copper smell assaulted her, and she looked down at herself in a detached sort of understanding, at the blood pulsating down her body from her punctured jugular, pooling at their joined bodies and spilling over onto the green fabric beneath them. He pulled her toward him, the blood between them sensitizing her to every touch of his body. His mouth returned to her throat.

Adam groaned against her throat, still aroused. She jerked her neck away from his mouth with a sob of pain and disgust mixed.

He left her body abruptly, turning Denise into his arms. Adam touched her face, his eyes wide and frantic. "What? What did I —"

"Vampire," she whispered, her stomach rebelling at the image in her mind as much as in the sick headache remembering gave her.

"What?" he demanded.

She felt her pale cheeks darken slightly. If she told him the truth, he'd send her to the psych ward; he'd think she had cracked. She'd never have a chance with him. But how else could she explain it?

"His delusion," she forced out. "He's playing vampire. That's why there's less blood at the scene than I... He doesn't carry it away, Adam. He dr... Oh, God!"

Denise clamped a hand to her mouth and staggered to her feet, bolting to the bathroom. Adam was at her back with a cool cloth in hand in the blink of an eye, smoothing her hair and whispering his assurances that she would be all right. When she'd emptied her stomach, he helped her clean up and guided her back to the bed. She snuggled into his chest, reveling in the warmth and comfort he offered.

"How did he draw the blood?" he asked, correctly assuming she had the answer to that now.

"I...don't know." How could she ever explain it? That rubber room beckoned if she tried.

"How could he stomach it? It should make him as sick as —"

She groaned at the renewed mental image of his blood-soaked face, compounded by the sick pain in her head and the one in her stomach as her nipples tightened.

"Forget I asked that."

"Thanks. I don't really know. Practice, I guess."

Adam paled. "Not an image I needed."

"Me, either." She closed her eyes, exhaustion dragging her down.

He stroked his hands over her back, cradling her to his chest gently. "Denise?"

"Mmm hmm," she yawned.

"What did he do to...subdue you? Do you remember that?"

"No," she lied. "I have no idea." That was one thing she would never share with Adam. She couldn't. "I hope I never do."

Chapter Thirty

Playing Games III: Daybreak

May 16th, 1987

Corwyn sank into bed, groaned, and wrapped Laura in his arms.

"Another one?" she asked quietly. It had gotten to the point that Corwyn didn't tell her about the attacks, unless she asked him directly.

Of course, he hadn't started lying to her about it when she did ask. "This one was a police detective. Veriel's game is getting dangerous."

Laura's mouth went dry at the thought of it. "What will you do?"

He rubbed a hand over his eyes. "We have to offer her protection."

"A police officer?" Laura squeaked.

Corwyn sighed. "Is she any less worthy? I have a duty."

She couldn't argue that. His dedication to his duty was one of the things she loved about him. Still — "What if she turns you in?"

It was a damned miracle that none of the other victims had chosen to do it. With no memories of the attacks, she'd been terrified at least one would. This was the eleventh attack in four months. Had their luck run out?

It has to run out soon. "What if —"

Corwyn brushed a kiss over her lips, tracing soothing circles over their squirming daughter. "We disappear. In fifteen hundred years, we've had to disappear countless times."

"What does he hope to gain by this? Having Polero attack people? Erasing their memories?"

She shuddered at the memory of the first. There had been no doubt the young woman had been planned to perfection. Her hair had been the color of Laura's, and she'd been left outside the doors of the Sentcare Clinic Laura had been working at then. It had been a warning...or a scare tactic.

Corwyn seemed to consider that. "Either he's frustrated and wants to cause me trouble and annoyance..."

"Or?"

"Or he's trying to split our ranks."

Laura didn't ask if it would work. She'd overheard enough planning sessions to know it wouldn't. Even if every human in their range suffered for it, there would always be Warriors surrounding her.

She nodded solemnly. "So, you'll offer her protection and hope for the best," she hedged.

"This isn't an option plan, Doc. It's a matter of honor and duty."

She winced at the exhaustion in his voice. "I know it. I would never ask you to abandon that."

Corwyn settled his forehead against her shoulder. "But?"

Her heart ached. "No buts about it. I'll be ready to move in a hurry. When will you offer her protection?"

"As soon as she's unguarded. Her protectors... The police are taking this seriously. So far, she's never been left alone."

"Will Veriel..." She couldn't finish the thought aloud.

"If he or one of his does come back for her, we'll protect her."

Laura nodded, holding to Corwyn, trying not to tremble. If she did, he wouldn't miss it.

Veriel is winning. I'm more afraid than ever because the entire family is in danger instead of just me.

* * * *

May 17th, 1987

Denise groaned, settling into one of the hard plastic chairs in the hospital cafeteria. "What is the point of taking more blood from a person who's lost so much blood?" she complained.

"Tests," Adam shot back.

"Oh, yeah," she grumbled. "Damned medical vampires."

"Stay here. I'll get us some juice and food." His fingertips feathered along her cheek, a silent promise that he'd be touching her a lot more intimately when he got her home. Then he was gone, striding to the far end of the huge cafeteria.

Denise buried her face in her hands, rubbing at her temples. She was aware that she was shaking, but she was too tired to care that she looked weak.

I am weak.

It had been six days of sketch artists and line-ups...six days of red hot spikes in her skull every time she tried to fill in the huge gaps in her Swiss cheese memories. As she'd feared, they'd made no headway toward finding their psycho, despite the information she'd dredged up from her uncooperative mind.

And now these sadistic doctors were siphoning off more of her blood. "Damned vampires," she repeated.

Denise looked toward the serving line, hoping Adam was heading back with their dinners, but there seemed to be some back-up. At a loss for anything to keep her occupied and awake, she started people watching.

It was the usual crowd for a hospital cafeteria.

There were weary-looking visitors and a few robed patients, one hacking up a lung and dragging a portable oxygen bottle behind him.

A young mother sipped juice while she nursed a baby.

An officer from another precinct ate heartily, a sure sign that it had been a rough day for him.

The rest were hospital employees on their dinner breaks. One sat alone, a woman with coffee and cream skin, maybe in her mid-forties, her hair in a beautiful fall of braids and beads. She read a book, her nearly empty plate pushed aside.

Denise's gaze locked on a movement. The woman was dangling a medallion on a long chain that was still looped around her neck. The medallion rotated back and forth, stirring a memory. Denise rose, needing to see the disc closer.

The woman didn't seem to note her approach, and Denise had scooped the metal disc onto her palm before the other reacted.

"Do you need something?" she challenged.

"It's different," Denise breathed. Instead of crossed swords, it had crossed arrows over a bow. The word was different, too. "But still German." She recognized the ä symbol. "*Jäger* not *Schwertträger*." Her mind spinning, Denise reached into her pocket for a pen.

The woman wrenched the necklace away and slid it beneath her shirt, clearly rattled.

"Where did you get that?" Denise asked.

"It was a gift."

"From who?"

The woman stood, tucking the book under her arm. "That's none of your business." She hurried toward the hallway.

Denise followed, the rush of adrenaline reviving her. "I'm a police officer, and that medallion is —"

"None of your business," she repeated, turning her head away to hide her face.

That move bared her neck. Denise's heart stuttered at the sight of the twin ovals on the other woman's neck, and she pressed a hand to her own. The truth struck her mute for a moment.

"It had both fangs. There's more than one vampire."

They stopped in unison, the other woman paling several shades at that pronouncement. Hadn't she known there were more? Or was it something else?

Her wide eyes locked with Denise's.

"Where did you get that medallion?" She had to know.

"I can't tell you that."

"You're part of this. You're working for them," Denise accused, forcing her voice to even.

"The beasts? Hell, no." She seemed genuinely horrified by the thought of it.

"Beasts?"

"What you call vampires...beasts."

"Then why won't you tell me where you got the medallion?" she challenged.

The woman swallowed hard. "I can't."

"Don't make me arrest you."

"You can't," she gasped.

"I've seen one of those before, at the scene of an attack. If you won't tell me how it ties in, I'll hold you for withholding evidence in an investigation. It's your choice."

She backed off a step, seemingly torn. "An — an old boyfriend gave it to me...ten years ago or so."

"And you still wear it?" Denise didn't doubt that she was lying.

"I like it. There's no crime in that."

"Where did he get it?"

"I never asked." She pasted on a look of disbelief.

"What's his name? Where does he live?"

"Michael Brown. Last I heard, he returned home to San Diego."

Denise raised an eyebrow.

As she anticipated, the woman hurried on with more — probably fictitious — information. "His company sent him here for six months or so. He did installations of machines for production lines."

"What kind?"

She shrugged.

"What company?"

"It was ten years ago. I don't remember. It started with a V, I think."

It was time to test her theory. "Well, then...I guess you won't mind me borrowing your medallion for the length of the investigation."

Her hand closed on the disc through her blue smock. "No."

Denise stared her down. The woman's gaze shifted toward the windows; Denise followed her line of sight.

Sunset. Vampires hunt the night.

"It protects you," she guessed. But who would want to protect the victims? Why would they?

"I — I can't..." She bit her lower lip, seemingly tortured by something Denise couldn't name.

"It's okay, Jewel. I'll handle this."

Denise turned to the male voice, disconcerted that it was so close. People didn't sneak up on her. It was impossible to...she'd thought. A mild vertigo told her it had happened before. But when?

He was nearly six and a half feet of leather and black clothing, dark hair and eyes. His jaw was locked tight in anger...or maybe stress. He didn't look angry. There was something sad in his eyes, something she couldn't name.

Realization that he was the mysterious second man in the alley from her notes assaulted her. The memory was right on its heels, the dagger disappearing and reappearing in the darkness.

Her stomach roiled. The pain in her head turned her knees to jelly, and her eyes slid shut.

Hands closed on her arms, easing her to a stop, supporting her weight effortlessly.

"What is this?" the other woman demanded.

Denise wanted to fight, but her body had gone leaden, jerking spasmodically instead of heeding her commands. Memories coursed over her, sending fresh shards of agony through her, making breathing difficult.

He lifted Denise into his arms, and she tried to scream without success. A sob half-escaped her throat.

She was going to disappear, and Adam would never know what happened to her.

* * * *

Corwyn muttered a series of curses in understanding. "She needs an amulet. Now, Jewel. Then... You disappear to the manor. We'll relocate you, if we have to." But erasing her life here would be impossible. Short of taking her off the grid, this was going to be problematic.

The protected didn't question him. She led the way into the construction wing, opened one of the nearly finished rooms, and waved him inside. She was gone before the door swung shut.

He laid Detective Roberts on the floor, pulling out an amulet. He had it halfway around her neck when the door burst open.

"Hold it."

Corwyn peeled his attention from the trembling and jerking detective and to the man who'd been a second skin to her for nearly two weeks...her boss.

Adam Williams had his pistol drawn and leveled at Corwyn. His green eyes blazed in fury, and his muscles were tensed for a fight.

"What did you do to her?" he demanded.

Corwyn took a calming breath. "I didn't. Polero did." He knew from watching the news that she'd come away with the beast's name. Now he knew how. "Let me help her."

"Get away from her. If you touch her, I'll kill you."

"If I *don't* touch her, I can't stop this." Corwyn didn't opine that this could kill her over time. It had been centuries since it had happened. The current crop of seizure medications might be able to stop that eventuality.

Williams stared at Corwyn, challenging him. His gaze slid to the downed officer. "You can stop the pain?"

"If she'll accept the amulet and my protection —"

His hand shook; the weapon wavered slightly...then steadied. Williams shook his head silently.

Corwyn ground his teeth in frustration. "This isn't about who can protect her best," he insisted. Though he could protect Roberts from the beasts and Williams couldn't, he understood the officer's need to believe he could do something positive for her. "I can stop the pain. Let me. We can discuss this later."

"Can you return her memories? Can you help her fill in the blank spaces?"

He hesitated and then shook his head. Whether Polero had left whispers of memory to start the cascade effect or Roberts was a psychic capable of fighting the memory tampering, it was beyond his power to undo.

The best he could do was give Williams hope. "Is she a psychic?"

The officer gaped at him.

"If Detective Roberts is a psychic, she may eventually recover her memories. I can't say for certain."

"Without pain and nausea?" Williams asked for qualification.

Corwyn hesitated. "Without pain. What she might remember..." He shrugged, discomforted by the fact that he couldn't do more for her.

"I've seen it." He clenched his jaw shut, then nodded curtly. "Do it." He didn't move the gun.

"Do you mind?" Corwyn motioned to the pistol.

"Hell, yes, I mind! If you make one suspicious move, you're through."

Corwyn sighed. If he could ignore Roberts' needs, he'd disarm Williams now and fade away. He couldn't; they'd failed her. Duty demanded he try to set this right.

He settled the amulet around her neck and leaned over her. At the touch of the amulet, the intermittent jerking stopped. She lay, shivering and sweating.

Corwyn placed his hand beneath her head, uttering the *Zeremonie des Schutzeses* in Gaelic. He paused a moment, then pressed his lips to her forehead.

Roberts went still beneath him, her breathing smoothing.

As he expected, Williams' hand closed on the back of his jacket and dragged Corwyn off. He allowed the officer to do it in an attempt to avoid hurting him.

The pistol pressed to the back of his neck wasn't part of the original plan though, and Corwyn stiffened in surprise.

"Damn you," Williams growled. "That wasn't necessary."

Corwyn tipped his head back, noting the other man's confusion and fury. It was almost as if — Corwyn winced. This was a man protecting his woman, one he had a claim on.

Whether Williams believed him or not, he had to try and defuse this situation. "It was. The ceremony isn't complete without it. I'll never touch her again." *Unless her life depends on it.*

"You're damned right, you won't."

"You're not the same one," Roberts stated weakly. "It was a different one in the alley."

"There's more than one?" Williams asked.

Corwyn didn't answer. He'd get out of this any way he had to, if it came down to his family's safety.

"More of those vampire beast things, too," she replied.

"How many?"

She eased to sitting, breathing heavily. "I don't know. At least two of each."

"How many?" Williams barked.

Corwyn didn't doubt the question was aimed at him. "A lot."

"What's a lot?"

He shrugged. "Thousands worldwide."

"What is this? Some sort of cult?"

Corwyn looked from Williams to Roberts. "You know what the beasts are. You said it."

Roberts lost all remaining color.

"Denise?" Williams called out.

She slumped against the wall, her gaze locked on Corwyn.

He nodded in understanding. "You don't remember it all, do you?" He kept his voice gentle...soothing. He'd had a lot of practice at that, of late.

Her negative shake of the head was wobbly at best. "He was drinking it," she managed. "His face...chin...covered in..."

"That's one memory I wish I could take away from you," he admitted. "Do you remember his fangs?"

Roberts hesitated and then nodded.

"Denise!" Williams protested.

"I remember them," she replied. "I remember them...covered in blood, but I don't remember what came before that. Just sitting there...holding a book...talking about..." Her color deepened slightly, and her gaze slid away from Corwyn's. "Something."

The faint scent of arousal told Corwyn all he needed to know. He ground his teeth in understanding. She remembered something of the seduction, but she couldn't admit that to her man. Maybe a half truth would put her at ease.

"The beasts read human minds and use it to manipulate people to what they want." That much was true and likely applied to her situation.

Her head snapped up, and she stared at him.

Corwyn nodded. "They also possess something of coercion. When all else fails, they can force someone to do what they want." Polero hadn't used it on her, but Roberts had been abused enough. If believing she might have been forced helped her, Corwyn would let her believe it.

She didn't reply to that.

"This is crazy," Williams interjected. "You honestly expect me to believe that he Jedi mind tricked her into submission?"

"What other options do you have?" Corwyn replied calmly. "No alcohol. No drugs. No injuries."

"An inhalant. Something new that we don't know to look for. Something fast acting that breaks down quickly."

"When you find it, let me know," he quipped in return. "Look for whatever you want to, Williams. I wish it was that simple."

"How do you know my name? You've been spying on us?"

"Protecting her," Corwyn corrected. "I stayed close, but I haven't been spying. If I had, I would have known you two were involved and warned you before I laid that kiss on her forehead."

Roberts pressed a hand to her forehead and shot Williams a questioning look.

Corwyn answered before the other man could. "The amulet and blessing will protect you. As long as you wear the amulet, the beasts cannot track you and cannot touch you."

She nodded. "That's why she wouldn't let me take hers."

Williams shot a look at the door that said he fully intended to track Jewel down and question her.

"Whatever you have to ask, ask me," Corwyn invited.

"Who are you?"

"For now, I'd rather not share that."

Williams glared at him. "Did I say you had a choice?"

"But I do, whether you wish me to have one or not," he pointed out. "I protect a lot of people. They all depend on me for that safety." Corwyn looked at Roberts. "This is your choice. You can choose to be protected, or you can return that amulet now and go back to the pain you were in before it...and the danger of the beasts coming for you again."

She didn't hesitate. "Are you going to make not talking about what I know a condition of keeping it?"

Corwyn wanted to lie to her. "About my kind? Yes. About the beasts? You take a risk in exposing them, but I won't stop you from trying to do your job."

"Trying to?" Williams ground out from between clenched teeth.

"You won't find them, unless they want to be found. If you do find them, you won't be able to kill them or incarcerate them."

"So all you do is clean up the mess?" he challenged.

Corwyn managed a weak smile. "I said you couldn't do anything. I never said I couldn't."

"That's it. I believe we have a lot to discuss, vampire hunter."

Corwyn barely managed to stifle the shudder at hearing his name on Williams' lips. He ignored the officer and focused on Roberts. "The choice is yours, Roberts. You decide whether or not you want to keep the amulet."

* * * *

Denise took a calming breath. "You are the good guys. I'm sure of that."

"They are vigilantes, Denise," Adam complained.

She nodded grimly. "Do they do worse? Do they do worse than what I know about?"

The vampire hunter sighed. "Yes. They kill. Innocents, sometimes. They rape. They torture. They enslave some people. They make more of their kind."

Adam grumbled a curse.

"And you do something about that?"

He hesitated and then nodded. "Yes." It was solemn, a vow, if she'd ever heard one.

"And I can continue to investigate them? I can continue to give the police everything I have on them...as long as I don't expose you?"

"Denise!"

"Yes." He didn't remind her that it wouldn't do any good.

I told Adam it wouldn't do any good when I woke in the hospital. Nothing has changed there.

"Denise, we have a duty to take him in for questioning."

"If I have questions, you'll answer them?" she asked.

He tipped his head to her. "I will. As long as it doesn't endanger my kind or those I protect, you can ask anything you want to, and I'll answer it."

"I accept." At least she could do her job with the amulet. Without it, it was looking like permanent disability for her.

"Denise," Adam warned.

"Look on him as an informant from inside an organized crime ring," she dismissed his concerns.

"You want to trust someone whose name you don't even know?"

She considered that. Flashes of memories from the alley she'd met Antonio in came without pain. "Tell me something," she breathed.

"What?" the hunter and Adam said in unison.

"The other like you called Antoñio Polero a baby-stealing monster. What did he mean?"

"You never told me that," Adam complained.

"Just remembered it."

"Without the pain?" he asked excitedly.

"Yes." She panned her gaze to the vampire hunter, noting the misery in his expression. Suddenly, Denise wished she could take the question back.

"It was my baby he helped steal. My daughter." There was a gruff edge to his voice. "Trust me now?" That was a challenge.

She suspected he'd never gotten the child back, but asking him might push him too far. Beyond that, Denise didn't want to consider what the beasts might have done to a baby. "Yes. I do."

He offered a quick snap of his head. "Then I should go."

Williams glared at him. "I didn't say you could go anywhere."

The vampire hunter looked up at him, a weary sort of smile on his face. "I didn't say you had a choice."

In the next moment, Adam landed beside her, his gun clattered to the floor, and the hunter moved. Denise scanned the room for him, but he was gone.

"Vanished into thin air," she whispered. Fractured memories attested that she'd seen similar things before.

Adam grunted out a curse. "No wonder no one can catch them."

The door opened, and he became visible to Denise again. The hunter tipped his head. "We'll see each other again, Detectives. Decide what you want to ask." He stepped into the hall and out of sight.

Adam scrambled to his feet, leaving the gun on the floor. He stopped at the doorway, looking both ways in seeming shock. He pounded the flat of his hand on the door frame.

"He's gone again," she guessed.

"How does he do that trick?"

"Ask him when we see him again. The other one did that too...and the beasts."

He turned to stare at her.

"I'm getting more memories back, now that I can think again," she defended herself.

"Not that." He paused. "You really think we're going to see him again?"

"Yes. I do." As sure as she'd been that they would never catch the maniac that had attacked her and with no more solid facts to base it on.

Chapter Thirty-one

Adam pulled Denise into his arms, his mouth closing on hers. There was something hard and uncompromising in his kiss, something possessive. Denise wrapped her arms around him, urging him on.

His hand inched up her stomach beneath her shirt, to the already-aching swell of her breast. He turned the palm, then fisted it around the metal disc hanging between the globes.

They both stilled, Adam's mouth leaving hers, muscles tensing. Denise forced her eyes open, regarding Adam's tight-lipped consideration of the amulet in stark terror.

"Adam?" she managed to gasp.

"I hate it," she grumbled.

"The amulet?" Who cared what it looked like, if it worked? The hours since she'd been gifted it had been bliss, pain-free joy in the making.

"The fact that we need some psycho vampire hunter's help. The fucking thing's like magic. The minute it touched you, you started getting better."

The moment the vampire hunter touched me, I started getting better. She was sure that offended Adam more than the amulet. "Thank God," she quipped.

Adam's scowl remained unchanged. "If I didn't know how much pain you were in, I'd ask you to toss it."

Her heart stuttered in fear. "You don't intend to, do you."

He fumed so visibly she could taste it in the air. "No. I don't intend to."

"Perhaps you should, Denise."

Denise startled at the voice she knew too well, then gasped as Adam pushed her behind him and turned to face the intruder, pulling his weapon. A whimper escaped her throat at the sight of Antoñio Pablo Polero.

He lounged on the breakfast bar, seemingly unperturbed by the handgun pointed at him. "Perhaps you should consider removing it."

It keeps him from touching me. "Not a chance in hell."

He laughed, baring the fangs that she knew would grow longer when he fed. "That is one down side to erasing your memories." Antoñio raised a hand as if in demonstration of his frustration. "You don't remember how much you enjoyed it."

Her breathing went ragged in the certainty that he meant more than just him drinking her blood. *Please, don't let him tell Adam that.*

The vampire hunter said they can force people to do things. But would Adam believe that?

Adam's muscles clenched at the comment. "How did you get in here?"

There was no question what he meant by it. There was twenty-four hour surveillance on her building.

Visions of both the hunters and the beast appearing and disappearing assaulted her. "The same way the vampire hunter disappeared right before our eyes."

He laughed again and focused on her. "Oh, I have better tricks than that."

Before either of them could question it, he melted into a black mist and streamed toward them, circled them once, and took shape again on the couch. Adam turned, keeping Denise behind him, though she no longer believed that would work.

Adam's breathing went harsh, and he shook his head as if he believed he was drugged.

"Sure you won't remove that amulet?" Antoñio asked.

Denise shook her head, sure that her voice would fail her if she tried to speak.

"Well then...we'll have to do something about that." He stared at her. "Won't we?"

The hunter said he can't touch me. I'm immune from him. Aren't I?

Adam's head rocked back, and his hand opened, dropping his weapon to the floor.

Denise shook him lightly. "Adam? What's wrong?"

He turned on her, his eyes strangely empty.

She backpedaled, coming up against the dining room table hard. He followed, and she slapped his face, hoping to break whatever spell Antoñio had him under.

It didn't work. Adam grasped the amulet in his fist, and started to raise it over her head. Panicked, Denise grabbed the leather and held on tight, hoping he couldn't snap it and pull it through her fingers.

She was so busy fighting with him over it, Denise didn't realize Antoñio was moving, until he had Adam by the throat. Adam released the amulet, and she recoiled, her hip hitting the edge of the table hard.

His eyes cleared, and he struggled against Antoñio's hold. "What the fuck did you just do to me? How did you make me —"

Antoñio's fingers morphed into deadly-looking claws, and Adam went still, his eyes wide and terrified.

He stared at Denise, paling. "This answers a lot." It was a weak joke, at best.

Antoñio's fangs lengthened a bit. "Unfortunately, we have no time for answers. Forcing me to coerce you to action has drawn the Warriors to us."

Denise closed the amulet in her fist, praying they'd get here quickly.

"I don't lose well, Denise." He opened his mouth and let his fangs down fully.

Her heart stuttered. He was going to feed on Adam.

I can't let this happen. "No! I'll take off the amulet. Don't —"

"Don't you dare," Adam roared. "Don't even think it."

The sharpened fang slid into his neck, and Adam howled in agony. Denise launched toward them, aiming a punch for Antoñio's face.

The backlash up her arm sent her sprawling, her right arm tingling and aching, as if she'd struck her funny bone. Antoñio flew the opposite direction. Plaster crunched as the wall between the living room and kitchen caved in. Adam landed between them, and his hand went to the bite.

The beast pulled himself out of the hole in the wall and started toward Adam again. His expression said he'd kill Adam when he reached him.

I am not letting this happen. She scrambled to her feet and launched herself at him, ignoring Adam's protests.

The second clash was no less spectacular. Antoñio went over the breakfast bar, taking the dish drainer beside the sink with him. Glasses and plates shattered, while Denise was trying to pick herself up off the floor again.

The front door burst in, and a flash of black bolted past her. Antoñio shot the newcomer a fang-heavy smile and dissolved into the same fine mist.

The drawn weapon disappeared into the sheath at the vampire hunter's hip, and he turned to Adam. Denise gasped at the sight of the hunter she'd seen in the alley.

"Your men are coming. We have little time. Will you accept my protection?"

"Doesn't seem to have worked too well," Adam snapped back at him.

He jerked his head in Denise's direction. "It worked just fine for her." He met her gaze. "Get something to put pressure on the wound before he passes out."

She hurried to comply.

"Is that when I forget everything."

"With the link to you open and bleeding, he can still do that."

Denise came back with a hand towel and applied pressure to the bite that made Adam hiss in displeasure. "Sorry. Will the amulet stop the beast from messing with his mind?"

"No coercion. No reordering or erasing memories."

Adam scowled. "How the hell do I hide that thing?"

Taking it for permission, the hunter knelt next to him, looped the leather thong around a belt loop, secured it, and shoved the amulet down the side of Adam's jeans. "A lot of male protected do this," he explained.

"Do it."

The hunter wasted no time. He raced through the words, laid a quick kiss on Adam's temple, and sprinted into the open bedroom.

Two uniformed officers came in through the front door a heartbeat after he disappeared through the other door.

"Through there," Adam ordered, pointing the way to the hunter.

They tore off that direction.

Denise gaped at him.

His voice dropped to a whisper. "He'll disappear. Hide your amulet. Quickly. If they take it, we're sunk."

She pulled his hand to the towel and used the same trick the hunter had. Denise had no sooner hidden the amulet than the two uniforms came back.

"He must have gone out the window and down the fire escape," the older one informed them. He squatted next to Adam and started checking the bite. "Good thing this was a vein and not an artery, or you'd be dead meat. Better call in the EMTs." He moved away to do it, motioning for Denise to put pressure on it again.

"He was in here when you got home?" the other asked.

Denise looked at the broken door. "And we just waltzed into a trap through that?" she offered sarcastically. "What do you think? No, he was in the building somewhere, I'd guess."

The older broke off for a moment. "I better call in reinforcements. He may be in one of the apartments."

Adam shot her a look that announced he understood what she'd said to him in the hospital now. They could look all they wanted. The police would

never find Antoñio Pablo Polero or the hunters that
were after him.

Chapter Thirty-two

June 25th, 1987

Corwyn stilled halfway across the foyer, turning his head toward the sound of breaking glass in the kitchen. There was no sound of either censure or soothing, which would have indicated that one of the children had knocked a glass over. There was no sound of one of the women cleaning up the mess or swearing over having caused it.

His heart pounding at the silence, Corwyn headed for the kitchen.

Laura appeared in the doorway, her hand pressed to the side of her womb. She took small, measured breaths. Her gaze locked with his, and she nodded in answer to his unasked question.

Excitement coursed over his nerves. It took a moment to kick himself into gear. Laura was in labor, and it was early enough in the day that their daughter might be born while it was light out.

Corwyn strode to her and scooped Laura into his arms, murmuring his assurances that he was there for her. *As I should have been there for Anna.*

He shook that thought away and headed for their room. He was here for Laura. That was all that mattered.

"Corwyn?" Jan called out from the Warriors' wing.

He didn't pause. If Jan wanted to talk to them, she'd have to catch up. Corwyn marched into their room, kicked the door shut, and eased Laura onto the bed. Her water had broken, most likely the event that had caused her to break the glass.

"Okay, Doc. Nightgown?"

Laura nodded. "And towels." She grimaced. "And Jewel, I think."

Her expression said she was sorry they'd lost Michael. Jewel was a nurse practitioner, but Michael had been a doctor. The death of one of their precious doctors — even of natural causes, as they'd lost Michael — was always acutely felt. It was one of the reasons the houses subsidized the further medical education of any protected that wished to pursue an MD.

Corwyn started helping her out of her maternity jeans.

"Corwyn?" Jan inquired from the other side of the door.

"Call Jewel. Then bring us some towels."

"On my way."

Corwyn stripped Laura and retrieved a nightgown for her. She had her arms in the sleeves when Jan returned. The other woman swung the door wide without knocking and launched right into commentary.

"Jewel is on her way. Stephen is bringing Gabby home to help. What else can I do?"

Laura groaned at the start of another contraction, pausing in smoothing the nightgown to press a hand to her womb again. "Go take care of the boys."

Jan paused in the process of laying out towels on the bed. "Not you, too," she complained.

Corwyn shot her a hard look. "You're too far along, Jan. There is a possibility that —"

"Yeah, yeah. I might go into labor," she grumbled. "And I could grow another ten inches this year, too. That's not likely either. You Warriors are always —"

"You could try listening," Colin offered from the doorway. "For a change, of course." His smile tempered the rebuke.

She stomped toward him, her jaw tightening in challenge. "See if I give *you* another child," she warned.

Colin tipped his head. "Your choice, as always." But his expression said he didn't believe it.

Jan pushed past him, miffed. In the wake of it, Colin looked skyward and cursed softly.

"Take care of her," Corwyn ordered. "Protect Jan and the boys."

He nodded and started to turn away. "Good luck to you both."

Laura looked at the clock, biting at her lower lip.

Corwyn turned it away. "You don't worry about that. We have fourteen hours until sunset."

"And if she's not born by then?"

"Then the birth is going to be really interesting."

"Whoever coined the phrase should be shot," she grumbled.

Corwyn smiled at the edge of annoying in her voice. "What phrase."

"May you live in interesting times. I think I've had enough of interesting, thanks." She smiled weakly.

"One more adventure. Then maybe we can get a rest from them." He didn't hold out much hope that it was true, but it was better than admitting what he believed right now. Until the Stone was done with him, there would be no peace for anyone in Hunter range.

* * * *

"Remind me why I wanted to do this again."

Corwyn winced, searching for the words to answer that. "Never again, if you don't want to," he vowed.

By her expression, he guessed that Laura didn't know if she wanted to or not.

That is probably for the best. But the thought still stung at him.

"Almost there, Laura," Jewel assured her.

"Thank goodness." She sounded weary.

Stephen shot a worried look at Corwyn that said he heard it too. His younger brother changed his hold on Laura's foot to give her more leverage when she pushed.

Gabby leaned into her hold on the other as Laura started pushing again. "I know, Laura. Warrior babies don't make this easy."

Corwyn hadn't been able to man up to helping with Gabby's labors, and he regretted that now. As small as she was, neither of her sons had been easy on her.

Laura cried out, drawing his attention back to their daughter's arrival. Corwyn watched in amazement as her seam bulged and parted and dark, slick hair appeared. He laughed aloud. "She's here."

"Not...yet," Laura panted. With hardly a break for breath, she started pushing again.

This is what I missed with Erin. The excitement put a potent edge on his nerves, sharpening his senses.

Push after push, his daughter emerged. Corwyn cradled her head while Jewel checked for any loops of cord that might cause a problem. It was a gift; the first human touch outside the womb had been his.

"Go, Laura," Jewel urged her. "She looks good."

Two pushes later, his daughter rested in Corwyn's hands. Tears stung at his eyes.

Though they still had hours until sunset, the urgency struck him. He had to free her. He had to protect her, and it had to be now.

The baby started punching her balled fists. Her bow mouth opened and let out a furious squall. Jewel took the opportunity to suction her nose and mouth.

Gabby settled a pink blanket on the mattress, and Corwyn took the hint and settled the baby on it.

I need my hands free for this anyway.

He drew his sacred weapon and sliced his palm. Drawing the blood marks on her body, the words of the *Zeremonie der Freiheit* spilled out of his mouth in a rush, and Corwyn tensed for the interruption that never came.

As if the release in his tension sparked something in her, the baby stopped crying. She stuffed her fist in her mouth and started sucking on it, looking at him with wide eyes that reminded him of a newborn Erin.

He hurried on to the *Zeremonie des Schutzes*, in an effort to quell that memory, and ended with a kiss to his daughter's quickly drying face.

The room had gone silent, and Corwyn looked up. Everyone was staring at him, and the urge to defend himself shocked him.

Jewel smiled and nodded to his sacred weapon. "You want to use your sacred weapon or my scissors?"

His brow furrowed in confusion. "For?"

"To cut the cord."

Corwyn's heart skipped in joy. He looked down, spotting the two clips she'd placed on the cord. With exaggerated care, he cut the cord between them with his sacred weapon, separating their child from Laura's body.

Setting his weapon aside, Corwyn wrapped the blanket around his younger daughter and lifted her to Laura's chest. "You did good, Doc," he breathed. "Now...what are you going to name her?"

They'd discussed this many times. To protect them all from the Council of Lords and to allow their daughter as normal a life as they could provide — *Veriel and his turned aside* — Laura wasn't going to name a father when she filed for the birth certificate...and wasn't going to give their child the Hunter name.

It is the only way she'll be safe. Corwyn repeated that to himself at least five times a day. It burned at him not to have his daughter carry his name, but there was no other way.

"Corwyn —"

He shook his head and motioned for silence. "I know. But if I'm not giving her my name..." Just saying it choked him. "I don't deserve to choose any part of her name. Please... Doc, please just do this."

Laura nodded solemnly. "To protect her," she agreed.

The length of time she took to continue proved she really hadn't decided on a name without him. That warmed Corwyn's heart.

"Stephanie Caroline Briony." She peeked up at Corwyn, as if gauging his response before making it official.

"If that is the name you want, that is her name." Corwyn tested it in his mind. "I like it. I know you're waiting to hear that."

She smiled. "But do you mean it?"

"On my honor, I do." Corwyn settled beside her and ran his fingertips down Stephanie's tiny fingers. "How did you choose it?"

"Caroline was my grandmother's name. She practically raised me, even when my parents were alive."

He nodded. "A good choice." His mind taunted him that it was a good choice, because it was untraceable to Hunter. "And Stephanie?"

Her cheeks darkened in a blush.

"Laura?" he prompted her.

"When I was still foolish enough to think I could have children, I'd always wanted to name a little girl Stephanie."

"Then it's a good thing you get the chance to, isn't it?"

Her smile was wide and heartfelt. "Now...let's see if Stephanie wants to eat."

* * * *

"You freed her."

All three Warriors turned to the sound of Veriel's voice, and the beast unghosted at the far side of the room.

"You know what this means. I will take them both."

Corwyn scowled at him. "Not a chance, Veriel."

"Then I will kill them both. Or perhaps I will give the other houses the information they need to kill you."

"Not a chance," Colin repeated.

Then again, would any Warrior alive believe Veriel? That was long odds, at best.

The beast leaned against Laura's dressing table, his gaze straying to the sleeping mother and child on the bed. That was enough of a threat to make Corwyn's blood boil.

"Lewis of Maher is first nighting. He will make a kill soon. There is nothing to stop the Council of Lords from killing you."

Corwyn laughed harshly. "Besides the fact that you will have no way to torment me when I'm dead?" he countered.

"And no one to torment me. No one to stand in my way when Erin is found. No one for her to cling to." He seemed to consider his options carefully.

Stephen snorted in disgust at that. "The entire Warrior world will stand against you when Erin is found, and I'm sure she will find some lucky man to protect her very personally."

Corwyn bit back a smile at Stephen's bid to infuriate Veriel into a fatal error.

Veriel didn't seem amused by it. Then again, he didn't seem annoyed by it either.

"Will you lie to the Council of Lords when they ask you if that bastard is yours? Or will you leave her fatherless?" He glanced around the room, his gaze lighting on first Colin and then Stephen. "All of the children fatherless... Who will train and first night the next generation of *Jägers*?"

Colin's *Blutjagd* spiked at that, but he tapped it back.

Corwyn faced him down, confident but for reasons he couldn't name. "That will never happen."

"Why? Because you'll kill me? You aren't capable. I am supposed to die by the hand of one Hunter born, but not her lord."

Colin snarled at him. "I would be glad to be that Warrior."

"Hold your place," Corwyn ordered. "He wants you to leave your position by the bed." A stiff smile pulled at the corners of his lips. "It won't happen, Veriel. The Stone won't permit it. She's not done with me yet. She's not done with you, either." He paused, a faint whispering in the back of his mind telling him he was on the right track. "And you know it."

It looked as if he meant to retort, but something in his face changed. Veriel's eyes narrowed. He recovered quickly, and a mocking smile settling on his face.

"Perhaps I will keep you alive a little longer. Torturing you is so very enjoyable."

"Perhaps you have no choice." *I certainly don't have one.*

Veriel pushed to his feet and offered a two-fingered salute. "Another day, *Jäger.*"

His smile widened, and he swept the bottles and jars off the top of the dressing table. They shattered against the wall, and Laura bolted to sitting on the mattress. Her gaze locked on Veriel for a moment, before the beast disappeared.

Stephanie started fussing, and Corwyn slid up the mattress and lifted her into his arms. He passed her to Laura with a kiss for his daughter, then his mate.

"He won't touch you," Corwyn promised. "You have my vow."

"And mine," Colin stated.

"Mine, too," Stephen's voice overlapped his.

* * * *

June 27ᵗʰ, 1987

Corwyn stopped at the foot of the stairs, abandoning the idea of forcing a smile to his face. "What brings you here, Kord?"

The return effort was nearly as weak. "Just taking a night of sleep on my way home. Have a spare room I could use?"

Colin shot a terrified look over Kord's shoulder.

"I do." He hesitated, seeking any way to dissuade Kord from staying at the manor. "But it might be quieter at one of the cabins."

Colin went an unhealthy shade of gray.

"Quieter? I'm no stranger to children, Corwyn. I just spent two days with James Armen's son tearing after his two daughters. Your boys would be a reprieve. No one screams like a little girl does."

As if in confirmation, Stephanie's wailing battered the walls.

Kord's draw dropped. "I thought Jannelle wasn't due for nearly two months."

Corwyn considered his options. "She isn't. Veriel and Polero have been threatening our doctors." *One doctor anyway.* Then again, Hunter range only had one doctor. The others were nurse practitioners and nurses. "One of them gave birth this week. She's safest here at the manor."

"Threatening our doctors? Why didn't you tell us? The other houses would have —" Kord snapped his mouth shut, his face going crimson.

In the distance, Stephanie quieted, probably feasting on breast milk. Corwyn cursed the fact that he wasn't there to share the moment.

"I'm sorry, Corwyn."

He nodded stiffly. Kord was the one person he truly believed would have disobeyed orders to help him. "I know." Saying that took all his strength.

"Let me call my father. I'll stay. I'll do what I can to —"

Corwyn's *Blutjagd* ignited.

Kord's eyes went wide. He cleared his throat. "It's a girl, isn't it?"

"Yes, and this is one child I vow on my life Veriel will never get near." Corwyn fisted his hand on the healed freeing scar.

"Maybe I should go."

"Colin, get the key to cabin five." He focused on Kord. "You can leave the key there when you go. It's yours for as long as you want it."

"I'll be gone tomorrow...and I'll let the other house lords know about Veriel for you."

Corwyn shrugged. "If you want. You know Veriel lives to torture me. Your doctors are most likely safe."

"Yeah." He glanced at the ceiling and swallowed hard. "Yeah, I do know that."

"He loses this round, Kord. *He* loses."

Kord headed to the front door, taking the key from Colin's hand. He paused in the doorway. "Oh...good news from Maher range."

The hair all over Corwyn's body rose in warning. "And that is?"

"Lewis has blood sealed."

His mouth went dry, and his stomach dropped out. "Good. Congratulate him for me."

"Don't get yourself killed, Corwyn. My son is too young to bear your burdens." In the next heartbeat — before Corwyn could find the words to reply to it — Kord was gone.

Colin waited for Kord's car to roar to life and start down the drive before he spoke. "He's blood sealed."

That meant there was someone that could take over Corwyn's duties with the Stone. Silence fell between them, an oppressive fog holding the entire manor in its grip.

"The Stone won't allow me to be caught," Corwyn attested, sure he was right, though the Stone hadn't said anything of the sort. "Not yet. The Stone isn't done with me." For one thing, Erin hadn't returned to him. He was certain he wouldn't be cast aside until that happened, at least.

His brother shuddered at the statement, but he didn't respond to it.

"I need to see if Stephanie is okay." Corwyn mounted the stairs two at a time, his mind spinning in plans to keep his mate and child safe.

* * * *

June 30th, 1987

"Fuck me," Colin grumbled.

Corwyn raised an eyebrow. "You have a mate for that. Don't you?"

"Funny." His voice didn't sound as if he found it so.

"Who pissed in your Wheaties?"

As if sanctioning him, Stephanie's lower lip came out in a pout.

"Todd Lord Armen. That's who I just buzzed through the front gate."

Colin's answer made his heart stutter. Corwyn made it to his feet and to his brother in a move that had Stephanie startling in his arms.

"Take her upstairs," he ordered.

"To Laura?"

"No. She's sleeping. To Gabby and the boys."

The sound of a car pulling up the drive to the stairs forced a shudder from him. Corwyn settled Stephanie in Colin's waiting arms. "Go."

His brother didn't hesitate. By the time Armen knocked, Colin was out of sight.

Corwyn took his time answering it. That gave him enough time to smooth his clothing and calm his hammering heart.

He glared at Armen across the divide of the door frame. "What brings you, Armen? Tracking in my range?"

Corwyn didn't suspect it. That was something house lords of a range had earned the right to delegate to others and typically did. *Armen is a Warrior rich range.*

His adversary didn't smile at the ridiculous statement. "May I come in?"

The urge to refuse him was strong. Corwyn stepped back stiffly, his muscles fighting his mind's commands.

"Can I offer you something to eat and drink, or would you rather go to the library?"

Armen's eyes narrowed. "Not your office?"

"Unless I need files, I avoid it at nap time." *A good reason to keep Armen on the ground floor of the manor.*

"Sensible, I suppose." He ambled past Corwyn and into the library. Armen settled in Corwyn's usual chair.

Corwyn chose to stand. This was anything but a social visit. Since he'd lost Anna and Erin, Warriors from other ranges had made a point of not attempting social visits to Hunter range.

"You still haven't said what brings you," he noted.

He sighed. "As the youngest North American lord, I drew the short stick."

"On?" Corwyn suspected he knew. *Time to piss them all off again.* Doing that was getting to be a lifestyle choice for him.

"I urge you to let us protect the doctor and her daughter."

"Why?" What were their aims in insisting on this?

"Because Lewis Maher is too damned young to be Stone lord, Corwyn. For whatever reason, Veriel continues to fixate on you. Maybe the damned Mad Elder is pissed off you only wounded him and is seeking a pissed off enough Hunter Warrior to end him. With him, no one can say.

"I don't question why you feel the need to fight him. I'd do so with my last breath, if it was me." He paused and shot Corwyn a pained look. "Let us show him a unified front."

"He is seeing one." Veriel was seeing all of Hunter unified, for certain. Stephanie was never alone. There was always one or more Warriors in the room with her.

"Of all the houses."

Corwyn scowled at him. "Because that worked *so* well last time." Sarcasm seemed warranted, given the circumstances.

"You faced Veriel alone, trying to protect Anna," he reasoned.

"Which was whose fault?"

Armen's hesitation had Corwyn's blood heating for a fight.

"The lords at that time, Corwyn. Is that what you want to hear? Will that justify your outrage enough to trust that we are being honorable this time?"

"Nothing you could say to me is enough to make me trust the lords again." It was the unvarnished truth. Beyond the particulars of this situation, all but two of the house lords were the very ones that had caused him to lose Anna and Erin.

"I am not my father, Corwyn. But you still doubt my honor." His *Blutjagd* burned lightly in his skin at that.

"Not your honor. Just your commitment. The houses don't play well together. Every lord wants to be the alpha dog. I'd rather keep the other alphas out of the ring, thanks."

"It wouldn't be the lords, and our Warriors would take orders from you."

And report to you. "Thanks, but no thanks. Warriors with divided loyalties won't do me any good. A Warrior can only pledge himself to one lord."

Armen's face darkened to blood red. "You're not going to give an inch, are you?"

"Not. An. Inch."

"Even if they are safer elsewhere and you're endangering them by doing this?"

His heart pounded at the challenge. Armen was insinuating that Corwyn was harming his mate and child. "Are you prepared to state that to the Council of Lords and face me as judge when they have to allow her to stay where she wants to stay?"

He purposely refused to use their names. Any information Corwyn provided to the other houses could be used against them later.

"I never said I intended to —"

"No. You insult my honor. You insist that I uproot a woman and child from their lives, and you suggest that I am being cavalier with two lives I am responsible for."

Armen opened his mouth to speak.

"And lest I forget, you wish to deprive me of my only protected doctor."

His opponent snapped his jaws shut. After a moment, Armen shook his head. "Only until Veriel loses interest."

Corwyn laughed harshly. "He's been obsessed with a dead woman for more than fifteen centuries. He chased Anna across three ranges. If you think time or distance mean anything to him, you are deluding yourself."

Armen's answer was cut short by Laura calling Corwyn's name from the top of the stairs. Corwyn stepped into the foyer, and Armen rushed to join him.

Laura's eyes narrowed at the sight of a strange Warrior.

"Do you need something, Doc?" Corwyn asked.

"Is the baby with you?"

Behind him, Armen went rigid.

Corwyn didn't react to it. "She's with Gabby and Colin, in the nursery. We figured you could use a break."

Laura nodded her thanks and started to turn away.

"If you have a moment, Doctor," Armen called out.

She looked back, straightening her robe.

And probably steeling herself for something unpleasant. Corwyn couldn't fault her for that.

"I was just suggesting to Corwyn, Doctor..." He hinted at her name.

"All the Warriors call me Doc, thanks," she lied smoothly.

"Well...Doc..." He ground his teeth at her refusal to offer her name. "I was suggesting to Corwyn that you might want to spend your recuperation in one of the other ranges. Just to discourage Veriel. A vacation of sorts."

Laura snapped a questioning look at Corwyn. He raised an eyebrow but remained silent.

"Well, that *is* a first, I admit," she drawled.

Armen rounded Corwyn, so they stood side-by-side. His brow furrowed in apparent confusion, Armen cleared his throat. "What is?"

"I didn't think there were any stupid Warriors."

Corwyn swallowed down a laugh.

"I beg your pardon," Armen offered crisply.

"If I was your wife, would you attempt to move me and a newborn hundreds or thousands of miles?"

Armen went from red to crimson. "I suppose not."

"Maybe you're not stupid. The stress of a trip like that before a few months isn't advisable. That is my professional opinion, anyway."

Armen wasn't done yet. "I can see your point." He was laying on the charm now. "What about extra guards? If you ask for them, Corwyn will allow me to bring in extra Warriors."

Corwyn bristled at his presumption. He'd agreed to no such thing, but Armen was trying to force his hand. If Laura asked for something to make them safer, and Corwyn refused her, Armen had a case to take to the Council of Lords.

Laura didn't even glance at Corwyn. "And introduce all those new germs to her before she builds up antibodies from my milk? Not a chance."

"If Veriel attacks —"

"The local Warriors have done a great job so far." She smiled a hard little smile. "Corwyn has survived battles with Veriel before. Have you?"

A tic appeared in the back of Armen's clenched jaw. "Think of your daughter."

"I am thinking of her." There was a bite of ice in her tone that said Laura was at the end of her patience and ready to strike.

"I am upsetting you. My apologies. Perhaps I could speak to your husband for a few moments."

Laura's cheeks bloomed with angry color. "I don't have a husband. Nor do I want one. One of the things I *like* about Hunter range is that all the men have printed. Now...if you will excuse me, I have a daughter to tend to." She marched away toward the nursery.

Corwyn turned on Armen. Under any other circumstances, he'd find the other lord's shock amusing. But Armen had just upset Laura; all Corwyn wanted to do was gut him and throw him to some hungry predator.

"I'm sure you can find your way out," he suggested, adding a glare that he hoped conveyed he'd do so bodily if given another minute to think about it.

"I'm sure I can." He turned on his heel.

"She's made her choice, Armen. Don't come back. Pass that message along to the rest of the lords."

He had no doubts Armen would.

* * * *

Laura looked up to find Corwyn watching her from the nursery doorway. He fidgeted as if he was discomfited by something. At his arrival, Colin took his leave.

"They can't force us to leave. Can they?" she voiced her greatest fear.

He shook his head. "You don't want to go, and you've made that abundantly clear to them. You've refused their protection. They can't push it any further than that."

But he still looked uneasy.

"Then what's wrong?" Something clearly was.

"What you said..."

Her head spun. Had she said something wrong. "What did I say?" And what problems would it cause for them?

"About not having...not...wanting a husband...?" His expression was tortured. "I'll find a way to marry you, if you want —"

"No."

Corwyn closed his eyes, looking weary.

"All our plans to keep Stephanie safe by separating her from you legally will fall apart, if we do that." Surely, he realized that. Not to mention it would provide a trail to use as evidence against him, if the other lords wanted him dead.

"I didn't ask that. If you *want* me to marry you, I will. I want to, Laura."

"You've already made a commitment most people never do. Why would I want a meaningless piece of paper?"

His eyes opened, and he stared at her.

"Want to know where my marriage license is? Bill tore it to pieces the night he left." Tears stung at her eyes at the memory of it. "I held onto them for a while, but the day the divorce papers arrived, I burned it. His promises literally were not worth the paper they were written on."

Corwyn's mouth dropped open. A moment later, he clenched it shut, and his face went a vivid red. Laura didn't need the sound of Stephen and Colin pounding down the hall to know Corwyn's *Blutjagd* was burning.

He waved his brothers off before they could question him. "I can't make that right for you, Laura." The admission clearly pained him.

She smiled. "Just being with you makes that right."

He nodded grimly.

"But...Corwyn?"

His head cocked to one side. "Yes?"

"Bill was never half as honorable as you are."

"What are you saying?"

"Don't even consider tarnishing your honor to beat him to a pulp."

The curving of his lips attested that she'd called his line of thinking right. "Is that an order?" There was a playful challenge in the question.

"As Lady Hunter."

Laura was sure the snickering from the hall was Stephen.

Chapter Thirty-three

August 29th, 1987

Laura laughed heartily, patting Stephanie's back. She motioned to the photo album, obviously unable to form words.

Jan obliged her by turning the page. She joined in the laughter as her gaze locked on a picture of the proud, blood-sealed Corwyn Hunter with Stephen on his broad shoulders, sparring open-handed with Colin and his wooden weapon.

Jan wiped the tears from her eyes. "Their mother got the most precious candid shots of them. I can't imagine why they hid these."

Gabby wrinkled her freckled nose, her eyes glittering in mischief. "Remember the lake shot?"

Laura held a hand to her ribs, hitching in laughter. "Three naked young Warriors frolicking. Stephen couldn't have been more than a year old."

"I know. I think I'll hang that one in our bedroom."

Jan turned another page and sucked in her breath. "That can't be."

Laura stopped laughing and looked close to tears. "It's Corwyn. Is that — ?"

Gabby nodded. "It has to be Anna. Who else could it be?"

Laura shook her head. "She was beautiful, wasn't she?"

Jan leaned over the photo, her brow furrowing. There was something she wasn't seeing. With her overactive sense for patterns, things like that had always bothered her.

Anna had possessed classic good looks, the kind most women hated you for. She'd had fine bone structure and had been so petite she'd been dwarfed by Corwyn. She looked familiar, though Jan knew she'd never seen a picture of Corwyn's first mate before.

Gabby sighed. "She looks so happy."

Laura swallowed what appeared to be a painful lump and rubbed Stephanie's back. "He looks so different. The beard —"

Jan groaned. "It was Anna's beard. That's what he called it. Corwyn didn't shave when he was printing on her, and she liked it. He cut it when he learned she was dead. He said he'd never grow a beard again."

Gabby scowled. "I've never heard that."

"Colin told me. Colin loved her, you know."

Laura looked up at her, clearly scandalized by something. "Anna?"

"No. I mean, as a sister, I'm sure. He loved Erin. He never got to see her. Not once. It was all Colin wanted. He'd planned to offer a vow of special protection to Erin when she was born, a blood oath. He did the ceremony without her. If she's ever found..."

Jan stilled, looking at the photo again. "Something familiar," she breathed. She searched the face again, knowing she was missing something elemental. "Something familiar."

The stone fireplace behind Anna and Corwyn caught her eye. *Stone. What is it about the stone?*

"What is it?" Laura asked.

"The stone." Jan pushed off the couch with the photo album open on her arm and scanned her gaze over the leather-bound ancient texts. She pulled out a thin volume and checked the cover, assuring herself that it was the same one Stephen had grabbed from her hand the first day she'd spent in the manor house. She rifled through it to the portrait of the woman on the stone.

"Jan, are you all right?" Gabby asked.

"It's her." The face was the same. If Anna had dark hair and eyes like a Warrior did, they'd be twins. The same cascade of long curls framed the aristocratic features and knowing eyes.

"Jan?" Laura called out in a soothing tone.

Jan turned back to them, stunned by the discovery. What did it mean? Anna and the dark-haired woman were connected somehow, but how?

Laura shifted a fussy Stephanie in her hands and brought a squeaky teddy bear up to the baby's eye level. "Momma's girl," Laura crooned.

The bear. She looked at the photo of Anna and then the portrait again. "Momma's girl."

Gabby's hand came down on her shoulder. "Jan, what is it?"

Jan shoved the books at her and headed for the door, grabbing her keys off the hook. Colin had insisted she park her car in the drive now that stairs were uncomfortable for her. She was glad of it. There was no time to waste.

"Jan?" Gabby stood in the library doorway, clutching the books to her chest. "What's wrong?"

"I have to go. I have..." She turned and hurried across the porch. "Why didn't I see it? It was right in front of me all that time."

Gabby followed her to the front door. "Jan, calm down. You're not making sense. Talk to me."

"No time. I have to go. I was blind, Gabby."

"About what? What didn't you see?" When Jan didn't slow, she continued. "Wait. Let me get Colin."

Jan shook her head, slid behind the wheel of her car, and started driving. The trip to the office seemed to take forever, despite her break-neck speeds. She made her way to her office, giving strained smiles and clipped answers in response to the pleasantries her coworkers offered.

She closed the door behind her and went to her bulletin boards. Her hand went to the spot she'd pinned the picture almost a year and a half earlier, a picture she looked at several times a week.

And I never saw it!

It was gone. Jan sucked in her breath, pulling paper off in a frenzy, hoping the photo was buried, that she'd moved it or covered it without remembering that she had. When ripped paper littered the floor, and the boards were empty save the map pins remaining behind, Jan sank to the floor with a sob.

She was crying openly when Devin stuck his head in. His smile faded, and the greeting he'd started to utter died half-spoken.

He stepped inside, pushed the door closed, and stared at the wreckage of her office. "What is it? Are you okay?"

Jan nodded, trying to staunch the flow of tears.

"Is it Colin?"

She shook her head, then took a shuddering breath.

"Jan, you have to talk to me."

"I-I h-had... There was something on my board. It's gone. It was there last week. I'm sure it was."

"Was it important?"

She nodded, biting back another sob.

"Can it be replaced?"

"I don't know," she wailed. "Maybe." *But where is it now? Who has it? What have I done?*

"What was it? Maybe I can help?"

He looked desperate to help. Jan was sure he'd put everything in his power toward making it better, if he could.

She shook her head. "It's a mother thing," she offered in half-truth.

Devin nodded solemnly. "At least let me call Colin for you. Or let me drive you home. I don't want you driving like this."

"Colin. Please." The sooner she told him what happened, the better.

Devin had made it halfway to the phone when the door opened and Colin bolted in. His look of relief melted into something between shock and concern. He raked his hand through his hair, panning his head back and forth to assess the catastrophe that was once her office. At last, he fixed his gaze on her.

With a jerk of his head to ask Devin for privacy, he ambled to her and lifted Jan into his arms. "Are you all right?" he asked softly.

"No. What have I done, Colin? I should have seen it. More than a year, and I never saw —"

"Not here. Whatever it is, we'll discuss this at home."

"But —"

"Jan...at home." His eyes pleaded with her for understanding.

"All right." Time was of the essence, but it was a Warrior secret. Maybe Gabby and Laura had made sense of her rambling and told Colin it had something to do with Erin. Maybe he was warning her that it wasn't safe to talk about it where there might be another minion lurking.

Jan didn't remember much about the trip back to the manor house. She supposed she must have slept most of the way, exhausted by her emotional outburst. She snuggled into Colin's chest as he lifted her from his car and didn't open her eyes as he made his way to their room, sending away concerned family members along the way. When she was settled in bed, she opened her eyes and waited for the interrogation to begin.

Colin raised her hand and kissed the back. "Now, what didn't you see?"

"Erin."

"I don't understand. How could you see Erin?"

"I had a photo, Colin. I've had it for almost a year and a half. Now..." She swallowed around the lump forming in her throat. "Now, it's gone."

His face drained of color. "A photo of Erin? You had..."

Jan grimaced and nodded.

"How can you be sure it was her?"

"Anna — The portrait — The same face." Jan took a deep breath and moved her hands aimlessly. "All three of them...have...the same face, Colin. It had to be her, and now the photograph is gone. It's *gone*. What have I done?"

Colin cradled her to his chest. "Shhh. You have to calm down."

"How can I when —"

"Calm."

She nodded, stifling her sobs into hitching breaths. When she was calm again, Colin settled her on the pillows.

"I'm going to get you a drink. When I come back, we'll discuss this calmly."

Jan nodded, and Colin kissed her forehead.

* * * *

Colin shook his head, looking back at the bed one more time before he jogged to the stairs and down. He'd like to believe Jan, but what she said made no sense. *A photograph of Erin?* She had to be mistaken. But she seemed so certain, it made the hair stand up on the back of his neck.

Where would she get a photo of Erin? And what did she mean when she said Anna and the ancient...something...had the same face?

He nodded to his assembled family grimly as he pulled out a glass and the pitcher of the apple juice his sons seemed so fond of making Jan crave.

"How is she?" Stephen asked.

Colin sighed, the muscles in his shoulders bunching in frustration. "I'd like to say she's fine, but she's not. She's so distraught, I'm tempted to have Laura and Jewel sedate her."

"What is she saying?" Corwyn prompted.

Colin avoided his eyes, pouring the juice while he considered his options. *Anything that doesn't give Corwyn false hope.* After their mad search for adopted babies, he couldn't bear to do that to his brother again.

"Colin?"

"Nothing that makes sense," he ground out more harshly than he wanted to. *It's not a lie. Until I make sense of it, I can't do this to him.*

"Try me." There was a hint of a house lord's order in that.

Colin paused with his hand on the refrigerator door and his back to the table, weighing what he *could* say. "Something about Anna. I'm telling you, Corwyn, it's not coherent enough to —"

"Come here."

He looked up at the group settled around the table in surprise.

"Come here. Let me show you something that might explain some of what she's saying to you."

Colin set Jan's glass of juice on the counter and crossed the room to the table. He glanced at the photo of Corwyn and Anna. "And?" It had been Anna's favorite photo, and Colin hadn't seen it in at least five years.

Corwyn laid *The Early Histories* by Gawen on the table and flipped it open to one of the illuminations. "Jan pulled this out when she saw Anna's photograph. She has quite a memory for faces, your wife."

Colin sucked in his breath in shock. "Regana." The Stone's words, as reported by Corwyn, echoed in his mind.

The mother's daughter and the mother's mother. Regana was the mother. She really was of Regana's blood...somehow.

Corwyn tapped the page. "I was so damned blind. I've had this book for more than ten years. I've read it hundreds of times, and I never saw it, Colin. How could I miss the resemblance? I was so busy reading it, I never *looked* at it."

I never saw it? How could I miss it? Jan was asking herself the same thing. Regana was the ancient she was talking about. *The same face. Anna...the ancient...*

Oh, gods! The photograph of the child has the same face. He fought for a decent breath, scanning the ceiling in disbelief. She'd done it. She'd actually found Erin. "The same face."

"Colin, what is it?" Stephen asked.

"Where in the hell would she get a photo?"

Stephen moved from his chair and guided Colin into it. "Sit down before you fall down," he instructed.

Colin looked up at Corwyn, his mind spinning. "Where could she possibly get a photo?"

Corwyn shook his head, clearly confused by the question. "Of Anna? We have a dozen, at least."

"Not of Anna, damn it," he snapped. "Of —" Colin forced himself to stop and consider what he was doing to Corwyn...just when he'd found peace with Laura. He averted his eyes, hating himself for it. "Where would Jan get a photograph of Erin?"

"What?" Stephen stormed.

"Colin, that makes no —"

"Oh, shit!" That was Gabby.

Everyone froze and turned her way, Corwyn last.

Gabby darkened. "A-a file," she stammered. "Just before Nicky was born, Jan called me about a file. I told her — It couldn't have been right. She destroyed it." Gabby faltered. "She said she did, anyway. I thought she had."

Colin bit back his fury and managed an even voice. "What file? From where?"

"I don't know. A file. Jan wanted to pull her own weight. She wanted to find Erin." She peeked up at Corwyn. "For you."

Laura took a deep breath. "She did it? She knows where Erin is?"

"I don't know. We thought it couldn't be Erin."

"Why?" Stephen asked. At his wife's questioning look, he continued. "What made you so sure it wasn't Erin?"

"She was jaundiced and...and tiny...and —" She shrugged.

Corwyn looked down at his hands, cupping them as he would to hold Stephanie. "She *was* tiny," he breathed. "Erin was. I'd never seen a baby that small before. Warrior babies are usually —" His voice cracked. "Much smaller than —"

Colin launched to his feet and sprinted for the stairs.

Stephen dragged him to a stop. "What are you doing?" he demanded.

Colin looked at the confusion in Corwyn's eyes and then back to their youngest brother. "The photo is gone. It has been stolen. You know as well as I do the only person that would want it. We have to get there first."

Corwyn nodded. "I'll find out." He met Colin's eyes. "Gently."

Colin nodded and accepted the glass of juice from Gabby's hand. He led the way up to Jan slowly.

Stephen looked at the retreating women and shook his head. "I have to talk to Gabby about what secrets she keeps from us."

Colin laughed harshly. "I have to talk to Jan about her research projects...again."

Corwyn shuddered. "Don't be so hard on her. She may be our only link to Erin."

Colin opened the door to the room. Jan looked up at him, her face swollen and her eyes red from crying. She glanced at Corwyn over his shoulder and started to retreat on the bed.

Corwyn took the juice from Colin and went to sit beside her. "Here. Drink this."

Jan took the glass with a shaking hand and sipped at it.

"Now, where did you get the file?" Corwyn's voice was low and soothing, though every muscle was strung tight. Only the fact that he wasn't burning in *Blutjagd* allowed Colin to give him space to do this.

She cleared her throat. "Abandoned babies the week Erin was — There were five. Two were older children. One was a baby boy. One was Hispanic, and one —"

"Was a white female neonate," Corwyn finished for her.

Jan nodded, fresh tears pooling in her eyes. "With black curls and brown eyes, but she was only six and a half pounds and jaundiced. It couldn't have been —"

She hiccupped and started again. "I thought it couldn't have been her. But...but it was," she hitched out.

"You told Gabby you destroyed the file."

"I did. I swear I did. I shredded it right after I talked to her."

"Except the photo?"

Jan blanched. "I couldn't."

Corwyn tipped the glass up to her lips, and Jan took another drink.

"You recognized her? That's why you couldn't destroy the photo?"

"I saw the portrait in the book the first day. I didn't make the connection. Not consciously. I swear it. It was just something I couldn't put my finger on. I had to figure out why the photo bothered me. So —"

"You kept it."

She grimaced, then nodded.

"Why didn't you bring it to Colin?"

"It couldn't have been her, and..." She glanced at Colin and then away.

His shoulders ached at the implication that she hadn't trusted him.

"And?" Corwyn prodded.

"And I was doing research I shouldn't have been." She bit her lower lip, then released it. "Again," Jan sighed.

Corwyn nodded. "Was there anything on the picture to identify it? Anything that could lead someone to her?"

"No. Nothing."

"You're sure?"

Jan nodded. "Nothing. I shredded everything with information on it."

Colin sighed in relief, and Stephen clapped a hand on his shoulder.

Corwyn took her hand. "Where is Erin, Jan?"

She met his eyes. "She was found in New York state."

"Now? Where is she now?" The slightest edge crept into his voice.

"I don't know. She was adopted, Corwyn. Most of the file is sealed, everything after she turned two and most of the earlier stuff as well. Just part of the initial report, medical, and a few photos are left in the unsealed portion. They don't leave the rest after the adoption. No foster parents' names. No adoptive parents' names. Just a case file.

"I can't get the full file. I — I don't know if anyone can. I'm sorry."

Corwyn nodded, released his hand and pushed to his feet. He turned away, looking tortured and defeated. As he reached Colin, he straightened his spine, burying his pain and loss again.

"Did she look happy, Jan? Was she...happy where she was?"

Jan bit back what was clearly a sob. "Yes. In the photo, she was laughing. She had a teddy bear...a huge one, and she was very happy."

Corwyn nodded slowly. "Good. I'm glad."

Stephen followed him out of the room, shooting Colin a look that said he'd take care of any fallout there might be.

Colin held Jan until she fell into a fitful sleep. He sighed and laid a kiss on her forehead.

In the stillness, he fingered the scar from his vow. Someday, Erin would come home to them. When she did, Colin would honor that vow. Erin would be under his personal protection, and there was nothing Colin wouldn't do for her.

* * * *

Jörg touched the child's face again. He couldn't stop touching the image, it seemed. If he wasn't careful, he'd destroy his only link to her.

If only he knew where she was, he could feel the silk of her skin and smell her scent on her hair as she slept.

No, it is better this way. Without Anna to soothe his blood, he wouldn't be safe with Erin. He would be driven to take her far too early, before she was ready for his attentions. That would never do.

Erin would be his true mate. She would carry his children. She would come to him at sixteen, when her body was ripe to carry his son, as Regana had.

Jörg sobered. He would find her at sixteen or soon after. Every year he was without her only added to his madness. Erin was the balm to his soul, and she would be his.

He pocketed the photograph, imaging the young woman she would be growing into, remembering what Regana had looked like at ten.

Jörg shook his head. No, it was better to remember the toddler in the photograph. Knowing her body was ripening for him would steal the last of his sanity from him.

He made his way to the streets, on the hunt for sweet young blood, a whore or maybe a gang member.

Definitely a whore. He needed to slake other thirsts while he waited for his mate.

The one he found seemed very young to his old eyes. Her blood was sweet with just the slightest taint of opiates. Her body wasn't so sweet, but he used her well, dreaming of his mate.

Not that I would take Erin to a filthy little room like this one. He'd made the mistake of showing such disrespect for Yzabeau, and it was a lesson he never intended to repeat.

No, Erin will have a castle...a mansion...silks and satins and furs. Erin will have whatever will make her happy...and nothing less than that.

Jörg returned to his home, wincing at the emptiness, at the stark lack of a woman's touch that Erin would soon remedy. He stroked the stiff photograph through the fabric of his jacket.

Jäger didn't know where Erin was. If he did, his drive to take her back into his care would be overwhelming.

So, where did Colin of *Jäger's* wife get the photograph? Did they not realize what she held, or did they find Erin only to lose her again?

Jörg smiled at that concept. It would be sweet justice for *Jäger* to have his dreams stolen from him as Jörg had so many times before.

Then again, *Jäger* didn't believe that he was Jörg. To *Jäger*, he would forever be Veriel. He laughed harshly at the thought.

"Veriel. The destroyer of lives. The mad elder. The mad deceiver. Your daughter's mate." That thought would keep him sane...or what passed for sane for another day.

Section Four:
The Lord's Daughter

Chapter Thirty-four

May 20th, 2011

Jacob Armen took a drink of his beer, panning his gaze around the club. He scowled. Why was he here? Did he really think he was going to find what he was looking for in a bar?

No. But I will find what I need — a way to stay sane for a few more weeks.

Like all Warriors, Jacob required sexual release on a regular basis. Unlike most Warriors, he'd tired of simple release early in life; at only twenty-seven, he was tired of one night stands and blade chasers.

What he wanted was a wife, family, someone he could call "home" when he returned from the hunt. What he needed was his "fix," just a little something to tide him over until he found what he really wanted.

Not all junkies love the drug, he mused. *Some loathe it as much as I do.*

So who would it be, tonight? What woman would save his sanity? Would she be blonde? A redhead? Or maybe — Jacob smiled and downed the last mouthful of his beer in a gulp.

"That one," he breathed. He scanned the woman at a table ringing the dance floor in hunger stronger than he'd felt in months. She had straight, black hair that curved at her shoulders, styled so it half covered her left eye, making her appear mysterious, giving her the appearance of a movie spy.

He nodded and started across the room to her. If she was interested, it was going to be a brunette tonight. That brunette.

* * * *

Stephanie Briony laughed heartily, setting her empty glass on the table. "Val, you are incorrigible," she complained.

Her roommate tossed her short, auburn curls, playing the party girl as she did so well. "Oh, come on, will you? This place is a meat market. Relax and enjoy yourself."

"I am relaxed."

She glanced around, trying to push back her unease. She didn't like going out in Armen range. Though there was no way they could know who she was with her amulet hidden under her sweater, she secretly feared that one of them would recognize her somehow.

Stephanie squared her shoulders in irritation. She had autonomy. There was no reason not to pick up any guy she wanted for the night. She'd done it before.

In Hunter range.

But what then?

She pushed her glass along the table with two fingers. Could she stand another one night stand? Worse, could her father overcome his Warrior nature and allow her to marry without causing a scene? Even if he did, how would she explain the eccentricities of her family to a human man?

There was no doubt that she'd have to marry a human...if she married. A Warrior was out of the question. If she slipped up and exposed her family somehow, the results would be disastrous.

"Yeah," Val chided her. "I can see how relaxed you are. I just don't get you. You are a completely different person when you're back home."

She opened her mouth to make yet another apology for how tense she was when Val dragged her out to clubs, but a rough, male voice interrupted her.

"Care for a dance?"

She glanced up at the speaker and froze. *Gods, no!* It was undeniably a Warrior, most likely an Armen, though she'd never been permitted to meet Warriors outside her own house, so she couldn't be certain.

"Care for a dance?" he repeated, his hand extended to her.

"Mmm," Val purred. "Just your type."

Stephanie elbowed her, her heart pounding. She knew she should simply turn him down and clear out, but the words stuck in her throat.

Never one to take a hint, Val continued, "You know, it's spooky how much he looks —"

Stephanie kicked her, then was off the stool before her roommate could say "ouch." She grasped the Warrior's hand, turning him toward the dance floor. "Dance? Sure," she stammered.

Gods, what am I doing? It was a senseless question. She had to get him away from Val. Two more seconds, and Val would have mentioned Stephanie's cousins or worse, the fact that he could pass for Joel's older brother — by name.

One dance, she soothed herself. She'd dance with the Armen once, then get out of Dodge as fast as she could. She'd rent a car and call Geoff's cell phone from the road if she had to.

She'd barely noted that the song was a slow one before he had her held lightly to his body, his hands on her hips. Stephanie hesitated, then placed her hands on his shoulders, her gaze darting around the room.

"Jacob," he breathed.

She looked at him, trying to ignore the response of her body when she met his eyes. It was too bad that he felt so right, because this particular encounter wasn't going any further. "What?" she asked, reminding herself that he'd said something a moment earlier.

"My name... It's Jacob Armen."

She nodded, feigning ignorance of his hope for her name in return. The less information he had, the better.

"And you?" he hinted.

She hesitated. If she refused to tell him anything, he'd get suspicious. "Stephanie," she conceded.

Jacob smiled a truly devastating smile, and she swallowed hard. He pulled her closer, his body moving against hers, a positively sinful promise of what he intended.

Stephanie closed her eyes, trying to ground herself. It didn't work. Jacob's hands caressed her back, his breath pulsing hot and fast against her temple. She laid her cheek to his chest, dizzy in her responses, arguing that it was just the drink she'd downed too quickly. She gasped as his cock hardened, the gyrations of his hips stroking his pelvis against hers again and again.

The song ended, and they held to each other in the silence before the next started, their breathing ragged.

Stephanie steeled herself to rebuff him, though being in his arms fired her under-indulged libido into a frenzy.

"Come home with me," he requested.

She opened her eyes, and for the second time in the space of five minutes, words stuck in her throat.

Dearest gods! What else could go wrong?

Joel and Geoff weren't supposed to escort her home until tomorrow, yet there they were, standing at the side door, looking for her. Stephanie turned, guiding Jacob with her, gliding with the music as if she were still dancing, her mind spinning.

If she didn't get Jacob out of here, he'd see her cousins. There would be questions — what a Hunter-protected woman had been doing in Armen range on and off for the last two years without notifying the Armens about it, why it took two of Hunter's best Warriors to escort her home to their range, and why she had a lord's amulet.

"Stephanie? I asked —"

"Yes," she decided. She had to get him out of there before Val tried to introduce them to Jacob.

He stepped back, touching her cheek and smiling again. Her heart stuttered at that. What was she doing? Was she crazy to chance this?

She took stock of his body as he guided her toward the front door. Who was she kidding? She wanted him. Protecting her father was just a fortuitous circumstance. She had autonomy. Why shouldn't she have sex with Jacob and walk away?

He was a Warrior picking up a woman in a barroom. He wanted release. The night was all he was looking for. Since her schooling was complete, the night was something she could give him without fear of running into him again.

* * * *

Geoff wrapped his arms around Val and laid a playful kiss on her cheek, thankful that she wasn't pursuing some other man for the evening. "Well, if it isn't Little Red Riding Hood," he teased. He was certainly the wolf that wanted to eat her up. *Until she screams for more.*

"Ooooh, he's early. Dare I hope you showed up tonight to ravish me?"

"Maybe." His cock rose at the invitation. In truth, that was precisely why he'd insisted they come a night early. He'd slept with Val several times in the last year, and he'd make it a permanent arrangement if she gave any indication at all that she was the serious sort.

Joel leaned his crossed arms on the tabletop. "Maybe she wants to trade up," he suggested, raising an eyebrow at Geoff in challenge.

Val leaned back into his chest, licking her lip as she presented her cleavage for Geoff's perusal. "Maybe she wants to be a Val sandwich on Hunter."

Geoff shot her a look of disbelief, feeling the slight burn of *Blutjagd* at the idea of sharing her with his cousin, then grinned at her glittering eyes. "Maybe I should change your mind."

"Maybe you should."

Joel groaned. "I think I need a shot of Bourbon — or maybe insulin. Where's Trouble?"

Val chuckled. "Dancing." She knelt up on the bar stool, using Geoff's shoulder for balance, peering over the crowd. Her smile disappeared.

Joel tensed. "What is it?" he asked urgently.

"She was there just a minute ago." She whipped her head around, nearly losing her balance as she started searching the other half of the room. "They were right there when you walked in. She can't have left. Her purse is still here."

"They?" Geoff asked, worry gnawing at his gut.

"Yeah. He..." She met his eyes, then looked at Joel, hesitating as if something of note had just occurred to her.

"What is it?" Joel asked again.

"He... Well, he looked so much like you both, I mistook him for Joel at first."

Geoff rubbed at his forehead, hiding a grimace with the sleeve of his long black leather jacket. *An Armen! Gods alive! What do we do now?*

* * * *

Jacob stopped the car outside a row house and turned to her. "Home sweet home," he offered in a voice rough in arousal.

Stephanie nodded, searching for signs of habitation and praying none of the other Armens were in residence. "Nice house."

"I try to spend a few weeks here once in a while. It's nice to get away from it all when you have the chance."

The tightness around her heart eased. There weren't any other Warriors in the house. "Yes. It is."

He got out of the car and came around to her side, opening the door and offering Stephanie his hand. She took it without hesitation, managing an honest smile.

Just one night, she reasoned as she stepped into the dimly lit foyer. Even she deserved a mad adventure once in her life.

Jacob turned, crowding her against the wall. "I've wanted to do this since the first time you spoke to me."

She didn't question what he meant. His mouth closed on hers, hungry, full of promise as the dance had been. Stephanie wrapped her arms around his neck and leaned into him, groaning as her amulet shifted against her chest. That was another problem to be dealt with. If only she hadn't left her purse behind, she would have some way of hiding the amulet; but if she could have returned to the table for it, she wouldn't be here to worry about it.

"Do you need anything?" he asked, the unspoken comment that he wanted no interruptions echoing in his tone.

"Yes!" She calmed herself. "Bathroom?" She felt her cheeks heat.

He smiled. "Sure. This way." He led her to a master bedroom and motioned to what was undoubtedly the attached bath.

She retreated inside and shut the door, sighing in relief. Stephanie dragged the amulet off, pausing in indecision. She'd left her purse at the table with Val. Where could she hide it that Jacob wouldn't feel or see it while they...

Who knew something so simple could be such a major problem? She pulled off her sweater and snagged the clasp on the inside threads, then folded it.

She took a deep breath and headed back into the bedroom.

Jacob looked up from the bedside, bare-chested, barefoot, and highly aroused. He panned his gaze over her as if he wanted to devour her.

She put the sweater down on the dresser and ambled toward him. *One night*, she reminded herself.

* * * *

Gods, she is beautiful. Stephanie's hips swayed enticingly as she made her way to the bed. Her nearly-black hair swung around her shoulders and followed the line of her jaw.

Jacob forced himself to breathe. What was it about her that made his heart ache? Was it her hesitancy? Her nervousness? Stephanie had a vulnerable quality about her that made him want to hold her — or maybe he was looking for something that wasn't there in hopes that he'd find a mate. If so, he was further gone than was prudent.

No. He was sane. He was certain of that. There was something in Stephanie that begged to be soothed and protected, little things that she seemed unconscious of like the way she sank into him even when he didn't pull her there.

Armens tended toward women in need of protection. *They also fall for them quickly,* he mused.

She ran her fingertips along the line of his shoulder, the silk of her camisole teasing at his ribs. He kissed her, turning and pulling her to the bed over him. She reached back and flipped her heeled sandals to the floor.

Jacob took the opportunity to slide his hands under the camisole, edging it upward. Stephanie met his eyes, unfastening her jeans, then raising her arms and ducking out of the cami as he peeled it away and tossed it over his shoulder.

She stared at him, seemingly uncertain. He eased her over him, cupping her cheeks and lacing his fingertips behind her head, feathering kisses over her mouth. Her eyes closed, and her hands pulled at the fastener on his jeans.

He pulled a condom from the front pocket as she pushed them away. He would prefer not to wear one, but he'd sensed her downstairs and confirmed that she was high cycle. By the rules of sanction, a Warrior never created life with a woman who wasn't sealed as his mate and never without her permission. His honor and his life made using the condom necessary.

He looked up as she yanked the jeans over his feet and dropped them to the floor. Stephanie stood there a moment, scanning his body and licking her lips.

"Come back to bed," he grumbled.

She knelt on the bed, peeling her jeans back. Jacob took the fabric in his hands and pulled them down to her knees. Her eyes closed and she sank to her back. He rose up over her, laying kisses down her body as he removed the last of her clothing. She shivered, laying a hand over her stomach.

"Are you sure?" he asked, trying to gauge her attack of nerves.

"Yes." Her voice was soft and wistful.

Jacob leaned over her, easing her thighs apart and laying a kiss at the pulse point a hand's width below her core. She sighed, running her fingers through his hair. He trailed upward with the tip of his tongue, and she groaned, her hand fisting. He traced the line of her labia, then circled her clit.

"My gods," she pleaded, panting as he sucked at her clit.

He flicked it with his tongue, and she muttered a curse in German. Jacob moved lower, parting her labia as he tore open the packet. He turned slightly and rolled the condom on, knowing it wouldn't take much to push her over.

"Jacob," she begged. Another muttered phrase followed that sounded Italian.

He played at her more urgently, reining in his need as her breath started coming in spasms.

"Now. Please, now."

That was his breaking point. Jacob pushed up over her and slid in fully in a single stroke. Stephanie met his eyes, sucking in her breath. Her eyes fluttered shut and her back arched up, as sweet contractions gripped his length.

Not yet, he pleaded as his cock exploded in sensation and climax rolled like thunder from the base of his spine and his balls up the length. He cried out harshly at her scream of pleasure. She relaxed to the bed beneath him, looking stunned.

Jacob laid a kiss on her lower lip. "Don't leave yet," he requested.

Stephanie bit her lip. "M — my roommate," she stammered.

"Is a big girl." From the other woman's show, Jacob couldn't believe that she was alone at the club for long. "Please, stay for a while."

She seemed to consider something carefully, then nodded. He smiled, relieved that she'd agreed.

* * * *

"Okay," Joel grumbled. "Jacob's here, and Stephanie is probably with him. What now?"

Geoff ground his teeth in frustration. *Of all the boneheaded moves Trouble has made over the years, this one takes the cake. What in the Christian hell is she thinking?*

Whatever it was, it was going to sound reasonable when she explained it. It always did. It wasn't enough to get her out of the trouble she was named for, but it was always rational...from a particular point of view.

"Geoff?"

"Load all of her stuff in the car and leave me here. Meet me back here as soon as you're through."

"We're running."

"As soon as she's away from him." *Back to Hunter range before anything worse comes out of this.*

* * * *

Jacob refilled her wine glass, smiling at Stephanie's red-faced laughter.

"Then what did he do?" she managed through hitching breaths.

"Kord?" He sipped his wine, savoring the burn in his throat. "He told Jack to collect his sister before he throttled her. It's amazing that those two ever married."

She nearly choked on a mouthful of the red liquid. "Oh, gods! I can picture their faces."

"So, tell me about yourself." It was the one thing she seemed to be avoiding, though he had no idea why.

Stephanie sobered and swallowed another mouthful. "Not much to tell."

"Where are you from?" She didn't have a definitive accent that would tell him.

She shrugged. "Around. We didn't keep much of a steady address while I was growing up."

"Dad was a drifter?" he guessed.

"No. Mom was a doctor."

Jacob raised an eyebrow in surprise. Doctors were typically sedentary types, building a practice and tending it painstakingly. "Really?"

She managed a weak smile. "Really."

"Brothers or sisters?"

She stared into her glass. "A half-sister, but we don't see each other often. You know the drill. She's older and has her own life."

"What about your father?"

She stared into the fire he'd built in the fireplace, sipping her drink again, her eyes sad. "I don't have one."

He winced. "Dead?"

"No. I...just don't have one. You know. The old blank line on the birth certificate. I think it might actually say father unknown or something. I never looked closely enough to find out."

"I'm sorry."

"Don't be. It doesn't bother me much."

He took a calming breath. Stephanie wasn't much of a liar. It obviously bothered her a lot, but she didn't seem to want to talk about that. A change of subject was in order. "So... Where do you live?"

"On campus."

He searched her expression, wondering at how closed she suddenly was. "It's a big campus," he noted.

"I don't even know you, Jacob."

"I've been telling you about me for the last two hours, and we've made love twice so far."

Her skin flushed a deep rose, and she met his eyes. Jacob felt the breath being punched out of him by the stark hunger in her eyes.

* * * *

Stephanie set her wine glass aside, needing this connection with him one more time. She crawled across the quilt to him, taking his length in her mouth and closing her eyes to his groan of pleasure.

"Gods alive, you're trying to kill me," he accused.

She pushed him to the edge in a few dedicated strokes, then knelt up and kissed him, grasping the condom he'd placed next to the wine bottle and ripping it open. His mouth came at hers more urgently as she rolled it down him.

He reached for her, but she smiled and turned away, dropping to her hands and knees. Jacob didn't question what she wanted. There were few words between them at moments like this; they didn't seem necessary.

His hands circled her hips, then one eased down to stroke her clit. Stephanie moaned, pushing back on him, and he eased inside.

"*Madre de Dios,*" she breathed.

Jacob chuckled, then groaned as he set a slow, easy pace. "Just exactly how many languages do you speak?" he asked.

She swallowed hard, glad that he couldn't see her expression — what was surely pure panic. "Only three fluently. Besides English."

"Only?" He laughed heartily at that.

She winced. How many mistakes could she make in one night? "I know a few linguists who speak a dozen," she reasoned. *And grew up with Warriors who spoke between four and eight as a rule.*

She closed her eyes, trying to push away her fear of slipping and lose herself in this fantastic sex. As if Jacob agreed, he dropped the discussion and paid full attention to the subject at hand.

He murmured words in the ancient language of the Warriors, but they were words she didn't recognize. For some reason, the sound of them increased her pleasure. Stephanie found herself screaming his name, riding waves of delight to a second crest as his heat swirled against the latex between them.

Jacob cradled her to his body and pulled her to their sides, still embedded deep inside her, his arm under her head as a pillow. He laid a kiss on the back of her head, trailing his fingertips through the curls that covered her sex.

She shifted against the arm under her cheek, too tired and comfortable to do what needed done. *Just a few minutes*, she assured herself. *I'll leave in a few minutes.*

Chapter Thirty-five

May 21ˢᵗ, 2011

Stephanie came awake in a jolt of realization. Sunlight was streaming through the windows. Geoff and Joel were going to kill her for this.

She left the quilts on the floor quickly and quietly, looking to Jacob to assure herself that he was still sleeping. She pulled on her clothes, guiltily noting the sticky feeling of her thighs that announced her misdeeds.

She was nearly to the door, her sweater thrown over her arm and her shoes in hand, when he groaned. She didn't hesitate. She had to get away before he came fully awake.

A grumbled curse followed, and she winced at the idea of a Warrior with a red-wine headache as bad as hers was. *His will be gone in an hour!*

"Stephanie, wait."

"I have to go," she replied brusquely, opening the bedroom door.

"You can't leave yet."

Her head pounded in terror. That was an order — an order he had no right to give. "I can't stay." She stepped through the door.

He moved behind her, and she hurried down the hall toward the stairs, praying he'd take the time to dress before he followed her.

"Stephanie, wait. This is important."

She glanced back at him, cursing aloud at the sweatpants he'd pulled on. Jeans would have taken longer. She started down the stairs.

"Damn it, I said wait." His hand closed around her wrist, pulling her to an abrupt stop.

Stephanie didn't look at him. The urge to scream the sanctions he was breaking at him in several languages was too strong. How would she explain knowing them in the first place?

"Now...I need to talk to you."

She nodded, swallowing hard and hoping that it was something mundane like an offer to drive her home that she would refuse kindly.

He sighed. "I don't want you to leave."

"I can't stay. I have a life — responsibilities." *Most notably the responsibility to protect my family. I'm only here for them.*

Liar! She couldn't even utter the words in her mind and not call herself a hypocrite.

"Even if you have no intention of marrying me —"

She stared at him, and he winced, no doubt reading her horror at that idea clearly on her face. "I don't do marriage," she offered coolly, silencing the traitorous voice in her mind that was pleased he'd asked.

Jacob was a wonderful man: funny, tender, loving, exciting, and great in bed. If he were human — or she wasn't what she was, she'd marry him in a heartbeat.

His face hardened, and he nodded curtly. "We still have to talk." His voice was strained.

"There is nothing to talk about."

"Yes, there is. We fell asleep after that last time — both of us. I was still inside you and —"

The blood rushing in her ears drowned out the rest. If he was concerned, she was high cycle. How dare he put her in this situation! She drew her fist back and punched him hard across the cheekbone, gratified when he released her arm to catch himself against the wall.

She turned and bolted for the door, knowing that punch wouldn't do more than stun him for a second. It wouldn't take him long to recover from his shock, and she had to be out the door and in public before that happened.

"Stephanie," he thundered as she pulled the door open.

"Don't come near me, you bastard," she shot back, slamming it between them. She turned to run, crashing into another broad chest. She snapped her eyes up, fearful that it was an Armen, then gasped in realization.

Geoff swept her to his back, drawing his weapon and planting it firmly in the lock. He hit the hilt solidly and snapped the tip off inside. Then he turned and dragged her to the car Joel had running on the other side of Jacob's Buick.

She scrambled into the back seat with her cousin at her heels, breathing a sigh of relief as they left Jacob Armen far behind.

* * * *

It was a full minute before Jacob recovered from her vehement exit enough to follow her to the door. The delay didn't worry him. She was a human on foot, and he was a Night Warrior. She couldn't possibly outrun him.

The snap of metal as he reached the door startled him, and the fact that the latch wouldn't disengage confirmed his worst fears. He sprinted to the living room window, intent on going through it if he had to, then stopped in shock.

A man in black had Stephanie by the arm, hustling her into a car driven by another. He wrenched the back door open, and she ducked inside with the man behind her. Before Jacob had recovered his senses and forced himself to motion, the car was gone.

He laid his head against the glass, his mind in a sick swirl. What in the Christian hell was this? Who were these men and what did they have to do with Stephanie? She went with them without a fuss when she'd proven only moments earlier that she could defend herself.

A niggling of unease ate at him. The men had looked roughly like Warriors, but they couldn't be. If they had been —

No. She hadn't been wearing an amulet, and no protected from other ranges were reported in Armen. Even if there was a slip-up, and a protected was here...

Without an amulet? He winced. Why would a protected risk that? Why would she feel the need to hide that she was protected from a Warrior? No. No protected would risk it, and no Warrior would have behaved as the two men had.

So where did that leave him? Did she have a boyfriend? After her reaction, Jacob was certain she didn't have a husband.

He sighed, pushing away from the window and ambling back upstairs. No matter who they were to her, the men were immaterial. Jacob had a duty to find her. He'd screwed up in the most monumental way possible. He had to find her and —

What do I do then? Good gods! Uncle James is going to kill me for this.

Where do I start? Jacob sat on the quilts he'd shared with Stephanie, replaying their conversations in his mind. She'd said maddeningly little about herself. He didn't even have a full name to go on. She lived on campus. It was the best lead he had — nearly the only lead he had.

He started collecting up the glasses and quilts, planning his pursuit. What in Ani's name was he supposed to do if she thought he was a crackpot? He had a duty to protect and train his progeny.

Jacob stilled at the bed, spying an amulet kicked under the edge of the dresser. He sighed, crossing the room and scooping it up. It was no doubt one of Tommy's. The boy lost at least three amulets a year. He tossed the amulet up in the air and caught it with a smile, envisioning Tim's scowl when Jacob returned his son's amulet to him...again.

His smile disappeared, and he stared at the seal in disbelief, then the dresser. Her sweater! She'd removed it in the bathroom and put it on the dresser before she came to bed.

Jacob fisted his hand around the amulet. So, Stephanie *was* protected. She'd taken off her amulet and played blade chaser. Well, that was just fine. If she knew about the Warriors, his reasons for finding her would come as no surprise.

He grumbled a curse, remembering the men who drove her away. Jacob took the stairs down and went out the back door, speeding around the end of the block, two houses down, and to the front door. He pulled at the piece of metal broken off in the lock, his jaw tightening in fury as the tip of a sacred weapon slid free.

"What are they doing? Are they insane?"

Jacob looked at the amulet again, wondering which of the Lord Hunter's nephews he had to thank for this damage. His eyes widened. *A lord's amulet!* Who was Stephanie that she had a lord's amulet?

* * * *

"Are you insane?" Geoff thundered.

Stephanie rubbed at her forehead, wincing in pain.

"Hangover?" he inquired.

"If you must know, yes. Between the mixed drinks with Val and the wine...and..." She groaned, looking ill.

"Good," he snapped at her. *Stupidity should be painful.* "You know that doesn't excuse you."

"Excuse me? If you hadn't shown up at the club last night — a *day* early, I could have turned him down and made a quick exit and run for the border. But, no! I couldn't let him see the two of you." She winced again, as if her own shouting was making her as ill as his was.

Geoff raised an eyebrow, his face burning in rising impatience. "Are you saying you slept with him to save —"

"No! Well...partly, I guess."

"Stephanie..." he warned.

"Well, if I wasn't who I am, I wouldn't have balked at the idea, but I only went for it —"

"Stephanie!"

She paled and fished for her purse, pulling her sunglasses out and settling them on her face. "Don't do that. Okay?"

"Did it ever occur to you that we could have lied our way out?"

She moved her mouth as if to speak, then shook her head, dumbstruck.

"We've been lying for twenty-five years. What's new? We could have claimed you were dating Joel or something. You could have pulled that off for five minutes, couldn't you?"

Stephanie laid her head back. "Yeah," she admitted. "I hadn't considered that."

"You never consider the possibilities, Trouble," he grumbled.

"But, Val! I danced with him, because Val almost said —"

"Do you think I couldn't have kept Val busy?" he challenged.

She sighed. "You could," she admitted.

Joel snickered. "Always knew we called you 'Trouble' for a reason. Wonder what your father will say about this one."

Stephanie looked at the back of his head in undisguised horror. "No. Don't make him worry, Joel. Just stop off somewhere so I can get a shower and change. It's over. Okay?"

"As soon as we clear Armen range," he promised.

Geoff cleared his throat. "What was that scene about when you were leaving?" He wasn't promising anything in regards to Corwyn until he had an answer on that.

She stared at the hands clutched in her sweater. "He asked me to marry him, and I refused." She peeked up at him through the hair hanging over her eyes and over the rims of her sunglasses.

"Oh, gods," he pleaded.

"I refused him," she repeated. "The sanctions say —"

"I know what they say," he snapped. He glared at her, his gaze settling on her camisole. "Put on your amulet, damn it!"

She sighed and unfolded her sweater into her lap, her brow furrowing as she ran her hands over the inside once — then again, even turning the sleeves inside out. Stephanie didn't meet his eyes. She paled.

"I think — I think I need to be sick," she managed weakly.

Joel groaned. "You lost it, didn't you? At Armen's house?"

"More likely on the way to the car," she suggested hopefully.

Geoff pulled an amulet from his pocket and shoved it at her. "Only if your luck has changed, Trouble."

She looked at him with tears in her eyes, scooping the amulet over her shoulders.

He sighed. All her life, it had been like this. Where every other Warrior daughter was indulged completely, Stephanie's life had been nothing short of regimental. She had always been watched...for nearly every moment of her life, whether she knew it or not. Losing her amulet had been punished harshly. Hiding from her guards had been punished even more severely.

With Veriel's threat hanging over her during her childhood, it had to be that way.

Worse, she was hidden — always hidden away like some dirty secret. When Warriors called to see Corwyn, Laura and Stephanie had been sent away. When Warriors showed up unexpectedly, they had been snuck out a back door. In order for Stephanie to have a feminine room, Corwyn had to buy a new house to share with his second mate and daughter, one the other houses didn't know about.

His duty demanded that Geoff tell Corwyn all of this, but one look at Stephanie was all he needed to convince him that he couldn't do this to her again. She wasn't a Warrior. She was a freed female of his house. Veriel was dead, and the only reason for this treatment was to protect the family name.

His honor wouldn't allow Geoff to let her suffer alone for the family. Not this time. If he could help it, she'd never suffer for no better reason than their name again. The worst part was, Stephanie wasn't even suffering for their honor; Geoff wasn't certain how much honor any of them had left.

"Come here," he conceded, letting her cry into his shoulder.

"I'm sorry," she whispered. "I never intended —"

"I know."

Corwyn once said that being found stole Jayde's life and freedom. In truth, it did far worse things to Stephanie than it ever had to Jayde. Erin — now Jayde — rejoining the Warrior world brought the eyes of the other houses down on Hunter range, effectively stealing her family from her when she needed them most.

It wasn't fair that Stephanie had to shoulder the responsibility for hiding her own birth. "I know," he repeated.

Chapter Thirty-six

May 26th, 2011

Jacob rubbed his eyes, staring at the computer screen in relief. After five days of intensive searching, he'd finally found her.

Who knew there could be so many Stephanies, Stefanis, Stefanys and any other number of variants of the spelling at one university? He'd finally given up and done a blanket search for any names containing Steph or Stef, but that had netted him every Stephen and Stefano at the college. He had even had to cross a George Stefani off of his list.

It had been painstaking. He'd whittled the printouts down by sex and then age. Finally, he'd taken five hundred and sixty-eight names to the individual computer files, pulling them up and eliminating them one by one. With no clue as to the spelling of her name, he'd made the poor choice of taking them in alphabetical order, starting with the Stefanis, solidified by the fact that most of the names fell in the Stef spellings. As a result, Stephanie Caroline Briony had been number three hundred and ninety-two on the list.

There she was, her black hair half-covering her left eye as he remembered it, laughing into the camera, wearing a skin-tight baby T. His heart ached. Why did she have to look so good?

He printed out the file with a sigh. It was a given that Stephanie wouldn't be happy to see him again, but that was immaterial. He had a duty to perform, a duty she was no doubt well aware of if she had a lord's amulet.

Jacob just hoped the Wonder Twins stayed away long enough for him to do that duty. In his endless replays of every moment with Stephanie, her would-be rescuers had become all too clear to him.

Stephanie's friend had pronounced him just her type, and she'd elbowed her. Then she'd commented that it was spooky how much he looked like someone; Stephanie had dragged him off before she could say who. There was only one North American Warrior who could be mistaken for Jacob... He glared at the amulet. And he was a Hunter.

Joel Hunter.

Joel Hunter and his cousin Geoff were laughingly called "the Wonder Twins." Exceptional Warriors in their own right, the duo were who Corwyn Lord Hunter sent in as a team when there was extreme trouble.

That word seemed coined for Stephanie — trouble! *Then why do I still want her? Why do I believe she's vulnerable and in need of protection?*

She has protection, he argued with himself. A lord's amulet and the Wonder Twins were protection enough for even young Erin *König.*

"Who are you, Stephanie Briony?"

An unwelcome thought lodged in his mind, making his gut twist uncomfortably. What if she was involved with one of the Wonder Twins? What if Stephanie had been playing him all along — getting a taste of a new Warrior cock?

He fisted her amulet, digging every line into his palm. Baiting a Warrior wasn't a smart move — not if she wanted to keep her protection for long.

He sighed, pushing away his uncertainties and pulling her school files from the printer. The best thing to do was to learn all he could about her before he approached.

He panned his gaze down the pages, noting an apartment she kept in Hunter range, her stats, and grades. He stopped in confusion when he reached her emergency contact information.

"Laura Briony, mother." The address was a house in Denver in the same area as her apartment, but the phone number...

It had been years since he'd had to check in at the Hunter manor when a track took him across the dividing line, but that phone number was definitely the manor line. The address wasn't one he knew of as a Hunter sanctuary, but the houses didn't share all their inner workings with the others. It could be one.

But the phone number... Why wouldn't her emergency contact phone be her mother's? If they were worried that Dr. Briony would be out of touch when Stephanie needed her... He shook his head. That went beyond any sane definition of protection he'd ever heard of.

Jacob scowled at the information, more confused than ever. "Wonder what the Hunter finances would show?" he mused. His uncle and father would surely disapprove of a hack into another house, but this wasn't a typical inquiry.

Four hours later, he was more confused than ever. The Hunter accounts had paid for Stephanie's condo and her mother's house. Monthly bills seemed to be paid from elsewhere — perhaps from Laura and

Stephanie's own earnings, though it was hard to track with so many cabins and sanctuaries.

He set down the file, staring at the amulet warily. "Who are you, Stephanie Briony?"

Chapter Thirty-seven

May 28th, 2011

"And there she is." Jacob smiled at the sight of Stephanie walking out the side door of the city offices and toward her car. From his place in the alley — and ghosted, she couldn't possibly see him.

Without warning, Geoff eased from behind a van and grasped her by the arm. She swung around, pulling a small dagger from a sheath behind her, but the Warrior's hand moved from her arm to the opposite wrist in the blink of an eye — in roughly the time it took Jacob to tense to kill him if he harmed her.

Geoff laughed heartily, and she reached her now-free hand up to smack him aside the head. He released her, rubbing his skull in mock annoyance, and Stephanie sheathed the dagger again.

She kissed his cheek, winding both arms over his right shoulder and dropping her cheek to the pillow of her hands. Jacob fought for a decent breath, feeling as if he'd been gut shot with a sledge. By the time he recovered, they were moving toward him, arm in arm.

Joel charged across the parking lot with a battle whoop and a punch at the sky, swinging Stephanie around and planting a kiss on her cheek. He shot Geoff a look of challenge and tossed her over his shoulder like a sack of training equipment.

His cousin crossed his arms over his chest, his eyebrow raised in silent censure.

"Let me down," she complained, laughing.

"Only if you tell Geoff that you love me best," he vowed.

"Are you nuts?"

Jacob placed his hand on the wall, shaking his head in denial of what he was seeing.

Geoff cleared his throat. "I think the lady wants to trade up now," he suggested.

Stephanie aimed a kick for his chest that Geoff deflected.

"And that was for?" he inquired calmly.

"Trading up, you creep! I talked to Val and heard your idea of trading up."

Geoff looked horrified, and Jacob bit back a laugh at the unexpected treat of seeing him this way.

Joel howled in laughter. "Geoff's in the dog house now."

Stephanie smacked him on the shoulder. "You're not exactly off the hook, either," she warned him.

Joel's smile disappeared. "Aw, come on, Stephanie. You know the Hunter sandwich thing wasn't my idea."

"Well, it certainly wasn't mine," Geoff countered hotly.

Stephanie huffed in annoyance. "Let me down, and we'll discuss who's at fault over dinner. Your treat, Hunters."

Jacob felt the need to be sick. He'd heard of blade chasers like this, but he hadn't believed it. How could he have called Stephanie so wrong?

Joel settled her back on her feet, and both men hooked an arm around her hips.

Geoff smiled at her. "Back where you belong," he sighed. "We missed you, Trouble."

* * * *

Stephanie locked the door to her apartment behind her, groaning. It had been a long day, and a hot bath followed by bed was just the ticket. She dropped her backpack on the table in the front hall and ambled toward her bedroom, pulling her shirt from her jeans and peeling it off her body.

"And the lady returns."

She stopped with a gasp, pressing the shirt to her chest and looking toward the bed in disbelief. She didn't bother to ask how Jacob found her. With Warriors, there were too many possibilities for tracking her to count. Her initial stunned indecision didn't last long. "How dare you —"

Jacob lifted his hand and opened it; her lost amulet unfurled and bounced back slightly before setting into a gentle swing at the end of its chain, looped around his index finger. "You lost something, Stephanie."

She didn't hesitate. She stormed across the room, ripped the amulet from his hand, and stuffed it in her front pocket. "Thank you for returning it. Now, leave my home. If you come back, rest assured that I will report you to —"

"To Geoff or Joel? Tell me. Which one of the Wonder Twins is it that you care so much for?" His eyes were hard and dangerous.

Stephanie felt her cheeks heat. "To neither. You've seen my amulet. You know who I'll call, if you don't leave me alone."

"Ah, yes. The lord's amulet. Tell me... Why exactly would you have one of those?"

She swallowed around a dry spot in her throat. "My... My mother is a doctor. She has the Lord's seal, because she's so trusted, and —"

"And, her protection extended to you?" He raised an eyebrow in disbelief.

"Corwyn is generous and kind," she countered hotly. "He chooses who he protects, and it's none of your business if he chooses to protect every child and spouse of every professional he —"

"But he doesn't choose to. Why you? And...why the Lord's seal?"

"That is something you need to take up with Corwyn — if you dare approach him and admit you've done this."

Jacob rose from the bed, towering over her. Stephanie grasped the phone receiver and reached for the autodial button to the manor with an outstretched finger. Before she connected, he cut through the cord with his sacred weapon, then sheathed it again smoothly.

"You have to follow the sanctions," she reminded him, trying to calm the pounding of her heart.

"Yes, I do, and the sanctions say that I must be certain that any progeny of mine is under my protection and trained appropriately."

She fought back the automatic response that any child of hers would be well-protected and trained. That was something she could never admit to a Warrior outside her family. "Let me put your mind at ease, Jacob. My mother is a doctor. If I do conceive, I guarantee she will take care of that for you. You will have no duty to me."

He tensed, grasping at her shoulders as if he would hurt her. Stephanie dropped the receiver, reaching automatically for the dagger at her back. His hand closed over hers, stopping the slide and shoving the weapon back into the sheath. His eyes bored into her, and she shuddered. She'd pushed him too far. Warriors were biologically and psychologically committed to their children. Her threat had snapped him.

Jacob released her and turned to the door, striding away as she sagged to the wall. He stopped in the doorway, his breathing harsh. "Stephanie..."

"Yes?"

"I'll be back to check on that. Don't think I won't." He didn't move for a moment. "I'll be at the Governor's Inn — if you have anything to say to me. Anything at all."

Then he was gone, the front door slamming behind him.

She sank to the bed, running a shaking hand through her hair. "Great," she grumbled. "Just great."

What was she supposed to do now? If she went to her father, Corwyn would end up dead when he revealed his connection to her. If she went to Geoff or Joel, most of the Hunter warriors would end up dead or judged. Her mother was her only choice.

Chapter Thirty-eight

May 30th, 2011

Geoff ground his teeth in fury, taking in the sight of the Warrior slouched against the medical building, a sour look on his face. How dare Jacob Armen stalk Stephanie in her own range! No wonder she'd been so edgy the last few days. She probably feared what Geoff would do if he knew about this, and she was right about that. She'd said "no." That should have ended Armen's involvement.

Jacob turned to him when he was still two body lengths away, glaring at him. "Hunter," he growled.

"You are inviting judgment, Armen. I suggest you leave Hunter range before I haul you in."

"I have unfinished business here —"

"She turned down your offer of marriage. By the rules of sanction —"

"I have a duty," he snapped.

Geoff's stomach rebelled. "What are you saying?" he demanded.

"Let me guess. She hasn't told you." His face was set in a scowl, his voice cynical.

Geoff fisted the hilt of his sacred weapon, fighting back the urge to play the role of judge. If there was judgment to be passed, it was Corwyn's place to pass it. "You took her unprotected at high cycle? Tell me you didn't, you bastard."

"Of course, I didn't!" He paced along the wall and back again, seemingly ready to snap mentally.

Geoff's breathing eased, though the answer confused him. If he hadn't taken her unprotected... Or had he simply asked the wrong question? "Then what are you talking about?"

Jacob ran a hand through his hair, mussing it more instead of straightening it. "We were drinking and... It's no excuse. I know that. I screwed up." The words seemed to torture him.

"How?"

"I fell asleep still inside her. I don't know how much spilled — If I spilled inside her at all. I don't...know."

Geoff grasped the wall, his legs uncertain beneath him.

"She felt so right, so comfortable, and it just happened. You must have some idea what I mean," he decided miserably.

"What?" Where had that come from?

"Oh, come on! I've analyzed what I've seen of you three so many times it makes me dizzy. You're the one she's sleeping with, aren't you? Joel is just taunting you about it like he does in training."

Geoff forced his mouth to shut, abruptly aware that he looked like an idiot.

Jacob laughed harshly, a half-mad sound. "She's not the marrying type, you know. She told me that. She's probably carrying my son, and she'd rather abort than consider being my mate."

Geoff looked at the building in sick horror; Laura would do that without question if Stephanie requested it. Stephanie wouldn't... But he knew she would, just as she'd done nearly everything else she thought would protect Corwyn.

"Get out of my range, Armen."

"I have a duty —"

He grabbed the other Warrior by the throat, just a warning of what would come next if he dared utter another syllable about staying in Hunter. "Consider your duty done."

His face paled. "What are you saying? She hasn't —"

"I hope not. If she chooses not to abort, I'm raising this child as my son. Get used to the idea." Geoff didn't give him time to answer. He pushed Jacob away and stormed into the medical building and up the three flights of stairs to Laura's office.

* * * *

"You did what?" Laura asked, her eyes wide.

Stephanie fought back tears. All those years of careful living, and she'd blown it. She hadn't even had the courage to go directly to her mother. She'd procrastinated two days, trying to figure out the best way to approach this. Now she was getting a lecture, when what she really needed was a solution.

"Oh, Mom! Please, don't. I screwed up. I know it."

Obviously realizing Stephanie had already beaten herself up for this mess, her mother wrapped her arms around her, sighing. "Okay. Planning session."

She winced. That term sent a cold wave through her. It was usually preceded by some stunt of Stephanie's that called for emergency action on her father's part. Out of all of her options, getting Corwyn involved was the lowest on her list.

"If you have conceived, what do you plan to do about it?"

"I already told him I'd abort," she admitted.

Laura nodded. "Are you sure about this?"

"What other choice do I have? Do you know any Warrior that would willingly give up his child?"

"No," she agreed. "They aren't wired that way. You're right. This is probably the best course."

"Right. Then I don't have a choice."

"Well... We better get moving. A blood test should tell us definitively."

"You can't go in there," the receptionist shouted.

Stephanie pushed to her feet, forcing herself not to bolt. Where would she run? "Oh, gods," she pleaded. "He wouldn't dare."

But the flash of black coming around the opening door told her that Jacob would. She backed toward the wall, bumping past her mother as she retreated, swallowing a whimper of fear and blinking back tears that it had come to this.

Laura didn't hesitate. She placed herself between them, pulling her amulet from under her smock, prepared to take on Jacob with her bare hands if it became necessary.

The coming Warrior wasn't Jacob. Stephanie sobbed in relief at the sight of Geoff, then pressed herself hard to the wall at his expression of pure malice.

"Geoffrey Paul Hunter," Laura snapped, throwing her full authority as Lady Hunter into her demand. "What in the hell do you think you're doing?"

He ignored her, rounding Laura and grasping Stephanie by the shoulders. He growled a series of curses. "Your luck couldn't be with us just once, could it?"

Stephanie's knees gave way at that proclamation, and Geoff supported her. She'd hoped — She'd secretly believed that it wouldn't happen, that the gods who'd cursed her from birth wouldn't dare do this to her as well.

Geoff hugged her to his body, letting her vent tears into his chest. "It's okay. You don't have to do this."

"I do," she choked. "I don't have a choice."

"Fuck that! There are always options. You just never seem to see them until it's too late. Now — Do you really want to abort?"

Her mind wouldn't seem to function. Want to? This wasn't an option, was it?

"Stephanie! I know how you feel about the subject in general. It's your body and your baby now. If you had another option, one that would let you keep the baby and not expose Corwyn, would you choose it?"

She nodded, her mind numb.

He sighed in obvious relief, smoothing her hair. "Then this isn't necessary."

"How? I don't understand how."

"Trust me. But there is one thing we have to do."

Stephanie wiped at her tears. "What's that?"

"We have to tell your father what's going on."

She swallowed a sour wave in her throat. "No. I can't."

"We have to. For this to work, we need his help. Be reasonable, Stephanie. If you have a baby, he's going to know details. He'll demand to."

She nodded. "Tomorrow," she requested. Anything but facing him at this moment.

"We'll meet for lunch," Laura added.

Chapter Thirty-nine

May 31ˢᵗ, 2011

Time to face the music. Stephanie squared her shoulders and headed for the restaurant entrance, scanning the cars in the lot. Her mother, Geoff, and Joel were here. Unless her father came with Laura or one of the guys, he'd yet to arrive.

She breathed a sigh of relief at that. She'd never been the type who simply wanted to get an unpleasant moment over with quickly. Avoidance was her unofficial middle name. Everyone around her knew her first name well enough.

She knew her cousins meant it as a joke, but she'd always hated the nickname. Calling her "Trouble" was too close to the truth of her entire existence.

A Warrior was only supposed to print once and only supposed to produce children with a sealed mate. From her conception, Stephanie had been an anomaly. Her mother had been nearly a month pregnant before she and Corwyn sealed printing — a printing that shouldn't have been possible.

Corwyn had already printed and lost a mate and daughter, Anna and Jayde. Was it his fault that the Stone decided to give him another shot at being a husband and father by letting him print again? Was it hers?

Stephanie came into the world at a disadvantage. As if Veriel's mad games, tormenting her father with the possibility of taking her from him, were not bad enough; the Warriors of Hunter saw her as a liability.

The threat of losing Corwyn to judgment had solidified the name "Trouble" with a capital T.

A hand grasped at her arm, and she sighed. Wouldn't Geoff ever get tired of this game? He'd played it since he'd started training, long before her father had gifted her the dagger she typically wore at her back.

She didn't reach for the dagger. Instead, she swung around and smacked his cheek — hard. Stephanie swallowed a scream as her gaze locked with Jacob's.

His face hardened. He pulled her behind a shade tree. "I need to talk to you," he informed her.

She pulled at his hold. "We have nothing to discuss." *And if my family sees you here, you will be dead without ever standing before a judge.*

"You're carrying my child. We have a lot to discuss."

Stephanie struggled to form words. She couldn't tell him she intended to abort when she didn't. She didn't know what Geoff's plan was yet, so she couldn't even offer that.

Jacob's hands gentled and he nuzzled at her lips. Her head swam. What was he doing to her? His mouth closed on hers, softly, seeking. She found herself responding, opening for him when he sought entry and anticipating his touch.

He pulled away, laying a kiss on her forehead. "You're not a blade chaser," he whispered. "I know you aren't. I didn't call you wrong that first night. I couldn't have."

She shook her head. Blade chaser wasn't a title she'd ever earned.

"Then marry me." His lips traced her ear to the line of her jaw.

Her mind cleared at that, shocking her back to the reality of the situation. She shook her head, pulling back tears. "No. I —"

"I've seen you with Geoff. He's fun, but you don't love him."

"I do," she insisted. *Too much to see him judged for killing you.*

"Not like this."

She couldn't argue that.

He nodded, his eyes pleading with her. "Then marry me."

"I can't." Geoff said there were always choices, but there weren't. No matter how much she wanted him, there were some things she could never have. "Please, let me go."

* * * *

Jacob forced his fury back. "I can't. Don't you see? You love me. You've all but admitted it, but you're going to go through with this travesty."

"What travesty?" she demanded.

"Isn't it bad enough that our child's been conceived before printing? Ani only knows what will come of that. It's never been done before."

Her jaw tightened, and her eyes flashed in anger. "Of course it has! You're not really that stupid, are you? Good gods —" She snapped her mouth shut, seemingly mortified at her outburst.

"What do you mean? What babies —"

Stephanie shook her head, her face paling.

He grumbled a curse. "You still expect me to take this offer and walk away, don't you?"

She didn't seem capable of answering. If he didn't know better, he'd swear she had no clue what he was talking about.

He reined in the urge to shake her. "You love me, but you expect me to walk away and let a Warrior you don't love raise our son. I can't! How can you ask me to?"

Stephanie lost what little color remained in her cheeks, shaking her head in seeming horror. "Who —" She winced. "Geoff."

Fury herded his thoughts on. She really *didn't* know Hunter's game. Did he really hope to win her hand — and Jacob's son in this dishonorable manner?

"Jacob," she gasped, no doubt reading the murder in his eyes. "Don't. You can't do this."

"Can't I? Watch me."

The blade was at his throat in the blink of an eye, and Jacob froze in understanding. If he moved against either the Warrior or Stephanie in any way, he wouldn't make it to a judge. The rules of sanction gave the Warrior defending his protected or an unprotected human that right.

She grasped at the wrist holding the sacred weapon, desperation in her eyes. "No," she gasped. "Don't kill him. Please."

"Release her." The growling voice left no room for argument.

He pulled his hands up and back in a sign of surrender. The blade moved back, and Stephanie went with it. Jacob turned to the Warrior slowly, expecting to see Geoff, but the eyes that stared back at him with the promise of death were those of the Lord Hunter.

Well, at least my judge is here. I won't have to wait long for him to kill me.

Stephanie pulled at his arm. "Leave him," she requested. "Let's just —"

"Are you insane?" Corwyn demanded. "I have —"

"Nothing to do with this. Geoff has taken care of it. It's over. Jacob won't be coming back." She met his eyes, pleading for his agreement. "You won't be back, will you?"

Jacob ground his teeth in frustration. She'd played him perfectly. If he gave his vow not to return, he would be bound by it. With Lord Hunter in a full *Blutjagd*, not giving his vow could see him dead.

Other Warriors came at a run — Joel and then Geoff. They stopped cold at the scene laid out for them, shooting each other nervous looks.

His mind kicked into gear. He faced judgment; that much was true, but so did Geoff. A sudden certainty that Corwyn had no idea what his nephew was up to any more than Stephanie had propelled him toward a desperate course.

"I demand my judge," he stated.

"No," Stephanie pleaded with him. "There's no need for this. I told you —"

He glared at her, panning his gaze to her flat stomach — to his child. "It's easy for you, isn't it?"

She straightened her spine, her cheeks burning crimson. "No. It isn't easy for me, but you are leaving me no choice."

Jacob shook his head. What was wrong with him that she wouldn't consider marriage with him when she wasn't so picky where she spent her nights? She loved him. He was sure of it. "I demand my judge."

Corwyn nodded. "I'm sure you can find your way to the manor. Leave your weapons at the door."

"Straight away," he promised.

The lord turned, sheathing his weapon and drawing Stephanie under his arm. Geoff took up position at their backs while Joel escorted another woman toward the cars. At the last moment, the woman slipped from him and took the shotgun seat in Corwyn's vehicle. Stephanie slid into the back, and Corwyn took the wheel. Geoff and Joel stood guard between Jacob and the car until it was in motion, then headed to Geoff's.

Jacob stood where they'd left him, his heart sick in what was about to happen. Stephanie didn't want this. She didn't want him to seek judgment. He only wished he knew if she didn't want to see him hurt or Geoff.

Her newest threat to their child stung. If there was any way for him to release their care to Corwyn and stay sane, he would do it, but Jacob was honest enough to admit that he'd have to be executed within a month of his son's birth if it came to that. He couldn't give his word to stay away. It wasn't possible.

* * * *

Stephanie breathed a sigh of relief as the restaurant fell behind them. She tried not to consider what would happen at the manor. She had thirty minutes to calm her father down so that he wouldn't kill a man who didn't deserve it.

She ground her teeth at Geoff's "plan." She should never have left this to him. It was her problem, and it was up to her to settle it. It always had been, and for once in her life, she had to clean up her own mess instead of letting the Warriors do it.

"Does anyone want to explain *why* I'm about to pass judgment on Jacob Armen?" Corwyn asked in a voice she knew to be deceptively calm.

There was no route but the direct one. "I...slept with him."

He swerved, then pulled the car into line again, his hand tightening on the wheel. "Any particular reason you decided not to tell me this?"

"I have autonomy," she snapped. "Do you know the names of the other men I've slept with?"

"All three of them," he growled.

That figured. The other three had all been in Hunter range. What had she expected? "Well, put your mind at ease. I had *planned* to tell you today — until..." She motioned hopelessly.

"He's printing on you?"

She groaned. "I guess so."

"If this is the way he accepts no... You *did* say 'no,' didn't —"

"I'm pregnant."

Corwyn slammed on the brakes, pulled off the road, and turned to her, his face a mask of pure dismay. "You're what?"

"Pregnant. Gravid. In the family way. In trouble — Trouble, just like always."

He buried his face in his hands. "Dear gods. This was what you intended to tell me over lunch?"

"Lunch was Mom's idea, but yes... In a slightly less dramatic fashion, of course."

Laura stroked his arm. "Corwyn, it's not how it sounds. I'm sure Geoff's plan — whatever it is —"

"No," Stephanie interrupted them. "There won't be a judgment and there won't be a plan. I'm out of options. I shouldn't have left this to Geoff. All he did was make it worse."

Her father lowered his hands. "If you're saying what I think you are, you're going to push Jacob over the edge."

"The same edge breaking printing is going to force him to. It's not too late for him."

Corwyn nodded wearily and put the car in gear. "I hope you're right about that."

She closed her eyes, praying to gods who didn't care whether she lived or died as long as her father stayed stable. Maybe they cared enough about Jacob to take pity on him and not see him killed over this.

* * * *

Jacob entered the manor, handing his weapon off to Joel, then his jacket. He followed the younger Warrior into the library, wincing at the line of Hunter Warriors against the far wall, most likely every Warrior who wasn't on trail or based at the far reaches of Hunter range — a full five of the eight.

Stephanie sat on a leather sofa, her knees pulled to her chest, the other woman's arm wrapped around her. He stopped in recognition of their resemblance. So her mother had been at the restaurant with the Warriors. *The plot thickens.*

"Dr. Laura Briony, I presume," he said with a stiff bow of his head.

Corwyn tensed as if his greeting were some sort of threat. "I believe I've been given the full story now,

Jacob. I'm sorry, but Stephanie's choice to terminate and to refuse you is beyond my ability to change with a judgment."

Jacob felt his legs weaken and grasped the chair back in front of him for support. "You don't want to do this," he breathed, seeking her eyes for confirmation.

"Of course she doesn't," Geoff countered hotly. "If you'd just drop this, she wouldn't be forced to —"

"You shut up! You face judgment for what you've done already."

"Me?"

"Yes you, you son of a —"

"What the blazes are you talking —"

"When did you plan to tell Stephanie what your plan was? How did you intend to get your lord to agree to it? You may want her, but she loves me! If you think I'm going to stand by and —"

"She *asked* for my help."

"She doesn't want to marry you, Geoff."

"I *know* that. I don't know where you got this mad idea that I want to marry —"

"Don't you?"

"No. I don't."

Jacob stopped in confusion. "Then why are you doing this?"

"Because I won't let you force Stephanie into a choice she doesn't want to make."

"You're saying you're not doing this to keep her in your bed?"

Joel put a restraining hand on Geoff's weapon hand, and every Warrior in the room lit in varying levels of *Blutjagd*. Jacob looked around in rising unease; it would be far too easy for them to kill him and lie about why they did it. It would be dishonorable, but it wasn't impossible. He'd obviously just made a monumental error, though he had no idea what it might have been, and the Warriors looked ready to take that dishonorable step at their first opportunity.

Stephanie pushed from the couch and stormed to him, slapping his face with a resounding crack. Corwyn winced at that.

"How dare you," she demanded in a shaking voice. "You unspeakable bastard! You want to toss accusations? How about one that you planned to get me pregnant so I'd have to accept your offer of marriage?"

"I didn't. You know —"

"No. I don't know that, but I do know that I have never — that's right, *never* — slept with a Warrior of Hunter range."

The silence in the room was absolute. Jacob reached for her, intent on apologizing for offending her so grievously. "I'm —"

She pulled away with a sound halfway between a sob and a growl. "Don't touch me," she ordered, running from the room in tears.

Corwyn sighed. "Doc?"

Laura stood and strode toward the door, her head high. "I have her, Corwyn."

Jacob met the lord's eyes, surprised at the older man's seeming indecision. "I suppose you intend to judge me for getting her pregnant...and for being an idiot."

"No. I intend to talk to you...alone."

"Corwyn, I don't think —" Stephen began.

"Alone."

Geoff pulled out from under Joel's hand, glaring at Jacob all the way to the door. Joel and Nicky avoided his eyes as they followed their lord's orders.

Stephen remained. "I think I should —"

"Alone," he repeated patiently.

"Should I —"

"You'll know soon. Won't you?" he replied cryptically.

He nodded and left the room, closing the doors behind him.

"Sit down, Jacob."

He hesitated, then circled the chair and sank into it.

Corwyn dropped onto the sofa Stephanie and her mother had vacated. "You're printing, aren't you?"

Jacob felt his face flush. "Yes. I am."

"Then this whole thing has to be agonizing for you."

"Yeah." Agonizing was a pale comparison to the actual sensation, but Corwyn hardly needed that reminder.

"She doesn't want to abort, you know. She loathes the practice."

Jacob winced at that. He didn't want her to do something she would regret, but he couldn't conscience walking away. "I don't want her to. You know I don't."

"If it came to a choice of knowing your child was safe somewhere else —"

"Did you spend a single day not wishing Jayde was with you?"

He sighed. "No. I didn't."

"Wouldn't knowing where she was and not being able to touch her have killed you?"

"I imagine it would over years of it. I didn't weather it well for even the few weeks after she was found."

"Then how can you ask this of me?"

"I have to. Either I ask you to do this or I allow Stephanie to follow a course you'll both regret for the rest of your lives."

"She respects you. Talk sense to her."

"I can't. If I could..." He opened his fisted hand and stared at it miserably. "Sometimes, I think she has more honor than I do. She'll never abandon it."

"So you would honestly ask me to stay away, to sacrifice my sanity this way? Can you imagine what it will be like for me to never be able to claim my child?"

Corwyn didn't answer. He stared at his hand as if lost in thought, tracing first one line and then another, over and over.

It took a moment for the significance to hit Jacob. *Two* scars. *Two* blood oaths. Jacob looked at the closed doors in shock, facts racing through his mind.

Corwyn granted Stephanie and her mother the Lord's seal. He bought their home and Stephanie's condo. He paid for her education. He sent the Wonder Twins to escort her "home."

Stephanie had the look of a Warrior-born daughter. She said she had an older half-sister, but Jacob had never thought to check if that sister had been Laura's child. *Jayde?* There was no father listed on her birth certificate. She was fluent in four languages and had moved a lot as a child.

Joel and Geoff acted like older brothers — teasing, protective, as they would be of any woman of their house. Their faces when he'd accused her of sleeping with Geoff... Outrage! Pure and simple outrage had been their reactions. And Geoff's look of shock the first time Jacob said it... How had he missed the significance?

He looked back at Corwyn's hand. The second scar wasn't for any other blood oath. He knew it. It was a second freeing scar.

"You do know," he whispered. "She's yours. That's why her contact information is yours, why you foot the bills. How could anyone miss it? When she... Dear gods! When she argued that children have been born out of printing before, she meant herself."

"My daughter is no bastard," he growled, an edge of *Blutjagd* burning in him. "Believe what you like, but it was never that. Yes, she was conceived before printing was... But...the Stone..." He closed his eyes with a pained look. "I stopped caring if I lived or died, so it arranged to give me a purpose in life. You probably don't believe me. I wouldn't believe me, but it's true."

"She's doing this to protect you."

He nodded. "If I thought it would make her happy, I'd announce who she is today, but it wouldn't."

"Because you'd face the judgment of the other lords." He didn't question it.

"I would give anything to make her happy, but I don't know how to do that. It's been too many years and too many lies. Even if I gave her permission to marry you —"

"You'd do that?" he asked urgently.

"In a heartbeat," he vowed. "But the mistrust runs deep. I didn't intend to make her so fearful. It just happened along the way, but you see why she can't trust you."

"She's afraid I'd expose you? Or that someone else in my house would?"

"Yes. To you, this is simple. You see it as her accepting you or not. For Stephanie, the choice is much direr. You're asking her to endanger or lose her family — or to go against what she really wants to protect us."

He fought for a decent breath, his mind grasping at the one possibility to work this out. "Maybe not." If there was any chance, he had to take it.

* * * *

Stephanie burrowed her face into the pillow, so exhausted that even sleep seemed unobtainable. She forced her eyes open as the door creaked. She stared up at her father.

"Is he gone?" she asked.

He nodded, crossing the room and sitting on the bed beside her.

Her heart ached at that, but she pushed it away. She had to do this. "Good," she grumbled.

"Is it?"

Stephanie blinked her eyes, certain she was dreaming. "What?"

"He was right. You do love him. Don't you?"

Breathing was abruptly difficult.

"That's why you wouldn't let me kill him."

"It would have been too hard to explain —"

"It wouldn't have been hard at all! You know that." His expression went hard as stone, a sure sign that he was calling her a liar.

She felt her cheeks heat and looked away to the bathroom door. Of course it would have been easy. Hadn't she considered that when Corwyn's blade had been at Jacob's throat? He could have been dead in moments, and even his own house wouldn't have questioned it once her father declared that he'd proven a danger to a human protected.

He turned her face back to his, searching her eyes for answers she couldn't seem to come up with in her scattered mind.

"What if I offered to take on the baby's care and training?"

Her stomach lurched. It was a terrible idea when Geoff offered, and it was still terrible. "No."

"No? You don't want to abort. Why say no?"

"Jacob...won't give up. He —"

"The truth!"

She swallowed hard. Nothing made sense anymore. How could she tell him the truth when her mind seemed mired in the complexity of this situation?

"Geoff didn't tell you his plan."

"No. He didn't," she admitted, her head spinning.

"What was your reaction when you found out?"

Jacob's face swam before her eyes. All she remembered was his pain.

"Disbelief? Horror? Fear? Pity?" he prodded. "Come on, Stephanie. What did you feel?"

No. She hadn't pitied him. Or had she? "I don't know."

"Did you consider what would happen to Jacob if you did that to him?"

"Of course, I did!"

"That's why you won't choose that course. Not because he won't give up. Judgment would make him give up — or he'd be killed for breaking sanction."

"No," she gasped, all too aware that Jacob would be killed, if it came to that.

"So...you do love him."

Stephanie rubbed at her forehead, trying to stop the room's incessant spinning. Why was he doing this to her? Why was Corwyn making this more complicated?

"What do you really want, Stephanie?"

She felt the need to laugh and cry at the same time. "I don't know what I want anymore," she admitted.

"If you weren't my daughter... If it was just you, with no worries about exposing our family, what would you do?"

Memories of her night with Jacob flooded her mind. How many times that night had she reminded herself that it couldn't be more, but only because of who she was? The rest of his comment filtered in slowly.

"I'm not giving up my family for him." That wasn't an option she would ever consider seriously.

Corwyn shook his head. "I'm giving you permission to marry him, Stephanie. At some point in your life, you have to start doing what's right for you."

"But...what about you?"

"You are my daughter. I can't let you —"

A block of ice settled in her stomach. "You told him that?"

"He already had a clear picture. All it took was seeing us all interact to put it into perspective for him."

She pushed from the bed, shaking her head in denial. That was it. It came down to accepting Jacob or endangering her family? In actuality, it wasn't even that simple. She endangered them either way.

"Just consider it," Corwyn soothed her. "If you want him —"

"I don't." She fumed at the thought that she ever had. If he did this, he had no honor.

"Stephanie —"

She turned and bolted from the room, pulling the spare keys to her father's car from the rack by the front door. If Jacob Armen thought he could bully her this way, he was sadly mistaken.

* * * *

Jacob raised his head at the knock, praying to Ani that it was the news he hoped for. Perhaps Stephanie would accept his offer of marriage once her father talked to her.

He opened the door, letting out a breath he hadn't realized he'd been holding at the sight of her on the stoop. He'd barely had time to wonder at the pale, strained expression on her face when she punched him hard across the cheek.

"What did you do?" she shouted, her chest heaving in dry sobs. "Did you think I'd agree to this blackmail? That I wouldn't fight you?"

Jacob grimaced. Was *that* what Corwyn told her? He'd thought the man was earnest in his support. "Maybe you should come inside," he offered.

"Why? So, I don't ruin *your* honorable name? Two can play this game, Jacob. You want to convene a

Council of Lords? How about one for yourself! I have nothing to lose now."

"There isn't going to be a Council of Lords," he assured her through gritted teeth.

"If I marry you, you mean," she countered sarcastically. "Or maybe I should just give you your precious son! Your damned duty is all that's important to —"

She stopped on a gasp as he lifted her by the waist and hoisted her inside the room, kicking the door shut.

"Wh — What are you doing?" she stammered.

Jacob deposited her on the edge of the bed and strode to the mini-fridge, thankful that he'd been taught to keep nutritious food on hand. He returned to her with a bottle of juice, noting that she seemed too stunned to move.

Or too frightened.

He nudged her clasped hands with the bottle, and she looked at it in confusion.

"Drink this," he requested, "and calm down." Being so upset while she carried was a bad idea.

Stephanie opened the bottle and drank down several swallows. She glanced at him, then away, scooping the hair that typically covered her eye over her ear. "Don't do this," she whispered. "Please, don't."

He grumbled a curse. "I don't know what your father told you, but —"

She looked up at him in undisguised fear.

"Stephanie, please... You have the wrong idea."

"Do I? Are you saying you didn't investigate my background until you had enough evidence to implicate him?"

Jacob felt his face heat. "I did, but I didn't realize what I was seeing until today. I swear it. If I did, would I have accused you of sleeping with..." He groaned at that.

She shook her head slowly.

"You just confused me. Nothing fit. You're hot for me, but you were *violently* against a relationship. You were panicked every time it was brought up. Your amulet. The Wond — your cousins. I never —"

"What was it? What led you to Corwyn? Was it my travel? He insists on —"

"Your schooling. He paid for it, and while he has the money to do it on a whim, the emergency phone number in your file —"

"The manor," she choked.

"The manor."

Her lip trembled. Stephanie tried to hide it by taking another drink, but she spilled some of the juice. She sobbed, pressing a hand to her mouth.

Jacob knelt before her, blotting at the stain on her shirt with his cuff. "What is it?" he asked.

"I can't do this," she wailed, tears spilling down her cheeks.

He winced. "Why not?"

"Someone would find out. I'd slip up. I can't —"

"Shhh," he soothed her. "We can do this. Corwyn and I —"

She shook her head fiercely. "No. I won't be responsible for bringing him down. I can't. All my life, I've avoided Warriors. One wrong word..." Her eyes pleaded with him. "It would be my fault. It would —"

Jacob pulled her to his chest, anger warring with his need to protect her. He'd wondered what it was about her that screamed for comfort, and now that he knew, he wanted to hurt the ones who'd put her in this situation.

"It's not your responsibility to protect him. It's never been. I'm sure you were told that, but you're..." *You're the one who should have been protected, not them!* "It wasn't right to do this to you," he raged. "It's too much."

He suddenly realized that he was rocking her. It felt right, so he continued. Stephanie was silent save her hitching breaths. Just when he thought she'd fallen asleep in his arms, she spoke again.

"What if I slip?" she whispered.

"It won't matter. We've taken care of it."

"How?" she squeaked, tensing.

Jacob pulled back until he met her gaze. He stroked at her tears with his fingertips. "He was willing to announce who you are, you know."

She paled. "He can't."

He shook his head. "He won't. I convinced him to take a page from my uncle's book."

"I don't understand."

He brushed his lips over hers, hungry for more. "My Uncle James married a widow with daughters. Your father doesn't dare admit printing again, but —"

"You believe him?" she asked urgently.

"Yes, I do. Look... The Lord Armen has raised human girls who weren't his own as his daughters. Can't you see —"

"You believe him." She laughed nervously, as if his acceptance was more than she'd dared hope for.

"Yes. I really do." He looked to her lips, wanting to taste her again. He met her eyes reluctantly.

"He needed something, Stephanie." *I need the same thing.* "You and your mother filled that need." *Please, do the same for me.* "The other lords won't begrudge him taking a special interest in a family that needed him, a family that helped fill the empty ache in his heart."

She laid a hand over his heart, as if she'd heard his unspoken comments.

"You were raised as his daughter from infancy, much as Michelle and Melissa were raised as James's daughters," he continued. "They call him Daddy. What child wouldn't?"

"I've never —" she managed.

Jacob cupped her head and brought her mouth to his in a slow, solemn kiss. "It's too much to do alone, Stephanie. You've had too many years of shouldering this. Let the burden go. Let the rest of us carry it for you."

"Give...give me your vow."

"You have my vow that I never had any intention of exposing or blackmailing Corwyn. You have my vow that I will live this version of the truth until I die. You have my vow that I will never let a hint of this harm you..." He swallowed hard. *It's time to risk it all.* "No matter what you choose to do."

Stephanie sank to his chest, wrapping her arms around his shoulders, grasping his shirt in her fists. She didn't answer him; she just clung to him until her hands unclenched and her arms slid away.

Jacob lifted her onto the bed and laid beside her, praying this meant she'd choose him.

As if she read his mind, Stephanie turned into his chest. "Take me home," she grumbled sleepily.

His heart sank. "Your condo or the manor?" He kept his voice neutral, though he wanted to hit something — hard.

She yawned widely and wrapped her arm over his waist. "Do you live at the Armen manor?"

He chuckled. "Most of the time."

"Mmm. Okay," she breathed, tucking her cheek further in. "But I need to pack first."

Chapter Forty

June 1st, 2011

Jacob pulled up to the manor house, scowling at the Hunter van full of Stephanie's gear parking behind them. *Stephanie's gear and the Wonder Twins.* How did Corwyn expect Jacob to pull this off with the circus in tow?

"Trust me, he says," he grumbled.

Stephanie winced. "Corwyn said we'd understand later."

"Does he do that often?" If so, her life had been even less fun than he'd imagined. It had taken all Jacob's control not to threaten Corwyn at the high-handed pronouncement.

She sighed. "He *is* the Stone lord."

It was his turn to wince. Corwyn was Stone lord and had made an enigmatic set of directives for her cousins and for themselves. By extension, that meant Corwyn was either as fond of games and puzzles as the Stone was Herself or that he might enjoy the perversion of watching this one bite Jacob in the ass. "Joy."

The front door opened, and Jacob pushed his car door out and slid to his feet. "Show time," he muttered.

Stephanie didn't wait for him to come around and play the gentleman as he'd intended. Her door slammed shut as an echo to his, and she met him at the front of the car. At his side, she grasped his hand.

Hard. "It will be okay," he assured her. He'd already called ahead and told his family he'd be bringing home his mate. Of course, at the time, he hadn't expected to be shadowed by the Wonder Twins while he did it.

"That's not what you said in the car."

Tim appeared in the doorway, his brow furrowing at the sight of the assembled Warriors. Jacob clearly heard his cousin call for James.

She is under enough stress. I shouldn't have said anything that made Stephanie more self-conscious. "I didn't mean it. It will be fine. I know my family."

Stephanie smiled up at him and motioned to the door. "Should we?"

Invariably. "Before the Wonder Twins have a chance to introduce my mate to my family for me? Not an option plan." He tried to insert humor into the situation, and his muscles eased slightly at the twinkle in her eyes.

His heart hammering, Jacob escorted Stephanie into the manor house, her cousins close on their heels. James strode out of his office as they paraded into the foyer. His look could properly be classified as "house lord unamused." Other Warriors, mates, and children came running.

James spoke first, a sure sign that no one knew what to make of this development. "Coming home with a Hunter escort, Jacob? The story had better amuse me."

Family stories had it that James had heard that warning from Carter more than a few times in his youth.

"Why don't you tell me what Corwyn stood as judge to, what judgment he passed on you, and save me time in deciding what judgment I need to impose as your house lord."

Women started herding children out of the foyer in anticipation of a trial to come. Only Jacob's mother and James's mate, Beth, held their ground, acting as Stephanie's support system, though they didn't know the new addition to their ranks yet.

Jacob's face flamed. He couldn't deny that he'd been judged in Hunter range, though he'd like to.

Geoff spoke up for him. "The escort is for Stephanie. Not for Jacob. Corwyn's orders."

James's eyebrows went up in surprise at that pronouncement. His gaze panned over Stephanie. The family members came to a halt, and everyone took inventory of her, clearly trying to figure out what would cause a house lord to evict someone that wasn't a Warrior so publicly.

This is dangerous. Jacob had to end it. "I did face a judge in Hunter," he admitted proudly. *Please, let them focus on that and not on Stephanie.*

"It was a misunderstanding," she inserted before James could open his mouth to order the children away. "There was no judgment and no need of one."

The tension bled from James's shoulders. "Very well. Why do *you* require an escort?" That was directed at Stephanie, and James swung his gaze to her to punctuate it.

Jacob bristled at the interrogation. Why was Corwyn inviting this? His life was on the line if James suspected the truth.

As if she was coming to the same conclusion, Stephanie's face lost all color, and Jacob prepared to inform his house lord that she was bearing. That would shame his uncle into —

Joel handed over a thick paper file folder he'd had shoved inside his leather jacket. "Stephanie is protected."

James took it with exaggerated patience. "And you are insinuating that Jacob was not protection enough to bring her a few hundred miles? Stephanie requires the Wonder Twins, Hunter's best?"

The two Hunters didn't protest the nickname. They stayed cool and calm in the face of his anger and scorn.

James flipped the file folder open with a sneer that said he'd rather have an electronic one. As it was, the paper would have to be scanned in. "How unlike Corwyn to send me paper." He scanned his gaze down the first page. "The Wonder Twins mean trouble and now trouble in my range. Who *are* you, Stephanie Briony?"

That seemed to unglue her tongue. "My mother is Hunter's doctor," she snapped back at him. "The manor's personal physician."

She'd stopped short of saying Laura was Corwyn's personal physician, though that's precisely what her father had told her to say. He'd said it would make sense when she said it, but it still didn't. Not to Jacob.

The older Warriors' stillness was so absolute it put Jacob's nerves on edge, and even the children fell silent and stared at them. Though that affiliation had meant nothing to Jacob, it was clear it held meaning to the older generations of Armen.

James recovered his wits enough to speak. "What amulet do you wear?"

He knows! Why would Corwyn hide her all these years, if the Warriors knew?

Stephanie pulled the Lord Hunter's amulet from beneath her shirt and let it flop to her chest over her shirt.

James stared at it, the color drained from his face, and his hand twitched as if he wanted to touch the amulet but was afraid to. "Oh...damn. It is you."

"James?" Jacob asked. He'd never seen his uncle in this state.

He didn't reply. Instead, he kept asking questions of Stephanie. "Are Veriel's turned still a problem for you? For us? For us," he repeated, as if reminding himself that she was part of his household now.

Geoff answered for his lord. There was no doubt, based on the words he chose. "Since Veriel's death, there have been few attempts on Stephanie, but Hunter never chances her. I trust Armen will not."

Jacob stared at her, his mind working fast. Veriel had an adversarial relationship with Corwyn during his lifetime. Rumor and stories said that the elder had tortured Corwyn every way he could.

Veriel knew Corwyn was Stephanie's father.

But he didn't turn Corwyn over to the other lords. If he wanted to destroy Corwyn, that would have been the easiest way to do it.

If Corwyn died, the game would end. Veriel wouldn't have wanted that, if he wanted to continue torturing Corwyn. Instead, he'd terrorized Corwyn's child. It must have driven the Stone lord mad in worry.

That's why the Wonder Twins were assigned to her. That's why he is so protective of her. It wasn't to save his own ass. It was to save her from the beasts.

474

"Jacob, why the hell didn't you warn me?" James asked.

He swallowed hard. "Corwyn left out a bit of information. I knew Stephanie was protected, that he'd raised her as his own, but I didn't know about Veriel. I swear it."

Now that he did, he wanted to gut every one of Veriel's minions and turned that still lived their damned lives. He wanted to thank Corwyn for keeping her alive. He wanted to berate his family for never telling him about Corwyn's doctor and her protected child.

Joel snorted in unkind laughter. "Corwyn doesn't want your promise, Jacob. As her mate, we know you'll die to protect her." He stared at James. "It is Armen that has to give his vow to protect Stephanie as Corwyn would."

"Corwyn trusts Armen, all of the sudden? When my uncle offered to protect Stephanie and her mother, he made it clear our help wasn't welcome."

Jacob gaped at him. "You are not seriously refusing to protect my mate." *I will take her directly back to Corwyn and appeal to the Council of Lords to let me stay with her. If they refuse me, I will die rather than see her and our child returned to Armen range.*

A murmur from the wives echoed his concern, and Stephanie sought the comfort of his chest.

"Of course not," James growled at him. "I just want to hear the answer to that question. Does. Corwyn. Trust. Me?"

Geoff shot a cool look of consideration at James. "Corwyn trusts Stephanie's judgment. She trusts Jacob. If you give your vow to protect her as Corwyn always has, he will accept your sincerity. After all, you are one of the lords he considers a friend. Your uncle never earned that place."

"My uncle was never given the chance to," he countered.

There was a tense moment of silence between them.

"Perhaps that is true," Geoff answered. "Corwyn had no reason to trust house lords then."

James sighed. "Corwyn has my vow. Stephanie will be safe in my range."

Beth smiled widely. "Dinner, everyone? Before it goes cold, that is."

* * * *

Stephanie sat between Jacob's mother and Jacob himself. He piled food onto a plate and set it for Stephanie.

Her eyes widened. "Jacob, I couldn't eat that in a day."

He smiled widely. "You will be amazed at how much a young Warrior will make you eat."

Silence fell around the table.

That time, his father cleared his throat and motioned for his attention. "Something you haven't told us yet, Jacob?" Mark asked.

"I almost told James," he grumbled in return. "Yes. Stephanie is carrying."

"For you?"

Jacob tensed as if he meant to take his father to trial.

"Mark!" his wife admonished him. Mariah turned to Stephanie and patted her hand. "That was rude of him. Forgive him."

Stephanie's smile felt brittle, but she nodded.

"It's just the timing," he complained.

Jacob darkened a few notches. "That...didn't precisely go according to plan," he offered carefully.

At his father's quirked eyebrow, Stephanie dredged up an answer. "Failure of preventatives would cover that one."

James leaned down the table toward them. "I will assume you were in my range when you met Jacob. In my range and without anyone telling me you were here?"

Her heart stuttered. It was a gross offense to knowingly send a protected into another range without letting the lord of the other range know it. Corwyn had not only done but it but done it for extended periods of time.

Geoff answered before she could. "Stephanie attended college here. Jacob met her just before she left." He hurried on before James had a chance to protest. "Years ago, your uncle offered her protection here in Armen range."

"Armen protection. And it was refused."

"If the lords would have let Anna and Corwyn stay in Maher range, he might never have lost his wife and child. Hiding Stephanie outside our range — with a proper complement of Hunter Warriors to protect her — seemed the easiest way to keep her safe from Veriel's turned."

Stephanie winced at the outright lie. She'd always been something to be hidden away and lied about. Now they were lying about the level of protection she'd had in Armen range.

Geoff focused on her for a moment and offered a smile. "You were never alone, Stephanie. We took turns, a rotating shift hiding ourselves in Armen range to protect you while you were here."

Sobs rose in her throat at that, and she swallowed them down.

Joel took over for him. "We were always with you." He shot a sly grin at Jacob. "Well, almost always. Nicky will never live down the fact that he waited outside and let you disappear with Jacob."

James interrupted. "That doesn't excuse the fact that Stephanie was in my range without me knowing it."

Geoff pulled out his cell phone. "Corwyn sends his apologies for that trespass. He only meant to protect Stephanie the best that he could, considering the circumstances. If you wish to take him to trial, he submits to you as his judge and will be here in a few hours to face you."

James didn't seem to know how to answer that. There were a few tense minutes of silence. At last he nodded. "Corwyn raised Stephanie as his own."

"Yes, he did," Geoff replied. "Corwyn couldn't have been any more committed to protecting Stephanie; he would have protected Jayde much the same way, given the chance to."

Stephanie's breathing hitched at the truth of that.

Joel stepped in. "Corwyn never told your uncle that the threat to Stephanie was specific. When Veriel learned Laura was carrying a girl, he felt he had a bargaining chip. Corwyn was— He couldn't stand the idea of a baby girl in danger. Even ten years after Jayde...it was too raw. Veriel terrorized Laura and proposed a..." His jaw tightened, and his eyes narrowed and went hard. He glanced at Stephanie, then averted his eyes.

"A deal," Geoff continued for him. "He vowed to kill or capture both Laura and Stephanie, unless..." He looked at Stephanie, an apology in his eyes.

"Unless he agreed not to stand in their way...to let them take Jayde when she was found," she whispered. "The beast that attacked me when I was eight told me. I asked Corwyn and my mother about it later."

Jacob's hand closed on hers.

Stephanie couldn't bring herself to look at him yet. "Corwyn wouldn't do that. I know it. I've always known it. But if you want to piss the man off royally..." She winced and glanced at the children's table, her face burning. "Sorry."

"Understandable," Beth excused her.

"Corwyn has been personally protecting me or hiding me my entire life."

James nodded. "And Jayde is now being hidden in other ranges as well. She was here two months ago. You can put that cell phone away. I forgive the breach of the rules of sanction. Corwyn had ample reason to do it."

Stephanie smiled at him, her muscles relaxing. Corwyn had been right. It all made sense now.

"I will assume Corwyn will be visiting from time to time," Beth guessed.

Geoff laughed darkly. "I can guarantee it."

The End

Hunter FAQ

Once upon a time, a couple of readers asked questions of me that I told them I'd answer when this book released. The scenes I wrote to answer them didn't quite fit into the book, but I decided to include them as a special gift.

Q: What did Laura say when she learned Corwyn hadn't told her that he'd found Erin/Jayde?

A:

Corwyn crawled into bed, wrapping his arms around Laura and pulling her into the shelter of his body.

She sighed. "How is she?"

"Stephanie or Jayde?"

Laura chuckled. "Both."

"Stephanie is asleep. Jayde...is recovering."

"Recovering? Recovering from what?"

Corwyn planted a kiss on her throat. "She'll always be hunted, Doc. I can't stop that." By the gods, he wished he could, though. He'd always wanted to protect Jayde from it. He'd simply been ignorant of the lengths the Stone would have to go to in order to extend that protection to her.

"Again? Tonight?"

Panic colored her voice. It was a sound that went through him, every time Corwyn heard it.

"At the manor?" Her disbelief was impossible to miss.

"Yes. She killed a high level in the master bath." He hesitated, weighing whether or not the beast's identity would be too much for her. No, Laura deserved to know that the last of their greatest threat was gone. "It was Polero."

Laura sucked in her breath, shuddering, then nodding. "Still... The bathroom, Corwyn?"

"I'm serious. She sleeps with weapons, and I don't mean wooden weapons, either. She carries them into the bathroom. I didn't want this for her." His anger and frustration ate at him. Even now, he was torn between the need to be there, guarding Jayde, and the need to be in Laura's arms, guarding his mate and younger daughter, though Joel and Geoff were doing just that.

Laura turned in his arms, seemingly fighting with herself. "When did you find her, Corwyn?"

He grimaced at the hurt in her tone. "Her husband found her almost seven weeks ago. A beast attacked her. Talon was using Jayde as bait. He didn't know who she was until it was too late."

"When did *you* know?"

"Before she regained consciousness," he admitted.

"And you didn't tell me." There was a question in that, one that went unspoken, a question of his trust...perhaps of his loyalty.

Corwyn stroked the backs of his fingers over her cheek, tortured by his duties and his wants and needs. It was enough to drive him mad. "I didn't want you living in fear. Until it was necessary, I didn't want —"

"To alert Veriel?" she guessed.

"Yes. Among other things. If he'd come after you and Stephanie, how would I live with myself?"

"If he went after Jayde, how would you?" she countered.

"It's not easy," he admitted.

"And...when you and Colin took that jaunt to Cross?" Laura had always been a perceptive one.

"Yes. It was to meet her. I had to see her."

Laura closed her eyes, looking weary. "What now, Corwyn?"

"Jayde likes you. She feels safe with you. I think she'll choose you to deliver the baby."

"So...I'm a doctor?"

Sick realization settled in his gut. "No! I wouldn't... Only until Gunther and Piers leave. They can't stay long. Their range is unprotected. When they leave, I want to introduce you. I want Jayde to know you...to know Stephanie."

"Is that wise?"

Corwyn stilled, searching her face in confusion. "What are you saying?" She didn't want Jayde to know her? She wanted to continue leading this double life?

"It's too dangerous —"

"I won't hide you," he growled.

Laura managed a weak smile. "You've hidden me for fifteen years, Corwyn."

"Not from family."

"What if —"

"I know her, Doc. I went to Cross to meet her. She won't begrudge me happiness. I know she won't."

"You hope she won't."

"You don't want her to know." His heart ached at that. Would he never be allowed to have a single family? The concept crushed the hope he'd secretly harbored since Gunther had contacted him to say that Jayde had to come home to them.

Laura sighed, and his heart pounded in anticipation of her answer. He'd waited more than fifteen years to have his family whole. She couldn't request this. It wasn't right.

Finally, she spoke. "I do want her to know us."

"But?" There was more. He was sure of that.

"I don't want to overpower her. The woman I met today is fragile, not physically but emotionally. I don't want to push her too hard. The introductions will come when it's comfortable for Jayde. Promise me, you won't push her."

"Are you sure about this?"

"Absolutely."

Q: Did Corwyn ever tell Jayde and Talon who Laura really was? Did Jayde ever meet Stephanie?

A: No...and that is yet another tale...

Laura shrugged her pack onto her shoulder and waved to Colin on her way into the training house.

Stephanie bolted away, a rolled towel wrapped around her neck, to entice Joel and Geoff to join her for a swim and whatever trouble she could arrange next. Stuck with Nicky and Brandon as her shadows for the last few weeks, Stephanie missed her absent "favorite cousins."

Laura gave Garrett, Colin's youngest son, a kiss on the cheek on her way up the stairs to the bedrooms. The young Warrior blushed and smiled sheepishly before waving her on. At twelve, he was proud to be trusted to stand a daylight watch over the Lady *König*,

Blutjagdfrau. No other Warrior would wear such a badge of honor. Even Geoff was a trainee.

She knocked on the door to the lord's chamber and waited for Talon's invitation before entering.

Jayde looked up from the bed, rolling her eyes. "Thank God. Laura, call these men off, please."

Laura stifled a laugh at that. "Why don't you start by telling me what the problem is." Though she had her suspicions, it couldn't hurt to confirm it.

Talon shot his wife a quelling look and spoke before she could. "She's sick," he grumbled. "And she's seeing a doctor for it, whether she likes it or not."

Jayde waved to him in frustration, her eyes pleading with Laura. "Warriors don't get sick, Laura. You know it, I'm sure. I haven't been sick since my *Krankheit.*" She waved Talon's move to interrupt off. "It's morning sickness. You've dragged Laura out here for no good reason."

"I will let her judge that, if you don't mind."

"Fine. In the meantime, make yourself useful. Go cook me some sausage, eggs, and toast." She motioned the Warrior standing over her, dwarfing his irritated mate, toward the hall door.

Talon stared at her in disbelief. "You've done nothing but puke yourself weak as a kitten for almost two days."

"Nothing in means nothing to feed our son on. That is unacceptable, even if I puke it back up. Move, Warrior."

Laura laughed at Talon's red-faced frustration. She waved him out. "She's right, Talon. Make her some food. Add milk and juice to that, and I'll check her over for you."

Somewhat mollified at her agreement to make certain his mate wasn't going to die of dehydration or malnutrition, he nodded. "I'd appreciate that, Laura. Can I get you anything, while I'm down there?"

"Just a glass of juice, thanks."

He disappeared down the stairs with a tip of his head.

Jayde sighed, then scrubbed her slightly-pale face, growling out what was probably a curse on men. "You'd think I was made of glass. I killed an elder and a high-level in less than a day."

Laura scooped up her wrist, taking the young woman's pulse. She chuckled. "They're Warriors. They are hardwired that direction."

She nodded. "Was Corwyn like that?"

"I didn't know him when your mother was alive," she answered smoothly.

"I didn't mean with Anna. I meant..." She darkened. "He doesn't think I'll understand, does he?"

Laura sucked in her breath in shock, searching for her voice in light of the tears in Jayde's eyes. "He does. Oh, Jadye... Corwyn wanted to tell you the first night. I swear it."

"Then why didn't he?"

"I was afraid for him."

Jayde swung her head up, and Laura blanched at the hurt she saw there. Laura hurried to continue.

"If Gunther or Piers got wind of it..." She forced a breath, the very thought of Corwyn being put to death nearly too much for her. "How did you know?"

"Little things. The pictures in your office, the way Corwyn looked at them...and you did, the Lord's seal. We stayed in the lord's chamber at the manor house...and here. There are some ladies' toiletries in the bathrooms, your perfume among them. The men... They don't treat you like they do most protecteds."

Laura nodded. They were all little things, easily overlooked, unless taken together. "It's printing, Jayde. Corwyn broke no laws. I want you to know that. The Stone...it gave him a double whammy."

"I don't care about that."

"What?" Her surprise, after years of Warriors as a threat to them, was so absolute, she almost couldn't force the word out.

"Those laws have caused nothing but heartache for me and for Corwyn. If you make each other happy, why would I care? Why should I? After Anna, he deserves some happiness."

That did it. Laura was rendered speechless.

Jayde shook her head, looking to the window. "Does — Does your daughter know who I am?"

Laura followed her line of sight, smiling weakly as Geoff dunked her daughter in the lake. "No. We haven't told Stephanie that you're Erin yet."

She swallowed hard. "Will you?"

The rest went unspoken. After so many years without her father, Jayde felt like the dirty secret Laura and Stephanie had always been.

"I'd like to, but I didn't want to push you too far, too fast."

"I've never had a sister, Laura. Do you think she'll be upset?"

Laura settled on the bed next to her, meeting Jayde's gaze. "Do you like to swim?"

Jayde furrowed her brow. "Yes, but what does that have to do with anything?"

"If you're willing to go swimming with her, play card games, and listen to your share of teenage boy-talk, she'll love you."

Jayde didn't hesitate. "Let's go then."

"Now? But...but Talon is cooking for you."

Jayde's eyes glittered in mischief, much as Corwyn's did at times. "I don't want to eat, Laura, but I had to get rid of him somehow. He's driving me nuts."

Laura laughed heartily. "Then, as your doctor, I order fresh air and sunshine. Hang on while I get a couple of spare suits for us."

The End

The Stone Alphabet

Ani (birth/the mother)- Regana first Lady Kreuzträger, Jayde Marie Albright

Baroo (thunder)- Olbrecht first Lord Kaufmann

Dobler (twin peace-bringer)- Ditrich first Lord Jäger

Fih (twin war)- Geldric/the beast Cerran, Cody König-Armen

Geil (iron)- Bryon König-Kaufmann

Hir (the cool wood)- Gerhardus first Lord Landwirt

Iol (immovable ice)- Redulf/the beast Carstol

Jee (justice)- Mikel of Crossbearer-König and all descendants thereof

Kor (the bear)- Corwyn of König-Maher

Len (mountain)- Wilhelmus first Lord Maher

Mul (flowing water)- Mitchell König-Farmer

Nul (stealth of the night)- Bertolf/the beast Draden

Ori (the sun)- Pauwel first Lord Kreuzträger, Hunter Lord Crossbearer-König

Pol (the horse)- Dado/the beast Lorian

Reg (intensity of the fire)- Jörg/the beast Veriel

Syth (the Stone lord)- Master Trainer Sibold, Gawen first Lord Schwertträger, Etienne Lord Kaufmann, Joseph Lord Armen, Carrick Lord Armen, Corwyn Lord Hunter, Lewis of Maher

Tes (stars and moon)- Kevin König-Smith

Vin (wind)- Cunczel first Lord Schmied

Wul (the wolf)- Tilbrand/the beast Resten

Zel (ending/death)- Erin of Crossbearer-König, Kaitlyn "Katie" of König-Maher, Skye of König-Armen, Victorious Ellen "Vick/Vicky" of König-Smith, Margaret Elizabeth "Maggie" König-Farmer, Colette "Lettie" Kong-Kaufmann

About the Author

Brenna Lyons wears many hats, sometimes all on the same day: former president of EPIC, author of more than 100 published works, owner of Fireborn Publishing, columnist, special needs teacher, wife, mother...and member in good standing of more than 60 writing advocacy groups.

In her first ten years published in novel-length, she's won 3 EPIC e-Book Awards (out of 15 finalists) and finaled for 3 PEARLS (including one Honorable Mention, second to NY Times Bestseller Angela Knight), 2 CAPAS, and a Dream Realm Award. She's also taken Spinetingler's Book of the Year for 2007.

Brenna writes in 26 established worlds plus stand-alones, poetry, articles and essays. She's a bestseller in indie/e fantasy and horror, straight genre and cross-genres thereof. Brenna has been termed "one of the most deviant erotic minds in the publishing world...not for the weak." (Rachelle for Fallen Angels Reviews) Milieu-heavy dark work is practically Brenna's calling card, with or without the erotic content.

She teaches classes in everything from POV studies to advanced editing, networking to marketing. Brenna enjoys hearing from people who read her work and can be reached by e-mail.

Website: http://www.brennalyons.com/

Facebook: http://www.facebook.com/brenna.lyons

Email: brennalyons4168@live.com

Also by this Author

Available from *Fireborn Publishing*

KEIF'S DEN AND PACK
Keif's Pack
Mother of the Keif
Keif's Den (Coming Soon)

PROPHECY
Prophecy: Revelations
Prophecy: Rapture
The Prophet's Mate
Prophecy: Rampage - Meet Gavin
Prophecy: Rampage (Coming Soon)

THE FANTASY CLUB
The Consort

Beyond the Veil
Fairy Wishes (Coming Soon)
Mine for the Night
Once in a Blue Moon
Overtime Pay
Stay With Me
The Fire God's Woman
The Punishment of Phoebus Apollo
Werewolf U

Available from *Phaze Books*

ANGEL-WING SAGA
Sons of Heaven: Beldon
Daughters of Man: Prize Match
Sons of Heaven: Unexpected Mates
Daughters of Man: Claiming a Princess

STAR MAGES
The Master's Lover

XXAN WAR
Daahan Rising
Crossbred Son
Raashh Decisions

Enslaved
All I Want for Christmas is You
Fates Magic
All's Fair...
Black Sail
Mama's Tales
Dream Walk
Unexpected Daddy
Phaze in Verse
We Shall Live Again
May the Best Man Win
Nevermore
Marked
And It Was Good

Available from **Mundania Press**

STAR MAGES
Written in the Stars

Fairy Dreams
Monsters of Myth Anthology

Available from **Under the Moon**

RENEGADES SERIES
TYGERS
Renegade's Run
Max Sec

URBAN GRIMM
Catch Me, If You Can
Three Wishes
Temptation of Eve

With Great Power
Undead in Blue
Evil Overlords Union Issue #1 Anthology
Undead Embrace
"*Playing Games*" in *Forbidden Love: Bad Boys*
"*Marked*" in *Forbidden Love: Wicked Women*
"*The Master's Lover*" in *Forbidden Love: Sacred Bands*

Available from **Logical Lust**

"*Mine for the Night*" in *The Cougar Book* Anthology

Available from **Coming Together Charity Anthologies**

INSTINCT SERIES
"*Foundling*" in *Coming Together: Into the Light* Anthology

"*Claim Mate*" (available separately and as part of the *Coming Together: Against the Odds* Anthology)
"*The Fire God's Woman*" in *Coming Together: Under Fire* Anthology

Available **self-published**

KEGIN SERIES
Earth-Born Lord
Graham: Training the Earth-Born Lord

NIGHT WARRIORS
Claiming a Lady
Stone Lord

Mother's Son

COLOR OF LOVE
A Safe Heart

Snapshots from a Poet's Life

Award-Winning Books

EPPIE/EPIC eBOOK AWARDS WINNERS
Coming Together: Against the Odds- 2010
Time Currents- 2010
Coming Together: Into the Light- 2011

EPPIE/EPIC eBOOK AWARDS FINALISTS
Fion's Daughter- 2004
Collected Poems: Book One- 2005 (now titled *Snapshots of a Poet's Life*)
Renegade's Run- 2005
Rites of Mating- 2006
All I Want for Christmas- 2006
Phaze in Verse- 2008
"The Fire God's Woman" in Coming Together: Under Fire- 2009
Three Wishes- 2010
Matchmaker's Misery- 2010
The Cougar Book- 2011
The Master's Lover- 2011
Bride Ball- 2011

DREAM REALM AWARDS FINALIST
Last Chance for Love- 2003

PEARL HONORABLE MENTION
Night Warriors- 2004

PEARL FINALISTS
Schente Night- 2003 (now included in *The Last of Fion's Daughters*)
König Cursebreakers- 2004 (now titled *Will of the Stone*)

JOYFULLY REVIEWED BEST BOOKS OF 2010
Written in the Stars- 2010

SPINETINGLER'S BOOK OF THE YEAR 2007

NOBODY: An Anthology of Dark Fiction- 2007 (Brenna's pieces of the anthology can be found in *Beyond the Veil*)

TRS's CAPA FINALISTS
Ultimate Warriors- 2004 (Brenna's portion is now available as *With Great Power*)
Written in the Stars

LOVE ROMANCE AND MORE CAFÉ BOOK OF THE YEAR RUNNER UP
Last Chance for Love- 2008

ROAD TO ROMANCE REVIEWERS' CHOICE AWARD
Prophecy: Revelations- 2004

LOVE ROMANCES REVIEWERS' CHOICE AWARD
Black Sail- 2003

ROMANCE JUNKIES BOOK CLUB STAFF PICK
TYGERS- 2003

FALLEN ANGELS ROMANCE RECOMMENDED READ
Devon's Price-2005 (now available in *Bearing Armen*)

JOYFULLY RECOMMENDED READ
Fairy Dreams- 2008
The Last of Fion's Daughters- 2009

TREBLE HEART FINALIST
Prophecy: Revelations- 2003

www.ingramcontent.com/pod-product-compliance
Lightning Source LLC
Chambersburg PA
CBHW030923020726
47498CB00001B/90